THE MAN WHO WALKED IN THE DARK

All Things Found
Book 1

ANTHONY W. EICHENLAUB

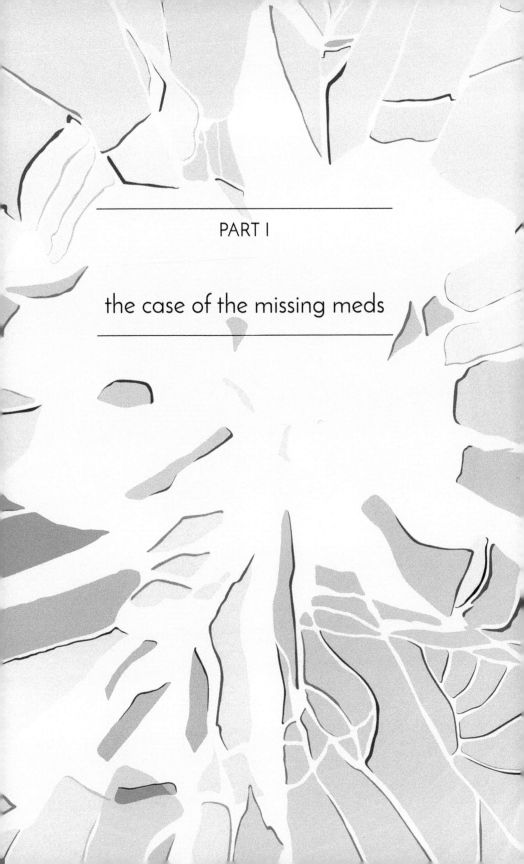

PART I

the case of the missing meds

Chapter 1

WHEN I'M dead and gone to the great beyond, somebody at my funeral, as my body slides through the chrome maw of the great recycler, will say, "Jude Demarco was a nobody, but he was the best damn private detective Nicodemia ever had from Heavies to Hallow. He was a bulldog who tracked down every lead and never let go until he grasped the bloody truth in his jaws. That man would never stop till he saw the way things really were, even if it got someone hurt. Even if it got someone killed. There was something we could all admire in Demarco, same as there was always something to hate. He found the good in people, even if deep down he always believed that that same good would eventually lose out against greed and vice."

More likely, though, when I'm dead and gone, they'll just say, "Jude Demarco was a nobody" and leave it at that.

I sat alone with these dark thoughts and a glass of cheap bourbon, drowning one in the other while the shadows of my unlit office swallowed me whole. An old blues tune played on my music rig, the guitar solo taking its own sweet eternity chasing away the loneliness of the empty room. It wasn't a nice office by any means, but I'd squatted in worse. It had the prerequisite desk and uncomfortable chair. There was a stained red sofa, which was where I did a fair amount of my sleeping. Through the glass storefront, the pulsing life of the spinning space station of Nicodemia rose and fell and passed me by. A sign affixed to the window read: *Demarco: Detective. Medic. Handyman. All things found. All things fixed.*

At least, the sign was supposed to be in my window. With a sigh, I crossed the room, picked it up from the floor, and propped it where it could be seen. A new crack ran right down its center, but I didn't bother with it. Just one of the dangers of setting up shop in an abandoned storefront. Nothing was permanent.

While I stood in my darkened office, the lights outside shifted, turning the mirrored surface into a window. A seedy man with a thin mustache spotted me and flinched. This lower segment of the station-city, where the simulated gravity was strong enough to make bones ache and joints burn, wasn't exactly the friendliest neighborhood. Unlike the other two beads of the station, Heavy Nicodemia's attitude was a glower and a clenched fist.

I glowered. I clenched my fist. I took another swig of bourbon.

Outside, black shadows pooled against static gray stone in the dim light of false stars. Down in the Heavies, shadows of nighttime marked a drop in the quality of clientele, but not the quantity. The bustle and swell of crowds through the lower district dragged on long after the false skies grew black. The city breathed deep of recycled air all night long and never, ever rested.

As I settled back into my lousy chair, a delivery boy entered, rolling right into the shop on a battered skateboard. He had a wisp of white-blond hair and thick-rimmed glasses that made his face look tiny under the wide expanses of smudged glass.

"It's a job for you," said the kid, offering a slender tab of white datasheet.

"Legit?"

He shrugged. "Nick said, 'Dump it on Demarco.'"

Nick Sully. I could always rely on Nick to bring me lousy jobs, but at least they were jobs. "Why won't the client come down here?"

"Fella's too fancy to go asking around for some excommunicated medic."

"Medic?" I looked down at the datasheet. It was rare anyone came looking for my skills as a medical tech. Rarer still that they tried to do it discreetly. Trinity, the station's AI, handled the medical needs of its people with the help of trained, registered medics.

The kid let the room fill all the way up with awkward silence. Finally, I tossed him a dime, and he rolled on his way.

The guitar solo finally finished, so I gathered the disparate parts of my music rig. The device was my only valuable possession, and it fit in the pocket of my trench coat with room to spare. After fetching my fedora from the garbage can, I stepped out of the office, not bothering to lock the door. Above, the darkened sky was dotted with sharp pinpricks of light. I let my eyes unfocus and felt a visceral instinct settle deep in my soul. I'd never been on a planet. Even though the Trinity generation ships had long since found their destination solar system, most folks still stayed on ship. No reason to go planetside, where colonies were as harsh and unforgiving as the worst parts of old Earth.

"It's funny how you all stare at that fake sky," said a woman down the street. Her accent drawled in a way I couldn't quite place. "It's like you've never seen the real thing."

"Who's to say what's real?" I said.

The woman's glasses caught the false starlight like a shattered mirror. Hair the color of communion wafers stuck out at odd angles, chopped like it'd angered the wrong kind of barber. Her long indigo coat almost touched the fiberstone cobbles, and one eyebrow arched dangerously high to contrast the narrow cigarette dangling helplessly from the suicide cliff of her lip.

I produced a thin lighter and obligingly offered flame.

"It's a nice city you have here," she said through a fresh haze of clove and spice.

"I hadn't noticed."

She gestured at a noodle cart someone had set up in front of the local noodle restaurant. The respective owners had started an argument that I wasn't sure both would walk away from. "It's colorful," she said.

I cast her a dubious look. She had a bit too much fashion to walk the lower shopping district, and the sparkle in her blue eyes said she knew it. It wasn't any of my business, but I couldn't let her blunder through the worst of the city unaware. "Hallow Nicodemia might be more to your tastes. The gravity down here in the Heavies is hard on the knees and worse on the temper."

She bobbed up and down a little with a sideways grin on her angular face. She wore sky-blue high heels that looked like they might surrender to gravity at any second. "Is it true they made three copies of the same city?"

"Heavy, Haven, and the Hallows. Is this your first time on a Trinity ship?"

"I've dealt with religious fanatics before."

"Most of us don't exactly qualify."

She looked up at the hazy sky. "You just live in someone else's paradise?"

Heavy Nicodemia was nobody's idea of paradise, but she could probably smell that all the way from the fisheries down below. The argument between the noodle vendors was getting so heated it was drawing a crowd.

As the woman watched the drama, a hint of amusement curled her lips. "My boss brought us to Nicodemia straight from Earth. Didn't even bother to stop at the planets."

Earth was five-years away for even the fastest ships. "Fresh off a long freeze, then?"

"You could say that." She held her cigarette between two immaculately decorated fingernails. The amber paint on her pointer finger caught the starlight with an iridescent sheen in the shape of an intricate Celtic cross.

When the noodle shop owner threw his first punch, I gestured for the woman to follow and she reluctantly complied. I took her across to the station's central hollow a few blocks away and crossed the trolley tracks to a railing overlooking the whole inner spiral of the city. The central throughway sloped up from a point far below, rising far above. We were just below the widest part of the spiral that made up the city, and high above, misty clouds blotted out the highest of the false stars. Everywhere, the bustle of the city swelled like a disturbed anthill.

Across the inner space, a cacophony rose from the crowded streets. Police lights flashed: just the blue in pursuit of their quarry. Above, fast transports shattered the stillness of the night sky.

I said, "Heavy Nicodemia isn't the kind of place a person wanders alone, miss."

"I've been worse places." She dropped her cigarette and ground it out with the toe of one shoe.

"Trinity doesn't care much for litterers."

"The ship?"

"Trinity is the AI that manages the ship. Its three-part mandate is 'Body, soul, community.'" Every school-age kid learned the history of Trinity and the Catholic missionaries who designed it.

"It's the god your ancestors built."

The comment hit a little close to home. "Don't let the wrong people hear you say that."

"Are you the wrong people?"

"I've been known to be."

"And which one is littering?"

"Excuse me?"

"Does littering violate body, soul, or community?"

I scratched the stubble on my chin. "Is there a reason you're here, ma'am?"

The woman backed away from the ledge, a smile on her ruby-red lips. "My name is Charlotte. Charlotte Beck."

"Demarco," I said reflexively.

"I work for Violet Ruiz."

People only name-drop for two reasons: to impress a potential contact or to get the measure of someone based on their recognition. I wasn't impressed by the name Violet Ruiz, seeing as how I had never heard it before, and if Charlotte Beck wanted to measure me based on who I knew, then she wasn't going to be particularly impressed. She watched me with those piercing blues.

"It's been a pleasure, Beck," I said, sweeping off my hat and giving a slight bow. "But a fella's got to get some work done if he wants a decent meal." With that, I hopped the spiral trolley as it passed, letting it sweep me upward and away.

As I left, she said, "Maybe I'll see you around, Jude Demarco."

It took me a whole half-turn of the station to realize she'd used my whole name—I had only told her my last—and by then she was a spec of color against the gray background of the city.

Heavy Nicodemia was a city of saints and sinners. Nights lumbered forward through thick gloom. The hundred miles of steel cord that spun us around the artificial star had spun as long as anyone's ancient great-grandmother could remember. Folks breathed the slick atmosphere of this bead as if it were the only city in all existence. To them, it was. A city was a city, after all, and no matter if that thriving metropolis was a blight on a green planet or, like this city, a pit in the gut of a once-majestic generation ship, it would live its own life. It would have a personality all its own.

Sinners, saints—we were all the same in Nicodemia.

Chapter 2

I HOPPED off the trolley where its track veered into a little residential neighborhood on the opposite side of the big spiral. Securing my hat on my head, I pulled my long coat close and walked the long road up into the seething mass of the city. The air grew heavy and wet, and the cool air tasted like the start of rain. Upward, along the central spiral, neon nightlife throbbed like the frantic pulse of a city that forgot how to sleep. The fastest path ran up the center of the spiral, and I took that until the crowds of revelers became too much.

All three cities of Nicodemia were beads along a single strand. Each bead was narrow at the top and bottom with a wide, bulging middle like a child's top. The address in my pocket led me to a location on the lower arc of the spiral, not far south of the gaudy jewel called the Cathedral of Saint Francis of Assisi, which marked the city's midpoint. Outside that central spiral stretched the fat belly of the city proper, where trouble lived and breathed every hour of every day. Unlike the other beads on the chain, Heavy Nicodemia's inner spiral teemed with humanity. Tiny booths pressed together like pixels on a high-def screen, and people ran and shouted as if there was something to get excited about.

There wasn't, and there likely never would be.

Music in my earpieces drowned out the city's endless chatter. My rig was loaded with ancient tunes from long before Nicodemia and her sister ships left Earth. When the Travelers converted their ships into permanent residences, music was their connection to the long-lost soil of their homeland. Johnny Lee Hooker filled my world with the blues, along with Muddy Waters and Howlin' Wolf. All the chaos of this tin can city dropped away into the endless void of space as Buddy Guy's "Whiskey, Beer & Wine" shook the contents of my skull.

The address the kid had given me was in a neighborhood called the Rook—a better part of town if such a thing existed this close to the raw stink of the fisheries. When I got there, I spent a long time looking at the front door to the client's apartment building. Two shrubs with big fat leaves flanked the red double door. From twenty feet away, it was unclear whether the shrubs were fake. Closer up, the fraudulent foliage was even less obvious.

My knife was almost out to check the plants when a stocky man in a suit keyed his way through the red door. I followed close knowing he would ignore me. The man took the elevator, but I took the stairs. An elevator wouldn't take an excommunicated man such as myself anywhere he wanted to go.

Because Trinity, the AI that ran the ship from Hallow to Heavies, wouldn't acknowledge my existence. It wouldn't turn on the lights if I was the only one in the room. It wouldn't steer a vehicle around me if I stood in the street. Terminals didn't respond to my touch. Few people knew how many excommunicated souls there were in Nicodemia, because, well, there was no record of us.

As situations go, excommunication was a teaspoon of freedom lumped in with a truckload of pain-in-the-ass. It was an odd system, and the full reasoning behind Trinity's use of excommunication made little sense to me. Was ignoring people supposed to bring them back into the fold? Starve them? It was punishment without explanation, and anyone who could fix it had died long ago.

In tall buildings, being excommunicated made for the fantastic cardio workout that I absolutely did not want. I made a mental note to check what floor potential new clients were on before agreeing to meet them. Anything above the third floor was probably not worth it. McCay lived on the fourth.

"Mr. McCay?" I said when he answered the knock at his flat. The fibersteel door frame gleamed in the too-bright light of the apartment hallway.

"Dr. McCay," the man said. The fat of his bonus chins wobbled as he looked me up and down. He stood taller than most, a giant by local measures, and his dark skin was blotchy in the harsh light. He'd probably never met someone who stood a head taller than him.

"Word is you need help."

He straightened the lapels of his suit, swallowed a lump in his throat, and motioned for me to step inside. "My usual guy—"

"You have a guy?" I cut him off. "Nobody said you have a guy." Last thing I wanted was to step on someone else's turf. I moved to leave, but he grabbed my sleeve.

"Hear me out," he said. Something about the puppy-dog plea in his eyes kept me from shrugging him off.

Paintings adorned the iron-gray walls like posters in a prison cell. Little hints of wealth dotted the room, from a vase made of real glass to a taupe sofa whose only hint of use was a single slightly askew pillow. The carpet was the kind of off-white that looked like it had never been stepped on. I stepped on it.

He led me farther into his house, letting me into what appeared to be either a cluttered study or an abandoned storage closet.

Unlike the well-kept living room, McCay's office looked like the dumping ground for a particularly messy gang of anarchist accountants. Binders overflowed with papers. Books cluttered the shelves that lined all four walls. The doorway was the only clear spot on the floor, which otherwise hid under mountains of discarded trinkets. Soccer balls, broken trophies, and a single glove hinted at sports in McCay's past. Based on the evidence, he'd been a goalie.

Back under the desk, almost out of sight, sat a single safe with its door wide open. Inside sat a box of plasti-ceramic bullets and a pistol to fire them. This was a plastic model designed to pass through detection scanners. The crimson barrel had a word etched into the side of it in curly gold letters: *Forsaken*.

"Interesting hardware," I said.

"We can talk in here without Trinity picking it up," he said.

This job was getting both sketchier and a whole lot more interesting. "Gun safes typically work better if you close them," I said.

McCay rushed past me to kick the safe closed, but he didn't engage the lock, which struck me as odd. The only people who left their guns unlocked were the paranoid and the sloppy. McCay seemed like a careful man, cluttered office notwithstanding. What was he afraid of?

"You're a Traveler, aren't you?" McCay blurted it out and then had the decency to look appalled at himself. "Descended from, I mean."

"You could say that."

"So, you'll understand. I have some Traveler blood, but it's been a long time since my parents brought me down here to the Heavies. They fell on hard times, you see."

"It happens to the best of us." And the worst.

It would have been a brutal transition for McCay's family. Travelers were the people who originally voyaged from Earth to the Paradise System. The first Travelers were chosen for their ability to metabolize efficiently, live long lives, and foster a stubborn tenacity on a ship for years without going crazy. The fast metabolism allowed them to pack on weight before enduring long hibernation cycles. Several generations passed with them alternating periods of wakefulness and hibernation, extending their lives for hundreds of years each. More often than not, those first generations were also lazy people, but I like to think that wasn't a genetic trait. The whole story stank of eugenics enough already. The original Travelers sacrificed their lives for the journey. Their children never had a choice.

Once the ship arrived, they had access to fresh resources, but the system proved much harder to terraform than anticipated. As immigrants from homeworld Earth arrived on faster and faster ships, the Travelers tightened their control over Hallow Nicodemia, taking the most luxurious bead as their own. They fashioned themselves into the ruling elite, with the immigrants as their servant class.

McCay was right about me. Both my parents were descended from Travelers. Most anyone could see it in my heavy stature, but the more observant noticed it in my patient demeanor and quiet stubborn streak. He was wrong about me wanting to ever go back to the Hallows.

"It stinks as bad up there as it does down here. Take my advice: forget about moving back up the chain."

His eyes narrowed.

I continued, "That's what this is about, right? You think you have a way to get back in good with the upper crust. Maybe a little deal going on the side or a friend of a friend who says he can get you in."

"It's a job opportunity."

"Sure. They need doctors up the Hallows as much as we need them down here. But, see, here's the thing. You've spent most of your life in the Heavies. Yeah, I can tell. The gravity here makes a person hard. Me, I've spent years down here and I can feel it in my bones every morning. You're not like that. Your body isn't accustomed to the lighter gravity up above. Sure, you felt great when you went to visit on vacation, but that wouldn't last."

"You don't understand."

He was right. I didn't. "It's your life, either way. I'm just saying that whatever you got going on here probably isn't worth giving up for whatever you stand to gain up there."

McCay really seemed to consider that. His lips tightened as the thoughts churned around in his head. "I still have to try. For my kids."

"You have kids?"

"No."

I sighed. Men and their ambitions. "What do you need a handyman for?"

"I need my medicine."

"You're a doctor."

"Word is you had medical credentials."

"*You've* got medical credentials. Just write yourself a prescription." I knew full well it wouldn't be that easy.

"It's not that easy."

Damn. "You want this off the books. You're talking about stealing the meds."

"I can just record that they're going to someone else."

"Like I said, stealing."

His shoulders visibly tensed. "Who is it stealing from? Trinity can print more and it's not like anyone is going to miss it."

When a medical technician dispensed meds, Trinity tracked where they went and what they were used for. The data got factored into a thousand equations in a thousand subroutines that kept the ship stable. I didn't explain this to McCay. All I said was, "Body. Soul. Community." The three competing optimizations of the ship AI.

McCay deflated like a stuck balloon. "My other guy had no trouble with this."

"So go back to him."

"He died a while back. New guy I found flaked out on me."

"Why didn't your new guy stock you up before he left?"

After a long pause, McCay said, "He did. It disappeared."

Odd that he didn't say it was stolen. A prickle of curiosity brushed the back of my neck. "When?"

"Last week. I usually need to take my meds every day to keep everything normal." He looked up at me, genuine pleading in his eyes. "It's a form of sickle cell."

A genetic disease. No wonder he didn't want it in the record. "You've been getting meds under the table your whole life."

He nodded. "Lester was always reliable, but he died a couple years ago. I found a new guy, but when I tried to contact him this week he wasn't around. He's nowhere. I'm having a flare, and—" he choked on the words. The poor sap was desperate, so he'd reached out. "It hurts so much."

"There's gene editing."

His cold eyes told me what he was going to say before he said it. "Not God's will."

"You don't seem like the religious type."

"I am when the Church makes the rules about who Trinity lets move up the chain."

He endured a chronic condition and the only reason he wasn't seeking help was that he wanted to trick the ship's AI into giving him Traveler status for children he didn't even have. I wasn't lying when I said he was better off down here where the gravity pulled half again as much as Earth normal. He was a medically trained doctor in a place that desperately needed his skills. The apartment was nice, even if I didn't necessarily like his choice of decor.

But, "disappeared" hooked me. Heavy Nicodemia was a closed system, or nearly so. Nothing disappeared. Ever. Anything lost could be found. Anything wronged could be made right.

I closed my eyes and drew a long breath, feeling McCay's penetrating, pleading gaze. He wanted me to order him some new meds. That job didn't interest me at all.

But this? Figuring out how something could disappear so easily? Finding someone capable of the feat?

"All right," I said. "Show me."

Chapter 3

"SHOW ME AGAIN."

He held out his reader to me. A grainy, tone-flattened picture of a much neater version of his office flickered to life. This was night vision surveillance, courtesy of the all-seeing eyes of Trinity. On the desk sat a single bottle of pills. He advanced the feed one frame, then another.

"Each frame is ten seconds?" I asked.

"Yeah." He advanced another frame. The pills disappeared.

Disappeared.

They didn't fall. The desk couldn't have shaken them loose to be buried in the clutter. Any disturbance would have dislodged the precarious book tower.

But where did they go?

No, that wasn't the important part. It didn't matter where they went or how. It didn't even matter who took them. "Why these pills?" I muttered under my breath. To McCay, I said, "I thought this room was off Trinity's grid."

"Only when it needs to be for my privacy." McCay cleared his throat.

"So, right now?"

"I'm in here." He sounded annoyed.

"Bring up the video of this room. Most recent capture."

He pressed some buttons on his console, and scratchy video of a dark room came up.

The video continued, its timestamp showing roughly the moment that I knocked on McCay's door. Then, it continued. The room stayed empty. "This is right now," he said.

The video didn't show us in the room. "Why aren't we there?"

"Lester changed the local logic override so that it edits us out." Then he corrected himself. "It edits me out."

His local hack of the surveillance system didn't *need* to edit me out. Trinity did that all on its own.

I picked up a stack of papers and moved them to the other side of the desk. McCay tensed. "Don't worry," I said. "I'll put everything back." It was a lie. If he hadn't wanted me touching his things, he shouldn't have asked for my help.

"This isn't the kind of help I was looking for," he said.

Right. "Leave the room," I said, "and hand me your screen."

"It won't work," he said. "You're thinking the pills were stolen while I was in the room, and I can tell you I wasn't here."

"You ever sleep in here? Work a late night and maybe doze off reading the latest medical reports?"

His chins wobbled at the affront. "Never."

I took the screen from him and ushered him out the door. "Humor me. I want to see what it does."

It wasn't often I had my hands on a live feed of Trinity's video stream. As far as I knew, Trinity didn't see me, but I rarely got a glimpse of how it worked. As soon as the door closed, I was plunged into darkness. Several seconds later, the stack of papers I'd moved disappeared from one place on his desk and reappeared in the other. Just like the pills had done.

I was not in the video at all. Trinity's system edited me out on the fly. It was a fancy bit of computing that I didn't exactly understand. It might as well have been the smoke and mirrors of a cheap stage magician.

McCay's hack looped in recent footage of the empty room. It wasn't as fancy as editing a person out of a video on the fly, but it got the job done. Just for kicks, I picked up the stack of papers and watched for the movement on the screen. Sure enough, the papers levitated, then dropped down where I put them.

The image on the screen felt uncanny, like one of those animations of characters who didn't quite mimic real humans. Something was off.

I set the screen on the desk face down and waited for my eyes to adjust to the dark. In the pitch black, the room felt like a vast cavern, as if it stretched on forever into the void of space. I spread my arms and closed my eyes, imagining what it might be like to drift in the nothing.

When I opened my eyes, I saw the light under the desk.

Why would anyone take McCay's meds? They were prescribed for an exceedingly rare genetic disorder, and it would have been clear that he had it since childhood. His parents had opted to illegally acquire medication for him. There were even gene therapies available for a more permanent fix. For what? He would never find acceptance in the Hallows. Not in a way he wanted. So, why would anyone bother to steal a med that was available for free?

Tentatively, I crouched down and felt my way over to the soft glow. I felt past the scattered papers, most of which were not present in McCay's disappearing pill video.

Or, they weren't scattered, anyway. The floor had been clear in those images. McCay must have torn the place apart looking for his pills. Given the pain that sickle cell patients endure, I had no doubt he was desperate.

Maybe he took painkillers too. Meds to help with pain mixed with the meds to help normalize his blood cells. A more extensive DNA adjustment might have been a more stable fix, but he couldn't get that without Trinity recording the preexisting genetic flaw.

Painkillers were worth stealing. That might be the why. If McCay's handyman mixed several drugs in the same pill, it might make for a tiny addictive cocktail. If that was the case, then McCay had something with some street value. Plenty of thugs would take questionably sourced pills if they were in enough pain.

I took off my hat and ran my fingers through my hair. Pain pills. A ten-second disappearance job. A cluttered office in the middle of a decent neighborhood. Something still didn't fit.

Pushing papers aside, I pressed my face close to the crack in the floor. An access tunnel? A vent? I couldn't tell. The line ran along a square the size of a large pizza box. My fingernails couldn't pry it open, so I slid a penknife along the edge.

It popped open, and I saw that it was an access panel to a maintenance shaft. Trinity's repair bots would work their way through this tunnel to fix broken wiring when needed. It wasn't big enough for a person, at least not a giant like me.

The light came from farther down the shaft. I reached in, extending as far as I could go. My hand closed on something small, and I worked it loose from where it had snagged on a wiring bracket. A spot on the object glowed from some kind of iridescent paint. I knew what it was from the heft, the shape, the slurry of memories it drudged up. Still, I needed a better look at it.

I pulled my lighter from my pocket and clicked it on. My eyes quickly adjusted to the faint glow.

A cross necklace glinted in the flame's flickering light. It held a screaming Jesus, but I couldn't tell if he was supposed to be angry or terrified. I stuffed it in a coat pocket and picked up the floor panel. Wires ran along its length, with contact plates installed along one side. So that's why there had been a gap in the floor. But who could have installed this?

Poking my head down into the hole again, I took a close look at the hardware. If it tied into the room's surveillance, maybe removing the floor panel would shut off the camera. Maybe this is how McCay's previous handyman had overridden Trinity's systems.

No, that wasn't right. This was something else. I shook my head. It would be impossible to tell without an expert hacker and a full disassembly of the tampered goods. Something told me McCay wouldn't be keen on a fully destructive investigation.

That left quite a few questions. I placed the panel back where I found it and scattered some papers over it. McCay didn't need to know about this just yet. There were still too many questions and too many people I needed to speak with.

I tapped lightly on the door and McCay opened it.

"Well?"

I pushed past him. "I'll take the job," I said.

"You will?" The high pitch of his voice betrayed his disbelief.

"I need to talk to some people, starting with anyone who's ever been in this apartment."

He followed me to his door. "Now, hold on. Nobody I've had in here would have done it. You saw the video, and that happened in the middle of the night. I didn't have anyone over."

Something in his expression told me he was telling the truth, but it didn't matter. "Someone knows you're on those meds, and someone thought you'd be an easy target. Now listen, I've got no reason to think you're into something bad here, but if I'm going to help you, you've got to play it straight with me. Who's your new handyman?"

The man held my gaze for a frozen minute before relenting. "My handyman is a guy that I only know as Rick, but he split. You won't find him around."

"Any girlfriends who might have been in here?"

He blinked rapidly, like I'd slapped him. "No, not like that."

"Like what, then?"

"They don't come here. My reputation, you understand."

For a man who cared so much about reputation, he sure

seemed willing to stuff more skeletons in his closet. "I'm not making any promises."

I left, and several minutes later I was out in the streets, flanked by the towering structures, boxed in by the unrelenting sky. The air had cooled considerably in the time I'd been inside, but nothing held back the heat burning on the back of my neck. A heat I knew all too well.

Someone was following me.

Chapter 4

A CLINGING MIST formed in the night air, caressed by a guitar bending a blues note nearly to the point of breaking. A sharp ache in my stomach reminded me I'd taken a fool's job, and like a fool, I'd neglected to ask for payment up front.

The narrow alleys among the tenements kept me in the city's gray shadow, but that prickle at the back of my neck persisted like the lyrics of a half-remembered song. I picked my way downspiral with no real destination in mind. I needed a fast turnaround on this job. A chat with the other handyman, Rick, would shed some light on the subject, but if McCay was right, he was a shadow in the darkness.

By all reasonable estimates, McCay's case was dead right from the start. An investigator needed options, and there simply weren't any good ones here. I'd need a look at the schematics for McCay's building. That vent was big enough for a bot. Maybe a drone as big as half a person if it was built skinny enough. There were machines designed to travel those maintenance tunnels, but Trinity restricted access to them. I could track down the few locals with access to that kind of tech. Maybe figure out what the other end of that duct looked like.

The blue-red of police had converged on a point across the spiral high above. Closer, the stone buildings caught the noise of men shouting and bounced it back like an angry bark.

Gunshots cracked like bones being broken. Angry shouts turned into furious screams. Guns were rare in Nicodemia, but not rare enough.

I pressed my hat down on my head, steeled myself against the cold rain, and soldiered on. Another crack of a faraway pistol echoed in the brick canyons like the reverb of a well-amped guitar. Securing my earpieces in place, I shut out the world with a heavy dose of trombone and pity.

Avoid trouble; keep moving. Head down; feet forward. That's the way to survive Heavy Nicodemia. If someone was following me after McCay's apartment, then that person couldn't keep my tail if I moved fast enough through the dark streets. Lights followed every citizen of the city. Trinity made sure that nobody moved in darkness, even in the deepest night. I stepped into the light of a pair of darkly dressed women and felt like a fish in a bowl. Someone out there was sizing me up, and the farther I walked, the surer I was of it. In the dark again, I was safe. I cast a glance behind me as I rounded the next corner, trying to glimpse whoever might be following me—the ghost in the streets.

And I rounded the corner, right into trouble.

Two groups stood on either side of a toppled hotdog cart. The vendor lay next to his cart bleeding from a hole in his leg. Dark blood spread across rain-slick pavement, and the whole mess mixed with a pile of spilled hotdogs. It was a damn shame and enough to spoil my appetite. I could have faded back into the dark. For a hitched breath, nobody in the intersection noticed me. One step back and I'd be gone.

That would mean leaving the poor vendor to his fate, though, and something about that settled poorly on my empty gut.

I took my earpieces out, and the blues faded away.

A man, clearly the leader of the three men on his side, stepped forward. He stood taller than most and dressed in black suspenders over a white linen shirt that clung to him in the rain. He had a pencil-thin mustache and couldn't have been much past his mid-twenties. The man was unarmed, but he acted like he had all the power in Nicodemia at his fingertips.

"Tell Jerome this is my turf now," he said in a quiet voice.

The hotdog vendor quietly wept and clutched at his wounded leg.

On the other side, half a dozen men fought for the chance to not be in charge. One guy finally lost. Sam Wash, an angry lump of a young thug if I've ever seen one. The muscles of his thick neck twitched. "Saint Jerome's not going to settle for that, Lauder." His hand inched across his chest toward his suit coat pocket. "This block is under his protection."

"And if your hand moves any closer to that gun of yours, you're going to lose it," Lauder said, slick as hell.

Wash tensed. His body language said he was going to go for it, and it didn't take a genius to see that he wouldn't walk away if he did.

"This is more guns than I've seen in the past year," I said, stepping forward and holding an open palm to each man. Past decade, really. Guns were such a rarity in Nicodemia that even the ceramic-shooting plastic garbage these goons were wielding warranted a big red circle on the calendar. "Exciting times."

The muscles in Wash's neck twitched. An empty smile flashed across his lips. "Demarco." I couldn't tell if he was disgusted at me or relieved. Probably both. "We need to chat once I'm done taking care of the riffraff."

"Let's just all walk away," I said, mostly to Lauder. "No need for trouble tonight."

The vendor started to drag himself away from his cart like a captain abandoning his sinking ship. He left a streak of blood across the slick stones. So much for not needing any trouble.

"So, you're one of Jerome's men?" Lauder asked me.

"I'm my own." It was a perfectly valid position, though there might have been some alternate views on the subject, depending on who was asked. "What you have here is a nice little group of friends, but it's not going to do you any good once you have the big man's attention."

Lauder's hesitant smile managed to pull his thin lips away from his teeth for half a long second. "You think I don't want that fucker's attention?"

"I think you'll regret it once you have it."

He shook his head slowly. "You don't want to be part of this, Mr. Demarco."

"Here I am anyway."

Lauder held my gaze long enough for me to grow a shadow of a beard. At last, he dipped his chin almost imperceptibly and the men behind him relaxed. He took two long strides to me and stuck out a hand.

I looked at it like it was day-old fish.

"You should work for me," he said, not withdrawing the proffered hand. "The winds are changing in the Heavies."

"But no matter where they blow, it always seems to smell the same."

A quick smile spread across his face. He reached up and plucked the fedora from my head. "You don't see too many of these around."

"Keeps the rain off my head."

Lauder tried the hat on. He turned to his men and modeled it for them, then turned to Wash and his boys. When he didn't get a smile from any of them, he put on a pout and handed back my hat. "Seems the boys prefer a naked head." He slicked his wet hair back. "And the precipitation's good for my look."

The rain smelled like chlorine now and fell in fat drops. "Seems these streets are in need of a good cleaning," I said. "You'd best get indoors."

Lauder held my gaze again for a long breath. He was sizing me up, and I wondered what he saw. A man past his prime? An investigator too big for his own ego? A potential rival?

He made an open-handed gesture of "whatever" and backed away. Soon I was left with Wash's goons and a wounded hotdog vendor.

"Saint Jerome wants a talk with you, Demarco," Wash said.

"He knows where my office is."

Wash gripped my arm with his big, beefy fingers. His sleeve slipped back to reveal a tapestry of intertwined tattoos, prominently featuring a bloody cross. "I'm taking you to him right now."

"I'm on a job."

"Fuck your job," He pulled me close, his brow tight in a pleading expression. "I need this, my man. I'll owe you one."

"Wash."

"You don't know what it's like." He gave me a tug, but he must have forgotten how big I was. Even a solidly built Heavy like him couldn't drag me wherever he wanted. When I didn't move, he hissed, "I need this, man."

I took hold of his fist and peeled off his grip. With a shove, I sent him stumbling away.

Wash scowled at me while his boys laughed at his impotence. By the furious press of his lips, I knew I'd humiliated him a little too much. Not a smart move.

He said, "I'll tell the boss where your loyalties are."

"You don't know the first thing about loyalty," I said.

"No, but I know about survival."

My mind raced, looking for a graceful way out. My gaze settled on the hotdog vendor. "Give me some time, Wash. I need to get this guy situated."

The gears clicked as Wash figured out that he'd won. "Come by my place in Dockside when you're ready."

He backed away, fixing me with a dark glare. He wanted to drag me back to his boss like a prize, but he knew I wouldn't go quietly. What confused me was why he even cared. Wash was young—fresh out of school, by the look of him—but he wasn't the sort to have done much schooling. Wash was the kind of unambitious lunk who avoided conflict whenever he could. If they were all like that, maybe there wouldn't be so much need for me.

But they weren't, and there was.

It was only after he left that I realized the symbol in his tattoo resembled the screaming Jesus in my pocket. I was going to need to honor the offer to visit him in Dockside.

"What's your name?" I asked the vendor once Wash and his boys were gone. I helped him to the shelter of an overhang to get him out of the rain.

"Those assholes," he said. "Those fucking assholes."

"Seems a protection fee doesn't buy what it used to, huh?"

"You should have let them shoot each other."

"No need for that. Not today." Once he was out of the rain, I took a look at his leg. "Clean wound," I said as if that made it hurt less. He was lucky the plasti-ceramic bullet hadn't shattered. "You'll want stitches, but I can give it a quick seal for now."

"You a medical tech or something?"

"It's complicated." I took out a couple of skin patches and slapped one on the entry wound, the other on the exit. "Those will hold for a couple hours."

He stood gingerly. It must have hurt like hell, but he limped to his cart. I helped him stand it up, and he was able to roll it a short distance. Without looking back at me, he said, "Thank you."

It was more than I usually get for my efforts.

Music back on, I let the city dissolve into a bluesy haze. The song had continued without me, and when I put the earpieces back in, I was shunted directly into the end of a long trombone solo. It was a somber piece, but one tinged with a sharp optimism. It made my heart ache.

The vendor took another step forward and his whole body shuddered. I felt his pain right down to the marrow of my bones. Cold, wet, bloody—all that was nothing compared to what he felt inside at that moment. His shudder was the sensation men get when they're faced with the fact that their world is full of snakes. It's the heavy, gut-wrenching sense of betrayal in that moment when the slick underbelly of the world has finally revealed itself.

My song ended, so I stopped the rig and took out both earpieces.

"Come on," I said, taking the cart from him. "I know a place you can get off your feet for a few."

Chapter 5

"YOU CAN'T KEEP DRAGGING every poor sod you meet here," my sister hissed through clenched teeth. Angel was a head shorter than me, but she was my older sister, and I'd never shaken the impression that she could kick my ass even after the accident confined her to a wheelchair.

The wreck of the *Benevolent* had killed our parents and destroyed our otherwise pleasant teenage lives. It had taken Angel's ability to walk. To this day, every time I visited my sister, a twisting lump of guilt roiled in my gut. She sat across from me at an accessible booth with a cleaning rag in one hand and a scowl standing the lines of her brow on end.

Her wife, Helen, peeked in from the kitchen as if trying to gauge whether there'd be violence. When she saw me, she gave a polite nod and disappeared.

I said, "He needed a hand."

"So, take him to a church."

She was probably right, but the Angel's Diner sign outside was off and any food she had left that late at night was probably going into the recycler anyway. Only a person who wanted to get smacked would mention that fact to my sister.

"You've got stock going to waste, and this is good for your Karma," I said.

She cuffed me upside the head. It stung worse than it had any right to.

"He's not bad looking," she said. "What's this guy's name?"

"He never said," I admitted, "and you know I'm not interested."

"Right," she said. "How's that working out? Meet any nice ladies recently?"

The image of Charlotte Beck's sideways grin flashed in front of me. "No such luck."

Angel sighed. "You really didn't get this fella's name?" Her raised voice carried through the diner. "I thought Dad taught you better manners than that."

"There's a lot Dad didn't teach us." For example, he hadn't taught us how to manage the family fortune or even where it came from. "They never thought we would need to exist without them."

"Maybe it's about time we start learning on our own," she said.

I gestured at the diner. "Seems like you're managing just fine."

"That *we* wasn't inclusive."

"And it was singular." This was why I tried not to visit very often.

The hotdog vendor sat in the corner booth with a blank-eyed stare. Even from across the half-dozen booths, I could see that he wasn't listening, and he probably wasn't going to talk. Angel rolled away from the booth and rounded the counter.

"It wasn't right to just leave him. He lost half his stock to those goons, Angel."

"You brought him so that I'd feed you both," she drolled.

"Maybe." Absolutely.

"I've lost half my stock to my leech of a brother who keeps dropping in." She spoke as she rolled around the counter. A display stood at the corner with the remains of an apple pie. Angel always managed to procure fancy food in a bead that dealt mostly in fish and mushrooms. She had done well for herself, putting together a decent place to stop for a bite. "When are you going to get a job, Jude?"

I gave her a dry look. She knew my situation. The meaning of her words was clear. When was I going to seek reconciliation? When would I rejoin society and beg forgiveness for what I had done?

"I'm not ready," I whispered quiet enough that I didn't think she could hear.

Angel brought a plate around, paused in front of me long enough so I could smell the rich gravy she'd slathered all over an open-faced salmon sandwich, and then brought it to the hotdog vendor. He stared at it blankly for several long seconds before smiling and thanking her. She shot me a dirty look as she passed me on her way back behind the counter.

"I'm on a case," I said.

She slid into the booth across from me, leaning forward with her elbows on the table and her palms supporting her chin. "Tell me all about it, bro."

"Someone's stealing meds."

Her brow furrowed. "Why? Meds are free."

"It's complicated."

She raised an eyebrow. "Does it pay?"

"Not everything's about money, sis."

"It is if you don't have any Karma, Jude." She poked me in the chest. "I won't have any, either, if I keep having to feed your excommunicated ass. Just reconcile, already." There. She said it.

I drew a deep breath. We'd been over this same argument a dozen times and I didn't have the energy to go over it again. Instead, I stood, placed my hat on my head, and said, "Thank you for feeding the guy. He should be able to get home on his own."

With that, I pushed through the glass door into the night. The rain had stopped, leaving a cloying mist clinging to cool streets. Far away, the red and blue of the police still pulsed warnings into the thick haze.

The door opened behind me. At first, I thought it might be Angel, out to apologize, but it wasn't. Of course, it wasn't.

Helen handed me a paper package. Her mousy face was hidden behind a pair of large round glasses, but I saw the sympathy there. The white plastic gloves she wore stood in sharp contrast to her brown skin. "I heard what you said back there."

"She doesn't know what she's asking of me."

"You're a decent man, Jude Demarco. Angel knows it."

Strong evidence spoke against that. "You think I should reconcile too?"

"I don't care about your status with Trinity." Her hand rested gently on my elbow. "You'd be welcomed back, you know. She would give you a job at the diner if you asked."

Helen was a Catholic with a capital C, just like my sister. Maybe just like me. I didn't know anymore. She was Christian through and through, descended from a long line of half-hearted zealots. Unlike Helen, my sister and I came from a family assured of its righteousness by the esteemed virtue of wealth. It's hard to imagine anything going bad in the afterlife when your whole life is so damned blessed. When things finally went sour for our family, her faith adjusted to the change. Mine didn't.

High above, a blaze of white light cut through the haze. Searchlights pierced the mist. More signs of trouble in Nicodemia. Same old, same old.

"Even if Trinity lets me back into the system, I'd still be hungry."

Helen shook her head. "You never have to be hungry, Jude."

I opened the paper package. "Mushroom sandwich?"

"Portobello and mustard." She waggled her gloved hands. "Freshly chopped peppers."

One of my favorites. Helen had a knack for that kind of thing.

I took a bite, my hunger getting the best of me. Through the mouthful, I said, "You know anything about a new gang rolling around these parts?"

She crossed her arms. "Is this about that job you told my wife about?"

"Maybe." I took another bite. The sandwich was a little slice of heaven, and I'd never enjoyed anything more. "If the meds had painkillers mixed in, then the new gang might have taken them to help with some off-books surgery."

Helen didn't look convinced, but she'd spent her whole life on the right side of the law. It was hard for her to imagine anyone operating in the dark, especially in a city where the AI watched everyone all the time to track their deeds, both good and bad, in the form of a currency called Karma.

But there would always be those willing to break rules. There would always be people willing to hurt others for fun or profit.

"Rumor around the diner is that the new guy's name is Frank Lauder. He's a hotshot, and nobody thinks he'll be around for long, soon as Saint Jerome bothers to take care of him." Helen's eyes followed the spotlight slashing through darkness far across the city. "I don't know. I never figured out why Saint Jerome got a pass on everything he's done."

"Body, soul, community," I said. "Trinity's an AI designed by Catholics for their long journey across the stars."

"Don't give me that shit. The Saint doesn't serve any of those things."

"Maybe he serves a necessary function of the community. The only one around here who doesn't do that is me."

"Says the guy who saved a hotdog vendor from certain doom."

"Yeah," I said. "What would happen to our souls if we ran out of hotdogs."

Behind us, the hotdog vendor picked that moment to leave the diner. He still limped, but he gathered his cart without too much trouble. He gave me a nod as he walked past, and I tipped my hat to him. He'd be fine. And once he got back on his feet, maybe I could depend on his charity for a meal or two. The kindness of those who owe a favor beats the kindness of strangers any day—and it all beats the hell out of the kindness of family.

I finished the last few bites of sandwich. "Thanks, Helen," I said, unable to confer the depth of the gratitude that I really felt. "You know I'll pay you back."

"No need," Helen said, slapping me on the back. "Just don't give your sister too hard a time."

"No promises."

"And stay out of trouble."

I stepped into the misty night, sure now where my next visit needed to be. The cross I'd picked up under McCay's floor felt heavy in my pocket, and if anyone knew where it came from, it would be the Saint.

Chapter 6

I MAY HAVE TOLD Helen that Saint Jerome was a necessary component of a functioning community, but there's a big difference between repeating the twisted tenets of an ancient religion and swallowing them whole. Jerome was a wart on the ass of society and about as essential as an eel in a vat of tuna. Fear of his gangsters made parents keep their children indoors. Maybe his iron fist and vicious territorial tendencies kept crime from running rampant, but the cost of organized crime was the wellbeing of everybody in the lower bead of Nicodemia. Jerome was the slug in the garden that kept the lettuce from growing too tall. Neither God nor machine could possibly see a benefit in keeping the gangster boss in power, but there he was, a testament to the imperfections of the powers that be.

Dockside was a misnomer for the district of the lower Heavies that held the fisheries. Sure, there were docks. It was all docks down in the pitted bottom of the station. There, the gravity was heaviest, making every breath a pull through gritted teeth. Every step was a marathon. This was Jerome's territory, more than anywhere else, but as I walked the streets, his thugs never stepped out to greet me. Nothing lit up the foggy Dockside night.

I was alone but for the fish in their pools.

The fiberoak grid splayed out across the pits where fish of various varieties splashed slick and dark in the night. Tuna, salmon, carp. Every fish had its use in the station, and every single one of them stank its own kind of ugly. I'd visited Dockside plenty of times, but that fish rot stench hit with an aching newness every single time.

There, in the small hours of the morning, with the air heavy with fish and fog, a person could almost feel alone, even with all the world on his shoulders.

A blue light flickered through heavy fog. I headed for it, ignoring the slosh of the fisheries on either side. Out there, in the cold docks, a person could fall into the open water and his body might be lost for days before anyone bothered to dredge him up. Those black waters swallowed sin and sinner alike, and to feed the fish was almost a kind of redemption. It helped the station, anyway. In a closed system like Nicodemia, death was a person's last good deed.

The solid click of a small firearm told me I was no longer alone.

I raised my hands into the air. "I'm here to talk, Wash," I said, letting a small fraction of my weariness slide into my voice.

After a long pause, Wash responded from the fog. "There's been a change of plans."

I said, "Tell me about that tattoo of yours." The screaming Jesus necklace sat like lead in my breast pocket.

He stepped closer through the gloom, his silhouette looming between rippling ponds. "What's it like working for Lauder?"

"Come on, I…" I took a step back. "What?"

"I got to thinking," he said, "nobody ignores the Saint unless they've got the backing of a rival, but that's not going to save you." He raised an arm, but there wasn't a weapon in it. I wondered who had the gun I'd heard. Wash's jerky movements betrayed the fear behind his aggression. Fear of what, I wasn't sure. Maybe he was afraid I would humiliate him again.

"Like I said before," I said, "I don't work for anyone."

"You're here to ambush us."

I looked around, double-checking the army I hadn't brought. "How exactly do you think ambushes work?"

The twitchy smile didn't settle well on his soft features. He made a faint whistling noise through his teeth. "You tell Lauder we're not falling for it. Not this time. You're not going to see the Saint tonight, Demarco."

"I thought Jerome wanted to see me."

Wash ran his fingers through his hair and breathed a deep, noisy breath through his nose. "You switched sides."

Where was this coming from? "You can't possibly believe that."

When Wash stepped close, an odor hit me above even the stench of the fisheries. Something raw and ripe, like the musk of an animal. Every muscle in his body shuddered with tension.

"I just need a few answers," I said, hands still raised. "That's all."

Wash glanced to the side. Two of his buddies stepped forward from the mist on either side. That's where the guns were. They both held blocky orange pistols with blue grips. Small caliber, but it wasn't going to matter once the bullets started flying. I was surrounded. Oh. *That's* how ambushes work.

"Pretty clever," I said to the guy on my left. "Hey, where'd you guys get all these guns?"

He shrugged.

I looked from one to the other, making a point of ignoring Wash. "I don't think your boss treats you very well, guys. Have you ever considered unionizing?"

Wash slugged me fast, hard, and low. My knees hit the fiberoak dock. He looked down his nose at me. My long arms might have given me some advantage if I'd been stupid enough to fight back, but I wasn't. Wash was a native Heavy: built like a brick and twice as smart. He might not be able to shove me around, but I didn't like my odds in a straight-up brawl.

"Tell me what you're doing for Lauder," Wash hissed. "Or you'll feed these damn fish."

I patted my pockets. "I think I left my fish food back at the office."

"I ain't talkin' about fish food."

"Flakes, chum, feeder fish. I don't know, man." I showed my empty palms. "I got nothing."

Wash sputtered. "With your body, asshole."

"We can't do that."

"Why not?"

"I use my body." I flashed him a crooked smile. "Almost every day."

His thick fist pounded the side of my skull. In all fairness, that one might have been deserved. Little flashes danced around my vision, and if I hadn't been on my knees, I'd have worried about toppling over into the drink.

The guy on my left had the good grace to look uncomfortable, but I had the feeling his discomfort wasn't going to help me once my corpse hit the bottom of a pond. I moved my hand slowly to my pocket, careful not to trigger Wash's twitchy paranoia. From it, I drew the small cross. "This," I said. "What can you tell me about it?"

Wash's eyes went wide. He took a step back, eyes darting around at the fog. "Where'd you get that?"

I could have taken the advantage to stand up, but I got the distinct feeling that my height was one of those things that really pissed Wash off. His newfound paranoia bothered me, but I tried to set it aside. I knelt on one knee, ready to stand at the first sign of trouble. Wash didn't appear to pick up on the irony of my genuflection. The cross dangled on its chain, its screaming Jesus spinning in the dim light. "Maybe I should just talk to Jerome about this."

"He's not here," said the guy on my left, putting away his orange gun. "Not for you, anyway."

"And here I thought he and I were friends."

"Nobody's friends with the Saint," said Wash.

"Really? That's a shame. We got along so well at singles bowling night."

Wash's brow furrowed as if he truly couldn't tell if what I had said was a lie. It was, but the fact he couldn't tell confirmed that he had some serious drugs in his system. That explained the lack of self-control and the severely dilated pupils now transfixed by the dangling cross.

"Well, he must be lonely," I said. "Having no friends."

This time when Wash swung that meaty fist, I caught it. Standing to my full height, I kept hold of his hand, trying my very best to ignore the two thugs.

"Just shoot him!" shouted Wash.

A dozen heartbeats passed. Neither of the guys shot me, for reasons I could only guess. I set my gaze on Wash, meeting his brown-eyed stare until he twitched.

He growled, "I said—"

"They heard what you said, but here's the thing, Wash—a good thug knows what his boss wants. These two guys? They're looking at you right now and they're seeing you wrecked off a bad high. They're looking at how you cracked after that encounter with Lauder, and they're asking themselves how long you'll be around." I shoved him away. "When they walk away today, they're going to report to Saint Jerome. Do you think they want to tell the Saint that they murdered his favorite bowling buddy? A powerful friend? An excommunicated man who can work outside the system to do things they've never imagined?"

"The Saint's not your friend," Wash said, his voice almost swallowed by the fog. "He's never been your friend."

"Maybe. Maybe not." I held out the cross like I was warding off a vampire. "But here's how it's going to go. You're going to tell me what you know about this cross. Then you and your boys are going to go tell the Saint that I'm busy with another job, and I'll get back to him when I'm ready."

Wash worked his mouth like a fish a few times before responding. "The cross is from a bunch of kids I used to run with," he said. "Nothing big. They're not trouble if that's what you're looking for."

"Kids?"

"Young," he said. "Some of them really young."

"Where's their turf?"

He stared at me, the twitchiness in his muscles fading. Whatever courage he'd dosed himself with was dying off. "It's not a good night for the guilty, Demarco."

"Hardly ever is."

Wash looked down at his big hands as if finding them for the first time. His bruised knuckles looked black in the dim Dockside lights.

"If you're going to talk about guilt," I said, "you'd best know I was raised Catholic too. Guilt is in my blood."

His expression darkened. "You don't know what it's like growing up on the streets."

"I know Trinity takes care of you." Homelessness couldn't exist on the station, present company excluded. Anyone under Trinity's purview could have a place to live and food to eat. Good Karma made the house nicer and the food more palatable, but shelter and calories were a human right. Only the excommunicated really knew hunger.

Karma was a currency in Nicodemia, managed entirely by Trinity. It was the paperless, coinless currency earned with deeds that supported the station AI's priorities. Good Karma could raise a man to the highest standing in life, couching him in luxury befitting a king. In theory, anyway. More often, bad Karma held a man down. He'd scrape his head on the glass roof of progress, running into problems whichever way he turned in a system that rarely explained itself. A citizen with bad Karma would still have his needs met, but he'd turn to the de facto hard currency of good old-fashioned dimes to make ends meet.

Wash shook his head. "You're wrong. There's so much more to this damn city that you've never seen. Nobody has." He pointed at my chest. "And people like you are the ones who go around wrecking things. You want to know who that cross belongs to, but you only bring those kids pain."

"Sometimes that's what's needed."

"Not this time," he snapped. "Not now."

"All I want is answers. Promise."

The muscles in his enormous neck tightened. For a fraction of a second, I saw fear in his dark eyes, then it was gone. "I got a girl," he admitted. The way he said it made me think there was more to the story, but he didn't elaborate.

"Is she nice?"

"Hell of a lot nicer than anyone else around here."

So, that was his deal. He wanted out, but he didn't know how to get there. My refusing to cooperate probably wasn't helping him. "I won't cause any trouble," I said, "and I won't get you in trouble with the Saint."

"Maybe it's time you visited the church."

"I keep hearing that."

"Lot of good answers around there," he said. "Maybe the kind of answers you're looking for." He nodded to the necklace. "A piece like that? It belongs to someone special. Someone who might spend time near Joan. That's where you'll find the Wailing Sinners."

"I'll meet with the Saint tomorrow," I said. "I'll put in a good word."

I left the docks to make the long slow slog up the spiral to the city's biggest cathedral. He thinks I should visit a church? I'll visit the biggest church in the whole damn city.

Chapter 7

THE CITY WOKE with the persistent determination of a bad hangover.

I walked up the long spiral. First, the sky cleared, mist siphoning away into reservoirs to be purified and returned to the fish. False stars became visible in the distant sky, then disappeared as the eastern arc lightened in a dazzling series of static grays. It wasn't the best sunrise sequence in the repertoire, but it was welcome nonetheless. It came with a wave of dry cool air that helped my damp bones realize how uncomfortable they'd been all night without actually making things any better.

At first, I hugged the inner rail where I could see the faraway city spiraling up on the other side. The view dizzied me, same as ever, so I veered through the meandering streets farther from the center. Navigating city streets farther from the inner space meant a longer walk, but my joints couldn't ache any more, and my muscles couldn't get any more exhausted. What was another mile or two in the early hours of the morning?

Anyway, I didn't feel the urge to wake Priest Cecilia by arriving at church too early. I was her lost sheep. That didn't mean I needed to be an asshole about it.

"Want a lift?"

I turned to see the woman I'd met the previous night. She now wore red slacks, a billowing white blouse, and sunglasses that covered half her face. Her ride was a slick electric motorcycle, and there was barely room on the back for half of me.

"Charlotte Beck," I said. "Quite a coincidence running into you again."

"Oh honey, you know there's no such thing as coincidence when brilliant minds are at play."

"I've always thought of myself as average at best."

"You sell yourself short."

"Still enjoying our little city?" I kept walking.

"I never said I was here for fun."

"It's a long trip for business. Your boss must pay well."

She rode along beside me, wrists draped lazily over her handlebars. "It's easy when you love what you're doing."

"And what would that be?"

"Art."

"You're an artist?"

"Not exactly." Pedestrians choked the narrow street, and she had to fall in behind me for a short distance. When the way cleared, she accelerated up next to me again. "I hear you're the best at finding lost things."

"Fixing things," I said. "I fix things. Sometimes I find people."

Beck shot me a sideways grin. "Sometimes people have things I want."

"Like art?"

"Expensive art." She searched the side of my face, but I refused to give her any reaction. "Stolen art. My boss wants it back."

"Violet Ruiz?"

"You've never heard the name?"

The name rattled around my skull a few times but still didn't stick. "Doesn't ring a bell."

"Took you a good long pause to figure that out."

"That doesn't make me interested."

She gave a little pout, still rolling along next to me. "It'll pay."

"Your job's too dangerous," I finally said. "I prefer to play it safe."

"Buddy, you're the kind of guy who's a little too bruised to play it safe."

We walked in silence for a while. Finally, I cracked and asked, "What art were you looking for?"

Beck gunned her cycle, accelerating ahead of me and cutting across to block the path. She leaned toward me and met my eyes over the top of her sunglasses. "Ever heard of a painting called *The Garden of Earthly Delights*?"

I gave a low whistle. "What's Ruiz want with a thousand-year-old painting from Earth?"

"It's pretty."

"This whole business smelled fishy since the moment you showed up."

Beck sniffed. "Everything smells fishy around here."

"And yet this job stands out."

A crowd gathered around the passage blocked by Beck's motor-cycle. A few people opted to go another route, but others pressed forward, zombies out on their morning stroll. Beck didn't budge.

I focused on Beck and her smug expression. "I'm helping a guy right now who's looking for meds to save him from excruciating pain. They might even save his life. Now, as expected, he's a certain level of upset about those meds being missing. He hires me, and when I help him, he's a certain level of appreciative. Maybe I get a meal out of the deal. Maybe two. I can't imagine wanting more out of life."

An elderly woman half my height elbowed her way through to the front of the crowd to scowl at me.

I continued, "When people from this town need me, I try to

help. There are things I can do that they can't. There are things they can do that I can't. But it all stays in the closed system. It all makes sense." I took a step forward, looming over Beck. "But when you show up with your out-of-town boss and an offer of amazing wealth? That sets things out of balance. That's not a single fellow worried about where his next meds come from. Now you're talking about art. Worse, you're talking about important art. Art that makes its way into the history books."

"You never wanted to be part of something important?" Beck said.

"Not one damn day of my life." I reached out, lifted the front of her scooter with one hand, and moved it to the side so the old lady could pass. It opened the floodgate of pedestrians. "People who care about art enough to cross the stars care about it far more than a few human lives. I'm not interested in becoming the gravel under the tires of that machine as it speeds forward. Let someone else take that job."

"There is no one else," Beck said in a quiet voice. "Not like you."

My chest clenched at the words, and my tongue went dumb for several seconds. Finally, I said, "I'm a dime a dozen, lady, but I'll listen to more of whatever you have to say if you're willing to tag along."

"Really?" She sounded hopeful.

"Once you've said your piece, I'll make my decision, and you'll be on your way."

I stepped past her through the narrow alley, elbowing my way through more morning traffic. Soon, the streets would be packed with commuters, making their way from residential sections of town down to the docks or up to the farms. We were headed upward, so we moved to a street flowing the right direction. Vendors appeared along sidewalks, selling everything from newspapers to falafel.

"So," I said to Beck as she struggled to maneuver her motorcycle through the crowd, "what's so special about Violet Ruiz?"

"There are too many ears around here."

Of course there were. "Follow me," I growled. We made our way farther upspiral until we found what I was looking for. A tall building that looked like it had been carved from a solid slab of granite stood sentinel against the crowded upper quarter. Beck left her cycle on the street, and we took the stairs to the roof. Once there, I found a corner covered in cigarette butts and broken liquor bottles. Standing close to the edge made my head swoon, but it gave me a good view of the surrounding area, including Heavy Nicodemia's largest cathedral.

Beck eyed me as she lit a cigarette. "It's not so far a drop, you know."

I looked down at the crowd only a few stories below. "At the current spin of gravity, you'd be dead as sure as if you jumped from the farms to the docks, and without the pleasant rush of a long fall to keep you entertained."

She leaned over the railing above the deadly drop. "You'd think they would have some kind of safety mechanism," she said. "Like a net or something."

I took hold of her arm. Her strength surprised me, even though my big hand easily wrapped all the way around her whole wrist. "Trinity has drones that can catch people, but not for short drops like this. And not in the Heavies."

A crinkle at the corner of her eyes hinted at a smile. "They don't use rescue drones in Heavy Nicodemia?"

I said, "When you fall from up at the peak, they're almost fast enough to save you by the time you hit the Docks."

"Almost."

I made a so-so gesture. "Sometimes they slow you enough that you can have an open casket."

Beck raised an eyebrow at my hand still gripping her wrist. When I didn't move it, she relented and stepped back from the edge. "Trinity wouldn't catch *you*, though, would it?"

I released her wrist and stared up at the cathedral. The Cathedral of Saint Francis of Assisi's dark spires reached almost to the bottom of the spiral above it. Gargoyles lined the parapets above, and the stained glass shone in the morning light. An alcove in the side of the church held a statue of Joan of Arc in full armor, her brilliant sword held high in the light. Beck's words irritated me, and I couldn't explain why. "There are blind spots all over the station, and this is one of them. If you've got secrets you want to spill, then this is the time to do it."

A cloud of smoke drifted lazily from her flaring nostrils as if to punctuate the irritation I was giving her. "I never thought I'd smoke another cigarette when I left Earth. Mrs. Ruiz doesn't allow fire on her ship."

"Some things are hardly worth it if they're not forbidden," I said. "And fire isn't so bad since nothing else in the city burns."

"People burn."

"Not very well."

"Surely vape rigs would be safer."

"People need the freedom to make bad decisions. It's a fundamental part of our nature."

Beck fixed me with half-lidded eyes and savored the curl of the smoke that kissed her lips. "My employer is a woman of considerable wealth, and I'm her personal assistant. She expects me to behave in a certain way. I make things happen, and it's not always easy."

"I figured."

Below, pedestrians moved through the streets, passing Joan of Arc as if she wasn't even there. A slender teenage girl lingered near the statue.

Beck continued, "What you probably didn't figure is how she got that wealth, how she keeps it, and what she plans on doing with it in her old age."

"Is there a Mr. Ruiz?"

"Mr. Ruiz died in the course of his work a few years before we left to come here."

"What did he do?"

"He was an art thief." She grinned. "A good one, and he had decent taste."

"Hence the Hieronymus Bosch painting."

"Oh, you were paying attention?"

"A little." The girl below moved on, lingering near a group of kids. None of them were over the age of fifteen, and the youngest looked like he couldn't have been older than six. Maybe this was the gang Wash once ran with. Maybe not.

"*The Garden of Earthly Delights* is a triptych. Three panels, and they fold together to close. The left panel is all about Adam and Eve meeting. The center panel contains images of earthly sin, and the third panel—"

"Hell and the afterlife."

She drew a lungful of smoke and let it roll out the corners of her mouth. "Yeah. The consequences of all that earthly delight."

The girl below returned to the blind spot and the other kids spread out among the commuting crowd. People moved along with their daily lives, hardly noticing the presence of the children among them—children who ought to have been in school or some kind of apprenticeship. It seemed an oversight that Trinity hadn't already gathered them up, and I wondered what the police would do if they knew what was going on in this particular blind spot.

"My boss has the first two panels, but she wants the third. A few years ago, we tracked it as it went onto a transport-class vessel, headed for this system. It's here somewhere, and she wants it."

"There are dozens of station cities rotating around this star, and there are settlements on the nearby planets. What makes you think they'd bring it here, to Nicodemia?"

"None of the settlements are established enough to support the kind of environmental controls needed for a thousand-year-old painting."

"But why Nicodemia? Why not Samaria or Alexandria? There

are a dozen different cities, and your thieving friends might have had enough money to get established at any of them. For that matter, why Heavy Nicodemia? There's no reason someone of means would pick the toughest part of the roughest stack."

Beck leaned against the railing, her elbows sticking out over the city below. The cigarette dangled from ruby-red lips. "I think you're starting to get curious, big guy." Her tone was enticing. Provocative.

"I'm always curious. It doesn't mean I'll be stupid enough to take your job."

"I heard you were average at best."

"Maybe a little better when I've got a cup of coffee in me."

"But you don't."

"True."

"Well, you're asking the right questions. Why here? Why this stack?" She closed her eyes and shook her head as if to clear it. "We don't know where it is, but we know where to start looking."

"That's all you're going to say before I agree to work for you?"

She tossed her cigarette into the pile of butts and stepped it out the way a fat cat casually snuffs a moth. "That's the sum of it. We're looking for stolen art, Demarco. That warrants a little caution."

"Good," I said. "Because I already have a job, and it's about to get busy."

Beck shot a glance at the girl below. "How about I help?"

I sighed. "I'm sure you're a busy lady."

"Tell you what. Let's say we finish this, then you help me with my thing."

"I'm not taking that deal."

She slapped me on the back. "Sure you are, Demarco. Sure you are."

"Right now, all I need to do is have a nice, civil conversation with Joan of Arc down there," I said. "That is the extent of my ambition."

"She's not going to want to talk."

"What makes you say that?"

Beck drummed the four iridescent crosses on her nails against the metal railing. "Are you sure you don't want to skip all this and move on to a better job?"

"Look at those kids working the crowd," I said. "Look close. Each of them carries a cross somewhere visible. It's a gang."

Beck got an expression like she'd just eaten a sour grape. She eyed the kids moving through the crowd for a minute, watching as they stole trinkets from the morning commuters. Some of them wore the cross on a sleeve. Others wore it dangling from their belt. Nobody wore it as a necklace, but one of the larger boys wore a cross as a single dangling earring.

"The girl by the statue doesn't have one," I said. "She'll talk because she'll want her necklace back."

"So we flank her? Rough her up a little?"

"I don't want your help."

"I'm on a tight timeline, Demarco."

"Patience is a virtue."

Her jaw clenched. "My job is about the greater good. It's about righting a wrong."

I couldn't find the words to explain why sometimes my job wasn't about what was best for those involved. It wasn't making the world a better place that drove me. It wasn't getting art into the right hands or even saving people from their own greed and misfortune. It was about the riddle. Cracking the case. I had a puzzle that could only be solved by chatting up a certain street urchin, and I was going to do that whether or not Beck helped.

It surprised me when Beck fell into step behind me when I headed for the stairs. Together, we descended to the cobbled streets. The doors whooshed open onto a dwindling crowd, and the young girl across the way looked up just as I took my first step into the yellow light of day. By the time I took my second, she was gone.

Chapter 8

I DIDN'T THINK about what Beck would do if she caught the kid. Didn't think about what *I* would do. Didn't think about the danger of rushing through a crowd after a stranger on a hunch so weak it would tip over in a stiff wind. I didn't think about a lot of things I probably should have.

I just ran.

The kid was fast. Sleek and slim, like a racing drone fresh off the track. She dipped and dodged through pedestrian traffic and skirted past trolleys like she owned the whole damn street. Maybe she did.

While the kid dodged pedestrians, I bowled clean through. The first few fell and shouted. After that, they moved and shouted, making a clear path for the rampaging giant in a trench coat chasing a little kid who was no doubt up to no good.

"Demarco!" shouted Beck far behind me, but I ignored her. Time enough for her to find me again later since she was so damn good at it.

The kid rolled over a stumpy automobile trundling up the inside spiral. Its driver reacted badly, pounding brakes and swerving hard into my path. I swore. The kid ducked down the outer loop, heading for the labyrinthine Warehouse District behind the cathedral. She'd lose me for sure in there.

"Demarco!" Beck gasped as she buzzed up next to me on her scooter. "What the hell are you doing?"

"I'm chasing that kid," I said.

"Why?"

I sucked in a fresh lungful of oxygen and sprinted, closing some hard distance as the girl tangled with a cluster of shroom farmers.

"Stop her!" I shouted, hoping there was a chance a decent citizen would help me out.

Not a *good* chance. She slipped their semicircle and burned turf upspiral, sticking hard to a row of grasslike vegetation forming the long crescent leading up to the cathedral's front door. I left Beck and her scooter in the dust as she got tangled in the choked confines of a busy alley.

Then the kid ducked hard right. I was only a few long paces behind. The dark alley swallowed her like a whale, and I charged right in.

A flash of red at the far end. Beck had circled around.

My lungs burned. My legs ached.

The kid scrambled up a dumpster, then leaped onto another, where she climbed a short fiberstone barrier.

The dumpsters were sturdy things, but the lid of the first collapsed when I stood on it. I skirted the edge of the next one. Lifting myself up—oh damn I was out of shape—I topped the wall just in time to see the kid duck into a warehouse only a block off the cathedral square, right in the shadow of the big church.

"Got you," I whispered to myself, mostly to convince myself.

I brushed the dust off my coat and straightened my hat. My knuckles cracked, letting me know that I was clenching fists. That wouldn't do. I loosened up. Got myself ready.

Then I thought better of it. Clever kid like that wouldn't lead me straight to a hideout. She'd lead me to a trap or somewhere sticky. Instead, I made myself as invisible as a giant could be among the mottled stone of the dimly lit bead.

Minutes passed long and slow. My hands shook, and the rare craving for tobacco danced on my lips.

There! She crawled out the side of the building where airlock shutters butted up against a garbage chute. The skinny kid squeezed right through the chute, landing in a heap of trash. Filthy, but in a whole lot better shape than I would have been.

Well, that was one mystery solved. If she was the thief, she hadn't sent a drone in to steal the meds. This kid, or someone her size, had slipped right past McCay's security through the maintenance duct, climbed through the air vent, and stole the meds. It was a hell of a job for a kid to pull, but it made more sense than anything else I'd come up with. Now there was only one other question:

Why?

I hunkered up against the building in the deepest shadow. When she looked my way, I held my breath. The sparkle in her mischievous eyes flashed so bright it nearly blinded me, but she didn't bolt. She sauntered off like she owned the damn district. This time, I was convinced.

There were places all around Heavy Nicodemia where the dim gray light of the false sky only helped the shadows thrive like a lingering mold. These warehouse districts with their flat fibersteel walls and grime-covered ducts bred the kind of low-grade trouble that had plagued humanity since the first time someone decided to put two houses next to each other and call it a city. Cockroaches skittered along the darkest corners, feeding on the long-forgotten trash that for whatever reason had evaded both automated and manual cleanup for weeks, months, and even years.

Only someone with a low sense of self-preservation let his footsteps echo against these cavernous alleys.

The girl stayed alert, but I'd done my fair share of following. She had a pattern about her. Move forward, stop, check. Innocent people don't move with that kind of caution. The kid had something to hide, and her eyes held the kind of desperation that made a person dangerous.

Why was she there? Trinity cared for the kids of Nicodemia. Somebody was always around to help raise children who really needed it, and the AI never had trouble finding the right parents when a kid showed up lost. Why, then, was she wandering the rougher parts of town?

When she finally ducked into an abandoned warehouse—one out of many—I stuck to my instincts and played it cautious. Heavy Nicodemia's Warehouse District was a relic of industry long gone. Over the centuries, much of the manufacturing had moved up the chain to Haven while the fishing industry stayed strong in the Heavies' lower quarter. That left places like this unwanted and unused.

Circling at a safe distance, I made a note of all the entrances and exits. Then, when I was reasonably confident that she hadn't left, I approached.

The utility entrance stood clean and red against the grime of the surrounding buildings. It almost invited a visitor, so I took the extra time to poke around. A dozen bottles arranged to topple when the door slid open. Clever. I disassembled the noise trap and squeezed inside.

It was a cozy space that almost smelled like a home. Food and sweat and dust swirled through the closed air. Once my eyes adjusted to the dark, I looked around, but the big open space was as black as the deep void outside the station.

Only one corner showed signs of life. Buried in a crook of shelving was a mess of padding and a collection of trinkets. To one side, a pile of paintings leaned against a short wall. *Paintings* wasn't exactly the right word. The work was exquisite, using hand-stitched textiles and debris from the ship to capture light in strange and interesting ways. A little video screen leaned against a small mirrored cabinet. Flickering images on the screen projected dancing lights on the nearby artwork, bringing color and shadow to a kind of haunted life.

But the kid was nowhere to be seen.

Maybe she had escaped after all. I crept forward, keeping my ears open to approach. My heart slammed in my chest. It'd been a while since I'd found anywhere truly off grid. Something this far in the dark was rare in the AI-surveilled ship, and it felt like it had been here for a long time.

I toed the mess with my boot, still unsure if this was really the kid's place or just another trap. She had dog-eared paperback novels, stuffed animals, and a series of little fiber army men, a cross-stitch kit. Kid stuff, mostly. Little kid stuff.

Now that I was closer, I could see the cabinet door was open just a crack. I reached out and pulled it open, careful to move slowly and quietly, as if something out there lurked ready to pounce at the first noise.

The cabinet only held one thing, and it wasn't what I had expected at all. It sat there slightly to one side of the center as if it had once been balanced by a second thing. Like two objects worshiped in a shrine.

And the one that remained was McCay's meds.

The jar sat there clear as day, McCay's name and dosage written right on the side. I picked it up and looked over my shoulder.

Sure enough, there was the girl.

"Damn, kid," I said. "You really know how to keep quiet."

She raised her hand out of a pocket and pointed a fabricated gray pistol my direction. It was the kind of makeshift weapon a person could build after rummaging around the back end of a broken recycler. "Put that back."

"How old are you?" I asked.

With her aim not wavering, not even a little, she took one step to the side, then another. "Old enough." Her slender body could have belonged to a young teenager or even a younger kid. Her blonde hair piled onto her shoulders in an unkempt mess.

I held up the meds. The red bottle was a dark blot in the dim light. "What's this mean to you? You trading this for money or food?"

Another step. Where was she going?

"You wouldn't shoot me," I continued. "Think of the mess."

"I know how to clean up a mess."

"Is that so?"

She took another step. "Well," she said. "Now it won't be so bad." She nodded at her previous position. "If I had shot you from there, you might have gotten blood all over my best stuff."

Damn. "The fella you stole these meds from sent me. You think he won't send someone else?" I took a step closer to her little hideout. If she was so concerned about making a mess, then maybe that could be my final revenge.

"They'll never find me," she said.

"I found you, kid."

"Retch."

"What?"

"Don't call me kid. People call me Retch."

I forced a smirk across my face. "Retch isn't the first name I'd have guessed for such a pretty girl." It was as much charm as I could manage.

"My parents called me Gretchen, but I'm not a girl."

"You look like a girl."

"Yeah, well, you look like a piece of shit." She—*he* jutted his jaw out.

"Fair enough."

"You got a problem with it?"

Some instinct in me relaxed, and I knew the boy wasn't going to shoot. His posture changed from the raw musculature of a coiled snake to the defensive stance of a threatened rat. Still dangerous, but not quite the same. "I have no problem," I said. "You live in the shadow of a church that's still figuring it out." It explained why he had decided to live out here on his own.

"That church keeps me from getting anything other than these bland gender-neutral clothes. It makes procuring bindings hard as hell."

At first, I didn't know what he was talking about, but then it clicked. His body was starting to betray him. "How old are you, kid?"

"Twenty-five." He couldn't have been more than thirteen. He raised the gun a fraction so I could see straight down the barrel. The tip of a bullet shone in the barrel's shadowy depths.

"Not too concerned about the truth, are you?"

"I need those meds."

"If it makes you feel any better, the Church still hasn't figured me out either. Probably never will." Gesturing with my open palm, I indicated that I was going to reach into my pocket. When he gave the go-ahead, I withdrew the chain and dangled the screaming Jesus cross in front of him. "This is yours, isn't it?"

The cross caught his gaze like a hypnotist's fob. "Where did you get that?"

"You left it at the scene." I had to lay my cards on the table. "You're right. Nobody else is going to find you."

Retch absently pressed an open palm to his chest. The gun drifted, pointing a little to the side. If I chose to jump at him and disarm him, I'd probably only get killed a couple times in the process.

A sharp rapping came from the gap in the wall where I'd entered. Then, in an explosion of gray light, Beck's statuesque figure emerged. She strolled across the open warehouse.

There was something in the worried look Retch cast at Beck that I couldn't quite interpret. He hesitated, stuck between pointing his gun at me or Beck. In the time it took to make the decision, Beck closed half the distance.

"Stay back," Retch said, pointing the gun at me.

It was the wrong choice. Beck kept walking.

"I'll shoot!"

Muscles clenched, I braced myself for the inevitable gunshot.

It never came. Beck took one last long stride and struck Retch with a backhand hard enough to send the kid sprawling. I grabbed the gun and ejected the bullets.

"You're welcome," said Beck, even though I didn't thank her.

I *couldn't* thank her. I was too damn angry.

Chapter 9

"IT DIDN'T NEED to get violent," I growled on our way back to the church.

"It got violent when the kid pulled a gun," said Beck. "I saved your life."

"Great."

"Now will you take Ruiz's job?" Beck asked.

"Not yet." McCay's pills were in the breast pocket of my trench coat, and the kid was slinging weapons-grade vitriol from the safety of his warehouse a block away. I'd left him the gun and the cross. With any luck, he'd calm down and offer a prayer of forgiveness for the unrepentant assholes who had invaded his home.

Forgiveness like that wasn't likely this close to the cathedral, which is why I had kept his bullets.

Beck stepped between me and the cathedral. "You have the meds. Drop them off with your client and let's go."

"That painting's not going anywhere."

"No, but my boss is," Beck snapped. "*I* am."

I looked up, letting my eyes unfocus at the gray noonday sky. "I have a client, and I have questions. So long as those two things exist, I'm not touching another case, no matter what the pay. You apparently know how to solve your problems, so maybe you should go ahead and work on your own."

Beck growled in disgust. "Does your client really want you tracking down all these loose ends?"

She was right, of course. If McCay was my excuse to keep following up on this, then he ought to have some input. He wasn't. I needed to know more about the situation, and something didn't sit right about McCay.

"Nobody's ever tried to hire me this hard," I sighed. "Why does your boss want me so bad?"

"You're the right man for the job."

I stared at her hard. When she didn't twitch, I said, "The right person for the job is a person who wants it."

"You want this job."

"I'm busy." I shouldered past her up the front steps of the cathedral.

She didn't follow me. "You need the money, and you need to know the truth."

I pulled open the massive cathedral doors and spread my arms to take in the whole elaborately decorated church. "If I was interested in the truth, why would I come to a place like this?"

"Please?" This time, there was a hint of desperation in her voice.

"I'm busy," I repeated.

Beck didn't follow me into the church, and I didn't blame her. The Cathedral of Saint Francis of Assisi was an intimidating structure, even for those of us raised in the embrace of the almighty Catholic Church. It replicated all the polished wood and shining metal of the cathedrals of Earth but added the deep resonance found only in the hollowed core of a massive space station and held the existential heft of a religious building that had actually journeyed through the heavens. It was a three-hundred-year-old monstrosity made all the more impressive by its absolute dominance of the center of the great downward spiral.

The Jesuits who had funded Nicodemia had long ago decided that this would be the biggest bastion of Christianity's journey, never mind that folks of other religions were welcome on the trip. Never mind that the sins and vices of common folk thrived just as well no matter how the scenery changed. A church aboard a generation ship was just another church, far as I was concerned. Just as full of itself. Just as fallible.

"Jude Demarco," drolled a woman's voice from behind me as I walked up the aisle. "Your parents would be so proud to see you in church."

I didn't turn around to respond. "Hello, Cecilia."

"It's customary to take off one's hat, my dear." She placed a hand on my elbow. She was a tiny lady, worn by the years, but her blue eyes sparkled with a clarity that only true faith in God or the gleam of snake oil can provide.

I swept my hat from my head, genuflected, and sat at the nearest pew, indicating the spot next to me for Cecilia to sit. She did, and for a while, the silence of the midday church seeped into my tired bones.

Addressing the hat in my lap as much as the woman next to me, I said, "The world's a terrible place, Priest. Full of terrible people."

She placed a hand on mine. Her skin was paper-thin and soft. "Are we having this discussion, again?"

"The world just doesn't shine like it used to."

She looked up at me, her features grim in the imitation candlelight. "There is a lot of good in this world, Jude. In all of the worlds."

"Sure." I wasn't convinced. We'd had that argument too many times. "But today my problem's with the Church."

Her hand tensed. "Is it?"

"There's a stray kid not far from here living in a warehouse. You know about that?"

A long time passed before she spoke. "I have seen some kids running around."

"See, here's the thing," I said, trying hard to keep the tension from my voice. "There's this boy who feels alienated from the Church."

"This friend have a name?"

"The Church has some funny ideas about sex and gender, don't you think?"

"Mr. Demarco—"

"The way I see it, the Church started in a place where reproduction was a competitive advantage. Makes sense those rules might exist way back then." I swallowed back a lump in my throat. "Now there's this boy by the name of Retch."

She tilted her head quizzically.

"Gretchen, maybe."

Cecilia nodded understanding. "I've seen her around."

I cringed at her selection of pronouns. "What can you tell me about the Wailing Sinners?"

"They're a street gang. Trouble. Every last one."

"Lost causes?"

She spread her palms. "Aren't we all?"

"I should have come here first, but…"

"You don't like it here."

"Never have."

Her eyes twinkled with amusement. "You should always come here first, Jude. It would keep you out of a lot of trouble."

"Retch needs help. He's on the street and afraid of everyone, especially you. He's armed, maybe dangerous. He's a thief, at the very least."

Her brow furrowed. "You think I'm not doing my best to bring these kids into the fold?"

"It's not about bringing them into the fold, and you know it."

She looked down at the hymn book in the pew in front of her. "There's only so much I can do."

"You could accept him."

"He's always welcome here."

"Sure." I put a little more spite into the word than intended.

"Just like you, Demarco. You're always welcome."

I drew the med bottle from my pocket. "What do you know of this stuff?"

She peered at the bottle for several seconds. "It's used to treat certain genetic diseases, but Trinity provides it free, thanks to God's good grace."

"Free to anyone who wants to register their genetic flaw officially."

"It's hardly a flaw, Mr. Demarco. A lot of people take medicine."

"You provide medical assistance to your flock?"

"The Church has access to a medical printer. Help is provided to anyone who asks."

It was just like the Church to push people away and pull them close at the same time. One more way to manipulate the populace. "Do you think this Wailing Sinners gang is a threat?"

"No, of course not. Just deviants and confused children."

I closed my eyes and drew in a long breath. Retch's determined gaze greeted me behind my closed eyes. "He won't come to you if you're going to judge him."

"I will have you know that I have experienced more of the Church's judgment on sexuality than most."

"Yeah," I said, keeping my voice quiet. "They only got woman priests two hundred years ago."

"Two hundred years." She gave the sign of the cross. "We can only hope another two hundred will erase the stigma behind it."

"What can I say, Priest? The world is a terrible place full of terrible people."

Her fists balled up at her sides. She looked like she'd just sucked on a lemon. "There isn't much I can do if this Retch won't come to me."

"I want to know he'll have someone looking out for him."

She shot a glance at the bottle still in my hand. "You took her meds."

"I took *his* meds."

"Right." She licked her lips. "You stole from him the thing he needs to survive, and you want me to make sure things are fine?"

"Kids steal drugs all the time. It's not for survival."

"Isn't it?"

I genuflected and stood at the end of the pew. I took a good look at the gold leaf on the ceiling, some of which had been taken from the Vatican itself back on Earth. "Who gets to call it stealing, anyway? I took back something that had been stolen. What's God say about setting things right?"

She walked with me back through the church to the large wooden doors. "What does your heart tell you?"

"My heart tells me the Church should stop being such an asshole."

Cecilia gave me a wry look. "What else?"

I looked at the pill bottle. I hadn't read the label closely before, but the prescription on the side was printed in a tiny font that I could barely read. No narcotics. No painkillers. Nothing that might be used recreationally.

"Damn," I said, provoking a scathing look from the priest. I pocketed the pill bottle. "Next time you have a chat with God, tell him... Tell him he's not making life easy, okay?"

"You could tell him yourself."

"I would if I thought he'd listen."

Chapter 10

I NEVER MUCH WAS ONE for prayer. Even as a kid, I was the one kicking and screaming just to get a chance to end my day without voicing my concerns to the ever-present God above. I hated praying to God, hated asking Trinity for favors, and I hated begging anyone for help.

Call it practical or call it stupid. If something could be done, I'd be the one to do it. For myself, for my sister, even for my parents.

I sat on the fiberstone steps of the Cathedral of Saint Francis of Assisi, my whole body wracked with the urge for a single cigarette. I flicked my lighter into the wind, watching as it blew out every time. The day's wind was a dry exhale, swirling around the spiral station like a lazy hurricane. Eventually, it would stop, and a new weather pattern would emerge. Weather was constant change like the souls of men.

Still air was bad air. People craved change, and when it wasn't flowing in the air around them, they found ways to produce it. Raw instinct in the human spirit detests a static environment. Heat and humidity can be high or low and people will happily adapt, so long as it changes.

Flick. The flame danced for a few seconds, then guttered to a cold death.

Sometimes we don't like the changes life brings us. I'd worked a hundred cases like McCay's, and a hundred had ended the same way. These nice safe cases always came down to a nice safe end. Not this time. I held his meds in my hand, but I wasn't giving them back. All that was left was to visit the good doctor and tell him he was out of luck.

Or...

A raw stone of guilt lodged itself in the back of my throat. Flick. The man was in pain. I could get the meds by using my credentials as a trained med tech. The flame danced. It was in my power to get him exactly what he wanted, but my guilt pushed me to do more.

The flame died.

I was invisible. As far as the blue were concerned and as far as Trinity knew, I didn't even exist. A man could back out of any deal with me and the only consequence he'd face was a frown and a few foul words. McCay knew it too. Soon as he had another source for his meds, I was gone.

Flick. The flame instantly died.

McCay was in pain not because his meds were stolen. He was in pain because he refused to get help through Trinity. His vanity brought him pain. His refusal to comply with the norms of society. Flick. Then again, wasn't that what had caused Retch's trouble?

Or mine?

The flame died.

No, not really. My pain was a long slow train wreck of a life culminating in a series of bad luck and worse associations. My excommunication wasn't my choice. Retch's identity wasn't his. The only one of us who chose what they got was McCay, but did that mean he deserved his pain?

I pocketed my lighter. A tired ache drenched my bones, but there was more work to do. This needed to be finished, and soon.

Upspiral from the cathedral sat a shopping district complete with gambling hall and a few dozen decent bars. Later in the evening, the place would be crawling with acolytes of the mighty dime. Midday, however, the shops remained sparsely populated and the gambling halls were all but deserted.

The first shop I visited was a bust, as were the next several. Finally, I ran into one staffed by a bored-looking teen in a scrubby button-down blazer and a narrow-brimmed hat.

"It'll cost you," he said.

"I'll owe you a favor."

He looked me up and down, a slight twist of disgust tweaking his upper lip. "I like your coat."

"It keeps the rain off my back."

He looked away, his relaxed body language a clear dismissal, but I wasn't ready to be done.

I leaned forward, the knuckles of my fists pressed down on the hard white of his low counter. I spoke in a low growl. "There comes a time in every man's life when he finds a need for power outside his norm. He needs a problem solved or an obstacle removed. Maybe he says a prayer to God, but God doesn't listen. Maybe he asks the blue, but police are just as bad as anything else out there. They've got better things to worry about." My voice hissed with a barely controlled fervor, and I leaned in close, my face an inch from his. "Listen. One day you'll need the man who walks in the dark. You'll want questions answered that don't need answering. You'll want problems solved, and nobody else out there is going to solve them for you."

He nodded almost imperceptibly. His Adam's apple bobbed.

"I'm the man who walks in the dark, and I'm offering to owe you a favor." I dropped my business card down on his desk. "But I'm only offering this once."

He swallowed. "I'll see what I can do."

He did fine, and when I left his shop, I had a sack full of cast-off clothing and something that might pass for a decent meal. I ate the hard protein bar on my way back down the spiral, but this time I took the outer loop through gray, cramped streets. The cathedral shadowed this whole neighborhood, and as the scrubby residential brownstones turned to ramshackle warehouses, I noticed the first watcher.

And he noticed me. Soon, they were all around. A kid in the shadows or a gangly group of teens watching me from under a warm yellow lamp. None of the lights changed for me as I passed. Kids fell in behind me, keeping their distance at first, then closing closer and closer. By the time I reached Retch's warehouse, a pack of thirty-some children nipped at my heels, bristling with makeshift weapons.

Retch sat atop a crate, arms draped lazily over his knees. "Didn't think we'd see you back here so soon, dead man." His makeshift gun hung from a holster strapped across his chest. "I was hoping we wouldn't see you back here at all."

"I was thinking we might continue our conversation from earlier," I said.

"The one where I had a gun to your head?" The kids behind me laughed.

"The one that was interrupted before a proper conclusion."

"Yeah, your girlfriend sure is a looker." More jeers from the audience.

I held the bag out. "I'm not here to cause trouble, Retch."

He gestured at the crowd around us. "And yet."

"He went to the church," shouted a kid from the crowd. "Was in there a long time too."

Retch raised an eyebrow behind a tumble of blond hair. "Did the priest send you back here to show me the light?"

I took several steps forward. "Seems to me you might want some of this said in private."

"We don't have secrets here," he said with a quirky smile.

68

"These people accept me for who I am because they know I can kick some ass if I need to."

A couple kids in the crowd snickered at that. They pressed in closer, cutting off any illusion of an escape route I might have thought I still had.

"They know you're sick?" I asked.

Retch made a show of looking around at his cohorts. "Hardly anyone here isn't sick with something." He looked straight at me. "What've you got?"

I chose to misconstrue the question and set the sack on the crate next to him. "Your meds and an apology."

He blinked.

"Bindings," I said, "and boy-themed clothes that I think will fit you, if you're interested."

After a long pause, he whispered, "Why?" The waver in his voice told me that my gift had had the intended effect. My guess was he'd never heard that kind of respect from an adult.

"Tell me," I said, "how did you know McCay had the meds you needed?"

"Anonymous tip," he said.

"You won't divulge your sources?"

He made a show of considering it. "Some of us keep our promises," he finally said.

I tipped my hat to him and turned to leave. The crowd of kids parted before me, and as I passed, I saw that they all wore shoddy versions of the same screaming Jesus necklace that I'd given back to Retch. This gang of kids—forgotten by the church and all but ignored by Trinity—had managed to find each other in this vast city. They'd accepted each other's strangeness and found a way to survive outside the system.

Maybe they'd even make it.

Maybe they would even thrive.

There was still work to do before I slept, and the burning ache of exhaustion gnawed at my skull. My feet took me downspiral, past the warehouses and through the twisting residential tenements. Down where the air grew warm like the pit of my stomach every time I thought about telling McCay that I'd failed to bring his meds. It wasn't failure that bothered me so much. Failure was a good friend of mine.

The lying, though, sat ugly in the back of my gut. I'd have to lie to the man, and maybe even threaten him a little if he gave me a hard time. Nothing serious. Just a part of the job.

That's why it hit me with a mixed sense of dread and relief when I saw the flash of police lights outside McCay's apartment. The blue brought the whole works: two light scooters, three heavy rescue vehicles—the kind that couldn't go everywhere in the bead's narrow streets, but where they could go, they got there fast —and even a lifter. The big metal vehicle looked like it'd seen better days. Its brutal angular form wrapped itself around a trio of powerful rotors. Some enterprising cop had been upgrading and maintaining this thing for a long time. Its paint job sported the modern blue and white of police vehicles, and every light on every vehicle screamed blue and red in a psychedelic, asynchronous pulse.

They could have been there for anyone in that building. This could have been a random raid on a suspected criminal and have nothing to do with my small-potatoes medical fraud. McCay's crimes were hardly worth the paperwork, let alone a full regimen of officers.

The poor chap they'd left to guard the entrance looked up as I approached.

"What's the excitement?" I asked.

The officer's eyes lingered on the shape of my face. No doubt he saw how the street lamp I stood near didn't light up in my presence. Some of the older cops might ignore me entirely for the crime of having been excommunicated by Trinity. The younger crowd tended to brush me off with short answers and a gruff attitude.

By comparison, this guy was downright friendly. "Fella's dead up there. They think it's a murder."

"In a nice neighborhood like this?"

The cop—Anders, by the name on his badge—gestured at the flashing vehicles. "Apparently, the guy had decent Karma."

"Justice follows wealth, I suppose."

He jutted out his jaw. "Well, it shouldn't." I got the impression he'd had this argument before. He'd eventually come to terms with the cold fiber underpinning his reality. It wasn't my job to force the issue.

"Who's the corpse?"

"Dr. Lawrence McCay. Some bigwig at the hospital."

"How'd he die?"

Anders shrugged. "They won't tell me much except possibly over drinks later." He shook his head as if to clear it. "Sorry if you live here, buddy. I can't let anyone in yet. Had to send a bunch of people packing for the night already."

It wasn't uncommon for the police to shut down a whole tenement for one reason or another. A single body in a single room didn't seem like the best reason to me, but the police had their ways. They worked directly with data from Trinity, and if the station's AI indicated that a whole block needed a shutdown order, then that's what happened.

I took a deep breath of night air. "I don't rightly live anywhere."

"Sorry to hear that."

A dead client meant no pay, and the deep hunger gnawed at me. As I walked away, an idea surfaced and I spoke from pure instinct. "Hey, Anders," I said.

"Yes?"

"Can I buy you a beer and ask you a few questions?"

"I very much doubt you can." He considered me for a moment. "If you find yourself up around Kinderson Creek tomorrow, I'd be happy to swap stories."

Tipping my hat, I turned to walk away along the dark city streets. It didn't take me long to spot Beck. She stood out like a canary on a foggy day, leaning against a building. Smoke wafted around her head from the stub of a thin cigarette.

"All right," I told her as I took her up on the offer of a cigarette. "I'm in."

PART II

the case of the saint's pride

Chapter 11

THE LUMPY SOFA in the glass-doored hovel I call an office served as my bed. When I woke the next morning, fresh as a day-old mackerel fillet, I was about as ready for the new case as I was likely to get. Reheated stale coffee left in its fibersteel pot served as my breakfast. I winced as much from the heat as the bitter aftertaste. Coffee in Heavy Nicodemia never tasted quite right. Something about the extra gravity and hard air pressure made even a fresh brew both bitter and sour. Day-old coffee wasn't so bad because, hell, it couldn't get much worse.

I congratulated myself on that line of thought, figuring the bout of optimism would do me well for a change.

After a shower in water that smelled of chlorine and a shave that stung like a well-deserved slap, I buttoned up a fresh shirt and brushed off my wide-brimmed fedora. It probably paid to look my best going to meet a fancy new client. At the very least, it couldn't hurt. There was that optimism again.

Behind the Cathedral of Saint Francis of Assisi, deep past the hollows of the Warehouse District, stood a building that butted up against the wall of the station itself. The architecture did its best to confuse and confound, making it appear to stretch and expand over the surrounding streets. It was a lie. The building was squat and storm cloud gray like those around it, but it was a façade designed to give entry to one of Heavy Nicodemia's few airlocks.

Beck met me at the entrance, a sideways smile on her violet lips. "You clean up well, Demarco," she said.

My best indifferent shrug felt phony all the way through. "She really won't come out here to meet me?"

"The boss isn't really the kind of person to come when called, and these airlocks are a chore at best."

She waved a hand in front of the building's security panel and the big fiberoak doors hissed open. A pair of goons moved a dozen crates out as we shuffled past them into the first airlock.

"Mass exchange," said Beck. "Every ship that crosses the void brings something and takes something."

Balancing the station's mass was as important as managing its consumable resources. I watched as the goons moved the last of the crates. When they were finally finished, we cycled the first airlock.

Seven airlocks penetrated the seven walls of every bead of every Trinity station. Seven walls of seven types. Seven designs for seven systems, themed after the first seven spheres of heaven. Some were bulletproof to stop superfast meteors, some flexible to adjust to the sway of the station's rotation. Some healed when damaged and others were harder than any other known material in all of space.

All of them were tedious. They were themed for the spheres of heaven, and because one wouldn't work until the previous had run through its whole routine, it could take an hour to reach the final liminal space.

Ships rarely docked directly with Heavy Nicodemia. The fast rotation around the false star made the beads at the end of the chain trickier to pair. The spin that produced the artificial gravity made for complex math and an extreme potential for disaster. For that reason, most ships docked on the Hallow beads. Hallow

Nicodemia rotated around the false star at the same period, meaning less actual speed and a whole lot less potential for catastrophic failure.

That was to say, Violet Ruiz had landed here for a reason.

"Maybe a phone call would have gotten the point across," I said as we passed through the final airlock an hour later. "Or she could have written a letter."

Then I stepped into the liminal space. It was the space between spaces where Heavy Nicodemia's Trinity AI touched the great void beyond. This was where Ruiz's ship, the *Thirty Silver* docked.

There were many liminal spaces like this in Nicodemia, but they all had one thing in common. They were the only places where Trinity acknowledged my presence.

I tasted the bitter bile of regret as I stepped into that last airlock. Tension crept down the aching base of my neck. This was where it had all gone wrong for me. Not this airlock specifically, but another just like it.

The screen at the edge of Saturn, the final airlock between station and stars, flashed a single word in a plain font.

Reconcile?

It was the first time Trinity had directly addressed me in years. I stared at the word flickering on the screen. A lot of bad memories were tied up in an airlock just like this. My palms went clammy at the memory of the day I'd been excommunicated.

"Not today, Trinity," I muttered. Not ever, was what I meant.

Then the final gate in the station's clear shell opened. Beyond was the *Thirty Silver*'s open foyer, decorated to give us an extravagant hint at exactly how rich my new client was. This sprawling room was a testament to waste. The space had no real purpose except for when the ship was in dock, yet it had been filled with artifacts of wealth specifically to impress visitors—and as far as I could tell she didn't have all that many of those.

The floor was covered in a lush soft carpet that bounced ever so slightly under my footsteps. Even the click from Beck's heels disappeared on that soft surface. The walls were papered in a velvety pattern, textured with a paisley swirl on an otherwise brutal architecture.

And there was wood. Not fiberoak or some other variety of simulated hardwood, but actual wooden surfaces. A desk of red mahogany stood to one side of the room, and next to it a display case of the richest black wood I'd ever seen held only a single occupant—a three-foot-tall metal cup covered in names.

"They called that the Stanley Cup," Beck said. "People on Earth used to worship it."

"They didn't protest when you took it?"

Beck shrugged. "Dead religion, I guess."

More displays were scattered through the ship's entry corridor. Ancient paintings were sealed in vacuum under thick glass. Wood and stone pedestals held marble statues. A porcelain depiction of God above a cloud loomed against one wall. Three doors opened from the foyer to the ship, and Beck led me through the largest of them.

A shiver of recognition ran down my spine as I stepped into the corridor, but I shook it off. Ships hallways had a different feel from the station like they weren't entirely convinced about which direction was down. The space felt eerily familiar. The last time I was on a ship was the *Benevolent*, and that hadn't ended well. Beck led me past a pair of armed guards into a sitting room decorated with more art.

At the center of the room stood two framed panels of an oil painting, sealed in a vacuum behind heavy glass with a conspicuous gap where a third panel ought to be.

"Is that it?" I asked, nodding at the paintings.

The first panel featured a scene of Adam and Eve, with God holding Eve's wrist. Around them, animals crawled from the primordial pool to dance around a lush garden. The scenes playing out behind the first humans and their God were rich and abstract, with unicorns next to elephants and a landscape both strange and beautiful.

The second panel was something else. It was an enormous square so that the narrow outside panels could fold in to close it off. This panel teemed with humans, like a plague of revelry crawling across the green earth. Men and women posed in odd sexual positions. On closer inspection, some even had fruit heads or animal bodies. Centaurs danced in a great circle in the background.

"Hieronymus Bosch's *Garden of Earthly Delights*," Beck said. "It's possibly the greatest piece of art surviving the fifteenth-century Earth. If it hadn't been moved, it would have perished along with everything else in the burning of Spain."

"But it *was* moved," I said. "Stolen. We're looking at black market goods, right?"

The response came from a woman's voice behind me. "That's right, my dear."

I turned to see a stately woman with her slate gray hair cut short and a tumbler of something that looked suspiciously like whiskey cradled in her long fingers. She wore a dress of scarlet and white, and when she walked, the trailing edge brushed the plush carpet.

Before I could think, I swept the hat from my head, clutched it to my chest, and gave her a short bow. "Morning, Ma'am."

She gestured with her glass. "You may call me Violet, and it's evening to me right now."

"Of course," I said. She hadn't adjusted to Nicodemia's clock. I glanced to where I thought Beck still stood, but she wasn't there. Damn this soft carpet.

"I must say, matching spin with this place has been inconvenient." She sauntered up next to me and peered at the painting. "Don't you find it hard on the joints?"

"Why not dock with one of the upper beads?" I asked.

"Has Charlotte told you why we've hired you?"

"You need someone to track down the last panel of this painting."

"Have a seat, Mr. Demarco," Violet said, waving a hand at some sofas.

"I like to stretch my legs if you don't mind." I started a slow stroll around the outer perimeter of her room. Where had Beck gone? There were several doors leading away, but none near where she had stood.

Violet lowered herself gracefully onto a fainting couch and slid one foot up to assume a look of casual elegance. She watched me through half-lidded eyes. "It's been nearly a decade since my thief of a husband stole that triptych."

I passed another display case, this one full of gaudy jewelry. "Art was never really my thing, but my dad taught me a thing or two when I was a kid. One of the first lessons was that we're not supposed to take art that isn't ours."

She waved a hand dismissively. "Ownership is such a fluid thing. I don't resent my late husband for being a thief. It afforded our lifestyle a certain luxury."

"Until it didn't."

Her eyes hardened for a split second, then turned to amusement. "When I first discovered his extra-circular activities, I was frightened—then thrilled. It was so exciting, wondering what he might bring me next."

Or if he wouldn't come home at all. A bookshelf stood against one wall, and on it were dozens of ancient tomes. Bibles with gold leaf stood next to the smallest Koran I'd ever seen. A first edition copy of Milton's *Paradise Lost* sat open, the signature inside a calligraphic scrawl. "Paradife Loft?"

"They had some interesting ideas about letters back when that was written."

"Let me guess. Your husband liberated this book before England burned?"

"Don't be ridiculous. England still enjoys all the protection as an Asiatic Colony."

"Of course." There was a whole semester of current Earth events that every law-abiding student learned on their way through grade school. Most of us didn't pay much attention to it, and the political machinations of a world so far away hardly ever made headlines. I continued on through the collection, passing a hunk of carved rock labeled as one of the Elgin Marbles, a pencil drawing of a soup can by Andy Warhol, and several Van Goghs.

For a long time, Violet Ruiz said nothing, content to watch me enjoy her collection of stolen artifacts. When she spoke again, I noticed her tense slightly, as if what she was about to say mattered a great deal to her.

"My husband loved me very much, Mr. Demarco."

"I'm sure he did."

"Over the years, he brought me all of these things. Mostly they were things he pocketed on the side as other jobs brought in the real profits." She swallowed the last of her whiskey, her thin tongue licking the last touch of flavor from her lips. "He was a real charmer, my Richard. Always knew the right gift to bring and the right things to say."

A man in a white suit emerged from a panel in the wall that I hadn't realized was a door. He took Violet's glass and offered her another. She waved him away and he disappeared back from whence he came.

Violet continued. "I couldn't honestly say it was originally his idea to take *The Garden of Earthly Delights*, but the logistics of the heist were his plan, and he was responsible for everything that happened."

I watched her reflection in the glass of a display case.

She stared into space as if speaking to herself. Her voice was laced with venom. "He was betrayed. That much I know. The transport crashed, destroying much of what they intended to steal."

She gestured lazily at the two panels of *The Garden of Earthly Delights*. "These were recovered from the crash."

"Are you sure you don't have enough art?" I passed in front of a large wooden square, slightly taller than myself. It stood in another vacuum chamber and was unlabeled. The artwork on the panel was that of a landscape enclosed under glass, and it was faded almost to nothing. It wasn't much to look at, but I'd have wagered a bucket of dimes that it was worth a fortune to an art collector.

"I have recovered these two panels at great personal expense," said Ruiz. "It would be a shame to keep them separate from the third."

"From hell, you mean." I peered at the painting from across the room. It stood in all its majestic glory alone against the textured gray backdrop of the spaceship's illuminated walls. "It'd be a shame to have all that revelry with no punishment, wouldn't it?"

Her slip of a smile didn't touch her eyes. "People might get the wrong ideas."

"And you're convinced the third piece is in Heavy Nicodemia."

She waved a hand dismissively. "Two of my husband's accomplices arrived here several years ago. After that…"

I glanced back at the big wooden square. The world under a glass bubble, like a snow globe without any snow. Lakes and mountains in the distance disappeared under the mottles of stained wood. Anything lost in that glass bubble would be found because nothing could ever leave, just like Nicodemia. In the glass reflection, I saw Violet approaching. "Are you sure I can't offer you a drink, Mr. Demarco?"

I retreated along the wall and peered closely at a small, ornate box. The label said it contained a relic of Saint Catherine of Bologna, patron saint of artists. The box was closed, so the display required a good deal of trust that I didn't possess. "I think I'll be leaving."

She raised an eyebrow.

"Look. You don't need me. You need a long conversation with Trinity to track down your lost merchandise, then you need to trade one of these priceless things for that priceless thing, if it even exists. If you're not willing to give that up, then maybe hire someone to do some stealing for you. Either way, it's none of my business."

In three long strides, she crossed the floor to me. I was tall, but somehow her slender form intimidated me. She had a presence even I couldn't stand against.

"Mr. Demarco," she said, "I have done my research. You are the only person who can move through the streets of all three Nicodemias without rousing suspicion. Because of your"—she waved lazily in the direction of my whole self—"background, you stand a chance at blending in with both the lowest and the highest echelons of society."

"Low, I've pretty much got covered."

She took my hand in both of hers. Her skin was boiling hot. "Don't be coy. You were born and raised in Hallow Nicodemia. Your family goes back generations."

I didn't ask how she knew that. People like her didn't give up their sources without a struggle, and I wasn't up for that kind of fight. Not for something like that. "So, you're convinced you want me. How are you planning to convince me that *I* want this job? Sounds to me like it's going to dredge up something I buried a long time ago."

"Nonsense. I don't need to convince you."

"You don't?"

"No, I don't, because she's already done it." Letting go of my hands, she opened her arms wide to greet Beck, who had appeared again while I wasn't watching. The two women came together in a polite embrace—the kind rich people used to greet each other after a long absence.

Beck separated and approached me. She looked me in the eyes and gestured toward the door. "Shall we?"

They were, of course, perfectly correct. I was taking the job. There wasn't much choice of that. I needed the money, and the challenge intrigued me. Pretending to be uninterested wasn't going to gain me anything, so I switched gears. "Who were the thieves?"

Violet Ruiz said, "The two men who came to Nicodemia were Maurice Ribar and Trey Vitez."

"I'll need a stipend."

Beck said, "You'll get it."

"Fine. I'll find your thieves, and if it still exists, I'll find your painting."

Violet gave me a peck on the cheek and said, "Thank you, dear. This means a lot to me."

Beck took my elbow and led me out of the *Thirty Silver* and through the airlocks into Heavy Nicodemia. With every lock we passed, my mood improved. A stipend. It only occurred to me what that meant after the third airlock. It meant food, clothes, and maybe even access to avenues of inquiry that would make my job so much easier. If this investigation dragged on, I might eat for a week, whether or not I found anything. From my position at the bottom of the barrel, things definitely wouldn't get much worse, and they stood a moderate chance at getting better.

And for the first time that day, I wondered if, "Things can't get much worse," really counted as a streak of optimism.

Chapter 12

SOON AS WE stepped free of the last airlock, Beck tossed me a roll of dimes packed tight in paper.

"What's this?" I asked.

"Your stipend." She turned to saunter away, lazily waving me off. "I'll see you tomorrow, big man."

I hurried to catch up. "You aren't going to stick around?"

"You have your job, I have mine. If you need me, I'll know."

"This isn't a lot of money for an investigation," I said, hefting the roll of dimes. "Hardly enough for a few drinks."

She turned on me. "How many drinks does a guy need to solve a problem like this?"

"Maybe not all the drinks are for me."

"And maybe they are." She jabbed me in the belly with a sharp fingernail. "Keep it straight, big guy, and you'll get a good payday out of this. If I come back to find you drunk in a gutter somewhere, I've still got the option to make things a lot worse for you."

Something about the way she said it dissolved all my doubts in a strong acid. "You make a hell of a boss, Beck."

"I'm not your boss, Demarco," she shot back. "We're just two independent contractors who happen to be moving in the same direction." She flashed a smile and disappeared into a crowd.

"Let's hope it stays that way," I said, but she was already gone.

The yellow glow of noon warmed the city streets. My feet took me through the market district, my feet wandering as aimlessly as my brain. That was sometimes the key to solving a puzzle, I had found. Let the mind wander. It knows how to make connections. Let it.

It wasn't much to go by, but I'd had worse. Two names: Maurice Ribar and Trey Vitez. The art itself might hold some clues. *The Garden of Earthly Delights* wasn't an unknown piece. Ruiz was right to covet it. It was unique.

Despite my reluctance to take this particular piece of employment, it did feel good to have a job. Working gave me purpose, and it was all I could do to keep myself from jumping in feet first. Instead, I picked my way meticulously through the narrow streets, moving closer to the busy corridors where the cathedral dominated the neighborhood. I took a random path, doubling back on my path half a dozen times just to be safe. It made sense to think the widow might have me followed. Even Beck might want to keep an eye on me for her own reasons.

It was no surprise when I found someone following me, but it wasn't who I expected. One of Saint Jerome's men blended with the crowd a block back, and when he disappeared, I discovered he'd handed me off to someone else. They were good, handling the handoff like true professionals.

I came to a shop tucked into a secluded corner of the marketplace where bolts of cloth lined the walls and yarn of every color filled the narrow shelves.

A man wearing a silver crescent necklace paused in the midst of a cut of cloth. "Can I help you?"

"Do you have a back exit?" I asked.

"One in the back and one down into the emergency corridors."

Down was an option, but I didn't like navigating the emergency corridors. They often were blocked in ways that didn't open for me. "Can you let me out the back?"

He made a show of considering it. "Are you in trouble with the Church?"

I ran a hand along a bolt of cloth. It was good stuff, and the colors were more than most people could afford. "There might be a couple guys looking for me."

His expression soured. "What kind of guys?"

"The kind you won't want to lie to when they come asking."

The wattles of his chin jiggled as he shook his head. "I'm not getting involved in that. You can go out the front."

"It's just a little—"

"No. If I let you through and they decide I'm causing trouble, then my shop is ruined. It's hard enough margins being Muslim in this city."

I took off my hat and ran my fingers through my hair. I didn't want to cause the man any trouble, but I didn't want to go out the front door. They'd be waiting for me, maybe they'd be impatient enough to jump me right there.

"I can pay," I said, cracking the roll of dimes across my knuckles.

He tensed. "You think that'll make things better for me? They find your dirty dimes on me, and I'll be taking a swim for sure."

The door swung open, and a woman walked in. She wore a home-knit sweater and comfortable shoes. She moved straight to a pile of cast-offs and flipped through the reds.

I whispered to the shopkeeper. "Look, you let me through, and I'll make it worth your while. You can tell them where I went when they come asking. If I can get out the back, I'll be able to give them the slip."

"I can't."

"Just open the door." I moved up into his space. He was bigger than most folks around the Heavies, but I still towered over him. "Now."

"Please." Something really had the guy spooked. For the span of a heartbeat, I thought I had him, but he stiffened when the woman spoke.

"Does this come in red?" she asked, holding up a bolt of blue velvet.

The shopkeep stuttered for a second, then answered in the affirmative.

"Good," said the woman. "I won't need to make any adjustments." Her other hand came up holding a small red pistol—the kind polite members of society carry to dinner parties. "Why don't you step outside while Percival cuts some cloth for me, Demarco? The Saint wants to have a word."

Dammit.

"I have a counterproposal," I said.

She raised a well-groomed eyebrow. There were creases in her makeup where it had been caked on too thick.

I said, "Tell Saint Jerome I'm busy right now, and I'd rather not talk about what happened last night."

Percival backed into a corner. He wasn't even trying to find the cloth for the woman, and I figured that was probably a mistake. She didn't seem like the sort to put up with slow service.

"Lady," I said. "Someone's bound to get hurt. Put the gun away."

To my surprise, she did. "He said you wouldn't react well to the gun."

"It used to be rare that I would have to."

"Well," she said, "times are changing. It's not about last night, Demarco. The Saint wants to hire you."

Now it was my turn to raise an eyebrow. "I bet he does."

"It's important to him."

Where Saint Jerome was concerned, everything was important. From the amount of salt on his sardines to the dimes flowing through his countless gambling operations and illegal drug trades to the karats of the gold he wore at all times. If the crime boss of

Heavy Nicodemia said to jump, it was best not to complain about knee pain. If he said to collect a certain handyman, that handyman got collected, brought kicking and screaming if need be.

So, it was clear to me that whatever Saint Jerome's business with me was, it was really damn important.

Because the door's bell dinged and Saint Jerome himself—head mobster of the whole of Heavy Nicodemia—walked in the door.

Chapter 13

SAINT JEROME'S eyes were hard flint from a long life as a criminal, and his smile a soft glow because he was good at it. The well-tailored baby blue suit draped over his large frame was trimmed with gold to match his three glittering necklaces. One necklace was a simple cross, the second held a silver locket, and the third was empty of any ornamentation as if he were a simple man of simple desires.

He most definitely was not.

At a wave of one of the Saint's ringed fingers, the woman shopper patted me down. "He's clear."

Saint Jerome touched the blue velvet at the top of the cast-off pile. "Do you have this in red, Percival?"

The shopkeep—Percival—pressed himself farther into the corner. "Yes, yes sir. I'll go get some." He slinked through the back door—the same one I wanted him to open earlier—without moving one inch closer to the Saint.

"It's been too long, Demarco," the Saint said. His voice was oddly high for the masculinity of his body. "I miss seeing you around."

I kept the woman in the corner of my eye. "I've been busy."

"Busy getting in a little tussle with some of my boys."

"Busy saving your boys from this Lauder character."

Saint Jerome set the blue velvet down as if it were a dead fish. "Lauder." He shot a look at the woman. "I'm hearing a lot about this Lauder."

I paced around the outer wall of the shop, trying to make my movements casual as if I weren't immensely intimidated by this man. Logic told me he wouldn't kill me in person, but logic and a roll of dimes wouldn't buy me a tomorrow. "Seems he's heard a lot about you too. Like he has a grudge."

The Saint spread his open hands, palms up. "There are a lot of grudges these days. Can't we find in our hearts for forgiveness?"

"Spoken like a true saint."

Jerome's eyes went hard and dark as the black void outside the station. "We all do our best, Demarco. Everybody but you."

"Maybe my best isn't up to sainthood."

He flicked through the bolts of cloth. "It's a good thing saintly behavior isn't expected of you today."

I found myself next to the bolt of velvet that had been so popular. It was nice, but they were right. The blue didn't really pop. Red would be better. When I spoke, I failed to keep the agitation from my voice. "If something is expected of me, it'll have to wait. I'm on a job." How many dimes would it cost to get me out of the trouble my mouth kept getting me into?

Saint Jerome shrugged his massive shoulders. The chains around his neck glittered in the shop's yellow light. "Maybe you can multitask."

"Where do you suppose Percival got off to?"

The woman's posture changed, and I could tell my words were getting to her. She knew as well as I did that Percival was hiding in back.

Unless he wasn't. Unless he was somewhere calling down Lauder's men, setting up an impromptu ambush.

The woman made a few quick gestures. Sign language, but the only word I picked up was "Go." She was paid to be paranoid.

"What's the story, Jerome?" I pressed. "Why go through all this trouble to track me down and talk to me face to face."

"I was in the neighborhood on some business that required a personal touch." His relaxed smile was unreadable.

"And you decided to cross the street and pop in on me when you happened to see me walk past? We're not friends. You have a reason to be here."

He pressed a palm to his chest in mock hurt. "Not friends? That's not what I heard."

So, Wash *had* talked to the Saint. I wondered if it had all been a sham just to measure me up. Maybe I could make a decent living as a paranoid bodyguard like the woman. I was practically a natural. "I told you before, I've already been hired for a big job. If you have something else for me, it'll wait."

This time, I'd pushed the Saint too far. His jaw hardened and his bushy eyebrows bunched up with anger. "Listen to me, handy-man. I'm offering you work and you're going to take it."

I listened.

"There's a bureaucrat who's been giving me trouble. You're going to get him out of the way for me."

What was I? His hitman? "You have people for this."

He flashed me a saccharine smile. "They're busy."

Crossing the store to me, the woman handed me a sheaf of paper. I didn't bother looking at it.

Jerome continued, "There's a little paperwork here that needs filing. That's all. The kind of paperwork that that nice sister of yours needs to file from time to time to keep her restaurant legit."

"You know, real friends don't make veiled threats."

"Who's making threats?" He lifted a bolt of white velvet and showed it to his bodyguard. "I like this one," he said.

The woman said, "It'll show stains."

"Filing where?" I asked, not wanting to know where the conversation was going.

Percival picked that moment to return with a bolt of red velvet. It was quality stuff, and he held it up like he was a fisherman bringing back a triumphant catch. He practically glowed with excitement, but a touch of fear lingered in his eyes. "Red," he said. "It was hard to find, but I knew I had it somewhere back there."

Saint Jerome looked at him with all the warmth of a tiger shark. "Get the job done," he said without bothering to look at me. "Everything you need is in the paperwork."

With that, Jerome and his bodyguard left, stepping from the store directly into a black vehicle, which sped away.

Percival cleared his throat. "Do you still want to leave out the back?"

I clapped him on the shoulder. "Percival, I need a drink."

He looked down at the red velvet. It spilled out over his hands like blood. He smelled of the sour sweat of fear. "I don't think I can help you with that."

I said, "This morning I didn't have a job at all. Now I've got two, and I don't want either one."

Percival nodded. "You need a drink."

"That I do."

Chapter 14

THE DAY WAS TOO young to track down Officer Anders for that drink, so I spent the next several hours pickling myself in cheap whiskey and consuming the kind of greasy rubbish starving men crave the most. Rory's Ramshackle wasn't busy in the early afternoons but stayed open twenty-four hours a day to catch a crowd of aimless drifters and discreet businessmen. That particular afternoon it was me and two men far too involved in the depth of each other's eyes. No doubt they both had men back home. Nobody met at Rory's for romance unless they had to. The place smelled of old fish.

Rory's son, Jason, sat on a stool behind the bar, cheering at a small screen showing the latest rugby match. I ate my grease and opened the papers Saint Jerome had given me. They were detailed reports regarding a restaurant called the Pelican. Health and safety filings. Boring stuff. I closed the folder and pinched the bridge of my nose.

"Snappers are in for a pummeling if they don't get their shit together," Jason said.

"That so?"

"Yellowcoats are looking sharp this year." Jason leaned closer to his tiny screen. "Gordan Snyder at blindside flanker? Man's a menace."

"I thought they cut him for Karma," I said through another bite of burger.

"The lug spent a weekend volunteering to help old ladies move furniture so they're letting him back in," said Jason. "Gaming the system if you ask me."

It sounded to me exactly the way the Karma system was supposed to work. Snyder wanted access to the luxury of membership in a sports team, so he'd spent some of his free time helping people who needed help. Being a member of the team also built community, so just being on the team ought to have helped his Karma. "He wouldn't need to do that if he'd refrain from all the extracurriculars."

"Guys like that never stop fighting," said Jason. He poured me a couple fingers of whiskey. "Try the new stuff, Demarco."

I took a sip. "It's not good."

"It's got smoky undertones."

"Sure, it does." I took another sip. "Smoky overtones too."

He shrugged. "It's a big hit up the chain. Rumor is they love it in the Hallows."

Trends filtered downward in Nicodemia. Sometimes it was fast, sometimes it was slow, but down in the Heavies, people liked to copy the trends of their betters. It made the grease in my belly churn when I thought of it. "You ever heard of anyone selling art around these parts?"

Without taking his eyes from the screen, he said, "Like paintings?"

"Something like that."

"There's a fella upspiral who teaches drawing classes. They say he went to university in the Hallows when he was young."

"You don't say."

"Me, I've always been more of a sculpture kind of guy. I got this one bronze statue of these two fish jumping out of the water and it's been in my family for a few generations."

"Ever worried someone will steal it?"

Jason chuckled a little, almost to himself. "Nobody's going to get worked up about a statue of a couple fish."

"No," I said, leaning forward, "but suppose they did. Suppose someone upstairs says that fish statues are the greatest achievement of mankind. Then on one of those broadcasts where they're always appraising people's old junk someone comes in with a bronze fish statue and suddenly it's worth a million dimes and a trip to the Hallows. Everyone wants fish statues, and yours is looking like a pretty good haul. What then?"

Jason took his eyes off the game for two-thirds of a heartbeat just to get a good look at my face. "Demarco, nobody gets that excited about fish statues, not even down here in fish gut central. Plus, you haven't seen this statue. It's not that great."

"Maybe."

He watched the game for a while, then said, "In my experience, folks who get excited about art are actually excited about something else entirely."

"It's a proxy."

"Sure."

I raised the whiskey to my lips, then thought better of it and set the glass down. A little whiskey sloshed over the rim onto the papers spread out on the bar in front of me.

"Yeah," Jason said, "A proxy. Some people are just not that good at processing emotions. You might know what that's like."

"I have no idea."

He looked at my spilled whiskey, then up at me, probably to see if I was joking. I'm not sure that I was. Shrugging, he turned back to his game.

"You ever heard of anyone named Maurice Ribar or Trey Vitez?" I asked.

His brow furrowed. "Not sure. Is this related to the art thing?"

"They would have been newcomers a few years back." I endured another sip of whiskey. It was still not good. "Likely they would have wanted to move some goods."

"Don't they know this isn't a capitalist society?"

"Every society's capitalist if supply and demand get far enough out of whack."

He nodded. We'd been over this conversation before, and it always ended the same way. I cracked the roll of dimes in two and slid half across the counter. I noticed for the first time that they were Nicodemian dimes with Trinity's triangle pressed into one side and the cross on the other. I wondered what mass Beck had exchanged for all this local currency. "Is this capitalist enough for you?"

"You think it's going to be that easy?"

"It never is."

"I'll ask around. Anybody with anything worth selling is going to move up the chain."

"Word is they docked here."

"On a Heavy bead? They must have been trying to hide something." He chewed his chapped lip.

I scooped up Saint Jerome's papers, shook the whiskey off, and crammed everything back into the folder. It had been a dry bit of reading, and having finished, I didn't feel particularly enlightened. Restaurant and bar inspection reports made for a bland afternoon, but these were particularly dry. Even the violations were boring, with the occasional rodent infestation and a few mild storage temperature fluctuations. The papers hadn't helped me much for figuring out the Saint's plans, but at least I knew where they needed to be filed. The government buildings had paper backups for all recent reports—a hardcopy in case of digital storage failure—and low-level documents like this would be covered only by minimal security. It was an easy task for someone like me. A quick one. All the more reason to be suspicious.

"Hey, Jason," I said.

"Yeah."

"Can you get me an address? I need to drop by and have a chat with a friend."

He glanced down at the dimes on the bar. "That's not a lot of money, Demarco."

"It's half of my worldly possessions."

"It won't even pay your tab."

"You and I both know I'm never going to pay my tab." I forced a serious look across my face as I swallowed the last of the harsh whiskey. The smoky undertones burned a hole in my lungs. "This is a simple lookup. Nothing fancy."

"What's the name?"

"I don't have a name."

"If you don't have a name, it's not a simple lookup."

I tossed a few more dimes on the fiberoak bar. "I need to know who's in charge of restaurant inspections for this address." I pointed at a line on the cover page.

Jason peeled the dimes from the bar before answering. "I'll see what I can do."

"Now would be helpful."

He raised an eyebrow. "You're the only person I know who'd come into my place looking for emergency restaurant inspection."

I made a show of looking around the place. "Maybe I'm looking for a seedier place to hang out."

"A new place to mooch off the generous owner and scare away customers? A fella can hope, I suppose." He swiped the rugby game off his screen and brought up a directory. Technically, everyone in Nicodemia had access to this same book, but as an excommunicated handyman, I had a harder time getting such information. Trinity's excommunication extended to all connected screens, so I depended on the kindness of strangers. It made it useful to know people like Jason, who rarely asked hard questions. He also happened to have his thumb on the karmic scales, when it came to deep info access. "The guy in charge is named Matthew Williams." He spun the screen to face me so I could see the address and a video of a silver-haired man pushing papers at a desk. I never did understand how Jason was able to get up-to-date video of anyone in town. "He's an uptown kind of guy, and he's at work right now."

"That's a hell of a walk from here."

"You want me to call you a cab?"

I tossed a couple more dimes on the bar. There weren't enough left, but he deserved more for being helpful. "You know a cab driver who'll cart a fella around for free?"

"Wouldn't be much of a driver if he did."

"Then I'd better get walking." I tucked the folder under my arm and headed for the exit.

As I pushed the door open, Jason called out to me. "Good luck, Demarco."

I didn't bother telling him that luck had abandoned me long ago, and I'd need more than that, anyway. My luck must have been particularly sour because on the way out, I ran straight into Nick Sully.

He shouldered me hard as we passed in the short hallway, then froze and gave me a hard look. I could feel his gaze digging into the back of my neck. "Demarco."

"Sully." I continued out the door into the open. Last thing I needed was to deal with Sully after how the job with McCay had ended. Sully followed me out the door.

The sky was a hurricane swirl of gray on gray.

"What the hell happened with that job I sent you?" Sully asked, standing at my elbow.

"You cut right to business these days."

He lit a cigarette and let it dangle from his lip. He was a scrawny guy, scruffy right down to his thin mustache and frazzled hair. "I do when business goes to shit."

"You gave me a bad job. Your guy died. Nothing to do with the job, he just died." I stared up at the swirling sky, peering into the cloudy mist. Anything to keep from looking him in the eye.

"It's a hell of a coincidence."

I failed to keep the frustration from my voice. "Med runs like these always go south."

"You needed the work. I needed my cut."

"Your cut's not worth much for work that doesn't pay."

His face went red with anger. "What I don't need is the hit to my reputation, Demarco."

"Then send better jobs."

"He would have paid if you hadn't screwed it up." He took a long drag on his cigarette. "McCay called me after you left, you know. He was mad as hell about how you treated him."

I finally looked Sully in his sunken eyes. "I did what I had to do."

"It was a simple fucking med run. Not even recreational. He just wanted some fucking medicine, and you couldn't give it to him."

Would McCay still be alive if I had done what he'd asked? The thought made me ill. "There could have been more to it."

"But there wasn't, was there?"

"He's not dead from what I did." All the frustration dropped out of me, leaving a big hole in my chest that felt something like guilt. "I swear, Sully. All I wanted to do was figure out where his meds went. I was on my way to give him a new supply when I saw the police."

This seemed to surprise him. He took a step back. "You didn't out him?"

"Why would I do that?"

"A man doesn't go from zero to suicide on a whim, Demarco. You figure it out."

McCay had been terrified of someone figuring out his genetic condition. Terrible as it was, he had staked all his hopes on finding a way to return to the Hallow. If he had been outed, that might have devastated his dreams, but suicide? That didn't settle well. "Maybe his old dealer sold him out."

There was something fitting about that answer that placated Sully. He stubbed out his cigarette and disappeared back into Rory's Ramshackle. As much as I didn't like the job he'd given me, it was at least better than placing fraudulent paperwork and tracking down stolen art.

Jason had been right about the walk back upspiral, and my whiskey-leaded legs weren't up for the task. It made me wish for a scooter like Beck's. Fast, agile, and independent. She'd have had this job finished in under an hour. The weight of responsibility was an iron cross lashed around my neck.

But how would she have handled it? It would be simple for me to drop the papers where the Saint wanted them. Something told me there was more to the story, and I needed a chat with this Williams character if I wanted to know what it was.

With a few dimes in my pocket, I had options. Even if I couldn't rent a cab or swipe a scooter, I could still take a shortcut. My feet took me edgeward, back toward the outside of the city where darkness reigned, and the idea of sky was a figment in the minds of sinners. As I walked, the afternoon wore on and the crowds thinned. Where I walked alone, the lights didn't brighten, and shadows wrapped around me like a bulletproof vest. It was cold out here, and the haunted eyes that glanced my direction came from the gaunt faces of the almost forgotten.

There are several elevators running along the outer edge of the station. This one was a beige box set into a fibersteel facing. Neon graffiti decorated the surrounding walls, and a short distance away someone had carved a symbol into the hard wall. When the carriage car arrived, I paid the ferryman my dime, and he let me board. There were few other passengers, but they didn't need dimes. Their Karma carried them upward. I leaned against the far wall and waited. Soon, the car bucked and we rose straight to the next loop of the spiral. There, a dozen more people boarded.

Outside, I could see the change in neighborhoods. Where below was a dark pit of the forgotten, this level was the bright cacophony of lights—like an eternal Mardi Gras parade looping through space. The sin quarter wasn't one I frequented. I had plenty of that already, and it wasn't the kind of place a person could depend upon for the kindness of strangers.

Then, the car continued upward. Neighborhoods shifted before me, becoming brighter as the teardrop shape of Nicodemia made for shallower ledges of the spiral and therefore more access to the concave sky at the edges. More, but still not much. At almost the top, I stepped out into the stifling gray at the top of the world. The government quarter.

Chapter 15

MATTHEW WILLIAMS WAS A DRONE. He left work at precisely five o'clock, same as a couple thousand other government employees. I picked his silver shock of hair out of the crowd and hurried after him through the well-lit streets. Buildings weren't as tall up here, and the resulting excess of light made my headache. The whiskey had worn off, and my mouth tasted like the kind of dryness that only another stiff drink could remedy.

Williams wasn't an after-work drinker, unfortunately. He broke from the herd of government types early, stopping by a falafel stand for some nutrition and a quick chat with a lovely chef. He was clever and quick, this Williams. Witty. I couldn't hear his voice from across the street, but I could see it in the woman's smile. She liked him. I wondered if there might be something there or if it was only the polite banter of long-time customer and merchant.

I wanted to like this Williams guy. Stuffy pencil-pusher he might be, but his next stop was to pick up kids from the local school. His stocky daughter was dressed for soccer, and his son—tall for a resident of a heavy station—looked like the kind of kid who competed in debate club or chess. Williams shared his falafel with the kids and the three laughed and ate at a public bench along the edge of a tiny public green space.

But sometimes people are more than what they seem. This laughing, charming father must have some dark secret; otherwise how had his paperwork gotten mixed up with someone like Saint Jerome? The papers from the crime boss had a purpose, and that purpose revolved directly around Matthew Williams. I needed to know what the original documents said. If I knew that, then I could figure out exactly what the play was. Maybe Williams wasn't involved at all. I needed to find a way to approach Williams that didn't tip him off.

A shadow passed over me, blocking out the steel gray sky. "What are you up to, mister?"

Williams stood over me, arms crossed. The friendly, charming face I'd seen interacting with the falafel dealer and his kids had twisted into a mask of rage.

"I'm enjoying the sunset," I said. Sunset was still a few hours off. "Eventually."

He jabbed a stubby finger at me. "You've been watching me and my kids. I picked you out following me since I got off work."

"Paranoia's treatable, mister."

"Like hell." He took several steps back, never taking his eyes off me. "You stay away from my kids, you hear?" His hand dropped into his pocket. Whether it was subconscious or deliberate, I couldn't tell, but the message was clear: he had a weapon and he'd use it.

I leaned back on the bench and hooked my elbows on the backrest. I didn't know what I'd say until I said it. "You're in too deep, Williams. I'm here to help you dig out."

That froze him in place. Behind him, still at the other bench, his kids laughed about something more hilarious than I could comprehend. It's good for kids to laugh like that sometimes. It's healthy.

"I know you're tangled up in a bad deal," I said. "And I know about the threats." I didn't, but what the hell. There were always threats. "If you want to clear this all up and land on a fresh slate, I'm your man. Otherwise"—I waved dismissively with one hand—"be on your way."

That must have broken something in his brain because his mouth opened and closed like a trout in hard vacuum. Finally, he stepped close to me—talking to this man was like dancing the cha-cha—and whispered, "You want to see your sunset? Well, this is a good spot for it. Lots of sky."

With that, he left, herding his two protesting kids away through the busy streets.

That left me with two hours to kill and not many options to kill them with. My search for the artwork was at a standstill until Jason got back to me. I decided to look for the cop, Anders, at the Kinderson Creek, which wasn't far away. The place had a fiberoak façade lit by old-style lanterns, and it was crawling with the blue.

I pushed through the officers, largely ignored by the happy hour rush. When I didn't see Anders, I asked around.

"He's on shift until seven," said a woman in a patrol officer's uniform. Most of the blue around carried stunsticks, but she packed an actual firearm. "Usually doesn't get up here till around nine."

I thanked the officer and moved on. Anders might be willing to chat, but I'd never track him down if he was working. Williams would be back, and he'd talk, so that made anything I did on that case a potential waste of time.

Potential.

There were answers, and I couldn't sit around not finding them. I walked back to the government buildings. The drab gray slabs squatted in a row like old dogs shitting in a back alley. They were emptier than they had been at five, but several workaholics still trickled out of the buildings. I timed my entrance to coincide with someone leaving, and just like that, I was in. I had to be careful because the doors here wouldn't open for me. Getting in was easy, but it would also be easy to get stuck.

A cold stillness filled the government center like the pall over a fresh corpse. All that bureaucratic potential was wasted when the day's short life came to an end. No matter, though. The next morning, its zombie corpse would rise like Lazarus with a fresh cup of coffee.

Once again, the potential to finish the job danced enticingly before me. A couple turns down the hall and I saw the records room door slightly ajar. Somebody hadn't locked everything down, but that probably wasn't rare. These paper logs only existed to shore up a flaw in Trinity's databanks. Nothing here was consequential, and ninety-nine times out of a hundred these hard copies would never be fed back into the system.

Which was why I couldn't figure why anyone wanted documents planted here.

Cameras covered every square inch of the government buildings. Corners, ceilings, ducts. Everything bristled with surveillance, none of which could see me. How it worked, nobody alive could really say. Either at the point of recording, in transit, or in the quantum tangle of Trinity's vast mechanical brain, any image of me was scrubbed clean. Every sound of my voice. Every shadow I cast. Gone. Excommunicated.

The practice of excommunication was a punishment broken right down the middle, and that made a job like this easy.

I placed a box of paper down on the floor to block the door from closing. There was a whole pile of information a person could learn by being locked in the records vault for a whole night, but I wasn't in any mood to learn it.

The records vault was a low-ceilinged room that stretched far enough to show the curved arc of the station interior. This high up in Nicodemia, circles grew tight, and buildings curved along their outer walls, giving the impression of a place that sprawled on forever. Brown cardboard boxes filled the fibersteel shelves, each labeled with an arcane series of letters, numbers, and symbols.

All this waste made my spine twitch. Who knows what bureaucratic nightmare happened a thousand years ago to start up this tradition. Someone no doubt deleted some information they thought was important and the paper backup protocol was born. Reams of data were printed and stored every day, and on the other end, the same amount was destroyed. Recycled into fresh pulp. How old those papers were, I didn't know. Maybe nobody did.

I found the symbol for the correct aisle and followed it until I found the right box. Pulling it free, I found it wasn't as stuffed full as I'd expected. Inside sat a single manila folder, just like the one I carried. Inside that was—

The same thing.

Side by side, page after page, the documents looked exactly the same. But why?

Hinges creaked in the distance, and the door closed with a resounding boom. With the door closed and nobody officially around, the room went dark.

I sat on the floor in black silence for the span of a hundred slow breaths. Nothing stirred. Darkness wrapped around me like an oversized cardigan.

Then, as I was about to flip on my tiny lighter, I heard the single scuff of a footstep. It echoed in from the distance, its location hidden by the rows of shelves. Someone was there, but they weren't triggering the lights. That left a few options.

It could be the cleaning drones. They didn't require light, and they'd work at night like this. That didn't seem likely. Cleaning drones didn't sound like a purposeful cadence of footsteps. They whirred more, and they smelled of lubrication and electricity. No, this had to be a person.

Someone might have manually disabled the lights, but why? Why wander around in the dark?

The only answer that made sense sent a chill down my spine.

This was another excommunicated soul like myself in the records room. A comrade doing bitter work against the all-powerful machine. The more I thought about it, the more it made sense. This was another person walking in the dark.

But what did they want?

I carefully, quietly, got my feet under me and stood. The darkness was so complete, so overwhelming, that my eyes refused to adjust, even a little. Keeping my head low, I worked my way forward. One finger running along the boxes kept me moving straight. How many boxes had I been from the corner? Fifteen? Sixteen? I counted them out, not wanting to hear another footstep.

I didn't hear the scuff of a step when I reached the corner, but a prickle at the base of my neck told me the intruder was close. I froze. The air moved, as if from breath. The shadow of a hint of the idea of cologne touched my nostrils. A man, then, or someone who wanted to smell like one.

Maybe he smelled me too, because I heard him swallow with a nervous click.

"What are you doing here?" he rasped.

I let him hang there for a long pause before I replied, "Seems a bit late for a man to be checking records in the dark."

There was a crash of noise and the thumping of steps. I flipped on my lighter, but the man was gone.

My papers still sat on the floor, along with the papers they were meant to replace.

The light caught a shadow of movement as he rounded a corner. He was headed straight for the door. If I ran, I could catch him in the hall before he left the building.

But the papers.

I ran back to my spot where I had been checking out papers and stuffed the originals back in the box. Or was that the duplicates? No time to check. When I turned, the lights in the room blazed back to life, blinding me.

The door was open but swinging shut fast. Once it closed, I'd be trapped in the dark for the rest of the night. I ran hard, slamming into the shelf as I took the corner too tight. Pain blossomed up my elbow. The door was halfway closed.

I sprinted and dove, catching it just before it snapped shut.

Breaths came in deep gulps, but once they slowed, I caught another whiff of his cologne. It had a hint of cedar and lemon, but the man was nowhere to be seen. I looked down at the papers in my hand. Were they the originals or the copy? I stuffed them in my pocket and made my way out of the government center.

Sunset approached, and there was one more thing I needed to do before meeting with Williams. Maybe it was paranoia. Maybe it was wisdom brought on by my years living in the underbelly of the system's worst city. Likely it was a little of both, but I knew I needed to walk the perimeter before meeting with Williams. It was extra work, but coming up empty on a sweep would give me the confidence I needed to deal with the bureaucrat.

Unfortunately, that's not how it worked out.

Chapter 16

THE TWO THUGS crouched atop the roof of the neighborhood square's squat church. The little building was nothing like the cathedral at the center of Heavy Nicodemia, but it bore evidence of meticulous care and exceptional craftsmanship. Those who lived this close to the top of the bead had the Karma and cash to build this place of worship and the desire to properly maintain it. It was a testament to their faith and their priorities.

Of course, the fact that two thugs sat atop it like warts on a nose didn't help its quaint appearance. The first, a woman half my height with well-muscled arms and gray hair, leaned against the crenelations of the upper balcony. The second, a gangly man with a thick neck and thicker wrists, peered at the court below, clearly watching for someone to enter the area of the fountain. He held a thin rifle close to his leg.

I stood behind them on the arched roof of the church for a long time while they watched the courtyard.

"What I would like to know," I finally said, "is if Williams tipped you off or if you've been watching him and looking for trouble."

They spun as one, but I was ready for it. I wrenched the rifle out of the man's grasp, casting it off the church roof, where it cracked against the hard stone. The woman swung a meaty fist at me, but her reach was too short. She slugged my elbow, which stung, but probably not as much as my reply of a quick jab in the neck. She gasped and stumbled away.

The man took advantage of my distraction, landing a solid kick to my calf. My leg buckled and I dropped to one knee, narrowly twisting to the side to avoid his wild haymaker.

He grabbed my arm and twisted. It would have been a good move and showed a significant amount of skill and poise, but the man wasn't used to fighting someone as big as me. His angle was awkward. Clumsy. I dropped my weight, pulled, and shoved him away. He crashed into his partner just as she was starting to stand.

"Apparently, it's amateur hour." My fists tightened till the knuckles popped, and I dropped into a fighting stance. "Do I need to repeat the question?"

The man was almost to his feet when the woman grabbed his arm. He shot her a look that let me know she was the one in charge.

Her voice was a ragged rasp when she spoke. Maybe I'd hit her harder than I thought, or maybe she'd stuffed her short life full of harsh cigarettes and strong drink. Maybe both. "What makes you think we're here for you?"

"An out-of-control ego mostly," I said.

"Seems to me it's within our rights to keep an eye on our assets," said the guy, earning an absolutely filthy look from the woman.

"Williams is your asset then," I said as if thinking aloud.

"He never said that," snapped the woman.

The man shifted uncomfortably, and the two stood across the roof from me. My elbow ached from the guy's joint lock. All things considered, it was a good move. I might have to try it sometime.

My blood was pumping, and the sky was just beginning to yellow at the edges.

"Who do you work for?" I asked.

At some invisible signal, the man lunged for me. Again, I was ready. I threw a sloppy punch, which connected with knuckle-bruising force. The man's head snapped back, and he landed in a heap.

I swore and shook the pain out of my fist.

The woman slugged me hard in the side. Pain shot through my ribs like cheap fireworks. She gave me a good look at her brass knuckles when she swung them at my head.

I twisted away, turning something that might have killed me into only the worst headache I'd ever have.

My vision flashed and I doubled forward. She cracked the back of my skull, no doubt trying to knock me out flat. Either my skull's a hell of a lot harder than that, or she only hit me with a glancing blow.

I snatched her arm and pulled, a cheap imitation of the joint lock the man had used on me earlier. My technique wasn't good, but with the size difference, it didn't need to be. I lifted and pushed until she was backed up against the balcony's edge. Her center of gravity went over the crenelations, and I held her in place until my breathing slowed.

"Who do you work for?" I growled.

Her answer was a dead-eyed stare. A challenge. Dammit. She was betting I wouldn't toss her over the side, and she was right. Already, this was drawing attention from below. I pulled her back onto the roof. Using the tie from the man's coat, I bound both of their arms together. They'd escape eventually, but it would take some time.

The man was still alive, thankfully. I hadn't hit him hard enough to kill him outright. Good, probably. I didn't need this man's death on my conscience. I had enough weighing that down as it was.

"Sure you don't want to tell me why you're here?" I asked.

She spat at me, which I took for a no. Unfortunately, I didn't have any time left to change her mind.

With my sweep of the area complete, I felt moderately comfortable meeting Williams by the fountain. The sky blazed yellow and orange as I approached the bench. He was already there, looking nervous and suspicious, like a rat being confronted in the back of the pantry.

I walked up to him and stood in silence for a while, watching the sunset. The longer I waited, the longer the quiet cracked his defenses. First, he fidgeted, then he glanced nervously at the church. Interesting. Did he know about the thugs?

Finally, he spoke. "When my wife left, it was all I could do to maintain partial custody of my kids. You understand this is all about them, right?"

"Sure." I didn't understand at all, but I needed to keep him talking.

"I can't do that on my salary. Trinity doesn't care about stuff like this. I'm not hurting anyone. Not really."

"So, you're on the take."

"Just a little extra on the side. All I do is give owners a little extra wiggle room. I'm not hurting anyone."

I shook my head in disbelief. The man endangered the food safety of the entire lower half of the city, and he was convinced it wasn't harmful. "What can you tell me about the Pelican?"

"You're better off not knowing."

"Try me."

"I—I don't know about the Pelican." A bead of sweat glistened on his brow. "Sometimes red flags pop up because the algorithm isn't quite right, but it's not really a problem. Inspectors are sent to the establishment to check things out."

"And that's you?"

"Oh no. I haven't worked inspections in ages. All I do is push papers around."

If the papers Saint Jerome gave me were any indication, it wasn't a very exciting job. "And you make problems disappear."

"No," he said, suddenly panicked. "I would never. All I do is delay them a little so owners have a little extra time to get things fixed."

"What kind of red flags are we talking about?"

At the edge of the square, near the little church, a man with a trombone opened his case and affixed a cup mute. His gnarled brown hands worked up the length of his ancient instrument like an old lover returned from a long absence. When he started playing, the emotion he poured into the instrument rolled across the courtyard in lazy brassy waves. Above, the sky darkened.

"Sometimes the same people eat at the same place every day," Williams said. "Maybe they like the music or maybe they're really hooked on the food. Every day. Same time, same place."

The muscle of my calf tightened where the man had landed the kick. It would ache more in the morning, but I let the pain color my expression for the briefest second.

"My job is to make sure the food's safe, so what do I care, right? Trinity's old. Maybe a thousand years ago food safety had to look out for restaurants slipping a little addictive opium into their food. I don't know."

It didn't add up in my head. "Body, soul—"

"Community. Yeah, I get it. But fuck that."

"You make a solid point. So, what's the gig? Someone pays you off, you lose the papers for a bit?"

Williams scanned the rooftops again. When he didn't see anyone, he said, "I've already said too much."

He turned to leave, but I grabbed a handful of his shirt and pulled him close. "I think there's more going on here and I want to know what."

"There's not, I swear!"

The trombone hit a high tremolo descending to a deep lull.

"Tell me, Williams." I pushed him up against the fountain. "I've had enough of this."

His lower jaw worked, and a line of drool dripped onto his coat. He mouthed something over and over, but the words didn't come out. A wet spot bloomed on his trousers.

I let go of him, and he landed in the fountain with a splash. The trombonist slowed his tempo and chewed a few notes till they were good and tired.

It was a dilemma. This sniveling, weeping fool knew something more. I was sure of it. He was sitting in the fountain soaking in his own urine and scared of what I might do—or what someone else might do. All I wanted to know was how he fit into the papers still in my pocket. What was he covering up and why was Saint Jerome interested in this particular packet of information?

Twilight descended, but the light from overhead lamps followed several little social groups as they wandered through the square. A single yellow bulb illuminated the trombone player, who still wore dark sunglasses under his felt hat. He ended his song and watched Williams squirm out of the fountain.

"They're not coming, Williams," I growled, shifting so he could get a better look at the church. "Your friends decided to take a little break instead."

He whimpered.

The blues man hefted his trombone and started playing something cheery with a lot of fast slides.

"I can't tell you anything else, all right?" Williams snarled. His expression was animalistic in the deepened shadows. "Please."

I don't know what did it. It might have been the dedication he'd put into actually pissing himself or the real tears he was crying on my shoes, but I couldn't bring myself to push him any further. I crossed the courtyard to where the trombonist played, dropped two dimes in his case, and walked down the dark street where nobody would see me for the failed investigator I was. By the time I circled back to the church, the two thugs had escaped.

The lights were bright outside the Kinderson Creek Pub. It swarmed with the smug righteousness of its police patrons. Vehicles parked outside ranged from electric scooters to the larger people-movers used to transport prisoners and troops alike. The slick cobbles outside smelled of whiskey vomit and cigarette smoke.

Problem was, it took too much effort to give a damn about McCay's suspicious death. For that matter, caring about all the trouble surrounding Saint Jerome's feud with Frank Lauder felt like pushing Sisyphus's rock up the hill. They could all go to hell as far as I was concerned. Damn. Maybe they already had. Ever since I'd landed in the too-heavy version of Nicodemia, I'd felt it pull down on my soul like concrete dragging down the feet of the doomed.

And Williams. He was a small fish swimming with something big. The Saint didn't want me digging into it, but mysteries don't die easy for me. I didn't even know if I had placed the right papers since I'd run out of there so fast.

I drew the papers out of my inside pocket. They were a little worn for all the excitement, but still in good enough shape to make the switch.

Except…

I put the papers to my nose and sniffed.

Nothing.

Rory's awful whiskey had spilled onto the papers Saint Jerome had given me. That meant these must be the papers that had been in the archives. I grunted to myself and put the envelope back in my coat. The job was done.

It wasn't a good idea to put off work on Violet Ruiz's job. Beck would want to see progress every day, and if I couldn't provide it, she'd make my life hell. My feelers were already out with Jason. There wasn't much else for me to do.

I stared at the busy establishment before me. Glass shattered and the cops cheered. Wild and unruly just like any other gang in Nicodemia. The door opened, and inside I saw Anders laughing with a group of young officers.

Kinderson Creek was another in a long list of places I didn't belong. The cops were another group who wouldn't accept me. Instinct told me that Anders knew something important about McCay's death. He might help solve a mystery for me, but one look at him and exhaustion beat me down to a useless pulp. It crushed me into the slick cobbles and ground me to dust. Right then, the idea of walking into a busy pub and chatting up the blue felt like hiking from the tip of the Heavies up to the tallest heights of the Hallows.

So, I turned to leave. Beck was right. I needed to learn to let things go. McCay wouldn't be any deader tomorrow. Or the next day. What I needed right then was one good night of sleep. I'd track down Anders another time.

"Demarco," said a voice from Kinderson Creek's shining entrance. Anders stepped out, and the gloom surrounding the pub surrendered to a soft glow. "Is that you out there?"

The section of walkway where I stood was still steeped in shadow. I drew a cigarette from my pocket and flicked my lighter, letting its glow wash over me. As the first tongue of smoke writhed around my face, I said, "Too much heat for me in there, officer. We'll have that drink another time."

"What? Oh. I see." This cop was fresh as the morning catch. "I'm sorry, I thought—"

"It's not a problem." I turned to face him, stepping up to the edge of the dark. "Just tell me how McCay died."

"It's an active investigation."

"Knife? Gun? Was it a burglary?"

"Th-They warned us," he stammered. "We can't talk."

"It's not rare to see the evil in the world," I said, stepping forward. The smoke still lingered around my face, and I could tell that my fedora still cast a murky shadow over my face. "Everyone sees it. It's all around us, from grifters taking dimes from poor mothers to businessmen grinding the bones of their workers to killers of innocents. Most folks see evil and get mad. Furious, right down to their bones. It pains them." I drew a long breath, causing the cigarette to flare so its light danced in the fire of my eyes. "But they do nothing."

I took another step forward. "Others fight. Maybe they join a gang to solve some injustice. Maybe they get involved in politics." Our eyes locked. "Maybe they sign up to patrol the streets and live in the front lines. Then they realize that evil doesn't stop at the blue line. It seeps into every corner of society, digging its claws into the soup-thick laziness and the twisted bureaucratic lethargy. It comes in the form of too many mysteries to solve and answers that are too convenient to be true." My lungs burned and my breath ached. "I'll ask you again. How did McCay die?"

"They're calling it a robbery," he said. "Random."

"Not a suicide?"

"He didn't die easy."

"What was taken?"

"Look, Demarco," said Anders, casting a look back at the pub, "a few of the guys saw me talking to you at the scene. You're not popular."

"I'm aware."

"His throat was cut." Anders swallowed. "Word is it was clean. Professional. Like—Like slaughtering a pig up in Haven. Quick death. Lots of blood."

"Forced entry?"

"No."

"What was missing?"

His face was pale as the silver sky. "I—I don't know."

I dropped my cigarette butt and stepped it out. A curl of smoke still lingered on my lips. "Thanks, Anders. I appreciate it." I picked up the discarded butt and flicked it into a nearby recycler.

As I turned to leave, he said, "What are you going to do now?"

I paused to consider. "I'm going to get one good goddamn night of sleep."

Chapter 17

I DIDN'T GET one good goddamn night of sleep.

Back at the office, the whiskey tasted like recycled cardboard, and the cigarettes smelled like burned plastic. Nothing settled well, and once I'd finished the protein bar I dubbed supper, I tossed on the sofa for a handful of hours in something that almost resembled sleep. An alert on the office screen blinked yellow with a message until I put my hat over it. In my groggy half-sleep, I almost believed Trinity had a message for me, which was impossible because I was nobody.

When at last the thin specter of slumber finally closed my heavy eyes, a sound came at the door like a parade of all drums and no musicians.

My eyes were barely open when the door crashed in. Wash and his two goons swept through like they owned the whole block. When my mouth opened to say something—I don't even know what—Wash closed it with a quick slug from his ugly fist, sending a shockwave of pain searing into my jawbone.

"You've done it this time, Demarco," he said.

My jaw felt like a bruise on top of a bruise. I looked to his two goons, but they didn't cut me any slack. "You're welcome," I muttered.

Wash hit me again. This time, his fist struck my solar plexus hard and sharply enough to knock the dumb retorts right out of me. "You know, a lot of bosses would off you right now. Bam. Brains on the wall." He slugged me in the gut, but my breath was already gone, so it didn't really make me any worse. That'll show him. "But the Saint wants us to have another word with you."

"Good thing you're not the boss," I gasped.

Wash said, "That'd solve a lot of problems, wouldn't it?"

When I opened my fool mouth to speak again, he thumped me in the temple so hard little flashes of light danced around his lumpy face.

Maybe I'd sleep better if I didn't wake up to this drama.

There's a look people get when they've been pushed too far, and Sam Wash was close. I dropped to my knees, palms flat on the floor. My head pinged with pain and my vision blurred, but I made like it was far worse. Like I couldn't even stand.

"I'm getting real tired of this, Demarco," Wash said, his voice dropping to a low rumble. He kicked my thigh with a sharp-toed boot. Damn, that was right where it was already bruised. "My life would be a lot easier if you just did your job."

I nodded and got my feet under me, hitching forward like he'd really injured the leg. Maybe he had.

"Give us a minute," Wash said to his goons.

After an exchanged glance, they stepped outside, and Wash shoved me hard. "Tell me," he growled.

"Tell you what?"

"Tell me why you aren't doing what the Saint wants. Is there something you know that I don't?"

"What do you mean?" My jaw hurt when I spoke.

"As far as I see—as far as I've *ever* seen, people move when Saint Jerome asks for something. They move *fast.*" He ran his fingers through his tangled hair. "But not you. Not now. Am I hitching a ride on a doomed ship?"

"Saint Jerome has been headed for disaster since he chose a life on the wrong side of the law. It's just that some ships take longer to crash."

"He wants you to fall in line."

"Why?"

"That's not your business."

"It's the definition of my business, Wash."

His knuckles cracked, but he somehow found it in himself to not slug me. "Work for me, then."

A single barked laugh fled my gut before I could stop it. "What makes you think you could be in charge?"

"I've got experience."

"Running a gang of pickpockets?" I shook my head. "You won't survive, Wash. When you find out the pool's full of acid, *deeper* isn't the right direction."

"With you helping me out—"

"Leave it, Wash," I snapped. "You and that lady of yours won't last in this business. You won't crash slow like the Saint."

For a dozen pounding heartbeats Wash didn't respond. Then, anger twisted his features, and he took another swing at me. This time I was ready, and I took his arm in a tenuous joint lock.

"Guys," he winced. "Help me out."

The goons stepped forward, but I wrenched Wash around so they didn't know how to advance. He struggled against the lock. I couldn't hold him for long. Soon as he got free, I'd have goons all over me. I was stuck.

Then, out of the corner of my eye, I saw movement through the plate glass wall. A sleek shadow moved in the dark street.

"Did I mention that I expect a visitor this morning?" I asked.

This got a sneer from Wash. "You have a lot of friends?"

"No, actually. Not many at all. That's why this visitor is so important. You see, she's a beautiful lady, and I'd like to make a good impression."

Wash snorted. "What kind of lady visits a mook like you?"

"What kind of lady wants her man busting heads for a boss like Saint Jerome?"

That hit home. Doubt flashed across his face.

A shadow crossed in front of the open door. I could barely make out the shape, but I recognized her immediately. Beck lifted a gun and aimed it lazily at a goon.

"We have you outnumbered," I said.

Confusion twisted Wash's face, so I twisted his arm even harder.

"Leave," I said. "Tell Jerome I switched the papers. The Pelican's set."

Beck ushered the goons out of the room, and they disappeared into the night. Wash finally relaxed against my grip, so I let him go. Beck had a crimson-barreled pistol trained on him.

Wash was a dangerous man when his ego bled. I braced myself against another blow from his powerful fists, but he stood for several ragged breaths before opening his mouth to speak.

I interrupted, "You owe me for the door."

His brow furrowed. "I'll be back, Demarco."

"That's great. Pretty soon, I hope. A place like this needs a good door to keep the riffraff out."

Once Wash stalked off, Beck stepped over the shattered door and holstered her gun. A flash of gold lettering shone on the side of the crimson barrel. Her coat covered it before I could get a better look.

"Nice place you got here," she said.

I propped the door so it mostly blocked the entrance to the office. "It's not my place. Ownership's not really a privilege I have an abundance of these days."

She gave me a wry look as we exited the building into the dim pre-dawn city. "Why is it I keep needing to rescue you?"

"How about that stipend?" I asked.

She slapped a roll of dimes into my open hand. "Any progress?"

"Feelers are out. On my way to collect right now." I hoped. If Jason didn't have anything for me, it meant I was going to need to do some real work to catch up. "Care to join me?"

For a minute, Beck looked like she was pondering the political machinations of a brilliant tactician. "You know," she said finally, "I believe I would like to accompany you."

"It'd be safer."

"How so?"

"If I get the tar beaten out of me every time we meet up, then I'd just as soon stay together."

"Who's going to rescue you once I decide to kick your ass?"

Beck had parked her scooter a short distance away, and somehow the several thrashings I'd taken in the last twenty-four hours had relieved me of the pride that kept me from settling my bulk onto the back of it. We sped through morning traffic, spiraling downward through the morning mists. The cool breeze on my face woke me and helped clear the fog from my brain. By the time we finally arrived outside Rory's Ramshackle, I had more than a few questions I didn't dare ask.

For instance, why was Beck following me? How did she know exactly when to intervene and help? No way was that coincidence. The only real coincidences were bad ones, and her showing up at the right time didn't fit.

Jason wasn't working, but his father Rory was cleaning the bar. Rory was a caricature of his son, with the same swoop of hair, but with larger ears and a larger, knotty nose. He ignored us at first, and we watched as he scrubbed a sticky film from the fibersteel walls.

"Seems like a fella ought to make his son do work like that," I said.

He looked up at me, spotted Beck, and broke into a broad grin.

He stuck his hand out for a shake, and she daintily took it. "Pleasure meeting you, ma'am," he said. "This fella could use a lady like you around."

She destroyed him with her charming smile but said nothing.

"Jason leave anything for me?" I said. That's me. All business. And I wondered why I didn't have any friends.

Rory crossed behind the bar and checked. He handed me a slip of paper. "The fool let a bunch of troublemakers in last night," he said. "Had the blue all over the place."

Police again. I hadn't seen this much copper activity since right after the sugar riots. It reminded me of another question I couldn't ask. Why were the police so lax about a known art thief's widow docking at a Heavy port? Shouldn't there at least be a detail tracking her? Shouldn't they be tracking Beck?

Or did they think Trinity's surveillance was enough?

Or did Beck have some way of avoiding notice? If she did, what did she need me for?

I glanced at the paper and stuffed it in a pocket. "What's the blue looking for down this far? They're a little low for their route, aren't they?"

Rory waved away the idea like it was a fly. "Who ever knows what the blue man's looking for? It's never something good, so good riddance if they stay away."

"They sure leave a mess, though."

"Something I've learned from owning this place for as long as I have," Rory said. "I'd rather clean up a mess like this than deal with the fellas who make it."

"Maybe I should try that sometime," I said. "Seems like all I do is deal with people making messes."

"From what I figure, you're usually the one making the mess." Rory went back to cleaning the wall.

"Where to, Demarco?" Beck said as I settled my weight onto the back of her scooter.

"Down. All the way. Nine layers of down till we meet the devil himself."

"That's where one of the thieves is?"

"If he's anywhere at all." She put on a burst of speed, and I struggled to steady myself. The scooter wasn't fast, but she drove it like a madwoman. "Either way, we'll get some questions answered down there. It's a liminal space, like the one between the airlocks and the stars."

Of course, there were more questions I wasn't ready to ask. One in particular came to me as we hit a hard corner and Beck's coat flew up, exposing the plastic pistol she'd drawn against Wash's goons. I wanted to know this answer more than anything since I'd woken up that morning, but it wasn't anything I could bring myself to voice. Not yet, anyway.

Was Charlotte Beck carrying Dr. Lawrence McCay's crimson pistol?

Chapter 18

BECK SLOWED as we turned from the traveled path and plunged onto the roads below the fisheries. The air changed in that space between the city and the vast void of space. This place was the bottom of the bottom—a tangled knot of wormtrail passages and twisted spiderweb walkways. Aurora blue lighting gave the impression of a depth of emptiness deeper than the purest black and swallowed the scooter's headlight with pulses of indigo and the angled reflections of the jagged edges of the narrow tunnel. This was the gullet of the great beast of the outer void. The farther we twisted downward, the colder the air grew, and soon our breath billowed as white as lies and twice as thick.

After weaving down the narrowing path for as long as she could manage, Beck pulled to one side and stowed the scooter.

We walked, only vaguely aware that the network of tunnels was no longer empty. People lived in these depths and grew accustomed to the darkness. They moved as quiet as shadow in the void of space, but their bodies pressed closer in the black. The scuff of my shoes on hard metal were the drumbeats of an invading force.

This was a space where none were welcome, and nobody stayed long if they could help it.

Nobody but the thief Maurice Ribar.

A woman emerged like a ghost from the blue-black shadows. Her eyes shone in the light like headlights on an empty street, bright and unfeeling as the metal under our feet. She locked that gaze on me and grinned a toothy smile.

"Who's this man walking in the dark?" she said. It wasn't a question so much as an acknowledgment that she knew who I was. She knew what I could do.

"I'm looking for someone." My voice boomed in the dark.

Beck tensed at my elbow as two more pale ghosts materialized. They had the same stringy white hair and luminescent eyes. They didn't speak but hovered at the edge of sight. The woman bared her teeth at them.

"They're addicts," I whispered to Beck. "But they might know their way around this place."

"You get us some electric mud," the woman said, "and I'll take you to whoever you like."

Electric mud. Another designer drug for a junkie down on her luck. "You'll need to take us to him first." It hurt my soul thinking about feeding this group's habit, but I needed to find Maurice. Whatever this electric mud was, I was sure I could find it.

The woman's nostrils flared, and the two men took a step forward.

"I bet they have some dimes," said a man behind her with a shaved head and a mangled ear.

"Demarco," Beck said by way of warning.

To the woman, I said, "You know I can get you what you need. Just tell me where I can find Maurice."

Her muscles twitched. A shard of metal flashed in her left hand. Behind her, the man with the mangled ear grinned, showing yellow teeth.

It wasn't looking good.

Beck pressed her back against mine. "What's the plan, Demarco?"

Jason's note had told me to come down here, and he'd never led me astray before. Of course, all it took was once. Best plan I could come up with was to ask again, "Where is Maurice Ribar?"

Beck whispered a curse behind me.

The ghost woman stepped forward, her twitching muscles giving her a judder like a bad video feed. The makeshift knife glinted in her hand. I didn't dare look behind me to see what Beck was talking about, but I didn't need to. Behind the woman, more pairs of eyes appeared, and more ghostly shapes emerged from the darkness.

Then they attacked.

The ghost moved like a pouncing panther. A blink and she was on me. I had bulk on her, but she had the wiry strength of desperation. I tried to shove her off, but her grip was a steel vise. She slashed with the knife, drawing a well of blood from my arm and a vicious curse from my lips.

I thumped a fist into her temple. Once, twice, a third time. Then the others hit, and I tumbled back into Beck.

Beck drew the crimson-barreled pistol and waved it around. The ghosts scrambled back into the darkness.

I heaved my attackers away. Three of them now. The woman didn't relent at all, stabbing again with her jagged metal shard. It bit into her hand as much as it cut my arm. Blood darkened her translucent skin.

The others piled forward, driving Beck and me together, back to back. I threw a solid punch and shoved with all my strength so that they tumbled back as a single mass.

"Run!" I said.

Beck didn't need to be asked twice. She bolted and I followed, weaving our way through the blue-black tunnels. Furious scrabbling, scratching at our heels told me they followed. Fast. Beck's light flashed left, and I followed down a narrow tunnel. The maze swallowed us, welcoming us into its violent embrace. The blue glow faded, and the ache in my knees told me we were descending even farther into the belly of the station. We neared the liminal space at the edge of the void.

"Hey!" A voice came from somewhere up ahead. "Follow me!"

Beck hesitated. I didn't.

I grabbed her arm and dragged her forward. Our pursuers were desperate. Dangerous. Following the voice into deeper darkness, trusting the instinct that kept us moving forward, we found ourselves ushered through a narrow gap between sheer metal surfaces. Beck slipped through easily, but my shoulders stuck.

"Go!" I said.

This time she didn't hesitate. I heard her scrabble away into the darkness.

Dammit.

I pushed. Bony fingers grasped my elbow and my leg from behind. They'd caught me.

They pulled and bit. Panic welled deep in the core of my chest. My heart threatened to leap through my throat. I punched. Pulled. Kicked. Scraped forward.

My shoulder twisted farther through the gap, but that only pinned my arm. My legs burned and I pushed harder. Another junkie grabbed my foot. I kicked again, this time connecting with something solid. The attackers staggered back. Blue eyes flashed in the dark.

A light flared ahead, blazing orange like a tongue of fire. Its brilliance blinded me and the junkies recoiled. A strong hand gripped my shoulder and hauled me through the narrow gap.

"Come on," said a gruff voice. He dropped a blazing flare to the floor and its cold light licked at corroded steel. "Before they recover."

I followed him, but there wasn't far to go. Feeling our way along the wall, we located an entrance to a side passage and entered a dimly lit chamber that smelled of old sweat and the heat of human habitation. Blank eyes stared up at us from filthy blankets on the floor. Beck stood in the center of the room, hands on her knees as if trying to keep from vomiting. She'd already failed at least once. It was a moment of weakness starkly contrasting everything I had built up in my mind about the woman. The incongruity dislodged something in my gut, and I couldn't help but think of her as not an employer, but an ally. A friend? Maybe something more.

I placed a hand on her shoulder, but she shrugged me off and glared at me so hard my hat fell off.

The man sealed the door with a heavy crossbar. He wore a torn leather coat, and his beard was a tangled mess of unevenly clipped wires. His dark skin was pressed with oil and grime, and when he smiled there was a gap in his perfectly white teeth.

"You going to make it?" I asked Beck.

She straightened. Something danced behind her eyes, and four lines on her collarbone oozed blood. "I thought that kind of thing didn't exist here."

"Junkies," said the man who had rescued us. He had an odd accent I couldn't place. It wasn't anything like Beck's accent, but it also wasn't something from Nicodemia. "They exist anywhere there are people."

"Those weren't run-of-the-mill junkies," I said.

A middle-aged woman with her hair in thin braids said, "Electric mud isn't your run-of-the-mill drug." She held two young children close to her and looked up at us like we might bite.

The man said, "You're lucky we heard you out there."

Beck's frown deepened, but some color returned to her face.

"What's the best way out of here?" I asked.

"Back the way you came," the man said. "It's a maze, but there are ways through."

"Won't they figure out where to find us?"

The woman said with a dry voice. "They're not exactly deep thinkers."

"You'll want to stick around a while before you leave," the man added. "Let things settle down."

I gave him a sidelong glance and waited for him to confirm what I'd already figured out.

"And because I'm the man you were hollering for out there," the man said. "I'm Maurice Ribar."

Chapter 19

"IT'S A MAZE DOWN HERE," Maurice said, poking a sausage with his fork.

"I'm aware," I said.

He took a big juicy bite and chewed for days. After rescuing us, he'd led us past open pits where men played with their children, a table where mothers ate with their kids, and a room covered with blankets where the snores of the content wafted out along with the stench of the disavowed. It was a true homeless camp, and never in my trips down below had I ever seen such a thing. Then he shuffled us all into a narrow room with a single table at its center. A gray-haired woman with dark eyes brought us food, bandaged my arm, and gave Maurice a peck on the cheek.

"Thank you, honey," said the man.

She disappeared back into the maze.

"Myrna is my wife," Maurice explained. "I've made a life for myself down here."

"Why not above?" I asked.

Maurice considered the next bite of sausage. "The spiral

continues, you see, at least in spirit. Downward spiral, all the way to the bottom."

"I'm aware," I repeated.

He shot a glance at Beck, his eyes narrowing with suspicion. "Story of our lives, don't you think? The spiral only goes down."

"Maybe for those junkies out there," I said, "but some folks manage to claw their way back up."

He shrugged. "We've got music. Family. The city still feeds us. We have everything we need, really."

"Everything but a decent light source and proper citizenship." I picked up one of the tiny sausages and gave it a sniff. Damned if it wasn't rat or some other rodent but it was good. Beck dropped a shade paler when I took a bite, so I finished it and picked up a piece of hard bread.

Maurice said, "That used to be me. Wanting things I couldn't have. Citizenship isn't in the cards for me, so why get worked up about it?"

I leaned in. "Is that what the art was to you? Something you couldn't have, so you wanted it?"

He froze. "That was a long time ago."

"Not so long to some people. Not long enough at all, actually." The bread was good. Peppery. "Some folk say there's a man by your description holding onto one last painting."

A deep chuckle rumbled in his chest. "Art was a means to an end for me. Never really rose to the level of a proper addiction like it does with some folks. I'd never hold onto something like a paint- ing. Sell it and be done." He gestured around the room with a dented flask. "And where would I hang something that big?"

"I never said what size a painting we were talking about."

He looked at me with half-lidded eyes. "It's a damn big painting we're talking about, and there's no need to dance around it."

"Dancing? You have a lot of that around here?"

"When there's music, there's dance." He patted the pocket of his shirt where a harmonica glinted in the dim blue light. "Not now, though. Not for a while."

"How long have those junkies been around?"

"We've always had junkies. This is something else. Someone's leading them down here and dumping them. Someone with access to the new drugs."

Access. That was what it was all about. If the drug wasn't something Trinity explicitly allowed, then someone must have an override. Or a recipe. Either way, it was bad karma.

Maurice opened his mouth to talk, but just then a girl ran into the room. She couldn't have been more than two, maybe three, years old, and she had greasy ponytails covering her ears. Myrna followed close on her heels.

"Come on over here," Maurice said, opening his arms. The little girl ran into a big hug, and he swept her up. To me, he said, "We're not looking for trouble down here. We keep to ourselves, and the world spins up above us."

Beck leaned forward and looked Maurice right in the eyes. "We just want the painting, Mr. Ribar. Don't care how we get it."

He shook his head. "I don't know…"

"It'd be a good thing to get that piece put back together," I said. "For the sake of the art, if nothing else."

The little girl sat nicely on Maurice's lap. Maybe it was his daughter. Maybe they communally raised children down here. It was hard to detect any familial resemblance in the dim light. Maurice pushed his plate away. Something bothered him, but it wasn't clear what.

"That job was fucked from the start," he said. "Every one of us knew it."

Myrna gave him a reproachful look, took the little girl by the hand, and led her away.

"If it was a bad job, why did you take it?"

A muscle in Maurice's neck twitched. "It looked like the perfect gig. Everything was lined up just right. We all had the perfect skills, and nothing could ever go wrong. Systems to hack that Ruiz had worked before. Safes—they had the newest model of Cryptliner Fortitudes. They're titanium and iron all the way through, and all the hardware is so finely manufactured it's impossible to hear even the first tumbler fall."

"You cracked safes?" I said.

Maurice's eyes sparkled in a way that told me I'd hit the nail on the head. He pressed his lips together. "It was damn perfect. I'd just figured out how to crack that safe, and there were only seven of them in the whole world." He cleared his throat. "Vitez had the connections lined up. There was supposed to be a drop at the silo —this place we worked for sometimes. It was a big center for space tourism, but they made an extra dime moving Earth artifacts to the colonies. There's a good market for people missing their heritage, you know. At least that's what Vitez always said."

"He wasn't wrong."

The man sized me up, probably trying to decide if I was pulling his leg. I wasn't sure of the answer myself. He continued, "The painting was bigger than we would have liked, but old Hector Chance stepped out of retirement to lend us muscle, despite his wife's complaints."

"She wanted him to go clean?"

"He had kids, but I think he was thinking about his kids when he signed up for the job. He wanted to provide for them. Between the four of us, it was a cake job. All profit, hardly any risk."

"Hardly any risk, hardly any fun," Beck said. Her voice hitched in her throat.

The distant look in Maurice's eyes indicated that he seemed to agree. "You know, that's exactly what Chance used to say."

"Why'd this safe job go bad?" I asked.

Maurice continued, "At that point, I wasn't much looking for risk. Things could have been a lot worse, and it was damn hard to pass up that kind of job, given my financial situation."

"So, you took it." I picked up another piece of bread and

started picking it apart and eating it piece by piece. "And it went spinward."

"It was a transport job. A bunch of art and other valuables were being moved out of Catalina due to the unrest in the area. Lot of things were getting sketchy round those parts of Europe. The idea was to move it to someplace more stable. Nigeria, in this case. They loaded up one of those big ultra-fast unmanned transports and sent it on its way."

"There was other art on the flight too?"

Maurice nodded. "Sure was, but the client only cared about *The Garden of Earthly Delights*."

Beck asked, "Who was the client?"

"You'd have to ask Vitez if you can find him."

"About that," she said.

Maurice grinned. He had a captive audience, and I got the impression he was going to soak it for all it was worth. "My part in the job should have been straightforward. Board the airship as it passed into space, crack the safe, and help Chance transport the goods back onto our ship. Painting goes to the Silo, the transport finishes its journey unsuspecting, thanks to Ruiz's hacks, and by the time anyone figures out something's missing, we've already unloaded the goods."

"On the moon," I said.

"On the moon. Pretty straightforward job, really."

"So, what went wrong?"

"Everything. First, Vitez was also going to be our pilot. He'd had training and we spent a whole month practicing the maneuver." Maurice chuckled to himself. "He always said being a painter gave him a light touch with the shuttle controls. When it was go time, he flipped us like he was supposed to, matched pace with the transport, and then froze up."

"He was afraid?"

"Something like that. It wasn't like him. By the time we talked him down, our window was drastically shortened." Maurice wiggled his fingers as if to dislodge the memories from them. "I can crack any safe you drop in front of me, but it takes time."

"You got the job done, though."

"See, here's the thing. When Chance, Ruiz, and I dropped in on that transport, we didn't find a Cryptliner Fortitude. It was the previous year's Masterforce. Not an easy safe to crack, but I could do it."

"Sounds like a good thing," Beck said, leaning forward. She was getting into old Maurice's story. "An easier safe means you got it done faster."

Maurice shook his head. "An easier safe, yes, but the *wrong* safe. You see, intelligence failures like that are not good in the business. Ruiz took it in stride, but Chance panicked. Tried to abort the mission."

"Wasn't your hacker in charge of gathering that information?" Had Violet Ruiz's husband been the one to screw up the entire job?

Maurice looked down at his own hands. "I should have double-checked Ruiz's sources."

"But you trusted what he brought you."

"I *wanted* to trust his information. Right there on the transport, though, it didn't matter one way or the other. We were either walking out with a painting or we were walking out empty-handed. I had my opinion on that, so I got to work. Ruiz kept busy too, making sure we didn't trip any alarms." The deep lines in Maurice's flesh darkened. "He bought me enough time to open the safe, but just barely. Soon as that safe cracked, the lights went red and two guys with guns floated into the storage compartment."

"On an unmanned transport?" Beck asked.

"Not quite as unmanned as promised, apparently. Chance dispatched them easily enough. That old man moved faster in a pinch than any of us, but even he wasn't fast enough to do it without getting himself shot."

"Killed?" I asked.

Maurice shook his head. "I don't know. Maybe. Doesn't

matter at this point. He wasn't in any shape to help move the painting, but the painting was stored in three parts and we were in something pretty close to zero-G. Ruiz and I were able to maneuver one panel of it into our own ship without much trouble."

"What happened to Chance?"

The old man sagged in his seat, looking a decade older. "Those two fellas were the pilot and copilot. We didn't know that at the time." He quickly added, "Chance's wounds wouldn't have closed in zero-G. People don't heal right when there's no gravity. He needed to land as soon as possible."

They'd left him behind to his fate. Whether that was prison or a fiery crash or death from a gunshot wound didn't much matter. "What happened to Ruiz?"

Maurice shrugged. "The timer said we had another minute before the transport was scheduled to reenter atmo, but everything started heating up. I tied down the first part of the painting, and Ruiz went back to grab the next panel. Right about then, Vitez decided to separate. We left Ruiz and two-thirds of the painting along with Chance."

"Leaving you and Vitez with one panel."

"Hell," Maurice said, his voice low and grim. "All we got was hell. The third panel, I mean. The transport didn't have a pilot, so it crashed, killing Ruiz and Chance. The one panel we had was too hot to drop on the Moon, so we had to look at our options."

Beck leaned back and crossed her arms. "You came to Nicodemia."

"Our ship had simple cross-colony support and enough fuel. Yeah, it wasn't meant for it, but it was our best option." He gestured around at the modest room. "Welcome to the reward for our earthly delights."

"Where did Vitez end up?" Beck asked.

I said, "More important, where's the painting?"

"You'll have to ask Vitez. The bastard thought this place was too heavy. Headed up the gravity well with the painting after promising to send me half of whatever he made selling it."

"Where can we find him?" I popped the last crust of bread into my mouth and chewed. "Who was he going to sell to?"

He looked from me to Beck, then back again. "I don't know."

Beck didn't move, but the air between her and the old man grew tense.

Maurice must have felt it too, because he continued, "He was leaving for Haven Nicodemia. Vitez always played his cards close to his chest, especially when it came to his connections. He knew a guy here in the Heavy, and that guy must have given him a connection up the chain."

"Who did he know in town?"

Maurice chewed his lip for a long time. I'm not sure if he was trying to remember or trying to decide whether or not to tell us. I didn't interrupt his thought process, and it paid off. "McCain or McCare or something like that. Fella seemed like he knew how to get upstairs."

"McCay?" I asked, dreading the answer.

"That might be it." Thin lines creased between his eyes. "How did you know?"

"Because he's dead. Any other ideas?"

Maurice went three shades paler and silent as a robbed grave. I made pleasantries for a while, then asked Maurice to show us out. Once we were near the edge of their settlement, he hung back, a shadow in the blue light.

"We appreciate your hospitality, Mr. Ribar," I said, tipping my fedora. "Give regards to your wife."

"Sorry, I couldn't help more," he said.

Beck watched him with her steely gaze the whole time he backed away. She might have drilled a hole in him with the look she shot his direction. "He's holding back."

"Doesn't matter. He'll keep holding back and there's nothing we can do about it."

"Where do we go now?"

"I have one more stop down here, then we'll go up the chain to Haven Nicodemia. We know Vitez went that way with the painting, and I still have some contacts that direction. Somebody had to notice a fella from Earth dragging a third of *The Garden of Earthly Delights* around."

She didn't seem overly convinced, but then again, neither was I.

Chapter 20

THE BOTTOM of the world was a temple, with high-arched ceilings and ancient floors inscribed with symbols of both the faithful and the faithless. This was the Pit, the opposite of the Apex at the top of the Hallows. I stepped over the cross of Christianity and the crescent of Islam to stand in the center upon a symbol of anarchy. The walls shimmered with the same iridescent blue of the tunnels above, but this space was brighter. Piercing. It was a liminal space between the station and the dark of space, and I could feel the weight of Trinity's gaze on my back as soon as I arrived.

"Trinity," I said. My voice echoed in the enormous room.

When there was no response, I looked back to where Beck stood at the entrance. "Some privacy would be nice."

She took a few more steps back, disappearing into the tunnels.

"Trinity," I said again. "Let's have a chat."

This time, a deep rumble swelled from the ground below. The blue lights on the walls shifted, brightening into dancing holograms. After a few seconds, a faceless blue figure appeared before me. Its baritone voice resonated from the walls. "Reconcile?"

"Not today."

The AI expressed neither disappointment nor regret, but the sensation of both lingered in the air. Trinity wasn't a person in the conventional sense, and those who believed in it as an individual understood it to be such a strange intelligence that it might as well be alien. Its three hardcoded goals of "Body, Soul, Community" were concepts we used to understand its enigmatic nature, but its real internal priorities were much more complex. Each bead on this giant rosary had its own instance of the amalgamation of programs that made up the Trinity AI, and each Trinity behaved according to its own habits and mannerisms.

Since my excommunication, every instance only wanted one thing from me: reconciliation. And I could have it too. I could be a citizen again. Walk streets in the light, take and give and be a part of the community. Balance my Karma.

But there was still work to do in the dark, even if that started with finding a painting for a widow.

"There's a gang war starting in your bead," I said. "I'm wondering why you aren't stopping it."

The blue hologram cocked its head. "There are variables at play." Heavy Nicodemia's Trinity could be a tidge obtuse. "Community emerges from chaos." It started walking, motioning me to follow.

"It doesn't seem to me like it's doing much emerging."

Blue lights formed into images of people walking the streets of Heavy Nicodemia. Dense, bright areas showed where many people gathered: churches, shopping centers, restaurants, streets. Each tiny pinprick showed a person moving through the city from the docks all the way up to the government district. It was a staggering number of people.

The image zoomed in on the cathedral, where Cecilia and the other priests preached. Then, it focused on another part of the city, where a stage play was being performed. A dozen actors entertained hundreds of spectators.

"Yeah, I get it," I said. "There are a lot of different kinds of community. Some of it's religion and some of it's built around the arts. There doesn't need to be any of it built around murder, so why are you allowing it?"

Trinity led me along the outside of the room as the indigo display on the wall danced and changed, showing years in a matter of seconds. Sometimes people went to church. Other times, people gathered at raves in the warehouse districts. Still later, people gathered down at the docks for water sports.

"None of these activities end with dead innocents in the cross-fire," I protested.

"None of these activities has resulted in zero deaths."

"Even *I* think that's pretty cynical, Trinity."

Again, Trinity was silent. We continued our walk—or rather I continued to walk, and the hologram appeared to walk next to me. On the screen, the image of the spiral city danced with blue lights. Masses converged and dispersed through the days. The hypnotic pattern of humanity held me in its thrall for a long time.

Finally, a man's voice broke the silence. Saint Jerome spoke, and a thousand points of blue light formed his face. "Kill him, then," Jerome said. In the image, his gold necklaces glinted with blue so bright they were almost white. "Kill the handyman. Nobody gets away with this."

Then the million points of light dissipated. The blue figure stood next to me, its inert, unseeing eyes pointed my direction. A pit formed in my gut. Saint Jerome had given me a death sentence. I'd expected a lot of things from the bastard, but not that. I thought it was only Wash who had it in for me.

"I need some meds," I said to Trinity.

The blue of the wall reformed into a standard med panel control. I selected the chemical formulas that I needed and started a print. "I need unrestricted med station access throughout the station." The basic med-ordering control I had wasn't going to be enough.

"Reconcile," said Trinity.

"No."

"Temporary access," I said. "Just for when there isn't time to reach a liminal space."

The AI didn't answer.

"Why did you show me that, then?" I asked. "That video of Jerome. I know you don't give a damn about my safety. What are you trying to get out of this."

The hologram cocked its head. Its blue eyes shimmered like guttering flames. "The value of one soul is immeasurable. The value of many—"

"Is just math," Beck said, striding through the door as if she owned the place.

Trinity's hologram dissipated, light diffracting into nothing.

"What was that for?" I asked, more than a little annoyed by the interruption. "It was just starting to get good."

She waggled her fingers, indicating the whole room. "Your little religious moment here is going to have to wait. The junkies saw the lights and they're on their way."

As I walked to the center of the massive room, the central symbol broke into four pieces and a platform rose. Atop it was a small package, wrapped neatly in plain brown fiber. I took it and stowed it away.

"It's not religious," I said.

"Says the guy praying for help."

"Trinity's not God, and this isn't a prayer."

"How can you tell?"

"Because prayers aren't answered."

She raised an eyebrow.

As we left Trinity's temple, I said, "We need to leave the Heavies. Right away."

"Trouble?"

"Saint Jerome's people are looking for me. I have a couple of stops to make, then we're gone."

"Fair enough." She put a hand out to stop me from talking. Her nails dug lightly into my chest. She nodded at the path to our left.

After several seconds, I heard what she had noticed. Someone breathed slow and rasping in the nearby darkness.

We backed slowly away, turning to another narrow passage. I didn't dare bring out my light, and if Beck had some way of seeing in the dark, she didn't mention it. Time stretched in the bending tomb at the base of Heavy Nicodemia, and the monsters who lurked there moved in patterns I couldn't discern.

After an eternity and a day, Beck and I emerged from the maze into the relative light near the docks. The stench of stale water and gutted fish smelled better than mock-orange on a bright sunny day.

"Well," Beck said. "Care to go back in and get a lady her scooter?"

"I think I'll pass on that job."

"Seems to me you're not very good at passing on jobs."

"I'm passing on this one."

"You say that, and then it sticks to you like fish stink. You walk around with a cloud of it tainting everything around you until you finally figure out you can't get away."

I stopped and turned to her, ready to tell her off, but she was right. "Fine," I said. The way was easy enough, so I plunged once more into the dark.

It was a surprisingly short distance to where we'd parked the scooter. I listened closely as I approached, straining to hear the furtive movements of the junkies who had attacked us earlier. When I was sure they weren't nearby, I approached.

"Do not trust that woman," a voice said in the dark. "She lies to you."

"Myrna?" I asked.

Maurice's wife stepped forward through the blue light. The whites of her eyes shone like fire. "Maurice trusts everyone he meets, so he likes you both well enough."

"Beck works for my employer. She's as trustworthy as it gets."

Myrna crossed her arms and hugged herself close against the cold. "Then you better not trust anyone." With that, she disappeared into the dark, leaving me to wonder about the warning.

With the headlight cutting through blue-black darkness, I easily picked my way back topside where Beck leaned against the back of a fishing shack.

"I'll drive," I said, pulling up.

Without complaint, Beck slid onto the back seat of the scooter. Either the scooter handled better with me driving or my sense of control made the ride more comfortable. I maneuvered through foot traffic, taking the inside track most of the way up the spiral. When I reached the cathedral, I took a hard right into the warehouse district. Narrow alleys zipped past as I navigated the confusing maze of passages.

When I found Retch's place, I stopped. "Wait here," I told Beck. "I don't think he likes you very much."

I only had to knock on Retch's hidden door three times before the telltale click of a makeshift gun drew my attention to a narrow gap in the fibersteel wall.

"I have a job for you," I said, holding up the med pack. "And medicine to help pay for it."

"I have medicine, thanks."

"This is dosed specifically for you, and you'll never get in trouble for having it."

A second click sounded, the loud clack bouncing off my nerves louder and harder than I thought it probably should. A few seconds of silence passed, then the door swung open.

Retch wore a baggy button-down shirt and patched trousers. He looked comfortable in the outfit. Confident. His blond mop was chopped short, completing the look. He took the bag. "So, I won't have some asshole handyman showing up at my place trying to steal this stuff?"

"Doubt it."

He opened the bag and peered inside. Apparently satisfied, he closed it again. "What's this job you're talking about?"

I produced the bundle of papers I'd taken from the government center. "Hide these somewhere. Keep them safe and don't let anyone know you have them."

"And what are you paying?"

"I just gave you those meds."

He put a fist on his hip and looked at me reproachfully. "That was a gift."

"Fine," I said. "I'll pay you by being your friend."

"That's not how friendship works, asshole." He took the papers and leafed through them. "The Pelican, huh? Upscale place, right?"

"It'll kill you with boredom if you try to read those."

Retch sighed and retreated toward his warehouse, then stopped. "That lady," he said. "You know you can't trust her, right?"

"I keep hearing that."

He shrugged. "We losers need to stick together, right?"

Back at the street, I met Beck. Surprisingly, she let me drive again. Whether that was kindness or not, I could not tell.

I took us to the residential area near the government district. The streets were busy with pedestrian traffic. This high up, the system felt physically lighter, which I knew would be nothing compared to what I was about to feel moving to Haven.

"What are you looking for?" Beck said as I stepped off the scooter.

"There's a guy I need to talk to."

She fell in beside me.

I knew something was wrong as soon as we stepped into the apartment complex. It didn't smell right, like the sweat of fear and anger permeated the walls. An uncharacteristic gouge decorated the steel wall next to the elevator. Fresh, with shredded fiber flaking its corners.

We took the stairs up to the third floor, where I knew Williams lived with his kids. He wasn't there. It was unsurprising for the middle of the day, but his door stood wide open, and the smell of cigarette smoke lingered in the hallway.

Inside, the apartment was a mess. Papers and electronics were scattered everywhere, and deep under a pile of torn sofa cushions, a radio wailed with a haunting electric guitar. The music had a lot of slides in it, like the bluesmen of an old Chicago club.

"What happened here?" Beck asked, startling me from a near-trance.

After checking closets and dressers both in Williams's room and the rooms of his kids, I came to a conclusion. "He fled," I said. "Maybe early this morning. I must have spooked him."

"People don't trash their places when they leave. Not like this."

"They don't pack their kids' most essential clothes and books either."

The whole deal still felt off, so I dug through the room again. A half-eaten omelet sat in the trash receptacle. Cold. Wires protruded from the wall where Trinity's sensors should have been in the living room. I found a hint of ash near the window, smelling faintly of cheap tobacco. The board game scattered on the floor had a hint of that ash too.

"Someone came here after they left." I sniffed the air, catching a faint hint of cigar near the doorway. The apartment's air hadn't fully cycled through the filters. "As recent as an hour ago. They're looking for something." Maybe the papers I'd given Retch, but I didn't want to say that out loud. "They didn't find it."

"How can you tell?"

"People stop searching either when they find what they're looking for or when every square inch of the place is torn to shreds."

Beck looked around. "Option two?"

"That's right." Almost. I peered at the apartment's layout for the span of a few deep breaths. It was similar to McCay's apartment, only instead of the veneer of wealth, Williams covered his home in the drab grays of a proud bureaucrat. In the kids' bedroom—which was the equivalent of McCay's office—I dug under the tossed contents of a dresser and found the utility panel.

I don't know what I expected to find. A man can hope for answers. He can pretend like the world is going to fit nicely together and complete all the puzzles with one universal solution. Life rarely works like that, though.

What I found was more questions. Deep in the utility tunnel was a single rectangle of film. The single segment held five photographs with inverted colors. Actual photographs, not pictures printed from a digital image. I held them up to the light and peered through them.

The first four were blurry messes. Images too dark for the physical media. Nothing would come from those, no matter how well they were projected. The fifth was an image of a man standing in shadow. Smoke curled up around his face to gather under the brim of his ragged fedora, but it was clear that the nearby streetlamps weren't lighting for him. He was excommunicated, just like me.

Looking out the window, I saw that the photograph must have been taken from Williams's window. The backdrop of the buildings across the street matched the background behind the man.

"I think I saw this guy at the government center," I said, showing Beck the photograph.

Her jaw twitched, but all she said was, "We should go."

An hour later, Heavy Nicodemia dropped slowly away as we rode a cargo elevator up the chain to the next bead. As I dozed on the long journey upward, the questions of the day swam relentlessly through my head. Who had killed McCay? Where had Williams gone? What had I done that Saint Jerome wanted me killed? All of that seemed a fair amount more pressing than simple questions about paperwork and plastic pistols, but it was all related. Maybe we could find some answers up in Haven Nicodemia.

Or maybe all we'd find were more damn questions.

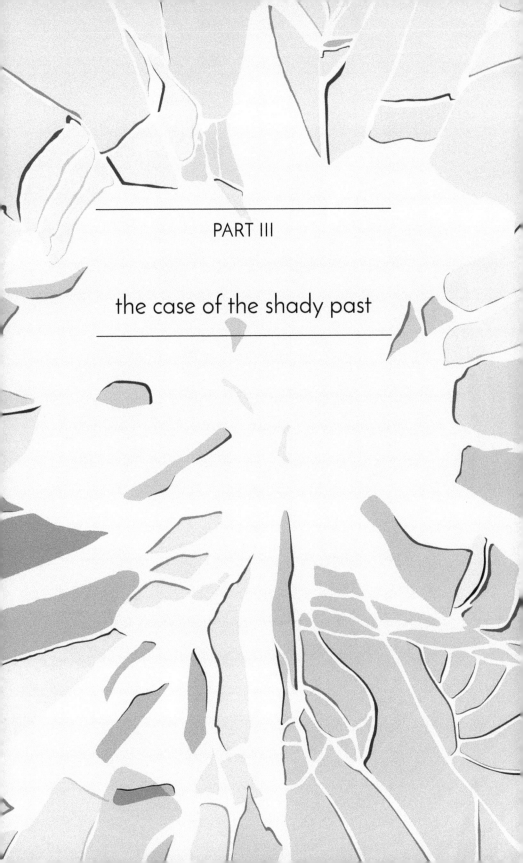

PART III

the case of the shady past

Chapter 21

THE ELEVATOR DOORS PARTED, and the turquoise brilliance of Haven Nicodemia burned a hole right through the ache in the back of my head. I squinted at the scintillating light, holding up a hand against the piercing illumination. Somewhere, a jazz saxophone wailed against the hard fiberstone corridors of the bottom reaches of the middle bead. The reception and customs room was much like Trinity's temple beneath Heavy Nicodemia, but with better acoustics and fewer judgy, asshole AIs.

A silhouette approached, but in my blindness, I couldn't tell if he held a gun or a scanner. Beck must have sensed my tension, because she stepped in front of me, one hand wheeling her scooter forward beside her.

"Charlotte Beck," she said, raising a hand. "Here on the travel authority of Violet Ruiz."

The man pulled the trigger. Once the scan finished, he turned to me.

"I'm nobody," I said. My vision cleared enough for me to get a good impression of his annoyed expression. I held up my hands. "Handyman."

The man shrugged. He wore a stiff gray uniform complete with a brimmed hat. When he scanned me, it came up clear, as expected. "Second one of you in two days." He holstered the scanner and patted me down manually.

"Who was the other guy?"

The customs inspector looked me straight in the eyes. "Nobody."

"Wise ass."

"You're telling me." The inspector moved on to scan the more inert cargo farther back in the container.

The tunnels under Haven were the same layout as in the Heavies, but here the space was well-lit in an eerie turquoise and reasonably well-populated. Travelers moved along cordoned-off lines to await inspections. Inspectors moved in packs, swarming and enveloping travelers in a tidal wave of paperwork and scans. Nobody stepped out of line the whole walk up. They'd be fools to try anything in this bead.

"We need to split up for a bit," I said.

Beck raised an eyebrow. "Already?"

"I know some folks up here, but they're not the sort to enjoy surprise company." Seeing the dubious look on her face, I continued, "We'll meet up at noon tomorrow by Saint Benedict's. Haven Nicodemia uses the exact same layout as Heavy. You won't have any trouble finding the cathedral."

"Never said I would."

"Head to the government district up at the top. Same place as the one in the Heavies. You ought to be able to pressure someone into telling you where this Vitez guy got off to."

"What am I paying you for?"

"My good looks."

We stepped out of the tunnels and breathed the open air of Haven Nicodemia. It stood in sharp contrast to the fish-gut smell down in Heavy, but it wasn't much better. The smell of wet fur rolled over us like a hot breath. Nearby were the pigs, guinea pigs, cattle, and goats. It all smelled damp and shitty to my unaccustomed nose, and by the expression on Beck's face, she felt the same.

"You get used to it," I said.

"How long did you live here before that happened?" She pulled her scooter to one side, opened the storage compartment, and withdrew the crimson-barreled pistol.

"You're lucky Customs didn't find that."

She holstered the weapon. "It'll make it easier to pressure government officials."

"How much pressure do you think you'll need?"

Beck shot me a sideways smile, and the charm of it almost knocked me off my feet. "Always a rule-follower, huh, Demarco?"

She tossed me a fresh roll of dimes and sped away. I marveled at how much faster it handled the slope here in Haven. The vehicle had probably been designed for an environment with one Earth-equivalent of gravitational pull. More Gs strained its motor, and adding a massive guy like me to the mix probably didn't help. Beck ignored the street signs and well-ordered rows of pedestrians and blasted her way up and away from the farm district, leaving me with nothing but my two lousy feet to get me around.

I strolled past hundreds of little pens, divided by narrow grassy rows. The animals inside were mostly pigs, but some contained goats or sheep. A few even had more interesting animals like capybaras or enormous rats. These gravity conditions worked well for the formation of meat, so that's what this whole damn bead smelled like. It wasn't a bad way to go. Better than fish. Barely.

Most of the little farm plots were organized into neatly curved grids. The workers wore coveralls arrayed in a spectacularly wide variety of grays. As I spiraled up past the farm district, I fell into the fastest pedestrian lane available. This wasn't the mad free-for-all of the city below. In Haven Nicodemia, people largely respected the traffic suggestions. Every time I wandered out of line, I earned a sour look from some well-dressed businessman.

I didn't have far to go. Something about the location of Rory's

Ramshackle made it the ideal location for a dive bar, and this copy of the city was no exception. Only here the place was called Ever Upward, and the glowing sign out front had its full array of letters like it was a fancy place or something. Hell, everything was fancier here. Even the sidewalks looked like they'd been recently polished.

Squinting against the bright sky, where real solar light filtered into the fortunate bead, I broke from the pedestrian stream and entered the bar.

The location was the same as Rory's, but everything else was completely different. High dividers sectioned off areas of the room, forming it into an ordered grid. Tables sat clean and polished in the early afternoon, every single one of them at perfect right angles.

At the bar, a man with an immaculate red beard and a dimpled smile perked up as I entered and said, "Hello, there! What can I..." The rest of his words must have got lost on the way because his dimples disappeared and all he had to say was, "Demarco."

"Aiken."

"I've been expecting you." He hardly moved, but now there was a stunstick in his left hand. It was as long as his forearm and the end crackled menacingly.

I showed him the palms of my hands. "This place always did have the friendliest service."

"Ever since you left."

"You're upset I didn't have time to say goodbye?"

Aiken took a step to the right and pressed a button under the bar. "Demarco's here."

I grimaced. "I was hoping we could keep this conversation between the two of us."

"Not after what you did."

My mind raced. What had I done? I had debts. Nothing big— well nothing *that* big. They were the kind of debts that went away if a person ditched out of town for a decade. It had been four years and that stunstick leveled at my chest told me they hadn't done much forgetting yet.

Slowly, while keeping eye contact with Aiken, I reached into my pocket and withdrew a dime. I walked over to the jukebox and dropped the coin in. They didn't have much in the way of blues around these parts. Everything on the list had a certain level of pep to it that didn't jive with my current mood. Finally, I found a soulful solo saxophone piece by Charlie Parker that hit all the right notes.

"Somebody's been telling stories," I said, approaching the bar.

Aiken shook his head. "I've seen the evidence myself, Demarco. We used to be pals and that's the only reason I haven't dropped you already." The icy look in his eyes told me he was telling the truth.

"There's plenty bad in all our lives, Aiken." I placed my hands on the bar. Heat from his crackling stunstick sizzled inches from my face. It was possible to crank a stunstick up so that it would deliver a killing pulse. I didn't know if Aiken had done that to his, but either way, I wasn't going to enjoy a zap to the face. "I'd be interested in seeing this evidence."

A voice crackled through his intercom. I could barely hear it over the crooning of the music. "Be a dear and show him the video." It was a woman's voice, with the weary hint of old age nipping at its edges.

Aiken pressed a few buttons and the screen behind him flickered to life. Grainy, gray footage of a large empty hallway came alive. A liminal space, not the crisp, powerful surveillance of one of Trinity's well-controlled areas. The video played for several seconds, showing the empty airlock, but he didn't need to show me any more.

I knew that place. It was burned indelibly into my memory.

My heart hammered as the video rolled forward.

"All I need is the location of a man who passed through here a while back," I said. "We don't need to do this."

Aiken's smile returned, but his dimples failed to reappear. "Your timing's funny. This video just fell into our laps."

"I bet."

The video jumped. Without sound, it looked as if the camera had been bumped, but I knew the truth. The cruiser docking at that airlock had just slammed into the station. Redundant fail-safes were failing, and every passenger onboard was in danger.

"Come on," I said, failing to keep the edge of panic from my voice. "What is it you want?"

"We want you to watch," said the woman through the intercom. The voice sounded achingly familiar.

"Who are you, lady?"

"Just watch the video," she said.

"She's just an informed citizen," Aiken said.

On the video, the airlock door opened, and the world shook. Several people rushed through: a man in a tweed suit, the janitor who worked for my family's estate for years, three women in their Sunday best, my sister, and finally, me. Young, gawky Jude Demarco in all his glory. I swallowed back my dislike for that boy. As he reached the console, another crash cascaded through the corridor. My sister flew straight up, smashing her back on the bulkhead. Others tumbled and flew, one of them skewing the camera with a solid thump.

"We know what you did on that console," the woman said. "We can prove that you were the one to engage the emergency release."

"You killed everyone on that ship," said Aiken.

But I was already on my way out of the Ever Upward. I didn't care if Aiken dropped me with his stunstick. They could make the video public for all I cared. Watch as the mobs came at me for everything I'd done. They were right. This was a damn fine piece of blackmail, and an excellent reason to hate me.

My pulse pounded in my throat. Bitter acid rose.

The crowd parted in chaos around me. Squinting against the searing light, I careened forward, not caring where I was going as long as it wasn't there. As long as I didn't need to relive that horrible memory. The day my sister was injured. The day my parents died.

And there were so many more who died that day.

A hand gripped my shoulder, and I swung a wild haymaker, missing Aiken by half a mile.

He shoved me against a wall. He'd left his stunstick at the bar. Nobody carried weapons in Haven Nicodemia. Not openly, anyway. Maybe that's all that saved me from a nerve-numbing pulse and a lousy day.

"Listen," Aiken growled. He shoved something hard into my ribs. Warm wet blood oozed down my side. "If it were up to me, you'd be a dead man right now, but that's not the play. I get a lot of money by turning you over, you asshole, and that goes away if you're dead."

"That'd be a shame, wouldn't it?"

He slipped something into one of my pockets and took a step back. By the time I turned, he'd concealed his knife. "Go where that sends you. Do what it says." His lips tightened into a thin line. "We used to be close, Demarco. I thought you were a decent guy. So, what's going to happen to you when people who don't even know you see what I've seen?"

I balled my fists, letting my pain channel into rage. My old friend turned on me. Blackmail. "All I want is the location of a guy."

"My brother worked on that ship, you asshole," Aiken said. "So, piss off and do what you're supposed to do. Maybe you'll get out of town without taking the long dive, but Demarco?"

I stared at him without saying a word.

"Don't ever come back."

A siren sounded somewhere far off in the distance. I didn't know if it was meant for me, but I wasn't going to wait around to find out. Without looking back at Aiken, I stepped into the pedestrian flow, allowing its massed anonymity to swallow me whole.

Chapter 22

THE BRIGHT DAYS of Haven Nicodemia burned like a bonfire against the sputtering torch of the Heavies, but the nights were just as dark. When finally nighttime fell over the city, the bleak, black alleys grew familiar once again. Grim pedestrians passed on the street under the neon glow of the jazz nightclubs dotting the cityscape. The world grew into a kind of mournful wail echoing in the emphatic insistence of brass and wood.

Trinity was different here, a separate instance grown from the same core program. "Body, soul, community" got a new interpretation in each bead, and in Haven Nicodemia, community was a building constructed on the rigid bedrock of obedience. Lights on the sidewalks told pedestrians which way to walk. Neighborhood curfews brought streets under control at night. In this city, everyone knew when to work, when to eat, when to play. It wasn't a terrible place to exist, but it wasn't exactly a free society.

Haven Nicodemia didn't have street food or free markets, but there were gambling halls nestled into its darkest edges. They called out to me—not with answers but with the endless siren song of cards and chips.

The first few haunts I visited were closed after my years away, no doubt fallen to the pressures of a world bent sideways in the winds of strict regulation. I finally found one with a dim lantern still glowing over its recessed stoop. Muted voices came from inside —an acknowledgment of broken curfews, suggesting that enforcement could still be lax. I entered and hung my hat and coat on the rack.

"Here for a game, sir?" asked the host, a swarthy Traveler with a mop of black hair and a double chin. The big man's mustache twitched as he took me in.

"Thought I'd tap a card or two," I said. "And grab a bite."

"Very well." The host led me to a blackjack table, where I exchanged a few dimes for gambling chips. "I'll send the server over immediately."

I was at a table with three other players: two women wearing fancy hats and a big man with more piercings than ear on the left side of his head. The dealer's hands danced over a deck of cards, and I landed a jack and a two. An easy choice, so I tapped and picked up a nine. Early victory.

From there, I was hooked. They brought food and drinks. Hours drained into an empty blackjack void. By the time my river of dimes ran dry, it was well past midnight, and the crowd was thinning. I blinked the bleariness away and realized the two women were gone and the fella next to me didn't have any piercings at all.

"Shot three times," someone behind me said. "Twice in the chest and once in the head."

The host responded in a loud whisper. "Professional?"

I twisted around to steal a look at the pair. The host was leaning close to a woman dressed like an off-duty police officer. Very trim. Very blue. Ten dimes said she was a detective of some sort.

"We're not sure," she said. "But it was ugly."

"We should shut down for the night."

"Probably. Maybe for the week. Blue's going to be wild after this."

I stretched my back, which felt as if it had been planted in that same spot for days. I left the gambling hall at the same time as a pack of men in business suits, the fog clearing from my mind. Reports of the shooting bothered me, especially after seeing that Beck still had that gun. Worry nagged at me, but I couldn't tell if I was worried that Beck had shot someone or that she was the person shot.

Something told me she hadn't been shot. I moved through dark alleys again, trying to organize my thoughts. Aiken's blackmail still made no sense. The paper with my instructions still sat in my pocket.

It was a name and a question. Jacob Donovan. Under it was scrawled the words: *Who crashed the* Benevolent?

The *Benevolent*. The Mark IV Cruiseliner that had crashed as it docked with Haven Nicodemia all those years ago. That accident had killed my parents and put my sister in a wheelchair. That crash left me with a burden of guilt so heavy it left me excommunicated. It burned in my dreams, and the fact that there was a recording of it made something deep in my chest ache.

Jacob Donovan.

I didn't want to find Donovan. I didn't want to ever think about that wreck. It was the one question I couldn't answer. My mouth went dry at the thought of it, and even though my head still felt fuzzy I wanted another drink. Maybe a few. No, I wouldn't track down Jacob Donovan. To hell with the blackmail.

Even through the blood-thick haze of alcohol, the memories of my youth refused to stay submerged. The woman's voice on Aiken's intercom had resonated with some bone-deep memory. It nagged at me.

I needed to track down Vitez, and none of this was helping. The blackmail, the gambling, it was all a distraction from finding that painting. If I could locate Vitez, I could get out of town before things got too bad. The blackmailer didn't *want* to release that video. She wouldn't bother once I was gone. There was no profit in it.

All she wanted was a way to interrogate Jacob Donovan, and the blackmail was a convenient way to make me do the hard work. I wouldn't do it. She could hire her own damn handyman if she needed a job done. I was busy.

But that meant I needed to finish my work and get out of town fast.

I started to walk, trudging upward along the open spiral, wholly absorbed by the shadows of the empty night.

But I wasn't so absorbed I couldn't spot when someone picked up my tail.

The Trinity in Haven Nicodemia wasn't very aggressive about lighting the way for nighttime travelers. Maybe that was because there weren't supposed to be many of them. Maybe it was because the contrast between light and dark was more drastic there. The piercing intensity of Haven days made the night darker. It seeped into the skin, and the gentle breeze that had been present in the day turned hard and cold at night.

A hundred steps behind me, a single streetlamp lit as someone passed too close to its detection radius. A while later, it happened again. The follower didn't step into the light as a normal traveler would. They *tried* to avoid it.

It was almost enough to make me wish I carried a weapon.

The cool breeze cleared my head of its alcohol haze, and I tried to think of who might be following me. It could be a random criminal, but not likely. This high up the gravity well, crime tended to be better thought out. Beck might have been tailing me, making sure I stayed on task. I liked to think she'd be better at it. Hell, the times she'd tracked me down in the Heavies, I'd never picked up her scent. Who else could it be? Would Saint Jerome have sent someone already? I wouldn't have put it past Aiken to tail me, the way he was talking at the bar.

After a long walk and a hard think, I decided it might be more efficient to figure out who *wouldn't* be following me. It was a shorter list.

By then, I'd reached the midpoint of the spiral, where the cathedral sat like a post-modern thumb on the pulse of the slumbering city. It couldn't have been more different from the Cathedral of Saint Francis below. Its stark, brutal angles loomed over half the square, and its broad, sweeping windows shone black in the clear night. This was as severe a church as I'd ever seen, and its people more so.

Behind me, now only fifty steps back, another streetlight flared to life. This time, a figure stepped out into the pool of yellow light. He wore a trench coat and a battered fedora, just like me. My doppelgänger's face was hidden in the harsh shadow under his hat, but I felt the gaze of his stare right through the dark of night. Was this the man from Williams's photograph? I stood in the blackness of the street, the cathedral as my backdrop, and he looked up at me from the darkness below.

He stepped forward out of the light.

I had a choice. Face my follower, or retreat to the safety of the church. I thought of all the bad bets I'd made earlier in the night. My nerves still jangled with adrenaline. I'd lost all my dimes at the blackjack table. Lost my knife and a fair share of my dignity too. What did I have to show for it?

Not one damn thing.

I stepped forward.

Thirty yards away, I saw a flash—a turquoise lenses fitted over his eyes. Night vision. That fit solidly into the loss column for me, then. Night vision gave him a significant advantage if he itched for a fight.

But I didn't back down. Fists balled at my sides, I strode toward my follower with nothing but starlight to light my path. My footsteps pounded like the drums of war, and if his goggles showed him heat, he'd surely see me like a man on fire.

Twenty steps. I heard the scuff of his boots. Ten, and he stopped.

I didn't.

"Demarco," he said. His voice was the gruff gravel of a long-time smoker. That voice told me two things about the man speaking it. First, it told me he was an older man, world-weary but still strong. Still determined. This was the voice of a war vet or a criminal—one who had survived the worst and come out the other end tough as nails.

Second, it told me exactly where his jaw was.

My first haymaker went wide, but it was a feint. At the sound of his sidestep I swung a hard backhand. Plastic and glass cracked under my blow. The guy swore.

He staggered back, but I caught his lapel. Three quick jabs and I felt blood slick on my knuckles.

"You got ten seconds to tell me why you're following me," I growled.

"I got nothin' against you," he said through dark spittle.

"The hell you don't." I lifted him and slammed him against the wall. To my gravity-accustomed muscles, he was as light as a toddler. I caught a whiff of cedar cologne. "I know a tail when I see one."

"Sure, sure," he said, his pitch rising higher. "He said to follow, that's it."

Lifting him with one arm, I finally got a decent look at his face. His lip was fat and bleeding, and the goggles were still askew on his face. He'd have a hell of a black eye in the morning, but nothing he'd learn much of a lesson from. A dark splotch of old tattoos marked the side of his neck. The symbols weren't a style I recognized from any local gang, but they were harsh and dark. Violent.

"You got some nerve, old man," I said. "Who put you up to this."

"Some guy," he said. "Some guy was paying debts and gambling with real coin, just like you."

"Tall guy?"

"Sure." He held his arms out indicating the coat. "Guy gave me this getup and said to follow you. Discretely."

"You didn't do all that great a job."

"He didn't pay all that much."

I dropped him. He landed unsteadily on his feet. "You were set up."

He rubbed his neck. "I've been through worse."

"What makes you think you're not about to get worse right now?"

His haggard grin flashed in the dim starlight. "Big softy like you? I bet you'd let the guy who killed your parents walk free."

"That's mighty specific."

The man picked his hat up off the ground and placed it gingerly on his head. "No hard feelings, all right? We're just a couple guys doing our jobs."

"That so?"

"Just be a dear and don't tell my boss that you spotted me. I'll leave you alone."

I let him walk, because what he said had dislodged something in the back of my brain. "Be a dear," I muttered to myself. The woman on Aiken's intercom had said that, and I now recognized the voice. Floretta Smith, my parents' long-time housekeeper.

The old man strolled away as if nothing bothered him in the world, and I wondered for a long time how much the old guy had been paid for his trouble. It wasn't until I'd walked halfway up the remains of the spiral that I reached into my pocket and found the note he'd stashed there while we'd scuffled.

It read: *Back off the painting, Demarco. Next guy I send won't be so nice.*

Chapter 23

FLORETTA SMITH.

The woman was a housekeeper. More specifically, she was my family's housekeeper. My mother dredged the poor woman up from the lower beads to clean the toilets of the Demarco estates. Smith had been a constant of my youth, always reprimanding the Demarco children for our sloppy ways, bitter at her position in life. As a kid, that didn't bother me. It seemed proper. I got the impression she despised us for our wealth and privilege. Young me was such a piece of shit.

I'd have never pegged Smith for a blackmailer, but impressions made as kids were about as accurate as a thrown dart on free whiskey night.

A quick stop at a jazz club upspiral from the church got me the information I needed from Smith's public file. As the musician whaled on his standup bass, a skinny man with a pencil mustache poked at the interface of the public terminal, my last cigarette dangling from his lips.

"She lives up in the Benedicts," the guy said. He showed me the address. "They pack 'em in pretty tight over there."

"This whole bead is packed tight."

"It's all relative, mister."

"Is that a real *Conversatio Morum* crowd up there?" I wondered if they expected Benedictine levels of poverty when they named the tenements.

He eyed me with a raised eyebrow, as if he couldn't decide if my rough clothing meant I was from the Heavies or my tall stature meant I was from the Hallows. He would have been right to guess either one. "There's a lot of activity around there at night," he said with a note of disapproval.

I made a point of looking around the packed jazz club.

"Some of us have trouble sleeping at night without a tipple or two," he said. "Up there they never sleep."

"Doesn't sound healthy."

He chuckled. "Thanks for the cigs."

"What about a guy named Trey Vitez?"

The guy punched a few buttons. "I got nothin' on that one."

"Might have come into town a few years back. He was from Earth."

He raised an eyebrow. "You serious?"

"Don't get many tourists?"

"Scientists and terraforming engineers sometimes."

"This guy was someone with an interest in art."

After half a cigarette, the guy squinted at the screen. "There might have been a guy a few years ago. Headed through on his way up north."

"The Hallows?"

He nodded. "Must have had some cash to spend."

It took more than cash to score long-term residence in Hallow Nicodemia. "Did he come back?"

"Not under the same credentials."

"And what credentials would that be?"

He showed me a series of ID numbers. "Names have been

purged. You might find it in cold storage, but someone didn't want this name in the public records."

The Benedict Tenements were upspiral and directly across from the cathedral. Not a long walk, compared to some, and I covered the distance without any trouble. As I approached that side of the bead, the glow of starlight gave way to the sulfur glow of streetlamps. Clusters of three or four people gathered in lonely pools of light. They spoke in low voices and pretended not to take notice of me. Buildings towered around narrow streets, the red fiberbrick façades stretched high into the sky, blotting out what false starlight might have lit the way. Spaces between pools of light became black voids of impossible darkness.

Smith's building was one of many, all identical. I pushed past a pack of teens on my way in, enduring their curses and the harsh stench of their cheap smokes. The elevator was broken, so I mounted the trash-strewn stairs to the eleventh floor.

The hallway was empty, and my footfalls fell soft on faded carpet. Instead of knocking on Smith's door right away, I stopped and listened for several minutes. There were voices, but they had the tinny, hollow sound of a drama. She was watching a show or listening to a radio. It struck me as shockingly mundane for my blackmailer to be alone and quiet in her home, watching entertainment, same as any curfew-obeying resident would in the dark of night.

Taking a deep breath, steeling myself against my memories, I knocked gently on the door.

When finally she opened the door, she stared at me for a long time under the rusted links of the security chain. She was smaller than I remembered, and grayer. Her cheeks sagged with loose flesh, but her eyes judged me with steel severity.

She closed the door, unfixed the chain, and flung it wide. Without a word, she walked back to her threadbare sofa and sat in front of the video screen. Her place had the thick odor of the elderly with a lingering mustiness that told a tale of filth deeper than surface trash. Books and trinkets heaped on tables and shelves. Dishes piled high in the sink at one end of her single room. There was no second chair, so I stood.

"If it ain't Wilson Demarco's kid. Aiken warned me you might come after me." She didn't take her eyes from the screen.

"I never forget a voice."

"It's been a long time."

"What is this about, Floretta? Reliving old memories?"

"Just like the spoiled brat you always were. You didn't even make an effort to do one damn job, did you, dear?"

"Why Jacob Donovan?" I stepped further into the room. Papers covered half the floor, and I was careful to step around what looked like cat droppings. "You think he was responsible for the crash."

She looked up at me. "What kind of fool do you take me for? He was the copilot. If he were responsible, I'd have figured it out." Her voice quivered with anger and age. "He knows something, though."

"You think I can get the truth out of him?"

"Donovan is a hack and a puffball. Anyone who can get close to him could get some real answers."

"What do you need me for, then?"

She frowned. "I said anyone who could get close to him." She pointed upward with her knobby finger.

"The Hallows?"

"Not quite that high."

"You think someone bought his silence?"

"My grandson died on that ship. Did you know I had a grandson?" She fixed me with her piercing gaze. "He was your age, but you never knew him. Your parents said he made them nervous. They were afraid what kind of influence a lower-class kid might have on their precious little brats."

"That's a lie."

"It's a hard truth learning that your parents were assholes, but it's something we all need to go through eventually. Maybe it's a good thing you got yours killed."

Anger boiled deep in my belly, but I swallowed it back. I didn't want her to see how her words affected me. "My parents were good Catholics."

Smith picked her way across the tiny room to me. Her head didn't even come up to the level of my chest, but she glared up at me with those fiery eyes. "They were good Catholics and shitty people. Not a mutually exclusive arrangement."

"They cared about the community. They were philanthropists."

"Art is the body and soul of the community," Floretta quoted in a deep, mocking voice. "Sound familiar?"

"Dad used to tell me that."

"Not the people. Not community for its own sake. He was the kind of philanthropist who loved squandering his money on pretty pictures instead of on feeding starving children."

"There are no starving children in Nicodemia." The lie tasted sour as soon as it touched my mouth.

"Tell that to the kids."

"That's enough," I growled. "Release your evidence or don't. I'm not finding anyone for you. I have business in town, then I'll be on my way."

"Just like your parents. An elitist all the way to the core."

"What?"

"You don't even know you're doing it. Let me guess, your client is wealthy? Important?"

"They pay."

"You would never work for a person like me."

I thought of Retch in his warehouse, but was I helping the poor kid or using him? It had certainly been convenient to win him as an ally. "Nobody likes a blackmailer."

"Call me names, then. You haven't changed one bit, have you? Still, the whiny, elitist brat you were when that ship crashed."

This time the rage took me fast and hot. With a broad sweep of my arm, I knocked the trinkets off a nearby shelf. "My parents died in that crash! You think I don't care how it happened?"

She stepped right into my personal space. "You never gave one shit about it. You know how I can tell? Because you never bothered to find who was behind it."

"It was an accident."

Her voice softened. "You know damn well it wasn't, child. Why didn't you find the person responsible?"

All the energy drained out of me, and my shoulders slumped. "I couldn't."

Smith put a hand on my elbow. "You found me, Jude. You found me with nothing more than a voice you hadn't heard in a decade and a hunch that I might be somewhere in Haven." She crossed to the kitchenette and put on a pot of tea. "You can find out who caused that crash." After a long while, when the teapot started to whistle its wailing moan, she said, "Do it for yourself, Jude. Free yourself from all that guilt you carry around." She switched off the electric burner.

"I'll always have the guilt."

She let out a deep sigh, and for the first time, her blue eyes went flat with the exhaustion she must have carried with her for decades.

"The life I live is my penance," I said as I let myself out.

As my feet hit the thin carpet in her apartment's hallway, I heard her quiet voice. "You were always a miserable little shit," she said. "But you always did your best to help people who really needed it."

And just like that, she had me working for her.

Chapter 24

THE DAY LEFT me with a powerful desire for either a good night's sleep or a massive amount of coffee. The good lord granted me neither, but when my feet refused to set themselves one in front of the other, I opted to find a place to crash.

Put like that, it almost sounds as if I had a choice. Atop one of the tenement buildings, I located a nest of threadbare cushions and damp blankets. It wasn't comfortable by any measure, but the rooftop was empty, and the access door was easy enough to wedge shut. I lay my coat over the cleanest portion of the nest, pulled my hat down over my eyes, and for a while, contemplated my discomfort.

Misery existed on many levels. The lumpy cushions over the black asphalt roof discomfited me well enough, but the real trouble lay on a less physical level. I realized that I would do anything to help Floretta Smith. She'd been there my whole childhood—more so than even my parents. She *knew* me. Smith had cleaned up after us—cared for us—and every complaint she had about us was true. Maybe I held a heaping, uncomfortable share of guilt over that fact. She'd been decent to us. Not good, maybe, but decent.

Yet, digging into the history of that crash terrified me. It always had. My parents died along with 123 passengers, the pilot, and a crew of twelve. So few of us survived that a more spiritual person might have called our rescue a miracle. That term never crossed my lips.

At the time, I had wanted to know the cause more than anything. I ignored my sister, even as she struggled with her recovery. I gambled. I fought. By then I was excommunicated for my sins, which should have led me to rely on the kindness of strangers and thus reintegrate with the community. It didn't work that way for me. Whoever designed that system had never heard of a teenager.

As I shifted on the cushions, the scent of dry mold lodged in my nostrils. It was the smell of a rot set in so deep that it touched everything. It was a rot that spread spores that itched on the skin. A rot that settled into the lungs.

This, I thought, was where I belonged. Right in the center of that rot. I couldn't know the cause of that crash because I didn't *deserve* to know it. At one point, I swore I'd uncover everything—and then I didn't. I let the world suck me down. I fled to the Heavies, bringing my sister the wrong direction to a place where her disability would be worse, not better.

But nobody ever ascends to better beads on this giant rosary. Eyes don't adjust to the light as painlessly as they settle into the dark. Down in dim bleak Heavy Nicodemia, my sister and I found a place to belong. A thing close enough to purgatory that it matched the dreary tint of my soul.

Somehow, despite the rot and the rocks and the wailing of the residents in the tenements below, I drifted into a fitful sleep to dream of danger in the liminal spaces—the danger I faced as a teen and the danger I would face still. Always, the black gravity of the Heavies pulled me back. All I needed to do was let go and fall.

I woke as the sky transitioned into a burning bright dawn. My bones ached and the cheery notes of a harmonica playing far below drove razor-sharp claws into the back of my skull. Three gray pigeons perched on the ledge nearby, watching my misery as I wrenched my aching body up from the uncomfortable impromptu bed.

"I've been worse," I said, surprised at the phlegmy gravel of my voice. I coughed and spat. Ran some fingers through my hair. The pigeons watched as if they were expecting the display. "I've been better too."

The pigeons looked unconvinced.

They say a good night's sleep is the best way to let ideas cook on the back burner. My terrible night's sleep had cooked my ideas, boiled them down to nothing, then burned them to a crisp. I figured they'd be fine once they were rehydrated with coffee, so I headed to the closest cafe.

A bleak coffee shop nestled into the corner of one of the tenements looked like the kind of place that had a regular clientele and an attitude toward anyone else. It had a faded sign out front that labeled it as Luke's, and the three tables set up on the sidewalk crammed three lonesome coffee drinkers into a space almost big enough for one. Inside, the decor was about as pretentious as my sister's diner, but without any of the friendliness. The lady behind the counter had wrinkles that looked like they would put up a good fight if she ever decided to smile. She didn't give them much of a workout when she finally looked up to greet me.

"Coffee," I said, sliding a dime across the counter. "Black."

She looked at the dime, raising one eyebrow. Without a word, she swayed over to her coffee pot and poured.

"Say," I said, trying to sound casual, "Any idea what weather's scheduled for the next few days?"

The woman finished pouring coffee. When she set the cup in front of me, a little sloshed out onto the counter. "What's a holy man like you doing slumming around down here?"

"Lady, I'm not holy."

"You from Hallows?" She must have picked it up from my size.

I'd lost my accent ages ago. "You're probably lost, mister. You're going to want to call a lift and go counter a spell."

Counterclockwise would take me upward, presumably to where I'd get out of her bead and take an elevator back to the Hallows. I was headed that way, but I didn't want to give her the satisfaction of hearing it. "You know of a lady named Smith? Floretta Smith?"

Her creases deepened. "Who's asking?"

"A concerned citizen," I said.

"I'm starting to get concerned. What if Floretta doesn't want you finding her?"

"She's already been found. What I'm doing is asking about her. She a decent person far as you know?"

She almost assaulted her face with a smile. "What kind of barista badmouths her customers?"

"So, she's a customer." I glanced down at the coffee. An oily film formed a sheen across the top. "Is she a black coffee kind of gal or is she more into the fancy stuff."

The barista glanced at the shelves, which held a few flavored oils that would have been decorative if they weren't dusty. "Honey, does this look like the kind of place that sells the fancy stuff?"

I shrugged. "Down below, all we have is burnt sludge and a kick in the face."

"Down below, huh?" She crossed her arms and gave me a hard look over. "You think I'm going to believe a tall fella like you comes from the Heavies?"

"I've had a long walk to get this far, lady. Sometimes that takes me where I need to go, and sometime that takes me where I should never be. But it's the only road I know how to walk."

She leaned forward, palms of her hands flat on the counter. "Floretta's a decent lady," she said. "She doesn't order fancy, tips well enough, and she isn't too nosy about other people's business. She likes it bitter and strong."

"So that's why she's taken such a shine to me."

"Must be a lapse in judgment."

It was about as I'd figured. If Smith had been a terrible gossip or a thorn in someone's side, the barista wouldn't have told me, but she would have hinted at it the way people speak with subtext that they think only they can hear. That didn't help my situation, of course. Learning that Smith wasn't a monster only made it harder to change my mind about helping her.

"One more thing," I said, sliding another dime across the counter.

"What is it?"

I tapped the fiberstone mug. "I need this in a to-go cup."

The barista took a lightweight disposable cup from the rack, dumped my black coffee into it, and slid it across the counter at me. More droplets of precious coffee sloshed onto the table. What a waste. I put a cover on and left, tipping my hat to the barista on my way out the door. She responded with a stony expression that had all the warmth of a stray exoplanet.

The coffee was life-changingly good, even though it wasn't the best coffee I'd ever had. It was a light roast, with notes of berries and vanilla. She'd scorched it with too-hot water, and by the time I took a sip, it was below that threshold where even good coffee starts to taste like bad feet. Not a great brew by any means, but after the garbage water they called coffee in the Heavies, I was almost ready to offer a hand in marriage.

Like I said: life-changing.

Chapter 25

I PATTED my pockets for a cigarette, coming up dreadfully short. There were only a few hours until Beck would ask me about my progress on the case, and I had a suspicion that "Oh, I haven't gotten around to it" wasn't the answer she was looking for. As much as I might have been convinced to help Floretta Smith, she needed to wait.

There weren't many ways to track a person passing through Haven Nicodemia that didn't involve asking Trinity for the appropriate records. Since the station AI wasn't spilling, and since Beck had been on her way to the government center, I decided to take the much simpler task of asking around about the painting. Only a few museums in the bead would ever have dealt with such work, and the nearest sat like a brick wart nestled against the unhealthy flesh of the Benedict Tenements. It had a banner that read Museum of Art History, and there wasn't a single window on the entire structure, even on its third floor, where nobody would even think of peeking inside.

Mobs of children clustered outside the museum—mostly pre-teens waiting with their unruly cohorts for educational field trips.

Elbowing past these groups, I muscled my way to the front of a long line.

"Excuse me?" said one adult as I passed. He had a goatee and inquisitive eyebrows. A mob of orange-shirted children orbited him.

I tipped my hat to him. "Just passing through."

The man pointed at the entrance, where a fibersteel sign extolled the exciting nature of early-era Earth art. "They're only allowing school groups today." One of the shorter kids slammed into his hip and bounced off but didn't seem to lose any kinetic energy in the process.

Small text on the sign explained the policy in great detail. Only school kids and their chaperones were allowed. It even went on to explain why. I read out loud, "So that children can learn in an environment suited for them." I turned to the man. "This sounds like garbage to me."

The chaperone shrugged. "It's so that they don't get as many kids wandering in on other days of the week." A cluster of tykes surrounded me like an amoeba devouring a fresh meal.

I made a quick count of the kids. "Twenty," I said. "Hell of a ratio."

"Their regular teacher is out sick."

"Need a hand?"

He smiled and stuck out a hand. "Lester," he said.

"Demarco." I shook his hand vigorously.

"We're up."

A tall man in a rumpled white suit that made his big belly look like a scoop of ice cream held the door open and waved our pack of orange-shirted children through. I dutifully counted twenty little heads. Hey, if I was going to chaperone, I might as well take the job seriously. The guide brought us to a large room: a central hub in the middle of a dozen other smaller curated spaces. A raised platform with a massive holographic projector dominated the space. The siren call of a jazz saxophone played on the overhead speakers.

"Welcome to the Museum of Art History," began our guide. "We are so glad to have you as our guests today." He said it with all the welcoming sincerity of a Hallows businessman inviting Saint Jerome over to meet his daughter. The guide rolled into a canned speech about the rules of the museum, and how breaking any rules would mean the immediate expulsion of the entire party.

Looking around, I saw no fewer than three kids from other groups breaking the rules.

I raised my hand to grab the guide's attention. When he made the mistake of glancing at me, I said, "Where is the art?" A couple of the kids snickered at that.

It also earned me the most annoyed look I'd seen all week, delivered by the guide. "I know we're all excited to see some art." Behind him, the holographic projector activated, projecting a seven-foot-tall marble statue of a man being attacked by snakes. Two boys struggled against the slithering onslaught. The image earned barely a flicker of response from the kids. "This is *Laocoön and His Sons*," the guide said. "This is one of the most famous statues of ancient Earth. Can anyone tell me why?"

A small girl at the front of the group raised her hand. "Because it's horrible."

The guide blinked. "It's famous because it is considered the quintessential depiction of human agony." He said it as if he were annoyed and correcting her, but I thought it sounded like they were saying the same thing. "The artist's depiction of the human body is exquisite, and when the piece was discovered in the sixteenth century in Rome, it was considered a true masterpiece. It was later discovered that this same statue was once praised by Pliny the Elder."

And he'd lost them. I entertained myself with another head-count. Twenty. Good. Lester spoke in hushed tones with one of the little boys.

The hologram changed, switching to the famous statue of David. David stood almost three times as tall as Laocoön. A couple of boys in back snorted and made jokes about the statue's nakedness. They stopped when I caught their attention and slowly shook my head. This wasn't going to get me what I wanted. I backed away slowly from the group so that I could peek into the other rooms.

The inquisitive girl raised her hand again. "Why is he naked?"

The guide's expression darkened. "Nudes are a tradition in art. During this period, artists would strive to depict the perfection of the human body. Many believe that Michelangelo achieved this with David, carving him from a single block of marble."

"But why?" the girl asked.

While the guide fumbled another answer, I ducked away. One long hall was gated off, but the others all stood open. They were lined with displays, mostly holographic depictions of art from the ages. A few protected alcoves contained actual paintings, and I lingered at these for a few moments. I'd been in museums like this before. The ones in the Hallows had a better artifact-to-hologram ratio, but it all amounted to the same thing. The digital displays were there so that we could remember our past. The actual artwork—that was where we could *connect* to that past. *That* privilege was closely guarded.

I stopped in front of a Van Gogh. Even though it rested in a hard vacuum under shaded glass, I felt the pace of my heart quicken. Long ago, one of the greatest painters that humanity had ever produced touched this, working the paint until the haystacks were perfect. It wasn't a photographic representative of the haystack—not that I'd ever seen a real one—but rather representative of the emotion Van Gogh was experiencing as he painted it. There, in the Museum of Art History, I connected with greatness.

That was why I never took jobs finding artwork. It matters too much.

"Excuse me, sir," said someone next to me. "Today is a school day here at the museum. I'm going to have to ask you to leave if you're not with a group."

Without taking my eyes off the haystacks, I said, "I'm with a group."

"You don't appear to be, sir."

I let my gaze lock on to him. He was dressed better than the guide, but even with his exuberant shock of hair, he was a good foot shorter than me. "What can you tell me about *The Garden of Earthly Delights?*"

He blinked quickly. I'd offended him.

I kept a thin veneer of friendliness on my face and rested an arm across his shoulders. "By Hieronymus Bosch."

"Yes, I'm aware."

"I'd like to see it."

"We don't have—"

"Hell, specifically."

"This is a—"

"Yeah, it's a school day for kids. My business can't wait, and you're going to show me that painting." I clenched my fist hard enough for the knuckles to crack.

The man swallowed, seemingly considering his odds. There were plenty of paid guards in the lobby, and I'd spotted a pair of police officers lingering outside. He'd probably do fine if he ran for it, but I wasn't going to tell him that.

"This way," he said.

I'd already walked almost the entire length of the hall, so we didn't have far to go. The room at the end was empty, except for a large holographic projector in its center. Unlike the one the class had gathered around, this one came complete with projectors that could make the walls disappear. The curator flipped a switch and the lights dimmed to almost black.

The curator split the world into darkness and light. Nothing else in the world existed but the painting. All three frames stood before me in a lifelike image, showing its messy depiction of a lonely Garden of Eden, a lustful Earth, and a torturous Afterlife. As I paced around the piece, it adjusted so that it was always facing me.

"It's a striking piece," the curator said. "Its history is a bit of a mystery."

"So is its current location," I said, watching his reaction closely. When his eye twitched ever so slightly, I knew I had the right man. "Can you explain why Hell in your hologram is of a different resolution than the other two panels?"

He shrugged in a feeble display of innocence, even though he had to have known I'd caught him. "The scans aren't always done under the same conditions. Even in a single piece like this, they can have differences in how the files are saved."

There were a few options I could take. It might be possible to smooth things over here a bit, maybe make friends with the guy and get him to spill. Hell, he might even tell me what I needed if I promised not to turn him in for buying illicit scans.

But I didn't have time for that. I could sense the stubborn edge in his hunched shoulders. This man wasn't going to spill. He'd probably lived his whole life hoarding secrets and hiding lies. As much as I detested it, if I wanted answers, I was going to need to take them.

In the dim light, I leaned my face close to his so he could smell my coffee breath as I whispered, "You saw the real thing, didn't you? A couple years ago."

"I don't know what you—"

I put one of my massive ham-hock hands on his shoulder and gave him just enough pressure to know I meant business. "A guy came here with it."

His Adam's apple bobbed like it was trying to escape. "He was trying to sell."

"Did you pay him?"

The curator shook his head. "We could never afford to buy something like that, even though the piece wasn't complete."

"That's not what I asked."

"We paid him well for the scan. The opportunity wasn't something we could pass up, and he seemed desperate. We didn't do anything illegal."

"The piece was stolen."

"We had no way of knowing that."

"Where did he go?"

"I don't—"

My nostrils flared.

"The Hallows!" The man tried to step back, but I kept him rooted in place. "Something like *The Garden of Earthly Delights* wouldn't be at a Haven museum without us all hearing about it. It probably wouldn't even be in the church."

It made sense. Vitez would have gone farther up, looking for a private buyer. This only confirmed what I knew, though. It wasn't helpful yet. "Who was buying?"

The curator opened his mouth, then closed it again. I released him, and he leaned back against the wall, hand on his chest.

"What was the guy's name?" I didn't think Trey Vitez would let his new alias slip to this third-rate curator, but it was all I could think to ask.

But a smug smile spread across the curator's lips. It was the kind of smile a perp gets when he's done answering questions— when he's figured out that there's a good reason why he doesn't *need* to answer questions anymore. A piece of the puzzle fell into place, or power had shifted.

Or backup arrived.

"Please take a step back, sir," said a voice behind me.

Shit.

Slowly raising my hands, I said to the curator, "What was the guy's name?" The guards had interrupted the one question I really needed answered. With a name, I could figure out where Trey Vitez went. At least, it would get me one step closer.

There was always the option of trading fists with the guard.

He'd be armed with a truncheon or stunstick, but nothing terribly lethal. No guns. Not in Haven. This didn't need to get messy, though. All I needed was for the curator to give me this one piece of information before I left.

"He came in just like the guy said he would," said the curator to the man behind me. "Started talking about obscure paintings. Stolen ones."

My palms went cold. "Like who said?" When the curator didn't answer, I turned around to look at the guard.

Only, it wasn't *a* guard. It was *two* guards. And they weren't guards. They were police, all geared up for a fight. One of them carried a stunstick—the baton's end crackling with electricity. Behind them, the orange-clad class I'd come in with shuffled up to the door and stared at me in silence. The girl who was interested in art watched me with wide eyes.

I tipped my hat to the girl. "I'll go quiet," I said. "No need for trouble, officers."

The officer slapped cuffs on me and ushered me out.

Chapter 26

"I TOLD YOU," I said, hating how exhaustion darkened my voice, "I was at the museum because I like art."

The officer across from me wore a striped button-down shirt and a badge that labeled him as a special investigator. His thin goatee failed to cover his weak chin, which only served to accentuate the lumps on his narrow nose, making it look crooked. "And the painting?"

I said, "I have an appointment."

"I'm sure it can wait."

"The lady I'm meeting isn't the kind of lady a person stands up."

He shuffled his notes. "Would that be one Miss Charlotte Beck? We'd very much like to speak with her as well. Where did you say she's waiting for you?"

I pressed my lips together. Any two-bit thug knows to say nothing at a police interview. Harder said than done. "I'm excommunicated."

Without looking up, he said, "That doesn't mean you're above the law, Mr. Demarco."

It didn't feel like the appropriate time to argue.

He continued, "I'm certain down in the Heavies they have different ideas about the rule of law. Up here, we take it seriously." His eyes locked with mine for the first time in the interview. "Quite seriously."

What a prick.

An officer entered and whispered something in the investigator's ear. The investigator never took his eyes off me, not even for a second. When the officer finished, he disappeared back through the door.

"Witnesses put you in the lower quarter since you arrived in the district."

"That's what I like about Haven," I said. "Everyone's so talkative."

"There was a killing up near the apex, so you might understand why we're so interested." He leaned forward as if an idea just occurred to him. "You know anything about that?"

"I was in the lower quarter," I said.

"The witnesses say you had a partner."

"More like an acquaintance."

"Miss Beck?"

"Rings a bell."

The investigator took a few minutes to make a long show of not being interested in me. He shuffled papers, clicked his tongue, and made notes with his pen. After a while, he looked up as if only then remembering he'd been keeping me in his interrogation room. "I'm going to go over everything one more time if you don't mind."

I definitely minded.

"A ship comes from Earth, landing in the Heavies because that's the best place to land if you don't want a full audit of your cargo. Once it's there, someone smuggles the goods—art or whatnot—into a shipping crate made to look like it's originating from the Heavies." At this, he pressed his pen to his lips and clicked his tongue a few times. "That right there is illegal. It's both a tax law violation and a violation of Customs and Imports. Important stuff, too, because foreign shipments can carry diseases or other problems for our enclosed habitat. Does this sound about right to you?"

No telling if he was referring to the disease transmissions or the smuggling operation, so I answered, "Sounds like a good reason to inspect shipments from the Heavies."

"I'm not Customs, though, Mr. Demarco. I'm police."

"Of course."

"It's a different department, you see, and they don't much like us telling them how to do their jobs."

"But that's what you'd like to do anyway." He probably wanted it even more because someone told him not to.

"We're just trying to keep crime down," he said. "So, once you have the shipment over here in Haven, you unpack it and shop it around to buyers. Not too many private citizens willing to deal in illicit merchandise, so you're left with a hard choice. Move up the rosary or start pushing to local museums." He leaned forward. "You and I both know there's no museum in this bead that'll take stolen goods, so your operation depends on being able to pass off fake documents."

I didn't much like how his description of the events sounded like I was involved. If he wanted me to say I'd been forging documents he'd need to lean on me a lot harder. This special investigator had put together so much of what I was still discovering. I leaned forward. "A trip up to the Hallows with the art would put that piece in front of a dozen wealthy buyers."

"A hundred." The officer said it with a puckered expression like he'd just bitten into a lemon. "But customs to the Hallows is a lot tighter than between the Heavies and Haven, isn't it?"

That's why Vitez stopped in Haven. He'd gone to the museum for paperwork showing that the painting was legit. Those weren't the kinds of documents he could forge—not being new to

Nicodemia's elaborate bureaucracy, anyway. He probably figured he could get approval from one of the museums in exchange for a new, accurate scan. Then he'd head up the chain to the Hallows to make his real sale—a sale he maybe already had lined up.

But to who?

"Who forged the documents?" I asked.

The investigator narrowed his eyes at me. "Funny question, Mr. Demarco."

"How come I'm not laughing?"

"Because the guy who authenticated the documentation just turned up dead." He drew a photograph from his folder and slid it across the table.

The man's face was a wreck. His left eye was a mess of blood, and the right side of his head featured significantly more exposed bone than was recommended by most doctors. He was an older man with dark skin and a white beard.

"Ceramic bullets?" I asked.

The investigator stared at me for a long time before replying, "How exactly do you think this interview is going to work, Mr. Demarco?"

"It had to have been up close for lightweight ammo to wreck a head like that," I said. "Personal."

"Or desperate." The inspector leaned forward. "We don't see a lot of murders like this around here, Demarco, but we know our business."

"You already know it wasn't me."

The inspector drew a long breath. "When the guy died, his stash of recordings went public. Turns out he was blackmailing half of Customs and more than a few police."

"He get you?"

"I'm still here."

"Congrats."

"I still want to know more about this Charlotte Beck," the investigator said.

"She's a looker. Nice sense of humor. Not really your type."

"You have a thing for her?"

"She gave me a roll of dimes. I gave her a few answers."

His eyes narrowed. "You work for her, then?"

I shrugged. I'd given up too much already, and anything else I said was going to get one or both of us in trouble. Not that I wasn't already basking in boiling water.

After a few more impotent hours of circular questioning, the officer led me back to a cell. One wall of the cell was clear resin, with holes providing inadequate ventilation. A tinny speaker somewhere spouted bubbly jazz, its relentless energy dissipating on the fiberstone walls like waves crashing on rocks.

"Can I get you to turn that off?" I asked.

The officer didn't even bother to answer. He slid the door shut and left me to slump on the hard bed. I lay back and closed my eyes. They'd taken my hat, my coat, my music. Everything I owned in the whole world was lost.

The music stopped mid-solo, which turned out to be the only thing worse than continuing. After several long, silent seconds, the lights dimmed, then switched entirely off. I let out a long breath. Darkness swallowed me again, welcoming me in its cold embrace. Would the police of Haven Nicodemia forget I was back here when their computer didn't register my presence? Would Haven's Trinity let me die of thirst here in a little fiberstone cell in the middle of its poorest district?

The long silence stretched thin. I sat up, unable to rest due to the jittery energy bouncing around my skull. My hands shook, but I wanted another coffee. Another cigarette. Another anything.

My eyes adjusted to a glow that I couldn't quite place.

They hadn't taken everything. I thought of Retch living in his little hole in the corner of an abandoned warehouse. Even Retch was wealthier than me, but was he happier? Was he more content? I didn't think so. I had my sister. After everything that had happened, I still had family. There would always be someone I could rely on for food and shelter. If I could contact her, she'd come get me.

When I looked up, he was there—a dark silhouette in the negative space of the abandoned hall.

"It's not visiting hours," I said.

His voice rolled through the gaps in the clear resin wall like broken gravel. "Wanted to check that you'd stay put this time."

I knew that voice. "You're the guy who followed me from the gambling hall."

"I have no problem if you do your job, Demarco. Just take a few days off first. Let me do what I need to do."

"Did you kill that guy up in the government quarter?"

His face was a blot of shadow in the darkness, but I sensed hesitation in his voice. "You'll get your painting when I've finished."

"See, I was thinking we could team up."

"You're on the wrong side in all this, Demarco."

My mind raced to grasp the implications of his words. *Wrong side?* What side was I on? I had an employer who was looking for a painting. What could the other side possibly be? Did this guy work for Vitez? If so, why was he so set on delaying me a few days? I'd have asked him, but there was no point in asking questions that weren't going to get answered.

Instead, I asked, "Did you kill McCay?"

I couldn't see his expression in the dim glow, but his weight shifted back on his heels.

"See, it must have happened in the room in his apartment that Trinity couldn't see. The only people who have access to that space are some kids. Kids can be rough, but I don't think these tykes are the murderous type." I pressed my palms against the glass. "But you could get in there without Trinity taking notice. You could murder McCay and leave a hell of a mess for the blue to clean up."

His back pressed against the far wall. I could feel his gaze rolling over me.

"Only, what I can't figure out is why? My best guess is McCay knew something about you, and he was threatening to sing." I glanced up at the speakers, which still stayed silent. "The wrong song is worse than none at all, don't you think? You thought he might spill once you stopped delivering his meds, so you did him in. Only, he didn't spill. He came to me. I had the meds for him, right in my hand. Ready to take care of his needs. He didn't need to die."

Shadows shifted, and my voice rang against an empty hall. The other handyman was gone. I crossed to the little sink, splashed some water on my face, lay on the bed, and breathed in a dark so oppressive it lingered in the brain.

Chapter 27

I POUNDED on the resin wall. "I'm ready to confess." It had been hours. How many, I couldn't say. Too many. I needed to get out.

Police in Haven were bound to procedure, and procedure made them lazy. They bring a person in, interview them, and then wait for the full confession. Once the confession comes, paperwork clears away, and they render a verdict.

Justice is always served in Haven Nicodemia. I've been in the system before, though not in the criminal sense. Police were good allies for a newly excommunicated handyman, and back then I took any ally I could get. I'd watched them roll over more than one hapless thug, and the next part wasn't pretty. I'd be pulled back into the investigation room, made to wait, and then given documents to sign. I had no intention of sticking around that long.

A new officer came to fetch me from my cage. It had been hours—long enough they could conceivably believe that I was ready. Long enough that I was dangerously late for my appointment with Beck.

I'd have to worry about that later.

The station was a bustle of activity. Officers pushed paper at nearly half the desks in the open space. To one side, a couple offi-cers talked in quiet voices, casting the occasional glance my direc-tion. One of them recognized me. They'd be trouble.

"Stay put," the officer said, sitting me down on a bench. I did my best to hide the smile. They made the same mistakes I'd seen them make years ago when I visited.

They assumed Trinity would sound the alarm if I tried to leave. That was wrong, of course, but I still felt guilty about it. After all, the young man was only doing his job the way he was taught. They needed to procure an interview room for me, and they needed to make sure it was prepped before I went in.

If only those two officers in the corner would look away.

I spotted my things on a desk not far away. My hat was wrapped in plastic, and the rest of my possessions were in a black fiberboard box. The man at that desk—the one who had inter-viewed me—had his head down, buried deep in paperwork. That was probably paperwork I'd made for him. It was going to get a whole lot worse.

The two officers talking in the corner glanced away, so I made my move. Strolling across the station floor was an exercise in patience. Every instinct in my body told me to run. The shuddering nerves in my chest told me to flee from imprisonment. They'd lock me away forever if they found me out.

One step, then another. Keep it slow. Don't draw attention.

Being excommunicated gives a person a sense of when he's being watched. It's a hypersensitivity to attention that comes from an awareness of exactly how we're all connected. This was what let me know when I was being followed. Hair prickled at the back of my neck. Somebody had looked my way.

But no alarm sounded.

Smooth as I could manage, given my frazzled nerves, I strolled up to the investigator's desk, picked up the box and hat, and mumbled, "I'll file these for you."

Then I veered toward the door.

I almost thought I'd make it.

"Excuse me," came a woman's voice from behind.

A chill ran down my spine. I didn't turn. "Yeah?"

"You think you could leave the box for us?"

The box? I looked down at the box in my hands. It held my coat and hat. I took the hat out of its plastic wrapping and placed it on my head. The coat draped across my shoulders like it belonged there. I set the box on the nearest desk.

"Thanks," she said.

Outside, I stopped across the street and watched the station until I was sure they wouldn't follow. They would see I was gone, check their records, and realize I didn't exist. Problem solved. Maybe there wouldn't be paperwork after all.

"Fancy meeting you here," said Beck as she strolled up to meet me. She wore a sharp blue business suit and thick-framed glasses.

"You found me," I said. "Again."

Beck lazily pressed her body against mine, her arm hooking my elbow. "You were late."

"I was busy with the jailbreak of the century."

She tossed me a roll of dimes. "Today's pay."

I hefted it. "Feels light."

"It's the same as the others."

"Those felt light too."

She gave a huff of frustration and disentangled herself from me. "It's always business with you."

"We have a business relationship."

"Yeah."

"What?" The simulated Haven sunlight had never felt so wonderful on my skin. "You pay me, and I find the painting. It's business."

Her eyes narrowed. "Do you, though? Find the painting, I mean."

"It's a work-in-progress."

We made our way upspiral through the winding streets. Unlike the Heavies, Haven Nicodemia featured a wide variety of plants, and the lush green growth lent an aroma to the atmosphere that was unmatched anywhere else in the city. Grasses grew in small decorative patches, vines that were stunted in the Heavies climbed high on fiberbrick walls, and there were even trees extending their branches toward the false sky and their roots into submerged containers.

"Do you ever want to leave this behind?" Beck breathed. "Just be one of the regulars rolling around in this little town?"

I watched a mother lead two small children across a busy street. "I *am* one of them."

Beck barked a laugh. "You're as much one of them as I am, Demarco."

"What about you?" I asked. "Ever consider giving up on being a traveling lackey for the rich and powerful?"

"Rich people have such broken priorities, don't you think?"

I met her gaze for several seconds, but if there was a hidden meaning in her words, I wasn't getting it. The warm impression where she'd touched me tingled in a cool breeze. I almost believed that she was showing a moment of vulnerability. Closing my eyes, I breathed deep of the scented air.

"Never mind," she said, spite dripping from her voice. She stalked down a short set of steps to her scooter, which she'd parked in the middle of a pedestrian walkway. The woman with the two children laughed at something the eldest said. She took both of their hands and disappeared into the crowd.

"Yeah," I said too quiet for Beck to possibly hear. "I *would* like to just be one of them." I followed her to the scooter, and she let me drive. "Where are we going?"

"You tell me."

I glanced up at the too-bright sky. Most of the day had passed, and the false sky grew hazy and indistinct in the waning glow of the afternoon. "I could use a drink."

"You didn't figure out where Vitez went either, did you?"

"I probably got about as far as you did," I said.

"I found the guy in charge of high-value imports, tracked down a paper trail, and located a meeting of art aficionados that was probably a front for an illegal art trade organization."

Why did she even hire me? "Yeah," I said. "About the same, then."

I twisted the accelerator and merged into the creeping traffic of other small vehicles. We spiraled upward for several minutes, and eventually, I spotted the entrance to a gated community called the Fixed Stars. Fancy. Just like Smith had said. The actual gate was a gilded joke, with bars not nearly narrow enough to keep out intruders. The walls, on the other hand, looked to be solid fiberstone of a marbled grain I hadn't seen anywhere else. This was the nice part of town, then. Nearly the highest point in Haven Nicodemia.

It was also the home of Jacob Donovan, copilot of the ship that had killed my parents.

"I need to chat with someone," I said, pulling up next to the gate.

Beck looked around, and I swear I caught a glimpse of wariness in her eyes. "About Vitez?"

"Not exactly."

Her expression flashed annoyance. "Make it quick."

I took out my music rig, relieved that the police hadn't messed with the device. I queued up a Muddy Waters album, reveling in his deep, throaty bass and exquisite guitar work. It reminded me of my sister, and Heavy Nicodemia, and the hard times we'd had as we scraped our way out of the ditch. With my earpieces in, the world faded away for several long seconds, but Beck was right. Time was of the essence, and I needed to move.

The bars were closer together than they looked, but with some effort, I squeezed my giant body through. The instant I passed into the gated neighborhood, the atmosphere shifted, both literally and figuratively. This was a safe place surrounded by safe spaces. The cool breeze outside the neighborhood disappeared, replaced by a warm glow from smooth streets. Here, pedestrians walked without worry, without the furtive glances over the shoulder or the paranoid flinch away from potential pickpockets.

The whole thing made me uneasy.

"Hey," a kid in short pants said as I stepped away from the gate. "You're not supposed to do that."

I murdered my music in the middle of a song. "Do what?"

"Step through the gate."

"I don't see why not. If someone wanted to keep me out, they'd make the bars closer together." I held up my hands, palms forward. "Therefore, I conclude that I was meant to come in that way."

"But it's supposed to stop you."

"I don't feel stopped."

He was a young kid, shorter than Retch and a whole lot better fed. He held a skateboard in one hand and eyed me as if I'd just stepped into the station straight out of the void.

"You know a guy named Jacob Donovan?" I asked.

He narrowed his eyes at me, probably trying to figure if I was there to murder the guy. The kid must have either figured I wasn't, or he didn't care, because he said, "What's in it for me?"

Typical capitalist mindset. "How's a dime sound?"

The kid scoffed. "Who spends dimes around here?"

"You spend something other than money?"

"Sure. It's all Trinity Karma. There's nothing you can buy with dimes."

So, he was still naive enough to believe the lies. I almost felt bad opening his eyes. "What if you want something Trinity doesn't sell?"

"Like what?"

I nodded to his skateboard. "Like a better board."

His eyes narrowed. "This is the best board around."

"It's a Heavy board."

"So?"

"So, this is the kind of board they make when it needs to work wherever you take it. It'll function even in the lower part of the Heavies, but the suspension's too stiff for this place." I scratched the stubble on my chin and wondered how disheveled I looked. They didn't teach kids about the danger of strange adults around here, did they? "What do you say if I trade your board for a better one, you show me where I can find Donovan."

The kid glanced at the sky. The sunset had turned the western horizon a deep violet. "It's almost curfew."

"I'm in a hurry."

He glanced down at his board, and I knew I had him. "Fine."

Ten minutes later, he had a new board, I had his old one, and my pocket was only a few dimes shorter. Folks always wonder at my uncanny ability to find things. They think the shady parts of their world simply don't exist because they can't see them. Turns out, the trick is in asking. Ask the right person in the right way, and the world is a flower opening to reveal a fistful of ants. To get the non-regulation board, all I needed to do was ask the tiredest-looking bloke at the sporting goods shop. He was tired because he was up late. He was up late because he was working late on some new gear.

It pays to be able to spot passion. Passion bends rules. Sometimes breaks them. That's the way of the world.

"He's usually at the Lucky Seven," said the kid. "If he's not there, he's passed out up around the Spiralview Tower."

"Lucky Seven? That a brothel or something?"

The kid screwed up his face. "Mom says people there drink and sometimes throw away money."

"What's he look like?"

"Big red braided beard. He usually wears these big sunglasses if it's bright out."

"It's not." By then, it wasn't. The sky had deepened to a burnt orange, soon to fade into the black of night.

That seemed to remind the kid about curfew. He kicked his

board down to the ground, rolled a few feet, then stopped and turned to me, big grin on his face. "Damn," he said.

I raised his old board to him in a kind of salute. "Damn."

With that, the kid skated away into the night. Maybe he'd make it home before curfew. More likely, the prospect of his new board would entice him to whatever ramp he was used to riding. If it was worth risking trouble to get a new board, then it was worth risking trouble to try it out.

The Lucky Seven was a dim little place set into the bottom corner of a towering high rise. It had a mood that reminded me a little of Rory's down in the Heavies, but with all the edges sharp and the surfaces polished. Outside, it had the air of a place abandoned and empty, left quiet as the curfew descended upon the district.

Inside, it was packed with gamblers. The kid had a few things wrong about the place. This wasn't someplace where people drank and sometimes threw their money away. Money-throwing sat top billing here. Drinks were an afterthought. I procured a gin and tonic and made my way around the outer perimeter until I spotted Jacob. The kid hadn't lied about the beard. He had hair like copper wire that made his green eyes glow under bushy eyebrows. What the kid hadn't mentioned was that Donovan's sunken cheeks and unkempt shirt made him look like a scarecrow.

The remains of my roll of dimes hung heavy in my pocket. The lights and the noise of gambling wins rang like Pavlov's bell in the back of my skull. I knew I couldn't win. That wasn't the issue. That's the thing about gambling. It's not about winning. Maybe I'd win sometimes, but deep down in the logic of my brain, I knew those winnings would end up on the table. I could turn anything into a loss, and those dimes were looking to be my next victim. There would always be more dimes tomorrow, right?

I shook my head to clear it. This required focus. Donovan was right in front of me, looking like he'd swallowed the poison of his lies for too many years. They burned a hole in his gut. All I needed was to give him the opportunity, and his secrets would come spilling right out.

I slapped my roll of dimes on the table and pushed in next to Donovan, not even really caring what game they played. "Give me some chips," I said. "I'm feeling lucky."

Chapter 28

"YOU KNOW, these places are all the same," I said as I tossed my last chip onto a truly staggering stack an hour later. The game was a form of poker where more cards were revealed after every round. "They drain your pockets but drown your sorrows. I'd almost call it worth it."

"Speak for yourself," said Donovan. It was the first he'd spoken since I sat down. Most of my chips sat in front of him. "I'm looking to pick up a few coins."

"Maybe a few sorrows too." All the other players had dropped out at this point. The table's dealer watched us across a battlefield of green velvet.

Donovan eyed me, no doubt trying to figure out my bluff. I wasn't bluffing, though. Not this time.

"A man like you knows a bit about sorrow, don't you?" I said.

Skin went pale under his copper beard, but his eyes stayed steely and hard. "Call."

I lay down my cards. Aces. He had kings. The dealer pushed a pile of chips to me and shuffled.

"I'm retired," said Donovan, not taking his eyes off my newly gained chips. "No time for sorrow."

"What did you do?"

"Pilot."

"I used to want to be a pilot." I stacked the chips into five stacks and lined them in a perfect row. "Then the *Benevolent* happened."

The muscles of his jaw clenched.

"Lot of folks died that day," I said after his ante was in.

Donovan gripped my arm and fixed me with his pale green eyes. "I'm here for the cards."

"No touching, please," said the dealer.

"Nothing wrong with a little friendly conversation," I said.

The dealer dealt. I didn't touch my cards, and Donovan did a fine job pretending not to notice.

"The way I see it," I said, sliding a bet into the center of the table, "a copilot's just as guilty as the pilot. I wouldn't want that kind of pressure."

A muscle in his jaw twitched. If I hadn't just picked up half his winnings in the last hand, he might have walked away. He knew exactly what my strategy was. That made one of us.

"Unless there was a technical problem or sabotage. Then it's the engineer's fault. You think the *Benevolent* was an engineering issue? Seems like I might have heard about that."

He scowled. He might have hit me if I didn't have most of his money. I probably would have deserved it.

"But you know all that, don't you, Jacob?"

Donovan raised the bet. I raised it right back. The dealer dealt us each another card. I still didn't look. My cards lay face down in front of me like a flock of dead birds.

"I'm just wondering," I said. "What really happened? Wouldn't it feel good to get that off your chest?"

"You wouldn't understand."

"That's the truth."

He raised the bet again, pushing a stack of ten chips into the center. I matched his bet.

"The thing is," I said, "I don't think you're guilty. I think you took a buyout for your silence, and I think that same silence is eating away at you. Pretty soon, you'll be out of that fat retirement cash, and you'll need to figure out what to do with the rest of your life. Maybe that'll mean getting a job here in the fancy part of town. Maybe it means rolling downspiral for something a little less reputable. Maybe it means landing in the Heavies, where nobody frowns at your gambling or your drink."

He gripped my arm hard enough to leave bruises. The dealer cleared his throat, but Donovan didn't let go. "I'm not in a downward spiral, buddy, and I'm not headed to one. Now, if you're here to play a game, play the goddamn game. If not, fold and get out of here."

A shadow crossed over us. Two of the hall's bouncers loomed.

"We're fine," I said. "No trouble here."

Donovan released my arm. "I apologize."

The goons stepped back, but not very far. The dealer dealt another card each, and Donovan raised the bet. I took my time deciding but still didn't look at my cards.

"You gotta look at them," Donovan muttered. "Play the damn game."

"You apologized," I said. "Was that for crashing the ship?"

For a hitched half breath, I thought he was going to hit me. When he didn't, I rolled my shoulders, stretched my neck, and pushed another stack of ten chips into the center. "I'll raise you," I said. Then I pushed in another stack. The pile in the center far outweighed the lingering remains in front of me. "You've been dealt a poor hand, Donovan, but at least you know what's in front of you."

Without speaking, he met my bid. The man was either the worst poker face or the best actor in town. Sweat beaded on his brow and his hand kept moving to stroke his beard. He must have known it was a tell because every few times he stopped himself. It didn't help.

He must have just then remembered his drink because he picked it up and downed the whole thing. When he was done, he crunched the ice, watching me the whole time. "There's a word we have for people like you."

"Is it *asshole*, because I can stop you right here. I've heard that one before."

"In the business, there are those of us who get things done. We follow rules, check all the boxes, take orders. We do things the way they're supposed to be done, and when there's a crisis, we make things right. We might not come up with the results you people like, but they're the best results given the circumstances, and we deserve medals for every safe landing you've never heard of." He glanced at his cards again and must have seen something he liked because a wicked grin crossed his face. He bid everything else on the table in front of him. "We're pilots, you piece of shit. We're the people who get you where you need to be. Now fucking drop out or play the game right."

I tapped my cards as if considering how much faith I needed to put in them. With my luck, this was a losing hand, dead before it ever got started. But I didn't need luck. Donovan might have been dealt a poor hand in life, but mine had been fantastic and I'd already thrown it all away.

Hadn't I?

Before I could second-guess myself, I pushed my chips in. What the hell was I going to do with a few dimes, anyway? They'd just burn a hole in my pocket until I wasted them.

"Thing is," I said to Donovan, "you say you take orders like a champ. Who were the orders from on the day you crashed the *Benevolent*."

One by one, he lay down his cards. Kings and sixes—a full house. He met my gaze, his eyes hooded with contempt. "You float through life. You let happen to you whatever's going to happen. When a ship crashes, it's not your fault. It's just something that your betters decided should happen to you." He stared at my face-down cards. "Whether that's your boss or your government or your god, there's always someone else to blame. You want to know who crashed that ship? It was me. Yeah, I was only the copilot, but my pilot showed up drunk. We were in the void before I knew it was going to be a problem. The *Benevolent* needed to dock somewhere, either up in the Hallows or down here. Might as well get people where they wanted to be, right?"

"Who gave that order?"

He reached for my cards, but I was too quick. I pressed them to the table.

He spat his words like a reflex. "Play the damn game."

"You'll see the cards when I get an answer."

"You're nothing," he said. His voice slurred, and I wondered how much alcohol was in that drink of his. "You people are all alike."

"Who gave the order? Who told you to keep going, and who told you where to dock?"

A wary smile touched his lips. "You wouldn't believe me if I said what." He swallowed hard. "If I said who gave the order."

What, not *who*. "It was Trinity."

His face flushed. "It was *my* call."

I held his gaze for several deep breaths. The bouncers took a step forward, but our dealer waved them back. With the kind of deliberate movements one uses to disarm a bomb, I upended each of my cards to reveal my hand: the hand I'd bet it all on.

"Pair of eights," I said.

The anger in Donovan's expression melted, giving way to an amused grin, then a light chuckle, and finally an all-out guffaw. He laughed in my face, breaking all sense of decorum.

A hand rested on my shoulder, and Beck said in a lightly mocking voice, "Was it worth it?"

I hadn't seen her come in. In fact, I looked around and saw that the whole gambling hall had been watching us, and I hadn't even noticed. I'd been so focused on the game and on Donovan's answers. A dozen blues rhythms about gambling and booze rang in my head. I'd bankrupted myself again between the brick walls of gambling and the truth. Every dime I owned was gone.

"There was something I needed to know," I said to Beck. "And now I know it."

"What's that?"

Instead of answering, I led her back through the crowd. The place had a short bar where servers picked up drinks to deliver to gambling patrons. I bellied up to it and ordered a couple of watered-down gin and tonics. When I couldn't pay, Beck made an exasperated sigh and dropped a couple dimes on the counter.

"How did you get in here?" I asked. "The gate was closed. Get close to it and Trinity will go nuts."

Beck made a face at the first sip of her drink. "Don't they have limes in this place?"

It wasn't lost on me every time she avoided a question, just like I assume it wasn't lost on her every time I avoided one of hers. "They're imports, either from up in the Hallows or from a different city."

"How many cities are there?"

"Twenty-seven originally, all in a row. Not all of them are populated now." That sober thought hung in the air for a few minutes.

"Not fifty-nine?"

It surprised me that she knew how many beads were on a rosary. "Budget constraints," I said.

She gulped her gin and tonic. "The maintenance tunnels below this neighborhood weren't secured. I was able to get in through one of those."

I decided not to ask her how she'd found me. "Those tunnels are tiny."

She flashed me a sideways grin. "You'd be surprised where a lady can fit if she needs to."

"Well, I think I'll use the front gate."

Beck swallowed the last of her drink and ordered something with some fruit in it. "Why would they make a gate with gaps big enough for even you to squeeze through?"

"Aesthetics?"

She didn't look convinced. "Is useless an aesthetic?"

"It's not useless. It's perfectly functional for almost everyone on the ship."

"But not you, and not anyone else excommunicated from Trinity."

"That's right."

"So, that's what I mean." She sipped her new drink and nodded with approval. "The design is specifically made to allow you through. Why?"

I'd never thought of it that way. "My life without the AI's help is inconvenient enough. Just leave me this one thing, all right?"

"One thing. Yeah. But what about getting personalized security threat alerts from Trinity? What about all the things you can do in the liminal spaces that nobody else can do?"

Gin soaked my brain, and I closed my eyes for a moment to block out the distracting noises of the gambling hall. For the first time all evening, I didn't want to leave. Not yet. "Tell me about Earth," I said. "What's it like growing up on a planet?"

She waved dismissively. "Earth is the rotting core of humanity. It's all stuck on being the cultural center of the expanding human universe, but nobody there bothers to notice that everything new is out here in the outer colonies. All the best new art, all the technological innovation. It's all out here."

"Nobody around here cares about our artists. Our planetside colonies are going to be another hundred years before they're sustainable."

"More, the way I hear it."

I shrugged. "Long enough it doesn't matter to me." There was an expression in her blue eyes I couldn't recognize. "Is that what Violet Ruiz is doing out here?"

"My boss wants the painting for sentimental reasons."

"But why? Two years in cryosleep for a painting, and then she goes right back home with her prize?"

Beck stared at the far wall for several long breaths. "We weren't asleep. Violet lives on that ship. It's the only place I've ever seen her, and I don't think she ever intends to set foot anywhere else."

I shook my head in disbelief. "I've lived my whole life on this station, and I think that's suffocating."

"Then leave."

The thought had never occurred to me.

"The *Thirty Silver* is the peak of luxury. She has everything she wants, and it's able to sustain her for her whole life, no matter where she goes. I think she plans to travel to all the colonies, just to see them."

"The ultimate retirement plan." I touched Beck's wrist with my fingertips. She didn't pull away. "Where does that put you?"

She sipped her drink and shifted her arm so that she was holding my hand. Her fingers were warm and light against my massive ham hocks. There was a sadness in the corners of her eyes that wasn't reflected in her voice. "I'll do whatever I want. It's a decent job, and when I'm ready to quit, I'll get off at the next stop." She led me through the crowd toward the exit. "Come on, you big lug. We have work to do." Her voice was all professionalism, but the bounce in her step told of a lighter emotion. It was distracting.

She pulled me along, and we slipped into the black Haven night. Even in this affluent neighborhood, very few people bothered to break the curfew. Those leaving the gambling hall did their best to slink away undetected. Only a few pinpoints of yellow illuminated the streets now, and the false sky above resembled the boiling gray of a cloudy night. A warm breeze tugged at my hat.

Beck led me to one side and climbed the stoop of a modestly appointed mansion. She stood a couple steps up, where her face was even with mine and looked straight into my eyes. "Demarco," she purred, the name like sweet wine on her lips. She leaned close.

For a moment, our breaths mingled in the soft breeze. My heart danced a rhythm too quick to be the blues, and I placed a hand on her hip.

"We shouldn't," I whispered. Why? I couldn't say.

She quieted me by pressing a sharp, painted nail to my lips. When she spoke, her breath tickled my nose. "There's someone beyond the gate."

A moment passed before her words made any sense in my muddled mind. When I finally figured it out, I turned slowly to look down the narrow line of sight along the long street that led up to the gate. A flicker of movement flashed through one of the pools of yellow light beyond. I would have recognized Sam Wash's solid silhouette anywhere.

Beck searched my eyes. "Isn't that the guy who wrecked your shop?"

"He must have followed me."

She turned to look, just in time to see Wash pass through the next lighted area. He wasn't even trying to keep to the shadows. Behind him, a dozen more shapes crossed through the light. They guarded my only public exit from the gated neighborhood, and they were cocky enough to not even be sneaky about it.

"Beck," I whispered, "how skinny did you say that maintenance tunnel was?"

She placed her palms on my broad shoulders and tilted her head. "You won't like it." Her eyes narrowed. "But there's a decent chance you'll fit."

Chapter 29

BECK WAS RIGHT. I didn't like it. The maintenance tunnel started with a lingering specter of claustrophobia. It was certainly bigger than the narrow tunnel Retch had used to sneak into McCay's secret room back in the Heavies. It was bigger than the passage I'd squeezed through in the bottom of the Heavies. It narrowed as we went, and the press of insufferable pressure drew sweat from my brow. My shoulders scraped both sides of the passage, and my head bumped endlessly against the ceiling. All the while, Beck led the way past the grimy machinery with a burning impatience.

Finally, the tunnel deposited us into a narrow alley with slick cobblestone covering the sloping street. The entrance was invisible from the street. How she found it, I did not know, but there wasn't time to ask.

The buzz of motors filled the night.

"Quickly," Beck whispered. "We can sneak away."

Beck liberated her scooter from a broad-leafed plant and waved me toward it. "You drive."

"Why me?" She was a better driver.

"You know this town and I'm a pretty good shot."

"You still have that gun?" I settled myself onto the scooter and refamiliarized myself with the controls. I switched it on, and the headlamp flared to life. "And are you sure that old thing still works?"

"Who says it's old?" Beck landed on the seat behind me.

Lights flashed across the buildings.

I twisted the accelerator, and the scooter's back wheel spun on the slick cobbles.

"Ease off a little," Beck said, gripping my coat.

When I eased off, the tire caught and the scooter lurched forward. We shot through the narrow alley, handlebars inches from the fiberstone walls on either side. The front wheel left the ground as we launched headfirst into Haven Nicodemia's dimly lit inner spiral.

There was no sneaking. Soon as we came out, they were on us. They swarmed from the alleys and buzzed along the spiral. Too many to count, and I didn't take the time to try. I twisted hard and a burst of speed took us past several of them. They fell in and followed.

The crack of small firearms rang out behind us. Beck swore.

"You hit?" I asked.

"Shut up and drive."

I banked hard into a side street, speeding from light to light as fast as I dared. Ahead, the bulk of Haven Nicodemia's brutal citadel dominated the churning gray sky. Its brutal spires were lit in effervescent purple.

Then I turned again, and the narrow streets swallowed us.

Behind, the high-pitched buzz of cycles spun onto our street. Beck shifted in her seat and fired a shot. There was no time to see if it hit because the street ended with a steep downward staircase, and I yanked the bars to keep from careening down it. With a burst of acceleration, we plunged into a narrow alley.

The burning white of a cycle's headlamp blazed at the other

end of the alley. The enormous mass of Wash's ride hummed with power.

Beck tensed.

"No," I whispered. "Wait."

"It's nothing personal," said Wash. I couldn't see his face, but I could imagine the rictus grin. "Just trying to earn some dimes."

"Everything's personal," I said. "There isn't anything else."

He rolled slowly forward. Behind us, two more cycles moved to block off our escape. We were in a narrow alley, hardly wide enough for one cycle. Wash's light shone narrow and straight, its white light piercing right into my skull. We couldn't see any of the intervening alley, but there was nothing between us. Nothing to duck behind for cover. It wouldn't matter anyway, trapped as we were.

Or were we?

I knew this neighborhood. At least, I knew the Heavy version of the same neighborhood. This was where Retch lived, in among the warehouses surrounding the great cathedral. I didn't just know these alleys in general. I knew this alley in particular. It was where Retch's hideout had a secret entrance.

My scooter edged forward at my command, rolling slowly, softly. "What is this about, Wash? I did everything Saint Jerome asked. What's his problem with me?"

Wash made a choking laugh. "Oh, you still think Jerome's still in charge? That old man is getting hunted down just like you."

"What ever happened to loyalty?" Forward a little more.

"You know what loyalty to the Saint got me?"

"Nothing."

"Not one damn thing. He doesn't see what kind of leader I could be." Two more cycles closed in around the alley behind him. More noise came from behind me, but I didn't dare look. I was busy staring defiantly at the space where I figured Wash must be, trying my best not to show how terrified I was. I only needed a few more seconds.

"So how does this go down?" I asked. "When you kill, Trinity will mark you as a murderer. You'll have the police on you."

"You and I both know that's not how Karma works."

"Demarco," Beck hissed. "What are you doing?"

"I'm interrogating him," I whispered.

"Usually that implies a different power differential."

"There's more to this."

"I can take him out." She was tense, and I saw she still held the crimson pistol in one hand, lowered to point at the ground.

There. Right at the corner of my light, I saw where the edge of fibersteel separated from the wall around it. It was narrower here, and better hidden, but it existed.

"Fine," I said to Wash. "One thing before you do this, though."

"What?"

I hit the accelerator and yanked the bars. We hit the wall hard, pushing the sheet of metal inches, feet. Wash shouted. Cycles revved.

Gunshots. Beck laid down a covering fire.

The metal tore with a scream like a wailing banshee. The hole widened and the scooter burst through into the warehouse. It really was like the one down in Heavy.

Only this warehouse wasn't empty.

The area around us was partially lit by the blinking lights of a robotic workforce. Shelves towered high up into the black above. All around, the sound of metal scraping and motors whirring filled the huge space. A robot arm swung at us, and I punched forward to avoid its grasp. It clamped onto a crate near the hidden entrance and lifted it high into the darkness.

Behind us, Wash's people wrenched at the wall where we had come through. Beck squeezed off two shots and they stopped. She gasped and shifted behind me.

"You all right?"

She squeezed me tighter.

I raised my voice so Wash could hear me behind the wall. "What's Lauder paying you, Wash?"

"Frank Lauder's on his way out the door."

"Who's the new boss, then? You?"

Wash and his goons pushed at the wall again. "The Saint wanted you dead, and he was right. You're a wildcard. Too much risk."

"Is that all it was? I thought maybe I did something wrong."

Beck fired another shot. "Move, Demarco!"

"It's gotta be more than that, Wash," I yelled. "Did I offend you when I kicked your ass the other day?"

"You didn't kick my ass."

Beck whispered in my ear. "Just drive."

I didn't. "A real leader's got to earn the respect of his people."

"I have plenty of respect."

"You have power. If you look around, who of your goons would have your back if they knew how weak you were?"

"Look around? You want me to look around? I don't see anyone out here, Demarco."

It took a few seconds for me to figure out what he was getting at. Beck got it first.

She said, "They're circling around to the front entrance."

I twisted the accelerator, and the back wheel peeled out on the slick fiberstone floor. The rows of shelves were narrow, and the headlamp shone only a short distance ahead. As fast as I dared go, I couldn't open up all the way. A robot blocked our path. I slammed on the brakes, and Beck pressed hard against my back. Behind us, metal screeched, and Wash forced his way into the warehouse.

Backing up, I found another side row and we were off again. Crates whipped past. The buzz of Wash's cycle echoed off the high ceiling. Faster. Faster. Stop. Another robotic arm blocked the way. Its blue light shone in the darkness, but my headlight blinded me to its glow until we were almost on top of it. I backed up again. Found another row.

Speeding along, we passed an empty shelf. On the other side, Wash matched our speed. He grinned his evil, manic grin for several long seconds.

The big warehouse door was visible at the long end of the row. We had a straight shot to the exit.

The door was closing. Wash's goons had made it around. The shapes of their shadows moved across the glow of their own head-lights. We could make it, but we'd be easy targets.

On the other side of the shelf beside us, Wash drew a long pistol. Beck fired a shot, but the plasti-ceramic bullet shattered against the metal shelving. Wash aimed.

The shelves were full again. Crates blocked us from Wash, but he was still there. I cranked the accelerator.

Time slowed. I had seconds to make the call. Seconds to decide whether or not we could shoot the gap before the door slammed closed. Seconds to calculate if we could do that without getting shot. Seconds to guess the best way to get out without getting killed.

"You know your streets," Beck whispered in my ear.

She was right. I knew these streets. These were the same streets I'd walked in Heavy Nicodemia. These same streets with lights that never lit for me, where I'd walked in the dark countless times looking for help. Looking for trouble. This was no different, only faster.

Nobody knows the streets quite like the man who walks in the dark. This was my territory.

This was my home.

I switched off the headlamp and cranked the accelerator. We burst from the shelving a cycle's length ahead of Wash. His head-light flashed across us for a split second before Beck unleashed her last few bullets. This time, she hit. His light shattered and his cycle's motor sparked. Died.

Ahead, the door lowered. I gave the scooter everything, and its little motor screamed in frustration. A split second is all it took to cross the space. There was a shout as they heard us approach, but they were too slow. We were too invisible. I yanked the scooter down and went into a hard skid with Beck clinging to my back. My boot grated against the wet fiberstone floor.

Then, the sound changed. We passed the door by inches. The air opened around us. We were out.

And blind in the dark of night. I popped the scooter back up and twisted hard, aiming for where I hoped the alley was.

Behind us, Wash's people mounted their cycles for pursuit.

From memory, I sped along the warehouse district streets, hoping against hope that no pavement would be broken, and no litter cluttered the streets. As my eyes adjusted to the gray of the Haven streets, the buildings around us became lumbering giants. My world was a thousand shades of gray. The deceptive dark wasn't as bad as it seemed.

Left, then right. I sped full speed through the shadowy streets. Soon, the noise of other cycles faded into the black. We were free.

I pulled to a stop in a nook at the base of Haven Nicodemia's monolithic cathedral.

Beck gave me a little squeeze from behind, holstered her pistol, and then slid off the bike, landing in a heap.

I rushed to her side. When I touched her waist, my hands came back sticky and wet.

Her eyes fluttered. "No hospitals," she whispered. "Take me to the church." With that, she slipped into uneasy unconsciousness.

Chapter 30

IT WASN'T the first time I'd kicked in the door to a house of God, and in all likelihood, it wouldn't be the last. Beck was a bloody sack in my arms—her body lighter than I would have imagined, considering the weight of her personality.

"Priest!" I bellowed without any respect to decorum.

Unlike the cathedral in Heavy Nicodemia, the Cathedral of Saint Benedict's stark gray walls gave it an institutional feel. Entering through the back deposited me in the business end of the church. Dark, empty offices lined the hall, and imitation ficus trees flanked an empty reception desk.

Without bothering to wait for an answer, I burst into the chapel. Beck groaned in my arms. She'd been hit in the side, and, based on a quick examination, the bullet had passed clean through. That was good, but I didn't know if it had punctured any organs on its quick visit. The ceramic bullets used in most guns tended to shatter on impact. That it hadn't might have been some kind of miracle. My medic training was a stress-panicked jumble in my head. I shouted again for the priest.

I shouldered through a pair of double doors into the narthex, where a crowd was gathered for the upcoming service. People gasped, startled by the appearance of a giant with a bloody body in his hands. Blood coated my hands and coat. Beck's skin was so pale in the warm lights that it glowed against the dark of the bloody smears. She'd bled so much. Why hadn't Wash shot me instead?

But that's not how life worked. People around me got hurt, and I walked away unscathed. Beck might die from this, even though it was me they wanted.

"Excuse me," came a kind but urgent voice. "Can I help you?"

"You the priest?"

The man was tall and long-faced, and the surgical starching of his white collar answered a whole lot of questions about who he was. His skin dropped all pretense at color when he saw the blood. "We have a medical station. Let me see if I can find a trained medic."

"I *am* a trained medic," I said. "Just get me the station."

The priest led me back through long, drab hallways. The lights activated for him as we passed through, bringing a sterile, clipped edge to the otherwise featureless space. This could have been any office in any financial district. Not a very successful one, I decided. Any successful finance office would have hung a painting or two. Maybe the ficus would be real.

"In here," said the priest, waving me through a wide double door.

The room was even more harsh than the hall, with a crisp, acid scent lingering in the cold air. Three steel tables stood spaced evenly in the room, and the far wall was a row of refrigeration units.

"A morgue?" I asked.

"Our facilities contain a standard medical station."

I placed Beck on the closest table. Her blood smeared across the reflective surface, rendering red storm clouds in a swirling sky. This wasn't a painting I ever wanted to see again. It took me back to the wreck of the *Benevolent*. To the death of my parents. I swallowed back that pain. There was work to do.

The medical station sat in a corner, its blue screen blinking a command prompt. I prayed that Trinity would allow the small shred of mercy that was the basic human right to proper healthcare.

I punched in codes for a trauma kit, painkillers, and synth blood. The first two emerged immediately from the slot. The blood would take a moment to generate. There was a complex system behind these medical stations. What it couldn't produce with materials on hand it would have transported from a storage location. It might even come from a warehouse like the one we'd just raced through.

Trinity had granted access, but would it be enough?

Beck's pale skin was cold to the touch. She was going into shock. I hit her with the painkillers, hoping it would help. Trinity used a blended mix of fast- and slow-acting pain meds, and the second I injected Beck she slumped into a deeper sleep. Good.

"Is there anything I can do to help?" The priest stood in the doorway looking as out of place as his parishioners must feel in the confessional.

Tearing Beck's shirt, I took my first good look at the wound. It was low in her abdomen, possibly near the liver. That was bad. I hadn't done a lot of internal work in my medical training.

"I'm good, Priest," I said. "Go tend your flock."

The medical station dinged and a pouch of synthblood arrived through the chute. I snatched it up and used the included hook to hang it from the low ceiling. Placing the IV was tricky. It took several tries to get a needle into her desiccated veins. With the priest gone, the lights faded. I squinted in the dim light, cursing Trinity and all of its automated systems.

Beck's breathing grew shallow, and her skin was ice. Little hitching sounds in the back of her throat caused her whole body to shudder as she slept. The wound bled, pooling on the steel table. I took a deep breath, braced myself, and dove in.

Wound care wasn't my specialty. In my few years of medical training, my focus was in comfort care. There were some things that artificial intelligence couldn't do well. Palliative care was one of them. I knew drugs, and I understood surgery, but the robotic appendages of a fully equipped surgical suite would do most procedures better than a human.

Beck wasn't going to last long enough to find one of those.

The station dinged again, and a surgery kit landed on the tray. Steadying my nerves, I set the thing down on the table nearest Beck. It had all the razor-sharp scalpels one would expect, plus some gadgets I barely remembered from my training. I fixed a pair of augment goggles on my face and took a moment to let them complete a scan.

Once I'd taken in everything, the augment goggles kicked in. With the device augmenting my vision, I didn't need the lights. I scrubbed in and gloved up at the closest sink. Instructions came with arrows pointing at where I needed to go and when. *Clean the area.*

I used the included cleaning kit to scrub the area around the wound.

Pick up the scalpel. Affix the ultrasound. Open the wound.

The piece I had never used was a flesh binder. It knit together torn flesh with a kind of resin glue, holding everything in place until it could heal properly. My hands shook as I used it on the nicked liver. I was a terrible surgeon.

Once the liver stopped bleeding, the augmented instructions walked me through procedures to clean the area. After it was cleaned—and several jagged bullet fragments were removed—the rest of the process was easy. The binder worked the pieces of her skin together, knitting it with an aerosol-applied semi-flexible mesh.

My head hurt. Vision grew blurry and unfocused. The back of

my throat tasted like bile. It was all I could do to keep from vomiting.

But she was alive.

Reconcile? The text on the medic screen said.

"Not today, Trinity," I said.

Remembering my training, I packed the remains of the surgery kit, including the augment goggles. They reminded me of the other excommunicated man running around town. He had used augmented goggles to see in the dark. It gave him even more of an advantage.

These wouldn't work for me outside of surgery. Trinity still controlled them. The whole kit went straight back into the medical station, and by the time I was finished, my joints ached, and every muscle felt weak with exhaustion. I fumbled in the near-dark. The only light was the soft glow of the med station screen.

I picked Beck up, afraid she would roll off the table when she woke. In a nearby office, I located a single reclining chair—no doubt a sinful luxury for some ancient priest. I settled into it, pulled Beck close, and arranged her so she wouldn't put pressure on her wound. Her holster dug into my hip, so I grabbed the gun and stuffed it in my pocket.

We slept with her wrapped in my arms. It was the first comfortable sleep I'd had in longer than I could remember.

Chapter 31

"PRIEST," I said, my voice a deep rumble in my chest. Beck still slept curled up next to me, her warm body rising and falling with each deep breath.

The priest was a silhouette in the office door. I don't know how long he'd been watching, but he didn't move when I spoke.

After a moment, he said, "I thought you would be gone by now."

With great effort, I extracted myself from Beck. She barely stirred. Her painkillers would wear off soon, but for now, they still kept her under. The nap had only lasted a couple of hours, but I felt more rested than I had after a long night's sleep. I smiled at the priest. "We appreciate the assistance, Father."

"Normally, you people are gone before I return," he said. A hint of peevishness lingered in his voice.

"We don't have anywhere to go."

"Everyone has somewhere to go," he said. "Trinity cares for us all."

"Not all of us," I said.

The expression on his face ran through a rainbow of emotions.

ANTHONY W. EICHENLAUB

Fear first. Fear was always first. He understood that I was outside the system. Then his eyes narrowed as his priestly greed considered how this could be turned to his advantage. Finally, resignation came in the drooping of his jowls. "I shouldn't have let you in here."

"I'm excommunicated from Trinity. Not from the Church."

He opened his palms in an accepting gesture. "Trinity does God's will, and if you have become excommunicated, then the Church shouldn't allow you access to its tools."

"Would you let a man starve?" I gestured at Beck. "Would you have let her die if you had known?"

The priest walked down the hallway, and I followed. "Trust in the Lord with your heart and lean not on your own understanding."

I shook my head in disbelief.

The priest pursed his lips. "You need to leave."

"No."

His voice went up an octave. "Excuse me?"

"She needs time to recover, Priest. Your duty is to those who need help."

"She is stable enough to move."

Before I could answer, Beck said, "I'm fine." She watched me with bloodshot eyes. "We can go."

"Beck, you can't—"

"Shut it, Demarco," she snapped. She winced as she pushed herself into a standing position. When I reached out to assist her, she brushed me away. "I've got this."

She didn't have it. When she stumbled, I got an arm under her. The ragged, bloody edges of her shirt still hung in scraps around her abdomen. The bandages covering her wound hadn't bled through, though, so I figured the glue was probably holding well enough.

"Beck," I said, "you need rest."

She flashed a weak smile. "You heard the man in black. We need to leave."

"Wash will be waiting for us out there," I said.

The priest tugged the cuffs of his black shirt and adjusted a thin silver bracelet. "It's really for the best if you leave."

"Demarco," Beck said through gritted teeth.

"Yeah?"

"I want my gun back."

I patted the pocket of my coat where the pistol sat. "You need it right now?"

"Yeah."

"What for?"

"I want to point it at this priest."

The priest took a step back and cleared his throat.

"What do you want to do that for?" I asked.

"It'll make it easier to shoot him." She pulled away from me and stood on her own.

"Now hold on." I took the gun out of my pocket. Its crimson barrel caught the light like a cardinal's robes. The curly gold letters said *Forsaken*, just like McCay's gun. "Nobody needs to point a gun at a priest."

Beck fixed her gaze on me with a hard stare. "We do if he keeps on being an asshole."

"First of all," I said, taking a step away from her. Beck looked weak, but her intense gaze made me nervous. "We need to discuss your criteria regarding who deserves to get shot."

She nodded at the priest. "He does."

"This guy was here for us last night when you were bleeding out. He showed us where to access the medical supplies that you needed, and he left us enough room so that I could perform the necessary surgery." I put an arm around the priest's shoulders. "None of that makes him an asshole."

"Give me the gun, Demarco."

"I think I'll keep it."

"I should be going." The priest tried to pull away, but I tightened my grip on him.

"Maybe we should finish that theological debate, Father," I growled.

His eyes locked on the pistol in my hand, which was pointed at the floor. "Are you threatening me, Mr. Demarco?"

"Hard to see how that could happen, considering excommunication means I can't even talk to you."

"That's clearly not what it means."

Beck stepped forward. Some of the color had come back to her skin. "This priest knows more than he's letting on."

The old man squirmed in my grip, but I had him tight.

Beck said, "I was tracking the paper trail. There's that ring of art aficionados in town. This guy was at the meetup."

"Was he?" I looked questioningly at the priest, but his face gave up about as much as a brick wall.

"He was in the wings, but I got a good look at him. His buddies wouldn't talk, and as soon as things got rough, he was gone. So, I know he's tied to the art theft in this town, and he's a coward."

I nodded. "Things got rough?"

"It happens sometimes."

"Hence, you wanting to point a gun at him."

"Get some answers."

We both stared at the priest. He cracked.

The priest said, "There's nothing illegal about what the Church does with the art trade."

"Trafficking stolen goods isn't illegal?"

"Trade is the lifeblood of Haven Nicodemia. Everyone knows that. If art passes through here, we make sure we have a handle on where it's coming from and where it's going. The church's interest is that religious works are preserved and accounted for."

"Exactly," Beck said. "He knows right where we need to go next."

"And you won't get that information from me. My goal is to

keep the art in the hands of those who care for it. Hands less stained with blood."

Beck hugged her arms close to herself, hiding her bloodied hands. It was *her* blood, but the move made her look guilty as sin.

"Listen, Priest," I said in my mellowest voice, "you might not trust her, but you can trust me."

"The excommunicated man."

"Excommunicated from the AI. I'm on neutral ground with the Church."

"They always say that."

I let go of the man's shoulder. "Priests are supposed to find the good in people. You're supposed to take confession and give penance. When someone comes to your door asking for help, you offer it. That's the job description."

He said, "I won't be a part of this."

"Shoot him in the leg," Beck said.

"You're not helping, Beck."

"Neither are you, Demarco."

I turned back to the priest. "I just want to get the painting back to someone who'll take care of it. It's one third of a triptych and belongs with the rest of the painting."

He took a step back. One more step and he'd bolt, I was sure of it. Beck was in no condition to chase him down, and I didn't think I could bring myself to tackle a priest in his own Church, whether or not he was an asshole.

I stowed the gun and held my hands up, palms outward. "Let me tell you what I know, Father. Call it a confession, so it's confidential."

He glanced at Beck. "That's not how it works."

"Look how much I don't care. *The Garden of Earthly Delights* was taken from its resting place in Madrid about a decade ago. Someone decided to move it to a safer location, and in transit, there was a heist. Things didn't go according to plan. The operation got dicey, and two of the thieves escaped with one of the panels. They high-tailed it out here to the colony, figuring they could find a buyer. Guy by the name of Troy Vitez sold his partner out and came through Haven Nicodemia with his prize. Following so far?"

He gave no response.

"Bringing hell with him in the form of an ancient painting, Vitez found a few things he liked around here. He brought the painting to a few museums in town, discovering that letting them do a full scan earned him a little spending cash. He used that cash to change his identity, which allowed him to move even farther north to the Hallows, that lucky guy. Walking into heaven with a crate full of hell."

The priest swallowed. His eyes darted to the exit at the end of the hall, but he must not have liked his odds because he stood still.

"But here's the thing. Fake IDs don't stand up too well to the Hallow Nicodemia customs office. He needed something real. Something that looked a whole lot like a real birth certificate. Maybe a First Communion or a Baptism or something to complete the picture."

This got the priest's attention. "You think I forged his documents?"

"I think someone here gave him real documents, with the assumption that he was telling the truth about needing replacements for them after his long journey. What did he tell you? Space accident? Asteroid encounter? Databank corruption? Whatever it was, I'm sure it was a thin excuse. You chose to believe it because that's how the Church justifies itself in the criminal underworld. You make sure people carrying important artifacts get where they're going safely, whether or not it means bending plausibility."

The air went out of the priest. His jowls sagged and his shoulders slumped. "What do you want from me?"

"I want the name, Father. Who did Troy Vitez become?"

"I don't know."

Beck spoke up, "Then find out." The threat in Beck's voice was bright enough to leave trace radiation.

The priest locked eyes with Beck and gave a slight nod. He led us down the long hall. The deeper layers of the church had more life to them than the upper layers. Carpets covered the floors and vacuum-preserved art decorated otherwise drab walls. I thought about giving the priest a hard time about hoarding all the best treasures, but he'd probably heard it all before.

Walking behind the priest, I leaned over to Beck and whispered, "How are you feeling this morning?"

She flashed a mischievous smile. "What did you give me? I feel great."

"Painkiller cocktail and a bag of synthblood. The synth they use here has a better O2 conversion than normal red blood cells. Keeps it so we don't need to give you quite so much."

Beck placed a hand on her side where I'd sealed the wound. "You fixed me up."

"Go easy for a few days. It's basically glue and tape. Any rough movement is going to pull it open."

She rolled her eyes.

"Yeah, I know. I sound like your mom. I get that a lot."

"Lester's going to run," she whispered.

"Who?"

"Lester." When I still didn't comprehend, she said, "Father Lester. Did you even read the bulletin?"

"I don't go to Mass anymore."

She shrugged. "I did my research."

"You were planning on coming after this guy anyway. That's why you wanted me to take you to the church." Once again, I was impressed by her ruthless efficiency.

"I trailed him back here, and then I had to go find your sorry ass."

"Sorry about that."

She flashed a wicked smile. "It's the least I could do."

Father Lester led us down another set of wide stairs. We were so deep in the church we had to be close to dropping out of the sky of the level below. I pictured us opening a door and falling straight into the tenements. It wouldn't be the first time someone fell from the sky, though typically it happened when maintenance workers were opening panels they ought not to open.

The hall opened into a record repository that dwarfed the one down in the government center of the Heavies. Row upon row of tall thin shelves stretched far enough that the floor sloped up along the spiral. All that separated us from the archive was a clear wall of fibersteel. There was no door.

"How do we get in?" I asked.

"We don't," said the priest. "We make requests to the archive, and it brings us the papers."

I wasn't a fan. "If Trinity decides what papers you see, how is that any better than letting the AI store it digitally?"

"It's not Trinity," said the priest in a grave tone. Something about his demeanor bothered me.

"You have your own proprietary AI?"

He gestured at a terminal on the wall. "Go ahead, request what you need."

"Records issued," I said into the terminal's microphone, giving it the dates in question. "And cross reference that with anything about Troy Vitez around that time period."

Father Lester took a step closer to the exit, but I kept him in my peripheral. Beck was right. He was a runner if I'd ever seen one. Only, Beck wasn't up for chasing him, and I'd never been the quickest guy around. "Priest," I said without looking up from the terminal. The numbers flashed up on the screen, but it was too much information. I needed to narrow it down more.

"Yes?"

I braced myself and asked something that had been bothering me. "When you said being excommunicated from Trinity meant the same as being excommunicated from the Church, what did you mean?"

Father Lester bristled. "It's just like it sounds. Trinity acts as an agent of the Lord our God, and if Trinity has decided your position in society, then we must respect it."

But the priest wasn't respecting it. That was what bothered me. "How long has that been policy?"

"As far back as the first time Trinity came online. The Catholics of the time designed the AI to be treated in this way."

It didn't make sense. "When I lived here before, I never noticed the policy, and it certainly isn't the case down in the Heavies."

"Well, even if that's true, I'm sure that won't last long. For the sake of consistency, it's important we all understand the doctrine of our faith."

"Sure." On the screen, the document collection had filtered down to only a thousand docs. I paged through the abstracts, looking for something I could use. "You worship the computer."

A flash of anger crossed his face before he returned to his placid, priestly self. "We do not worship Trinity any more than we worship the saints."

"So you say."

His fists clenched at his sides. "There is no god but God, Mr. Demarco. You know that."

I found what I was looking for. A document for someone in the right timeframe matching the right description. It even had a set of Customs documentation for a rather large piece of luggage. I poked at the screen. "Retrieve this document. I want to look at it."

Inside the sealed room, an arm descended from the ceiling and zoomed off through the room.

The priest took another step toward the door.

"I wouldn't do that, Lester," Beck said. Her voice dripped with a threat I'm pretty sure she couldn't follow up on.

"Let him go," I said. "We have what we want."

"But—"

"Nothing," I said. "Priest, go in peace."

"What?" Beck snapped.

"We never meant you any harm," I said to Father Lester. "I've got nothing but respect for the Church, even if your branch does lean a little too machinist for my taste."

His jaw worked like he wanted to respond, but better judgment won out, and he slipped out the door. The sound of his footsteps faded down the hall.

Beck got up in my face. "That guy was scum, Demarco."

"He was a priest."

"I sure as hell hope you have a plan."

"Plan?"

"Did you notice how he kept stalling?"

I thought *I* had been the one stalling. "We were having a nice conversation." I picked up the paper as the robot deposited it in the slot. "August. Vitez's new name is August Savior."

"You've got to be kidding me."

I considered my options and cycled through the interface for older records. "I'm looking for anything on the wreck of the *Benevolent.*"

"This again?" Beck asked.

"I'm opportunistic."

The machine cycled for several seconds, then delivered a single thin document. It was worse than useless. A couple paragraphs that could have described any docking crash in the history of Nicodemia.

"Using Church resources for personal gain?" Beck asked.

"Something like that." The comment gave me an idea. "How did you know about the maintenance access?"

"Pardon?" She put a fist on one hip and narrowed her eyes.

"Back outside the Fixed Stars. How did you know?"

Her eyes focused on something far away. "I was the kind of kid who always got into places she shouldn't. I liked to spy on my father and his friends, and this one guy was really good with computers. He showed me a thing or two about how to sneak around in a digital system the way I was already sneaking around in real life."

"You hacked Trinity?"

"Nothing quite that dramatic."

"Can you do it again?"

She eyed the computer screen. "That isn't Trinity."

Good point. "Computer, I need a map of this church and the surrounding maintenance tunnels." The arm sped through the shelves and retrieved a slender folder containing a single sheet of paper. On it was a diagram of the cathedral's maintenance tunnels. We'd be able to follow it for several blocks, avoiding Wash and his gang. In a few hours, we'd be in Hallow Nicodemia.

"You devious hacker," Beck teased.

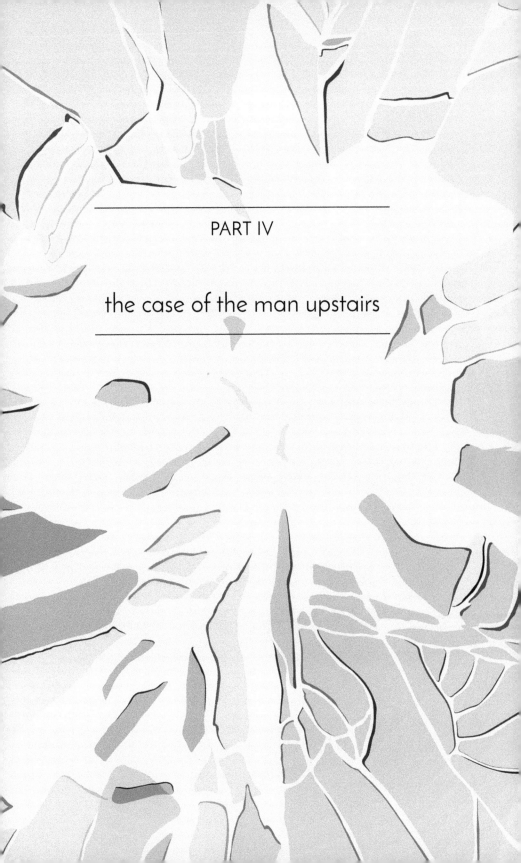

PART IV

the case of the man upstairs

Chapter 32

THE SUIT FIT. *Really* fit. I looked down at Reginald, the tailor, like he was some kind of genius artisan. Maybe he was. The blue undershirt shone in the shop lights. It was the kind of blue that had depth. A person could lose themselves in its indigo haze if they weren't careful. Atop that, I wore a coat of purest synthetic fibers with gold embroidery along the sleeves and shoulders. Matching slacks hung loose around my legs, breezy for the hot Hallows night, and cut to move with my body like the ocean against a shore. The whole outfit came with a blue bowler hat because hats were in style again in the Hallows.

"I prefer my old hat," I said.

"The bowler is an upcoming trend and will stay in style for quite some time."

I adjusted it on my head, but it still didn't feel right. "My old hat was ruined. Got all bloody and shot up."

Reginald cleared his throat. He was a small man. In the Hallows, the working class was often imported from down the chain. "A good-fitting hat is important to the outfit. I could find something more like your old hat if you like."

"You have a fedora?"

He winced.

"The bowler suits you," said Beck from behind.

"The suit suits me," I said. "The hat strikes like a bad chord."

I turned to behold the most stunning sight I'd ever seen. She wore a red sleeveless dress with a loose skirt and matching gloves that came to her elbows. Her hair was colored a deep crimson and she wore it slicked back and woven with flowers. When she smiled, her teeth gleamed white.

"You look amazing," I said.

She touched the embroidered sleeve of my suit coat. "You're not so bad yourself." She held me at arm's length. "Keep the bowler, though."

"It feels wrong."

Instead of answering, she hooked her arm in my elbow and pulled me toward the door. "Thank you, Reginald," she said as we left. "You've been lovely."

And we stepped outside into the Hallow Nicodemia night.

The air was clean and pure, scoured by a million million plants growing throughout the district. Great purple flowers of the nicotiana family bloomed their aromatic nighttime blooms around the almost-hidden entrance to the tailor's shop. Higher up, the view of the sky was blocked by an interlacing of thick vines heavy with grapes at even intervals. A warm breeze coursed through the wide alley, first from right to left, then left to right, like the whole world was breathing.

The place felt familiar but also very strange. It had been over a decade since I'd set foot among the upper crust, but the words of wealth fit my lips same as the suit fit my body. My accent changed in my ears as soon as I stepped into the buoyant gravity of the Hallows. I only hoped the changes wouldn't stick.

I led Beck through the wide streets of the lower city. Where Heavy Nicodemia had fish and Haven Nicodemia had livestock, Hallow Nicodemia had plants. For the most part, these were crops that could be harvested, but the city was designed to show that agriculture was not its main export.

In the central swell of the landscape, streets fell away so that the space resembled a park. The sky opened, and far above, through the vast open space, we could see the city above.

Hallow Nicodemia's basic layout was the same as the other two beads, but this district had taken liberties with that original design. The upper spiral had been pared back to allow more light from the fusion core to penetrate to the lower levels. All along the spiral's inner fence, hanging plants draped down, lush and glossy green in the sparkling light. The sky in the lower city consisted of a false depiction of stars, but in the Hallows the sky was a clear dome, allowing the light of our power-generating false star to shine directly into the habitat. At least, that's what it did during the day.

At night, the dome closed, and the sky filled with the sparks of a million fireflies.

"It's beautiful," Beck said, holding my elbow in both of her hands.

"That's why it's such an exclusive club," I said. "Can't let everyone enjoy the spoils of heaven."

"Is that why they call it Hallow?"

I gestured up at the open air above. "The way they tell it, it used to be the Hollow Nicodemia because they emptied more of the open space in the middle. Somehow that changed to Hallow, but it fits well enough."

"That tailor back there. He wasn't native, was he?"

"Anybody shorter than six feet probably isn't a lifer up here. Also, anyone working a real job is probably an import from a lower district or a rebellious teen trying to tweak off his parents."

"Is that what you did?"

I led Beck around the central hill. There were few others around to witness the morning light, but another couple passed us, smiling. It was the smile of acceptance, which had been foreign to me the last time I was here. These people believed that I belonged, and what's more, they believed Beck belonged. It wasn't a hard sell. She was slender and tall. Beautiful in her red dress. She was the perfect kind of stunning that residents of the Hallows appreciated.

"There's something you need to see," I said, leading her to the eastern side of the hill. We found a bench and sat in silence for a time. She leaned her head on my shoulder.

"Do you miss it?" she asked.

"Hallow Nicodemia?"

"Home."

It took me a minute to understand what she was saying. "Home is like an abusive partner," I said. "You miss it, but you want to get away. Sometimes we succeed, but it's not always worth the cost."

She looked up at me, taking measure of my expression.

"Yeah," I said. "Leaving was probably worth it in my case."

"But you still miss it?"

"Watch," I said, nodding to the base of the upper dome. "Just watch."

The first crack of light appeared as a scarlet line piercing through the misty haze. It ran laser-sharp straight across the city, where it seared a line on the opposing side. The red-refracted light gave way to orange, then a piercing yellow. Brightness intensified, and the line of light walked down the wall behind us until it touched the lower levels.

Then, it hit us. Pure white light from the fusion core of the generation ship washed over us like the scouring hand of God. Its light burned through me, and its fire scoured every sin in my tainted soul. Burned it clear. When I looked down at Beck, I saw her dress glowed in the light. The crosses painted into her nails shone with gold. The embroidery in my own coat did the same.

Still, it got brighter. More of the dome opened and even with my eyes closed, the bright light hurt. It pierced through all the aches and exhaustion of the past few days to energize and purify. Through my closed eyelids, I witnessed the actions of Saint Jerome and the new gangster Frank Lauder. Visions of Retch flashed in front of me, his clever grin watching me as I fumbled through life. I saw Violet Ruiz in her luxury ship and the strange excommunicated man. Who he was, I didn't know, but his face burned itself into the back of my skull with a crystalline clarity only available in this hallowed light.

Beck slid on some sleek sunglasses, and when I couldn't stand the light anymore, I did the same.

"I used to be able to handle the light longer," I said. "I've adjusted too much to the dark."

"Maybe that's for the best." Beck tossed me a roll of dimes.

"Still feels light," I said.

"How many times have I paid you?"

"I don't know. Three. Maybe four."

"And how many of those dimes have you gambled away?"

"A few more dimes might buy some better luck."

"You can buy all the luck you need once we find that painting."

I drew in a long breath. "It's somewhere in the city. I can smell it."

"This whole place smells like mulch."

"That's what money smells like."

We left the hilltop garden to find transport along the inner ring where the spiral led upward. Where the other districts had trolleys, the Hallows invested heavily in flying transports. In the lighter gravity and thick air, these became the cheapest, quickest way to move people around. I'd never been convinced of their safety, but even after the energizing effects of a Hallow Nicodemia sunrise, I wasn't up for a walk halfway up the city. We found a piloted transport, its long, loping rotors lazily spinning overhead.

"Two to the cathedral," I said, tossing a couple dimes to the pilot. He waved us aboard and soon the transport flew through the hollow inside of the ship.

"You really like cathedrals, don't you?"

"After the one in Haven, I'm not so sure." I watched the green city fly past as the transport quietly rose past each of the levels.

"But if I'm looking for a religiously themed painting, it's not a bad place to start."

"What about Trey's new name? August Savior?"

"He's around. We need to figure out what connections he's made before we try to find him. It's all about who you know up here."

She pulled away from me and took a good look at the side of my face. "We should just find him. He'll know where the painting went."

"No."

Beck's fists clenched at her side. "I'm tired of this, Demarco. You did this in Haven too."

"What?" I was genuinely confused.

"You fucked around. When we had clues to follow, you went off and what? What did you even do?"

I wasn't ready to tell her why I'd been sidetracked. "It was important."

"I'm paying you, aren't I?"

"Is that what this is all about?" I took the roll of dimes from my pocket and held it up. "It's still all dimes and business between us?"

"Well, it's not sunrises and—"

I held up a hand. "Quiet."

She glared daggers at me but stayed quiet.

Layers of city flew past, and I strained at the edge of the transport to get another look at the others around.

There! The transport below and clockwise held a single occupant. He wore the same hat and coat I'd seen him in when he'd acted the drunk outside the gambling hall. His face was the grim mask I'd seen when he'd last confronted me at the jail.

It was the stranger. The excommunicated man. Alone in a transport that shouldn't be recognizing him. How was he doing that? Trinity had protocols it ran when a transport flew empty. It would return to its base location. Nothing more. The man's transport didn't do that. As our own drone swooped along the spiral toward the cathedral, his transport followed.

"It's him," I whispered.

Beck peered out the side of the transport next to me. "Vitez?"

"No," I said. "This is the guy who's been following me."

She slumped back into her seat, her eyes wide. Her hands went to a place on her leg where I knew she hid a knife. I still hadn't given back her gun, though she'd asked plenty of times. I don't know if I wanted the extra protection or if I just didn't trust her to not shoot anyone. Maybe a little of both. Plus, I couldn't shake the idea that it was McCay's antique weapon.

I drew the pistol and held its crimson barrel up to the light. Etching along the side said *Forsaken*, but was it the same as McCay's pistol? I figured I wouldn't like the answer, and not knowing was just another reason not to give the gun back to Beck. How many of these cheap, printed pistols had flooded the streets of Nicodemia recently? The more I stared at the weapon the more I didn't like where the train of thought took me. I put it away.

She said, "Nothing's ever simple around you, is it?"

"We're going to need to move fast," I said as we landed in front of the cathedral. Our follower swept past. "And things are going to stay a lot simpler if we don't shoot any priests."

I mounted the steps in front of the shining cathedral and threw the doors wide open.

Chapter 33

THE CATHEDRAL OF SAINT Lucy of the Light was a monument
of mirrors and glass befitting its name. Inside, stained glass
refracted the candle's soft glow to make the whole of the structure
burn with the powerful illumination of a hundred false suns.
Entering Saint Lucy of the Light was like stepping under a magni-
fying glass when the sunlight was already too bright to bear. In the
center of the halo stood two priests.

"Just distract them," I said to Beck. "I'll go downstairs and take
a look at their records."

Beck's footsteps cracked like whips in the otherwise silent space,
drawing the grim attention of the two priests. I abandoned her to
their judgment, ducking into a side passage that I remembered
from the Haven version of the same cathedral. The decorations
and even the materials that made up the walls were different, but
the layout was exactly the same. That meant I could find what I
wanted by going down to the documents room.

Or, at least, I thought I could. As soon as I veered from the
main network of back offices, the lights grew dim. The walls
behind the narthex were steel and stone, lit by the remnants of

Trinity's benevolent glow from the open doorways. Beyond, the space was completely dark. I took out my lighter and navigated by its flickering dance.

These walls were sharply different from the ones in Haven or the Heavies. They held art, sometimes ancient paintings or vases decorated with depictions of the stations of the cross. Salvador Dalí's *Christ of Saint John of the Cross* stood sealed under glass at the end of one hallway, its sharp perspective lending the space a greater depth. Gold-framed fragments of the original Notre Dame stood on a vacuum-sealed pedestal. These were the halls of a fully decorated and wealthy Catholic church. A Space Vatican. I followed along, picking my way through to where Haven's cathedral had its morgue. This morgue sat empty, but the smell of preservatives lingered on the air. Beyond that, I found the stairs where Father Lester had shown us the document room.

If the records of Haven were any indication, this church might contain every answer I needed. I could learn about Trey Vitez's new identity, August Savior. These records might have more about my parents and the crash that killed them. Or I could learn about my childhood and all the things we never think about when we're growing up that bother us so much as adults. What exactly did my parents do? Where did our wealth come from? Even as a teen, I was protected from that information, and something now bothered me about that.

Those were distractions. I didn't know how much time Beck could buy for me.

The third level down I hit a snag. Where Haven's cathedral had another staircase, this version had installed an elevator—one that wouldn't respond to my lousy excommunicated face.

"Come on," I said to the wall. "Open up."

It didn't.

Prying did no good. The systems kept the doors shut solid, like the heavy steel of a security gate. There was a panel in the wall that might have offered an override, but it sat dormant. No need to power up if nobody was around. The same status that let me sneak in unnoticed also kept me from reaching my destination.

I was just thinking about finding something to smash it open with when a light came on around the corner. I hurried away from the elevator and doused my flame, letting the shadows surround me.

"Father said the guy came down this way," said a voice. It had the deep resonance of a large man.

The second guy had a thin, reedy voice. "Security doesn't show any movement at all."

"There are ways around security."

"You think it's the thief?"

The two men approached the elevator door and the panel flared to life. One of them was a big guy with muscles that tested the elasticity of his humble acolyte robes. The other was shorter than me by a head and thin as a rail.

The one with the deep voice spoke, surprising me that it turned out to be the thin man. "Father said to have a look down here, so we'll take a look."

This wasn't the door to an unguarded apartment complex; it was an elevator. The likelihood of sneaking up behind these men, riding the elevator, and getting where I needed to go seemed on the low side, so I took a more direct approach.

"Greetings, gentlemen," I said, stepping from the shadows. "I was hoping you might help me."

The thin man took a step back.

"Surprised?" I asked. "Don't you take everything your priest tells you as gospel truth? He *said* I was down here."

The big man flexed, no doubt an attempt at intimidation. I did my best to not show how much it worked.

"We're going to have to ask you to leave, sir," rumbled the thin man. "Immediately."

"I'm just here to take a look at some documents," I said. "I'm investigating some stolen art."

"You won't find any documents down there."

The big man made a grab at my arm, but I twisted away.

Without taking my eyes off the big guy, I said, "When I'm done, I'll leave. We'll both be happy. You can watch to make sure I don't steal anything."

For a brief second, I thought they might do something smart. I wasn't really a threat to them or their church. What could the church possibly have to hide that would interest me? Even if it did have something to hide, they could easily steer me away from it if only they accompanied me to the document center.

The thin man clicked his tongue.

Big guy lunged, but I was ready for it. I dropped my weight and stepped forward, coming in below his center of gravity. It had been a long time since I'd fought in lower gravity, but schoolyard scuffles take a long time to fade from a boy's memory. I hit him low in the stomach, lifted, and threw him behind me as hard as I could. He flew down the hall and slammed into the wall.

By the time he hit the floor, I was on the thin man, but he wasn't such an easy target.

He blocked a dozen grabs in half as many seconds. The thin man moved with a fluid grace that could only have come from rigorous martial arts training. His center of gravity was low and balanced, and he protected his center. If I overcommitted, I had no doubt he would throw me. A kick snapped out at my head, but I twisted away, turning it into a glancing blow. A punch to my elbow sent spikes of pain through my whole arm.

I swore.

"Have some respect," said the thin man. "This is a church."

"I give the church all the respect it deserves," I said. Angry heat burned behind my eyes. Too much anger. It made me sloppy.

A scuff on the hard floor was my only warning the big guy was up. I turned just in time to catch the full weight of a charge. The blow pushed me toward the thin man, but I kept my footing. The big guy was taller than me, and he had a lot of muscle.

But I'd just spent a decade in the Heavies. Years of hard living had turned me into a slab of granite.

His legs pumped, trying to force me to the ground. I shifted my weight, took hold of his wrists, and shoved. He moved. His eyes went wide, and he looked at me like I was some kind of monster. Maybe I was.

The big guy was a distraction. The thin man struck me in the back, first with a kick to the back of the knee, then a punch to the kidney. Damn, I'd be pissing blood after that. A searing roundhouse kick to the side of the head made the world spin.

It also made me mad.

Hollering in righteous fury, I pulled hard at the big man's wrists, yanking him off balance. Still staggering from the blow to the head, I switched grips, picked the big man up by his acolyte robes, and threw him as hard as I could at his rapidly backpedaling ally. The two collided and collapsed, landing in a tangle on the ground.

I strode forward, fists clenched at my sides. "Listen up," I said. The big man tried to stand, but I slammed a fist into the back of his head. "I've got some business here, and you're going to help me out."

"Never," gasped the thin man. He was pinned and couldn't extract himself. "This is the Church you're messing with, and we are bound to protect it."

"I didn't say you'd have a choice," I said. "And I'm not doing anything against your Church." I wondered again what the Church had that was so worth protecting.

When the big man tried to get up again, I took his wrist—he was so slow—and locked his elbow. Keeping the thin man in the corner of my eye so he wouldn't try to sneak up behind me, I used the big man's hand to activate the console. The elevator door slid open.

That was when the big man started to struggle. I could barely keep him under control. He dipped low and lifted, but the weight of my body against the joint lock became too much. He couldn't lift me.

"That move might work on lighter folk," I said, "but I'm heavy right down to my soul."

This time, it was the big man who swore, earning him a scowl from his partner. I pulled the big man into the elevator, used his hand again to activate the controls, and soon we were going down to the document level.

My heart pounded with anticipation. This would have information on my parents, August Savior, and any number of answers I so desperately wanted. They would know something about the wreck of the *Benevolent*. Apart from the government—maybe more so than the government—the Church was the greatest record-keeper in the whole of Nicodemia. The Church thrived on its history, and the long memory of the Catholic Church was the sole source of its power.

Only, when the elevator opened, it revealed a long expanse of empty space.

Nothing.

"They ditched the documents a while ago," the big man said, a touch of sadness in his voice.

"Why?"

"Blasphemy, they say."

At first, it didn't make sense. How could documentation be blasphemy? How could a long record of a storied history work against the word of God? Then something Father Lester had said clicked. "Paper documentation only exists to contradict Trinity."

The big man nodded. I dropped his elbow, and he didn't move to fight me. There was no need. I knew their secret. The Church was dissolving from within, succumbing to machine worship.

"My parents were Catholic," I said. "How long has this been going on?"

He shrugged.

"You just work here, don't you?"

249

"It feeds the family." Suddenly I felt bad for hitting him so hard.

"Let's go," I said.

He reached for the button to bring us back up.

"Wait," I said. "What do you know about art thieves?"

He shrugged. "Sometimes we catch them. Trinity won't prosecute anyone who's going to take care of the art, so we usually end up letting them go."

I furrowed my brow. "How does that work? Shouldn't the blue step up?"

"Police defer to Trinity, and Trinity goes easy on art collectors. It's a revolving door prison system."

"Ever heard of a painting called *The Garden of Earthly Delights*?"

The big man slowly shook his head. "Look, I'm not an expert."

"No, that's fine. Where would you go if you were trying to track down a piece that got stolen?"

"I wouldn't," he said, and my hope faded. I thought for a brief second the big man might just be able to point me in the right direction. Then, he continued, "I'd talk to Augie and figure out when the next auction was." He pushed the elevator button.

"Augie?" I asked. "As in August?"

"Nice guy. He's a collector, and he always seems to know when the black market is active. He's been known to buy up stolen paintings and donate them back to the Church where they belong."

"Sounds like a real saint."

"Don't let him hear you say that. He's pretty much the humblest rich guy I've ever met."

"You're kidding me."

He shrugged. "The guy likes art, and he's been a big help for the church." Before I could respond, the elevator dinged and he turned to me. "So, Gregor probably had time to get some backup."

"I'll go quiet."

He winced by way of an apology. "No," he said. "It's probably not going to be quiet."

The elevator door opened to reveal the thin man flanked by two stocky, suited men carrying truncheons. They grinned at me through ugly teeth. Muscle from the Heavies, if I had to judge. Hired muscle.

I put my dukes up. "All right, then," I said. "Let's do this."

Chapter 34

"THEY TELL ME YOU'RE AN INVESTIGATOR," said the priest, hands folded behind his back. He stared at me through thick glasses.

"They tell me you're a crook," I said. Thin rope bound my wrists behind my back. Next to me, Beck sat slumped in her chair, her hands similarly bound. I was starting to not like priests very much.

A wry grin crossed the priest's swollen lip. He was a tall man with heavy rings on his long fingers and a frayed beard. He held himself like he was the guy in charge. Beck's idea of a conversation had apparently resembled my own, and by the look of it had ended us up in the same place. The fiberstone walls in this part of the church had a medieval feel, complete with a fibersteel barred window in the door.

The priest paced, and it grated on my nerves. "You come into Saint Lucy of the Light with the intention to steal information, you assault my acolytes, and now you wish to libel my good name? I think you might consider your situation, Mr. Demarco."

I wasn't sure how he knew my name, but several things concerned me more. "I don't think I caught your name," I said.

"Theodore Barton," said the man.

"Is stolen art something that concerns you? Sounds to me like you're awfully agnostic about the subject."

"This Church collects artifacts of art and the relics of its saints in order to preserve our culture. We have always done this."

"How do you know that? You've disposed of your archives."

"We've digitized our archives, preserved for all time." He stopped pacing, which made me even more nervous. "Paper decays and can be easily corrupted."

"And digital files can't? You're entrusting everything to Trinity?"

Beck snorted and sputtered in her sleep. When she shifted, I saw a red welt on her neck. Somebody had hit her with a stunstick.

Barton resumed his pacing. His hard-soled shoes were a steady drumbeat on the rock-solid floor. "Why do you think you're in this room?"

At first, his words made little sense to me. Then I looked around the room. "No Trinity sensors."

"Not a single one."

No Trinity meant no law. The Church had built its own little bubble where it could get away with anything. Trinity might know that people came into this room and bodies came out, but the strange idiosyncrasies of the AI meant nobody could be held accountable for what happened in here. Not that all that elaborate subterfuge was needed if all the priest wanted to do was kill me.

"What do you want?" I said.

"I want you to do your job." The smile on his face would have been frightening if not for the asymmetry of his swollen lip. "We'll pay, of course."

I tested my strength against the rope binding my wrists. "Why doesn't anyone ever ask nicely?"

"We're not going to kill you, Mr. Demarco. In fact, we're not interested in harming you in any way. Might I remind you that you were the one found sneaking around our catacombs?"

"What about her?" I nodded to Beck. "Are you going to tell me she's just sleepy from listening to your elaborate theological justifications?"

The priest absently touched his swollen lip. "Mr. Demarco, we know that you're interested in August Savior."

He knew about August. I wondered how much more he knew. "Go on."

The priest continued, "It occurs to the Church that a man of your talents might finally get to the bottom of a mystery we've been facing."

"You want leverage on Savior so you can get a better deal on his stolen art?"

Barton blinked quickly. "Not at all." Definitely at all. "In the several years since Mr. Savior has been in business, we've seen a marked decline in art originating from Earth finding its way into the colony. In that same period, there has been increased interest in such art."

"You think he's cutting you out of the illegal deals."

"Render unto Caesar, Mr. Demarco. I care not of the legality of the trade. What's made for God ought to be given to him."

"To you, you mean."

"To the Church. The Church safeguards the most precious artifacts of Christian history. Statues, paintings, even the bones of the saints."

"You must be very proud."

His swollen lip turned white when he clenched his jaw.

"Cut me loose, priest. You're looking for missing art. I'm looking for missing art and the guy who stole it. There's no reason to tie me up for this."

"My acolytes think otherwise."

"We exchanged some harsh words."

The priest cut the bindings with an ornamental knife. Blood

rushed to my hands, flooding them with pins and needles. When he finished freeing Beck, he said, "I trust you understand your situation."

"Sure." My gaze went to the pistol on the table, but the priest shook his head. "You won't be needing that."

"Things might get rough out there."

His expression flattened. "Mr. Demarco. I will absolutely not send you out armed with a gun and unaccountable for your actions. There is nothing Trinity will do to keep you from killing, and from what I have heard, a swath of death and destruction has followed you all the way up from the slums."

"And it'll follow me back down again if I can't stop it."

He gave a slight shake of his head. "Figure out where the art is going and learn how they're stealing it from this church. Then I'll give back your weapon."

"So, once you have what you want, the swath of destruction can continue?"

"There is an auction tonight," he said. "You will want to start there."

With that, I nudged Beck until she groggily woke. Together, with everything but that gun, we made our way out of the church and into the harsh flaming light of the Hallow Nicodemia day.

Chapter 35

"A LOT of people think the Catholic Church's reverence for saints is a kind of idolatry," I said, popping a grape into my mouth. The burst of sweetness exploded on my tongue.

Beck squinted in the harsh light. Even under the shaded canopy attached to an open-air restaurant, the brilliance of Hallow Nicodemia pierced even the best sunglasses. She nudged the fruit tray between us with a look of distaste on her full lips. "Is that what you believe?"

"I'm not a theologian," I said.

"You seemed pretty upset about how those boys back there felt about Trinity."

"Those *boys* are blurring the line between the AI and the divine."

"That's exactly what a theologian would say." Her eyes twinkled. She had recovered significantly since the ordeal of the Church, but if she didn't eat, she would fade fast.

I pushed the tray back over to her. "It's relevant to my situation."

"Is that what it takes to get an opinion out of you?" She warily nudged a strawberry with the tip of one painted fingernail.

"Those guys study theology their whole lives. Who am I to fight them if it doesn't really matter."

"But it *does* matter."

"I'm opinionated but uneducated."

"You think you're the worst kind of opinionated, then. Fair enough." She plucked a peach from the tray and bit into it. The juices dribbled from her lips and a laugh escaped as she tried to contain the mess. "I'm starting to understand why people like it here."

"Give me a bowl of noodles and a dark cafe any day," I said.

She took another bite and let the flesh of the peach linger on her tongue as if its flavor were the grace of God. "We don't have these on the ship. I think Violet is allergic."

"You gave up a lot to travel with her."

Beck took a huge bite of the peach, this time not even trying to stop the juices dribbling down her chin onto her plate. She didn't break eye contact with me until she swallowed. "You have no idea."

Heat rose in the back of my throat, and suddenly the suit that had fit so perfectly was suffocating me. Instead of responding, I searched the crowds passing by outside the restaurant, keeping an eye out for the stranger.

Amusement laced Beck's words when she finally spoke again. "Do you think Wash followed us up here?"

"I doubt he could gain access to the Hallows," I said without thinking. "Saint Jerome might have that kind of pull, but if Wash's on his own, then I don't think we need to worry about him as long as we're up here."

"Do you worry about your sister?"

Always. "She can handle herself."

"That's something, at least," she said. "You don't think he's working for Lauder?"

"I don't even know at this point." I met her heavy-lidded gaze. "We'll have to deal with him eventually."

"You will, maybe," she said. When she saw my curious expression, she said, "I'm an optimist, remember? I still think I can probably get away with the painting before he catches up to me."

Her words smothered my mood like a leaded blanket. "You're right," I said. "You'll probably be gone." The embers of old anger boiled in my belly, and I didn't even know why. It was all I could do to keep my voice steady. "That's the kind of person you are, aren't you?"

"What's that supposed to mean?" Her face went pale and gray and flat.

"Why did you leave Earth?"

"It's complicated."

"Life is complicated."

Beck gestured at the too-bright Hallows. "Why did you leave this place? They seem to welcome you back well enough. A guy like you could do well around these parts. A whole lot better than being crushed down in the Heavies." She leaned forward. "Or are you punishing yourself like Maurice?"

"I think you mean to say, 'Thank you for saving me back there,'" I snapped.

"If I'd had my gun—"

"Neither of us has a gun now," I snapped, as if it were her fault.

She held her palms out. "I'm not saying we need one."

"Sounds like you are."

Her attention shifted to the meandering crowds. "I had a rough time on Earth." She plucked a grape from the fruit tray and rolled it between two long fingernails, puncturing it slightly. "Ever since my father was killed…"

The hairs on the back of my neck bristled. With the hint about her past, I got the impression that she was trying to manipulate me, and something in me hated it. But when *wasn't* she trying to manipulate me? After all, I was supposed to be working for her. Her whole job was convincing me to help her out.

Again, I wondered why.

"The priest is right," I said. "We won't need a gun for what we're doing."

She popped the grape into her mouth. "I hope not." Again, she watched me through half-lidded eyes. "For your sake."

"The auction is in the warehouse district behind Saint Lucy's," I said.

Her expression grew so serious I thought she might be mocking me. "We seem to spend a lot of time back there."

"This time it's for the job," I said, remembering Retch and his secret home. "I promise. I'm done with distractions."

She ate another grape, chewing it slowly, extracting every possible molecule of pleasure from it. "Are you sure?"

I wanted to tell her that I knew the second I had stepped into Hallow Nicodemia that this could never be my home again. I felt it in my bones. It could never offer answers that would satisfy my curiosity. I'd never find any justification for the way my parents were killed, and I'd never find the connection of friends and family that I'd once only found here. My sister lived down in Heavy Nicodemia. She was happy there. That was my family. She was my connection to a life that had otherwise rejected me. I wanted to tell Beck all of this and confess to her that I didn't give one good goddamn about this whole place or the people in it.

But I couldn't. All I said was, "Let's find that painting."

With that, we pushed the plate aside, paid our bill with a scattering of dimes, and allowed ourselves to be swallowed in the afternoon crowds of Hallow Nicodemia.

"Do you know the problem with being an optimist?" I asked.

She raised an eyebrow.

I pointed up at the sky, where the harsh sunlight was starting to fade. "It doesn't matter how much of an optimist you are," I said. "When it's going to rain, it's going to rain."

Chapter 36

RAIN IN HALLOW Nicodemia was infuriatingly pleasant. Fat raindrops fell through Hallow Nicodemia's orange sunset glow. Beck pressed her body close to mine under a black umbrella, her ivory skin glowing against the encroaching darkness.

"This isn't so bad," she murmured.

She was right, of course. Rain in the Hallows wasn't anything like rain in the Heavies. A warm, almost pleasant spatter of rain watered the lush plants and cleaned the streets. Many of the residents ignored the rain, preferring the refreshing embrace of cool water to the inconvenience of carrying an umbrella or rushing for cover.

We approached a castle. According to the locals, it had been converted from a warehouse many years ago. By a coincidence that could only be attributed to a divine sense of humor, this castle sat in the same location as the warehouse where Retch made his home and where we had risked our lives on Beck's cycle.

"We keep ending up here," I said.

"Maybe it's fate."

The air was warm to me, as it always had in Hallow

Nicodemia. Warm, humid, and full of the oppressive odor of a thriving ecosystem. Ivy grew up around the castle before us, and the grounds surrounding it featured red stone paths through lush gardens. Lights in the front of the mock castle flickered as if made of real flame. They welcomed travelers from a long journey, like the glow of a lantern in an inn.

Others were gathering in the castle. One by one and sometimes in pairs, tall, dark figures converged upon the heavy wooden doors. Each spoke through the small window, and each, in turn, was granted access.

Beck said, "Too bad the secret side entrance isn't there in this version."

It was the first thing we'd checked. The building's modifications were extensive, and the stone façade covered anything that might have resembled a poorly configured wall joint.

I said, "We're better off if they know we're here."

"Not if the painting's in there somewhere."

"We'll deal with that later."

Beck pulled back. "You're really going to do what that priest wanted?"

"Are you talking about the priest you punched in the face?"

"It was a kind of prayer." She pulled close again. A fit of shivers ran through her body.

"Are you sure you don't need another infusion of synthblood? It's not cold here."

"The priest's goons hit me with something to knock me out," she said. "I think this is just an aftereffect."

We made our way through the garden, lingering to enjoy a cluster of flowering hibiscus. It had been so long since I'd been in a real garden. The closest Heavy Nicodemia had was a few glossy green shrubs in the fancy districts and some stunted trees that struggled against the gravity. Hallow Nicodemia had the corner on the plant market. Heavy Nicodemia got fish.

It wasn't a great deal.

Rows of nicotine flowers opened as the sky grew dark. Great, purple inflorescence broke under the heavy raindrops, the scent spreading like a thick haze. It was a beautiful thing, and it reminded me of home.

But this wasn't home. Not anymore. The lighter gravity made my stomach churn, and I bounced a little too much. It made everything feel off.

As we approached the door, the little window opened. "Guests?"

"Friends," I said. "On behalf of Lucy."

The window closed and the door opened. A man with a bushy goatee ushered us inside. He stood several inches shorter than Beck, and if my eye was correct, he bore the gravity like a native of Haven. He took our umbrella and helped Beck out of her coat. I kept mine.

"Keeps me warm," I said. I didn't want anyone to see that I'd bled on the blue undershirt. Also, the suit coat looked good on me. It's hard to give up something like that. Instead, I gave him my bowler.

The outside of the building resembled a castle, but the inside resembled one open courtyard. Above, a false daytime sky shone blue around a great yellow orb of a sun. Below, people mingled in open spaces, sitting on the scattered benches or walking along meandering paths. A fountain bubbled happily in the center of the dust-strewn yard, and small trees provided shade. The light ached in the back of my eyes.

Beck remained unbothered. "Let's split up," she said, strength returning to her voice. "Work the crowd a little."

"Don't ask anyone about *The Garden of Earthly Delights* yet," I said. "Just try to gain their confidence and engage in small talk."

She scrunched up her nose. "Small talk?"

"Trust me. These people know when it's appropriate to do business. Before the auction isn't that time." I watched the crowd for a moment. It reminded me of the times my father had taken me to his business events. "My father used to always say that the most interesting deals happened after."

Without another word, Beck wandered to a group of women and her charm drew her into the fold as if she'd always belonged there.

"Beverage, sir?" A young woman stood next to me with a tray of tiny glasses.

I took a tumbler of whiskey and sipped. The smokey undertones were obliterated by smokey overtones. I still hated it. The flavors lingered in my mouth as I walked through the garden. At the first chance, I swapped it for a fruity white wine, feeling the flavor and memory wash over me with a wave of sweetness.

How far had I come since that day the *Benevolent* crashed?

The next hour passed in a haze. Rumors bubbled to the surface of the conversations again and again. The Lancasters had a daughter who had decided to travel rather than fulfill her familial duties. The Howards got caught in the market crash. Oxygen levels were good, but everyone agreed that the help coming up from the lower two nodes was subpar, and quality had been steadily dropping.

"They're just not very good at managing their economy down there," said a heavyset woman with a flowing violet dress and matching hairpins. She was the very model of Hallows beauty, plus about ten years. "We give them as much freedom as we can, but who's going to scoop them up again when they crash their markets and can't afford to keep a stable society? One must wonder what their Trinity even thinks community is?"

"They don't have our appreciation for art," I said, tipping my glass at the far end of the courtyard, where various works were displayed. "Here, our community thrives because we value art. Down below, all they care about is work." The words tasted like ash on my tongue. These were the kind of lies people up here were too likely to believe.

"As they should, I suppose," said the woman. "It seems that

many of them work, but nobody thinks about what they're working on. Shouldn't they be working on expanding food production to meet the growing population? Who is managing their technology industry?"

"Nobody, it seems," I said, hardly paying attention to the conversation.

"Exactly. They require a stronger influence from above. From us."

Her words caught my attention not because of their content but because of the intent she placed in the words. She wasn't spouting the idle ideas of an upper crust aristocrat. This woman in her violet dress actually advocated stronger control over the lower districts. The idea reeked of danger and should never be allowed to fester.

"They do well enough." I drained the last sips from my glass. "You'll have to excuse me. I have a painting or two calling to me."

We bid our goodbyes, and I left with a lingering sense of abstract dread. Her words bothered me, and even if she had the best intentions, her lack of understanding Heavy or Haven culture would cause problems if the Hallows ever went down that road.

But that was how it went, wasn't it? The upper echelons of society always misunderstood those beneath them, starting with the idea that those other societies were *beneath* anything. Not that they were alone in this belief. How much better would McCay's life have been if he had only learned to truly see the problems of those higher up the chain? Instead, he had idolized them, and it had gotten him killed.

I picked up another glass of wine on my way through the crowd. The courtyard wasn't packed by any means, but crossing from one side to the other meant picking my way carefully past small clusters of guests. They chattered about art and culture and moaned about their servants and praised their own brilliant leadership. It brought me back to my childhood. As a teen I'd been forced to attend more than one of these little functions, and the memory of it refused to go away, no matter how much wine I drank. Wine was good, after all, but it took something stronger to flush away the past.

A fedora in the crowd caught my eye then disappeared behind a group. The stranger was here. Doing my best to avoid tipping him off, I worked my way in his direction. Circling a group, I meandered along a stone path between a koi pond and a hedge row of currants and viburnum. I leaned close to the blooming viburnum and sniffed a flower. It had no scent, but I closed my eyes and tried my best to look like it brought me peace.

The angle from bending down got me a better look at the man. It was him, all right. The bastard wore a pinstripe suit with a matching fedora and looked good in it. Dangerous. When I'd seen him outside the gambling hall, he'd been disheveled and lumpy. In the flyer, he'd worn a tan overcoat and looked as plain as a man could look. This man at the auction bore himself like the upper of the upper crust. Like royalty.

He moved away, pointedly wandering a zigzag path. The pattern was clear, however. He was aiming for the exit. He maintained a calm demeanor, and so did I. Keeping my pace without purpose, I followed him.

Then, he hopped a short hedge between paths, a social faux pas if I ever saw one. I strode after, but I kept my steps on the designated path.

"Excuse me," a woman said at my elbow. She wanted me to stop to chat, but I didn't have time.

"Sorry, Miss," I said with as much propriety as I could manage. "I see someone I absolutely must speak with before I leave."

She huffed and let me go, but the distraction had been too much.

Where was he? He'd worked his way into a group of three men wearing brightly colored tuxedoes. I recognized them as the Vincent triplets, and though they didn't look anything alike, they all had the stature of pure-bred Travelers. They dwarfed the man I was after, but soon as I spotted him, he took his leave.

The distance between us closed. He was only a dozen paces from the door, but a steady stream of guests was still pouring inside. I needed to catch him before he left. He needed to get out through a crowd flowing in the wrong direction.

Discretion was my friend, but not my boss. I raised a hand and opened my mouth to hail the man.

"Mr. Demarco?" interrupted a man's voice behind me.

I turned to see a man in a scarlet suit and matching tinted glasses. He wore a scarlet top hat and carried a black cane topped with a ruby larger than any I'd ever seen. His smile deepened the creases in the corners of his eyes.

It was Trey Vitez.

"August Savior," said the man, sticking out his hand for a shake. "You may call me Augie."

The man in the fedora bolted, pushing his way out and through the incoming crowd. I'd lost him again.

I shook Vitez's hand in my massive paw. "Pleasure," I said. "It's nice to meet someone who takes such an interest in art."

"Where I come from, we have a saying: Art is the body and soul of the community."

His words were like a fist of ice over my heart. I'd only ever heard one person say that, and I'd be willing to bet it wasn't from anywhere Vitez had come from. The last time I'd heard that saying was years ago when my father talked to me about forcing me to yet another art gallery party. He had spent hours teaching me about the value of the statues, even as I persisted in ignoring him as only a teenage boy can. "Art is the body and soul of a community," he had said, echoing the "Body, Soul, Community" of Trinity's triple directive. At the time it didn't occur to me how important his use of those words was. Now, the inkling of its value scratched at the back of my brain.

But Vitez had used the same phrase as my father. I might never know who had originated the saying, but was it possible Vitez knew my parents? Was it possible they dealt with the illegal art scene?

Was it possible they were involved in manipulating Trinity?

"We have a lot of catching up to do, Mr. Demarco," Vitez said.

I didn't doubt him one bit.

Chapter 37

"I'VE WANTED to meet you for a long time, Mr. Demarco," Vitez said. "A long time."

We walked through the catacombs beneath the castle, where dimly lit walls were lined with art from across the ages. It should have been maintenance tunnels this deep, but wealth warps the very world around it.

Beck was at my elbow, and Vitez led a leisurely stroll through one grand arch after another. I could sense her pain in her stiff movements, but she otherwise hid her injuries well.

"You look just like your father, you know," said Vitez.

"So, you knew him," I said, pausing to take in a Renaissance painting of a mother and child. Mary and Jesus watched me with shining eyes. Two old men flanked the mother of God, and two fat cherubs lazed about near her feet.

"I visited Nicodemia when I was a young, adventurous man," said Vitez.

Beck's grip tightened, but she said nothing. Such a trip would have taken years, and even a man with enormous disposable wealth and a lot of time on his hands would balk at such a trip. Beck herself was in the middle of a similar trip, and I wondered what toll it took on her.

"You own all this art?" I asked.

Vitez waved a hand dismissively. "I did a stint as a collector, but now I mostly connect collectors with suppliers."

Without much interest in keeping things legal, I thought. "This painting of Mary. Is it Raphael Sanzio?"

His eyes brightened. "It is! I see you have some of your father's interest in the arts?"

"Not always willingly."

The next room opened into a wide, arched ceiling. At first, the space was dark, with only the floor illuminated by a trickle of ambient lighting. By degrees, the light increased, and the ceiling became visible.

"Is this a replica of the Sistine Chapel?" Beck asked, audibly impressed.

Vitez took a moment to gaze at the ceiling. The fresco depicted the creation of humanity and Earth in bright, powerful detail. "A near-perfect imitation. I'm afraid we've done some extemporaneous repair to parts of the image lost during the bombings of World Wars Two and Four."

"Those even-numbered World Wars were the worst," I said.

Beck scrunched her nose as she studied the painting. "Is it really like this in the Vatican? It's so bright."

Vitez laughed. "Well, not anymore. The original collapsed years ago. If anyone wants anything like the real experience, they'll just have to visit us here in Nicodemia."

I stared at Vitez, trying to decide if he was joking. "This is open to the public?"

"Once the displays are properly secured, this will be a fantastic museum for the people of Nicodemia."

Hallow Nicodemia, he meant. "It's not secure?"

"There's Trinity, of course, but we all know how fallible that system can be." He gestured at the paintings on the walls. "No, we'll add more layers of security before really opening things up."

Beck detached from my arm and strolled through the room, all the while staring at the ceiling.

"Trinity does a fine job," I said.

"You're living proof it's not quite good enough."

He had a point. "Some would say art like this should go to the Church."

Vitez laughed. "Saint Lucy's isn't any more secure, and from what I hear, you figured that out already too."

"From what I hear, so have you."

For a flicker of a second, his blue eyes went dull, the wrinkles at their corners flattening. He looked away from me, suddenly fascinated by the painting of Mary and her son. He folded his hands behind his back and stood perfectly still for a long time.

The silence shattered under the full force of an alarm siren. Red lights blared and a garbled voice came over the audio system.

Beck pulled back, hands raised. "Sorry. Just wanted to see the next room."

"It's fine, it's fine," Vitez said, rushing to her side. He opened a panel in the wall and punched in a code. When the alarm went silent, he said to Beck, "I'm afraid the sensors are a bit sensitive."

Beck pressed a palm to her chest. "It's a bit startling, isn't it?"

"It's off now." Vitez waved at a couple of guards who had appeared at the door, and they disappeared back up the stairs. "No more disturbances, I promise."

Beck walked back to me and took hold of my arm. The warmth of her hands burned, even through my suit coat. An impish smile flashed across her red lips. "I'll behave."

"This way," Vitez said, leading another direction. We have more than Renaissance art down here. I have a wide selection of found object art from the early 2000s, and a small selection of the incredible bronzeworks of Olympia Freeman."

The name dislodged a memory of my father's lectures about

art. "I've heard that improved techniques allowed Freeman to make more statues during the second half of the twenty-first century than all of the previous three centuries combined."

Vitez's smile filled his whole face. "Very good! You remember your art history."

The lights of the next room came on in a flash, revealing bronze depictions both large and small. Centaurs bedecked in American Civil War garb fought tigers with long, wicked claws. Fairies danced above the corpses of fallen soldiers. Men and women stood in protest in front of the bronze façades of banks and churches. The entire scene encapsulated the tumultuous years that preceded Nicodemia's journey into space. These statues were part of our shared history and held lessons for our shared future.

Vitez only smiled. "Prolific doesn't even start to describe Freeman and her acolytes, but many wrongly believe mass manufacturing to be the source of that increase in production. In truth, it had more to do with passion. Each piece is unique, with its own message and its own burning desire to make the world a better place."

"The Artistic Bronze Age," I said, remembering the lesson.

"Correct. Statues of the earlier ages were replaced with these new bronze visions of the future."

"It's amazing," Beck said. "And you transported all of this out here when you came?"

"Oh no," Vitez said. "These were brought out here over the years." He nodded to me. "I only wish your father would have seen the look on my face when I saw this display he'd assembled."

I blinked, but my eyes blurred with tears. My father had created this collection. I never knew. "My father was an asshole."

The sparkle returned to Vitez's eyes. "He was a brilliant artist and an even more brilliant curator. When he said something had artistic worth, he was always right. We stayed in contact after my visit to Nicodemia. Our correspondence over the years was a lesson in the entire artistic history of both Earth and the colonies."

His words described my entire childhood. An art lesson. "Tell me, then, what was the deal you made with him? You send art and he sends you—what?"

Beck answered for him. "Art. Poetry. Media. Earth is as fascinated with colony culture as this colony is with Earth. I've seen some of the work coming out of this place and others. It's different. Raw. It speaks of experiences we only dream of back on Earth."

Vitez grinned. "It's enough to inspire a person to make the trip to the stars, isn't it, my dear?"

Beck rolled her eyes. "I am here in a purely professional capacity."

His expression fell. "I do hope you're able to enjoy your stay."

She looked up at me and said, "The company's interesting."

I didn't know what she meant, but something bothered me about what Vitez had said. "Let me get this straight. You send art here via freighter because it's the cheapest way to safely transport your treasures. My father maintained your property here, getting it ready for your retirement. Meanwhile he'd send you art from Nicodemia's best and you'd use that to fund your purchase of more of Earth's treasures?"

Vitez led us into the next room without a word. Marble statuary stood on the fiberstone floors of reconstructed temples. At the center of the room, a worn milk-white statue of a beautiful woman lounged with its eyes cast at the entrance. It was only upon venturing farther into the room that the figure's hermaphroditic nature became apparent. Upon further inspection, its expression was more mischievous than enticing.

"With all that legitimate business happening, when did you have time to steal anything?" I asked, figuring it might as well come out straight.

He shook his head disapprovingly. "I prefer the term *rescued.*" He gestured to Beck. "Your friend here can confirm that the nations of Earth are in disarray. Art is being destroyed by the truck-load, and if—"

"Yeah, you're a real hero," I said. "Funny how it made you so rich."

"Demarco," Beck said, a warning in her voice.

"Sorry," I said. "You're right. It's no business of mine."

Vitez spread his hands wide. "I'm not wealthy, you know. It might appear like wealth, but I'm the steward of something very important here. I tend the treasures of old Earth, and my legacy will last a thousand years."

"Sounds like wealth to me." I looked at a statue of Laocoön with snakes biting him and his sons. "Maybe you're not like the Travelers here, but you've got something they don't."

"What's that?"

"Purpose. You're bending the rules of this place, and you don't care if it breaks everything as long as your precious art gets preserved."

Vitez smiled, but this time his eyes remained cold. "Guilty as charged."

We didn't speak for a long time, the silence stretching through Vitez's museum as we walked through one display after another. He had ages of human history gathered in the place, displayed as if in a public museum. The lack of patrons rang strange in such a place. It was a public museum designed for one person only.

Or, maybe for two.

"When did you learn of my father's death?"

Vitez's voice was quiet when he spoke, but the acoustics of the space made his words travel. "He was silent for a long time before I came out here. It worried me, but I didn't learn his fate until after I arrived."

"You came because you were worried your museum's art would fall into the wrong hands." A thought occurred to me. "It already had, hadn't it?"

He answered, but I wasn't listening because thoughts raced through my head. Of course, that's what had happened. When my father wasn't around anymore, nobody managed the museum's collection. Saint Lucy started picking up pieces of religious-themed art for their own archive. Under the pretense of preserving Christian lore, they became complicit in the robbery and financial dismemberment of the legal organization of Vitez's museum. One way or the other, they acquired his art. When Vitez finally arrived in Nicodemia to take control of his property, he found it missing some vital pieces.

That's when the church started getting burglarized. Vitez couldn't stand the idea of giving up his art, so he arranged to have it stolen back.

That's where the clever bit came in. Vitez wasn't just a thief. He was a painter. Maurice had mentioned that his abilities as a painter gave him a light touch as a pilot. It wasn't much of a stretch to pin Vitez as a master forger. He donated back to the Church, but instead of giving them the originals, he gave them the fakes.

These thoughts ran through my head as I stood in front of Salvador Dalí's seven-foot-tall *Christ of Saint John of the Cross*, and as closely as I looked, I could not see the difference between this version and the version in the basement of Saint Lucy of the Light. They were the same down to the small damage in one corner and the scuff marks on the golden frame.

"The perfect forgery," I said.

"Nonsense," Vitez said. "I would know."

"What happened on that last job, Vitez?" I said. "The one for *The Garden of Earthly Delights*." In the corner of my eye, I saw Beck tense. "Why did you try to back out at the last second?"

Vitez's face grew dark again, and his pinched cheeks deepened until he looked ten years older. "That was a long time ago."

"To some."

Vitez stared at me with cold calculation. "Your father never cared about how the art was acquired."

"I'm not my father."

"Who hired you, Mr. Demarco?"

"I like to keep that between myself and my client."

"You're the one who's been following me these past few weeks?" In a fluid movement, he drew a small iridescent blue pistol and pointed it at me. "You think you'll get me that easily?"

I blinked. "What?"

"That's right. I know you've been following me. I've got eyes everywhere, remember, unlike the complacent idiots of this node, I'm not dependent on Trinity for everything."

"Who paid you to get *The Garden*? Who were you working for?"

"That was a long time ago," he snapped. "She's long gone by now."

"Vitez," I said, raising my open palms, "we're not here to—"

"My name is Savior," he spat. "August Savior. You will not use that other name. That man no longer exists." He backed up and an elevator opened where I hadn't seen a door at all. He gestured with his pistol. "Get in."

I didn't have any particular desire to step into his box. "You got this all wrong, Savior."

Vitez spun on Beck, who had moved too close. "You too," he said. "In."

She shot me a questioning look.

"I don't care about the forgeries," I said. "In fact, I'm impressed. Your forgeries are an art all themselves. Your Sistine Chapel is stunning. *Christ of Saint John of the Cross* is staggering. All I want to know is where the third panel of *The Garden of Earthly Delights* is. The real one."

His eyes widened, and he took another step back. His lips pulled back against his too-white teeth, and his posture became oddly defensive. Wary. He jabbed the gun at Beck. "Who sent you?"

"Leave her alone, Augie," I said.

Beck was the picture of calm. She said nothing.

I raised my hands even higher and showed my palms. "It seems like longer, but she's only been in Nicodemia a few days. She wasn't following you, and neither was I. I've been in the Heavies for years."

"How do I know that?"

"Ask Trinity if you want," I said. "Don't trust the machine? Do you want to know what she did on her second day here? There was this kid. His name is Retch." Beck nodded. "He's a tough kid, living on the streets down there in the Heavies. He lives off the city, and I'd wager his art would be something you could put right here next to these Earth classics. They're every bit on the pulse of human life as Dalí or van Gogh. Every bit as beautiful."

Vitez took another step back. Beck watched his eyes like an owl watching a mouse.

"Thing is, Retch is a passionate kid. You talk about the passion of artists throughout the ages? Well, this kid's got some feelings. We were in a bit of an argument when Beck found us. Do you remember that, Beck?"

"Yeah," she said. Her voice was low and smooth, flattened out by her tension.

"That was really something," I said. "Kid had a gun on me." I took a step forward. "Just like you, Vitez."

Vitez raised his gun, aiming at my chest. "Savior."

"Thing is, Vitez," I said, hoping Beck's injury wouldn't slow her down too much. "The lady's quicker than you would think anyone in high heels could be."

With a crack, Beck closed the distance and landed a solid strike to the side of Vitez's head. He hit the floor like a bag of bricks.

Beck spun on me. "He could have killed you," she hissed.

I raised my hands in surrender. "He didn't have it in him."

"You *know* he's killed before."

"There's a look people get in their eyes when they're ready to pull a trigger. Vitez didn't have it. I don't know what his history is, but this life has made him soft." I kicked the gun, and it skittered across the hard floor. "He's not dangerous."

Vitez stirred.

"He is if he wakes and triggers the alarm," said Beck.

She was right, but something didn't settle quite right. "It should have already triggered. An attack like that?" But, no. He had disabled the security system.

Beck pursed her lips. "You need to give us some cover. Go let the guards know Vitez and I will be a little longer."

"You're still looking for the painting?"

Her brows knit in a pleading expression. "I need to look, Demarco. We're so close, and if we run now, he's going to lock this place down. I know it."

"Why don't you talk to the guards? I'll have a look around." It would be easier for me to slip away unnoticed. Maybe.

Beck pressed her red lips into a hard line. "What do you think is easier to believe? That Vitez wanted to spend time alone with you?" She spread her arms, displaying her still-stunning dress. "Or with me?"

"I was hired to find that painting."

"By me," she snapped. Vitez stirred again, and Beck flashed him a look of disgust and anger. "As your boss, I'm telling you to beat it. Give me some cover."

The intensity of her anger shocked me, but she was right. If she was going to find that painting, she'd need time. And I was the only one who could buy it for her. Without another word, I walked away into the dark.

Chapter 38

BY THE TIME I stepped back into the main courtyard, the auction was well underway. The auctioneer displayed a golden device that looked like a sextant that ancient Earth seafarers might have used to find their way under the stars. The device was utterly useless in Nicodemia, which made it quite valuable. I watched the bids rise as irritation spread like ants under my skin.

"Savior wants to be undisturbed," I told the first guard I saw. "For a while, he said."

She rolled her eyes. She was a petite woman. Severe but pretty in her own way. Apparently, the scenario was not unheard of.

I figured Beck wouldn't find *The Garden of Earthly Delights*. The more I thought about it, the more I was convinced that Vitez didn't have it. His reaction wasn't right. What bothered me more was Vitez's connection to my father. Had Violet Ruiz known about that connection when she'd insisted on hiring me? There were connections all over the place and I couldn't see the pattern they made.

That left me idly wondering about the rest of what we'd learned. Someone had been following Vitez. Could that be the same guy who had caught up to me in Haven? It felt likely, though

I couldn't pinpoint why. If that was true, maybe that guy was still around the auction. I'd very much like a chat, but with bidding underway, I couldn't question the other guests.

Now, my best bet was to ask the staff and find any clues he might have dropped.

At the front door, the bouncer still waited by the windowed door. He tipped his hat as I approached. "Leaving already, sir?"

"Did you see a fella come this way about an hour ago?"

"Quite a few, yes."

"A guy with a fedora."

He took off his hat and scratched his head. "Can't say that I did."

Figures.

Outside, starlight and a false double moon lit the garden paths. Here in the Hallows, even the nights were uncommonly bright. The dark was enough to cloak the tips of grasping trees in shadows, but not enough to hide the searing lump of guilt in my belly.

Beck was putting herself at an unnecessary risk. Everything in my gut told me the painting wasn't there, but what happened when Vitez woke? If she wasn't careful, he would reactivate the security and Beck would be in a mess of trouble. I remembered the look on her face when she looked down at him. She'd been upset—more upset than I had ever seen her.

Even if she found the painting, she couldn't move it out of there on her own. All she could do was find it and report back to her boss. Ruiz could certainly figure out a legal way to return the painting to its rightful owners, whoever that might be. She might even be able to gain temporary custody of it.

The Garden of Earthly Delights wasn't going to shatter the world if it disappeared forever. Nobody would mourn its loss except for a few art fanatics.

My father would have mourned. He would have raged for a full day if he heard I hadn't done everything I could to recover the painting. I'd never thought much about his job when he was alive.

He had tried to share his passion with me, but he had hidden that he curated his own private museum full of stolen artifacts. That he was a dealer of both legitimate and stolen art. That he had a contact on Earth who sent him illicit goods in the hope of one day coming to Nicodemia to live out his days.

Beck didn't care about any of this. What was she there for? The painting? She'd be there for hours looking for a painting that Vitez didn't have. The look in his eyes when I mentioned it told me everything I needed to know.

No, not everything.

A shadow moved in the garden. A glint of moonlight caught the shape of a battered fedora.

I patted my suit pockets and found a pack of cigarettes. Lighting one, I gazed up into the moonlight, keeping the man's shadow in the corner of my eye in case he made another move. The smoke lingered around my head, hanging heavy in the post-rain humidity.

I needn't have bothered with the subterfuge.

The familiar scent of cedar and lemon alerted me to the stranger's presence a second before he announced himself with the crackle of a stunstick. "Thought I warned you to back off." He stepped forward and the light of my cigarette fell across the deep creases of his face. Even in the dim light, I could see the half-moon of a black eye poorly concealed under makeup.

A drag of acid smoke burned my lungs. "Vitez is sitting on half the Smithsonian down there, but a fistful of dimes says he doesn't have *The Garden of Earthly Delights*."

"I could kill you right now. Nobody's here. Trinity doesn't care if you live or die."

"Here's the thing, though." I turned to look him full in the face. "I don't think this is about a painting. This lingering feeling that there's something more at play keeps cropping up. Did you know Vitez is making forgeries down there and donating them?"

This didn't elicit any reaction from the stranger, except possibly for the deepening of the creases at the corners of his mouth. Somewhere, an owl called in the night.

"There's history here that I'm not privy to," I said, "and it bothers me like a loose tooth. How do you fit into all this? Vitez, my father, Ruiz, even Ribar down at the bottom of the Heavies. They're all connected. All part of the same scheme. But what do you have to do with any of this?"

"You're asking the wrong kind of questions, kid. Making it real hard for me not to end this conversation the hard way."

I took another drag on the cigarette. "It ends or it doesn't. I'm just looking for answers."

"There's a play for power going on that's got nothing to do with that painting." He circled out of reach. "Frank Lauder's coming after Saint Jerome, and I've been hired to keep an eye on you. Lauder thinks you're the Saint's main killer."

"I'd hardly call myself a killer." I showed him my palms. "I'm not even armed."

"Big man like you hardly needs to carry a weapon to be considered dangerous. Just ask Lawrence McCay."

"McCay? What's he got to do with this?"

"You tell me. Fella was a client of mine for two years. One of my first contacts on this bead. You show up one day and the next he's dead."

"It wasn't me."

"Sounds like a song I've heard sung before."

"What did you do to get excommunicated?" A rude question, but manners go out the window at the crackling end of a stunstick.

The stranger twitched. "There aren't a lot of rules I won't break, and having no rules at all makes this whole thing easier."

"Meaning?"

"I heard you killed your parents to earn the ultimate punishment."

That hurt, but I did my best to hide it. My best probably wasn't much good, because a hint of a smile crossed his face. I said, "I couldn't have saved them."

"That's not what the records say. Records say you had plenty of chance. The controls were up and active. All you had to do was keep the ship connected. Instead, you blew the seals."

"Saving Haven Nicodemia."

"Maybe."

He was right. I fought a shudder deep in my chest. "It wasn't a risk I could take."

"Most kids would do whatever it took to save the ones they love. Either you didn't love them, or you made a hell of a sacrifice that day."

The image flashed in front of my eyes again, bright as the day it happened. The screen with the release in bright red. The big choice. Tear open half the ship by releasing the bad link or take the risk that the gate would hold and allow the passengers of the ship a chance to escape.

It wasn't a choice. It was a goddamn tragedy. "You don't know a damn thing about it," I said.

"No," he said. "I wasn't there. All I have is what Trinity kept of the record." His accent changed timber and cadence. I'd heard that accent recently.

"You're from Earth," I said.

He smiled. "Sure am. It's easy enough to pick up a Nicodemia accent." This time he spoke with a pure Hallows accent, with lingering vowels and lazy trailing consonants. "Amazing what an accent and a few local sayings can do to help a person blend into a new society. Languages have always been a hobby of mine, and picking up accents is fascinating."

"How long have you been here?"

"Long enough."

My cigarette neared its end, so I dropped it and stepped it out. Once it was cold, I picked it up and flicked it at the nearest recycler.

"Trinity doesn't like a litterer, does it," the stranger said.

"Trinity doesn't much care how folks like you and I litter. Part of the punishment, I guess. We don't exist."

That got a chuckle out of the man. "You still haven't figured it out, have you?"

"Figured what out?"

"It's not a punishment at all. Trinity excommunicated you because it trusts you." He nodded at the trashcan. "Looks to me like it was right."

"Bullshit."

He shrugged. "Hey, it's all in the code."

I took an involuntary step back. If what he said was true... If that could *possibly* be true, then everything I knew about my situation was turned on its head. Was it possible that I wasn't a person punished for a crime, but a person being rewarded for my loyalty? What did this mean for the other excommunicated people out there? What did it mean for the Church, which increasingly considered religious excommunication and AI excommunication to be the same thing?

"The generation ship's original design had a dozen handymen per bead. Those people were exempt from the normal AI operations so they'd be able to bypass what they needed to help keep the ship's systems in balance. They could retrain the AI if the parameters got out of whack, or they could access forbidden sections of the ship. They'd be able to do whatever they needed, even murder, if it was required to fix the closed community."

It almost made sense, but I couldn't believe it. "They'd have to be the most trusted members of society."

"That's the problem, isn't it? Trust."

"Always has been."

"Like when you tell a man to back off for his own good. That seems like something a trustworthy man would do." He raised his stunstick. It crackled with what I suspected was an overcharged killing pulse.

"If you're going to kill me, then kill me." I raised my hands. No use giving him the satisfaction of claiming self-defense. Something occurred to me. "If you're excommunicated, does that mean you're trustworthy too?" It seemed such a stretch that Trinity would trust someone from Earth.

"That what you think is going on here?" he said. "Kid, I'm not like you. I didn't kill my parents to earn the ship's dubious trust. There are other paths to greatness, you know. There are better ways to make a living around here."

"Such as?"

He patted his pocket. "I'm a computer guy, Demarco. Always have been. The right lines of code in the right place can do wonders to win a little trust with the machine."

"Even when it's not deserved."

"Especially when it's not deserved." He swallowed hard. Sweat glinted on his brow in the moonlight. The stunstick shook almost imperceptibly in his hand. "I'm sorry, Demarco," he said.

"It is what it is," I said.

He thumbed the stunstick controls and jammed the business end into my gut.

The ground rushed up to hit me, and everything went black.

Chapter 39

I WOKE to a sound like chattering geese. It took me a while to realize the honking and sputtering formed hushed words. Voices swirled through the fog of my addled brain, sickening me. I turned to one side and wretched hard, producing nothing of substance. A crust on my suit coat and the taste in my mouth told me it wasn't the first time I'd suffered this reaction. Common thing after getting hit with a stunstick.

The events flooded back into my head. The stranger. Beck. Vitez. I needed to do something, but the details slipped from my brain like sand through fingers.

Shrubbery surrounded me. The stranger could have killed me, but instead, he knocked me out and dumped me in the thicket. How long had I been out? It felt like days.

Darkness still wrapped the hazy garden, and the moons had only moved a fraction of their journey across the false sky. Ten minutes? An hour? My whole body ached.

Stunsticks are a kick to the organs, only the kick hits every organ simultaneously. The heart stutters and lungs flail. A person's lucky to avoid a full release of the bowels in all relevant directions.

As I cleaned myself as best I could, the final effect of the stunstick hit me, and it was the worst of them all.

It is the profound effect of the modern stunstick that sends a person down a long spiral of self-doubt. What had I done to put myself in that position? What kind of fool had I been? Most people live their whole lives without experiencing the gut-twisting agony of a stunstick. Why wasn't that me? What would it be like to be married, hold a regular job, and accrue Karma like a good citizen of Nicodemia?

The stranger's words returned in a mad jumble. He thought I wasn't being punished? He was a damn fool. Trinity didn't need me any more than I needed Trinity. We were separate. Excommunication works both ways, after all. Neither talked to the other. Neither gave a damn.

But I *did* give a damn. I'd help the citizens of this damn ark till the day it crashed into the sun. I'd answer questions for people— hard questions—because they needed answering.

The painting wasn't in Vitez's basement. I was sure of it. That question had been answered.

Almost.

Almost wasn't good enough. Doubt crept down my spine like a bad memory. Giving up on my fancy coat and shirt, I stripped down to an undershirt and pants. It was a rough look, resembling Frank Lauder's thugs down in Heavy Nicodemia. My bowler went too. A bowler was a chump's hat, and I'd had enough of feeling like a chump for one night.

I emerged from the hedge when the coast was clear. Flowing clusters of chattering guests migrated from one end of the garden to the other, taking in the artistry of the exceptionally maintained space. Branches scratched my bare arms, but I pushed through anyway. No use slowing down. Once through, I paused to get my bearings. The auction must have only recently ended, because the bulk of the crowd was still reluctant to leave the grounds. That made my job easy.

The bouncer at the entrance recognized me. "Mr. Demarco," he said in his reedy voice. "We're currently ushering guests into the garden for a toast."

"I'll be just a minute," I rasped, brushing past him. "Need to use the facilities." The words tasted strange on my numb lips.

They must have sounded odd to the guard too, because he signaled a couple of his buddies with a flick of one finger.

Elbowing backwards through the flowing crowd, I ducked to avoid them, but it didn't last. The crowd thinned, and in the open room, I had nothing to do but talk or run.

"What the hell am I doing?" I muttered to myself. It was one thing to sneak into an auction as a spy. Quite another thing to push past guards and run even when they said to stop.

And the guards said it pretty damn loud. The petite guard with short-cropped black hair paired with a stocky man with two granite boulders for fists. They didn't bother with niceties as they shoved guests aside, which surprised me. They meant business.

I ran full out, leaping the barrier between the auction room and the starlit hallways beyond. Sprinting, I rounded the corner at full speed, almost crashing into a pedestal holding an expensive-looking vase, and spun full circle to avoid an errant waiter who looked almost as stunned as I'd felt only a few minutes prior.

By the time I was a dozen steps past the waiter, I plunged into the cold darkness of Trinity's staunch disapproval. Blackness engulfed me, even as it retreated from the guards who followed. I ducked down a side hall, careful not to make too much noise. The guards rushed past.

Black wrapped around me like a blanket. Fine, maybe this wasn't so bad, but the harsh darkness still felt like punishment. Feeling my way forward, I located the door Vitez had taken us through to reach the museum below. It opened for me, and I carefully stepped onto the spiral stairs.

Security was still disabled, which meant I could walk in undeterred, but so could the stranger if he was still around.

I pushed open the double door leading into the first museum chamber, the one with the impressionist paintings. Light flooded through, blinding me with a piercing whiteness. That's not how I remembered it. The lights had been pleasant. Perfect for viewing art, and even going so far as to emulate the color spectra most favorable to each piece. With the lights all on, I could see into other sections of the museum. A few steps forward, and the whole place lay out before me, sectioned loosely into rooms by the heavy arches, but in truth, the entire museum was one large space.

The lights must have been Beck's doing because it made the task of searching for *The Garden of Earthly Delights* simple. From the top of the stone stairs, I could see it standing in the center of its own room in the far corner. The space had been cleared around it, and a single spotlight shone on it from above. A haze settled in that room, suspending the painting as if on a cloud.

I blinked hard and shook my head to clear it. I had been wrong. Vitez had fooled me with his reaction. The painting was there, clear as broad daylight. Then why had he acted as if he'd lost it?

Something was on the floor in front of the painting, so I descended the stairs to see what it was. As I got closer, a lump of dread rose in my throat. The shape was a crumpled mess like someone had tossed a rag doll aside and left it in the middle of the floor.

Only, it wasn't a doll.

The man's body lay prostrate in front of the painting, so I couldn't tell who it was until I was close. My stun-addled sense of smell told me the fog was a lingering alcohol haze, but that couldn't be right. Whatever it was, it flowed from somewhere behind the painting. By the time I arrived, the fog had nearly enveloped the body.

Bending down without touching the corpse, I peered at the side of the body's face. Blood covered his features and pooled under him. A knife wound in his back bled sticky blood into a red suit. I circled to the other side to see if I could get a better angle, already knowing who it was.

Trey Vitez.

Murdered.

There were two suspects, as far as I could figure. If Vitez had woken and threatened Beck, she might have reacted poorly. I bent down and peered at the wound, despite everything in my body telling me how wrong it was. This was an angry strike. The kind of attack born of hatred and fury. It was ugly and ragged and the main wound was one of a dozen plunged into the man's body. If Vitez had threatened Beck—even if he had surprised her—would she have reacted like this?

The memory of her face when she had confronted Vitez earlier flashed in front of me. Where had that anger come from?

The stranger could have killed Vitez. He had admitted to knowing the man. Vitez thought he had been followed for weeks. If the man had come here to assassinate Vitez, why would he wait until we were here to do it?

To frame me.

Dread in my belly threatened to choke me, but I forced myself to take in the scene. This was one question I wouldn't get to return to, and I needed answers.

The painting. Here it was, the third panel of *The Garden of Earthly Delights*, displayed in all its hellish glory. I stood in front of it and studied the image, keeping clear of Vitez's body. Lingering fog licked at my feet.

This piece was darker than the other two-thirds that I had seen in Ruiz's ship. It featured the hideous depictions of an afterlife earned by the pleasures of mortal flesh. Human bodies, hollowed and suffering, housed the sorrowful few. Creatures consumed naked flesh, swallowing whole the pale damned. The abstract monsters writhed around the painting. Giant knives with giant ears crushed a crowd of naked men, and armored dogs devoured a helpless knight. In the background, the broken ruins of a city burned.

For a long time, I couldn't shake myself from feeling that maybe this was us. Here, in the afterlife of Earth, we lived in a Garden of Earthly Delights, experiencing the suffering brought by the debauchery of the revelers of our past. Here we were, devoured by each other, consumed by the city in the heavens. This was our fate, to wander in the dark forever, lost in our suffering.

I don't know how long I stood there taking it all in. Minutes. Maybe longer. The guards would come soon, and I needed to be gone.

The fog swirled higher around my feet. Bending down, I took another whiff. Alcohol. I wasn't imagining it. Maybe something related. Methanol? I didn't know my chemicals very well, but the fog only lingered in that section of the gallery. The ventilation system sucked it away as soon as it neared the edges of that particular room. But why? Was the fog part of the display? Something strange with how Vitez preserved old paintings? That didn't make any sense. In all my years following my father's work with art, I had never heard of anything like that. I circled the painting to find the source of the fog.

That's when I saw the bomb.

A small canister leaked thick fog. On the side sat a red striped box. The pressure of the releasing gas kept a switch open. That would be the trigger. Close the canister, and the circuit closes. It would also close when the canister ran out of gas.

Which could be soon.

I didn't dare move the device. The fog must be flammable, and interference might ignite it.

But why?

The question spun in my head. If Beck had done this—no, she wanted to steal the painting. She'd never burn it. It must be the stranger. He was working for Frank Lauder. Why would Lauder want this painting destroyed?

Footsteps sounded from the stairs, but when I looked up, all I saw was half of a faded image on the back of the painting. When the triptych was complete, the left panel would close to form a full image, and what I saw there struck me in the solar plexus, driving me back a step.

There was no time to process it because there was a bomb at my feet. Any touch might set it off. The contact of the switch was hidden behind clear casing. If I could get the casing off without setting off the spark, maybe it would be possible to slip something in between the contacts.

The footsteps approached. Muffled voices carried off the high museum ceiling. I had seconds at best, even hidden behind the painting.

I checked my pockets. I had my music rig and a lighter. Nothing that resembled the tools needed to disable the bomb. Nothing at all.

Nothing.

The painting stood before me, rooted in place by mechanical arms embedded in the hard floor. If I couldn't stop the bomb, then I needed to move the painting. For that, I would need help.

I stepped out from behind the painting, hands raised. The two guards who had chased me circled the room, stunsticks drawn. They would have found me in seconds anyway.

"Don't move!" shouted the woman.

"We need to move this painting," I said.

The man didn't waver. "Hands behind your head." The twitching muscle in his neck told that he was serious.

My hands edged toward the back of my head, and I stepped away from the painting. "All I want is to move this painting," I said, "on account of the bomb."

The woman scrunched her nose at that, sniffing the fog. She got it. Taking a few steps to one side, she peered behind me at the little canister. "Um, Max?"

"Step over here," Max ordered.

I stepped forward. "It's going to go any second. We need to save the painting."

But as I stepped forward, the fog shifted and Max got a good look at the body. He took several steps back. "Is that…"

"I didn't do this, Max. We need to move this painting or it's going to burn when the bomb goes off." I spoke with the calmest voice I could manage. "Help me out, here, then I'll come quietly."

The woman said, "What do you care about a painting?"

"This is more than just a painting," I said. "This is the heritage of our humanity. It's the ugly truth of Christianity's hell, and it's a piece that revolutionized art through the ages with its gruesome, abstract depictions of suffering. This painting is one-third of something staggeringly great, and it's worth more than a hundred August Saviors. The art of humanity through the ages is a collection of our ability to rise above our filthy day-to-day lives." I indicated the threatened painting. "This painting is worth my life and yours, and when we're dead and gone it'll be worth the lives of anyone who comes after. This ugly thing has a thousand years of history and if we can move it right now it'll have a thousand more."

Finally, the woman holstered her weapon and stepped forward into the fog.

"Michelle!" said Max.

"Hit him if he looks at me funny." To me, she said, "Get that side and lift."

She took the other side, and between the two of us we dislodged the massive frame from where the clamps held it in place.

Almost.

It snagged on a clamp. I tried to force it, but the piece lodged in harder. Swearing didn't help, though I tried.

"Twist it that way," I said, casting a nervous glance at the bomb. Gas still hissed from its top.

"Back toward me," Michelle said. She pulled and I pushed, but the clamp held. "Max, get over here and break the clamp."

"No."

"Get over here!"

Max didn't move. He kept his stunstick ready to swing.

"Max," I said. "You know what your boss would want. He loved his art more than anything. Enough to steal it. Enough to forge fakes to give away so that he could keep the originals. He loved it with everything he knew, and if you ever want to work in this town again, you'll respect that love. It's the kind of loyalty people in this town expect from the help. Every single day."

"Fine," Max said.

The hissing stopped.

It's not easy coming across enough flammable substances aboard a space station to create a decent bomb. Oxygen is prevalent and available, but fuel is always needed to supplement anything that might be more dangerous than a flash of light and a gentle wave of heat. For that, a bomb needs something that burns hot and loud. Those substances are controlled tighter than any drug, any weapon, or any political belief. The fact that the bomb existed at all was a miracle. That it worked, even more so. Still, compromises had been made. The explosive potential of most available substances was low, but there were still chemical combinations that might generate enough heat. This was nothing like the true explosive potential of bombs found on Earth, but at the cost of speed and a concussive blast, it was no less destructive.

That was why I almost had enough time to get Michelle and myself free from the blast when the bomb exploded.

I barreled into Michelle, carrying both of us out, away from the fog. Behind us, a flash of light flared with the white-hot phosphorescent glow of the center of a star. It seared across my back, flashing through my hair and biting naked flesh.

My body blocked Michelle from the brunt of it. The initial flash wave was followed by a low slow burn like the embers of a dying flame.

Michelle shoved me, and I collapsed onto my injured back. I didn't want to look. I couldn't look. I had to look.

The painting burned, devoured by the flame. The empty husk of its frame crumbled from the grip of the clamps, tumbling onto the dead and burning Trey Vitez.

The three of us sat wide-eyed, unsure of how to proceed.

Pain stretched across the exposed flesh of my shoulders and back.

Michelle pushed herself to her feet. "Go." Max made a move to protest, but she cut him off. "If he stays, we'll have to detain him. If we detain him, we'll need to get the police involved."

I said, "If the police are involved, they'll want to see what's down here." They would need to be involved anyway, once the record showed Savior's death.

"We can't just let the guy go," Max protested.

Michelle helped me up. "He's right. Mr. Savior cared about this art more than anything. If we fail that, then we're sunk in this town."

Max grudgingly holstered his weapon. "Michelle will show you the way out."

She led me to a back exit, where the gallery connected via maintenance tunnels to an exit several buildings away. I stepped through the screen of a hedge to be greeted by the double moons low in the false sky.

"I'm sorry," I said as Michelle left, but I don't think she was as devastated as I was.

The Garden of Earthly Delights was gone. Burned to nothing. Destroyed. My mission was a failure. It was all I could do to stumble to the gilded pub in the analog of Rory's Ramshackle, where I found Beck waiting in her gorgeous red dress: a flash of color in the bleak blue light of the double moon. I collapsed into the booth across from her, buried my face in my hands, and wept.

Chapter 40

MY MUSIC RIG played a twenty-first-century jazz revival, heavy on the guitar and sax, while Beck applied ointment to my burns. She sat with her legs straddling my waist so she could look out over the ravaged field of my burned back. The scorched remnants of my fancy shirt lay in a crumpled heap on the floor.

The apartment Beck had chosen contained a bed and a single dresser. Our only lighting was a couple of flickering candles. In the hazy mirror atop the dresser, I watched Beck's tender expression as she tended my wounds. This was a servant's room, nothing like the luxurious extravagance the natives of Hallow Nicodemia might have expected.

"It's probably not as bad as it feels," she said.

"It feels pretty bad."

"Does it hurt worse than a bullet wound?"

"Maybe." Probably not.

She gave me a light slap with an ointment-laden hand, which hurt more than pretty bad. "You've been through worse, big guy," she teased.

"That doesn't make it hurt less."

She finished in silence, bandaging the worst spots and leaving a large portion open to the air. When she finished, she pulled me close, careful not to touch anything that hurt. "I'm sorry," she said.

Not knowing if she was talking about my burns or the painting, I said, "I just can't figure what that guy wanted. Why destroy the painting?"

Beck answered by nibbling on my ear. It didn't hurt, but it was terribly distracting.

My fists clenched. "I had him. He was right there in the garden, and I could have stopped him."

Her kisses migrated from my ear down my neck. Her arms wrapped around my body and her fingernails raked gently across my chest. My body responded to the touch, and if moving weren't so painful I might have turned around to her right then. Beck met my eyes in the mirror, and I saw her mischievous intent.

"My father would have disowned me if he found out I was responsible for destroying that painting. He'd have murdered me. He cared about art more than he cared about us." I remembered seeing the back of the panel. Something about it had been so familiar. "Then again—"

Beck took my head in one hand and turned it so our mouths met. She kissed deep and hard, and I rose to meet her. For a long time, we were lost in each other, pain and world disappearing into the fog of her warm embrace.

She took a handful of my hair and pulled me backwards, landing me flat on my back. The bandages stung, but the pain was nothing against the wave of heat and pressure as she swung her leg over atop me. She took both my wrists and pinned me down, kissing me hard until I gave up my feeble attempts to speak. Until my mind gave up its attempts to think.

And then, all we knew was passion.

Later, she curled up against my side, both of us naked. She ran her sharp nails through the hair of my chest. "What is it like living in a station?"

I had never known anything else. "I suppose it's like living in any other city, only the city limits are a hard vacuum and there's nowhere to go if you piss off your neighbors."

She got a mischievous smile. "Oh, is that what makes you so friendly?"

"You say that as if I'm not."

Beck pulled away from me with a mock frown. "Body, soul, community. That's what's important. Grump, grump, grump."

"You're not supposed to pronounce the 'grump'."

She sprung to her feet and marched around the small room. "Grump, grump, grump."

The absurdity of it got to me, and I laughed harder than I had laughed in years: big belly laughs sending pings of pain through my burned skin. There may have even been a snort at the end of one long, breathless laugh, which sent Beck into a downward spiral oscillating between grumping and hilarity. When I couldn't stand it anymore, I reached out across the tiny room and pulled her close to me again. We fell together and the whole world disappeared.

It could have lasted forever. She fell asleep in my arms, but I lay awake for a long time, thinking of the future as a last desperate grasp at avoiding the past. Violet Ruiz, my employer, would be upset. The widow wanted one last piece to remember her late husband by, and it had to be the one Vitez had taken. The piece her husband had gotten killed over. I couldn't pretend to understand the twisted nostalgia wrapped up in her motivations, but it could only lead to one outcome now that the painting was destroyed.

Maybe she would blame me or maybe she would blame Beck, but she'd be mad. Whatever deal she had going with the other powers of Heavy Nicodemia would falter. She would want to leave town.

But would Beck leave with her?

I wanted to ask, but it seemed rude to wake her for that conversation. After such a perfect time, why worry? Why grump endlessly? Ruiz would do whatever she did. The stranger would keep walking the streets unless I tracked him down and made him pay.

The more I thought about the man, the more I convinced myself that he was a danger to Nicodemia. He knew more than he let on, and what he hinted at was nothing short of the ability to ignore all the rules. He was excommunicated but still had manual access to Trinity's systems. He could do anything and get away with it.

So why burn the painting? That question ran through my head over and over, and each time the answers got worse.

Or nonexistent. There *wasn't* a good reason to burn the final panel of *The Garden of Earthly Delights*. Not greed, not revenge, not even as an artistic scholar fighting a rival's claim.

Unless the painting was a forgery.

With a forgery out of the way, the authentic copy might rise in value. With the forgery out of the way and the forger murdered, there wouldn't be any chance of confusion in the market. Whoever owned the whole triptych could monopolize the attention caused by the piece. They could make their case about the origin of the painting and its significance to the Church.

The Church. Why were the higher churches leaning toward machine worship? The trend hadn't gotten down to Heavy Nicodemia yet, but it was rampant in the Hallows and well established in Haven. The Church was changing in the way the Church always changed: by saying, "We've always been this way." The only things that stood in the way were the strong paper record and thousands of years of art.

The Garden of Earthly Delights displayed a core tenet of the Christian faith. It depicted the Garden of Eden and humanity's temptation. It showed the revelry of humanity as it discovered the pleasures of the flesh, and it showed the punishment of an afterlife caused by such revelry. Without that painting and others like it, a church might craft its own nuance to the story of creation. With modifications to Biblical translation, they might even find room for machine and God to truly become one.

This was too much for my sex-addled brain. It came down to one thing. In the morning, I would track down the stranger and confront him about the painting. Beck and I together could surely trap the man, and with a little luck, we'd get him to spill about who's paying his bills. I needed to know how Frank Lauder played into all of this, and what Saint Jerome's motivation was to call for my death.

As sleep finally tugged at my exhausted brain, another thought about the future wandered through. What if Beck wanted to stay? What if she'd had enough of the traveling life and she'd found a city she could live in? What if she wanted to be here with me?

The thought filled me with warmth, and I pulled Beck closer as I drifted off to sleep.

When I woke, Charlotte Beck was gone.

Chapter 41

MODERN FASHION DIDN'T ALLOW for trench coats in Hallow Nicodemia, so I settled for a new white button-down shirt, some comfortable slacks, and a subdued burgundy tie. Everything fit nicely, but that and an egg sandwich burned up a whole roll of the dimes Beck had left me before she disappeared without a trace. There were plenty more. It wasn't everything I was owed by Ruiz, but she hadn't left me with nothing.

She hadn't left without a trace. A note pinned to the dresser read: *Goodbye, Demarco.* Funny how a woman can stab a person through the heart with so few words. Beck always had been efficient.

I wandered the city unsettled and alone. With Beck gone, my only conclusion was that Violet was no longer my boss, but there were still questions that I couldn't let drop. The first one I couldn't shake was about the stranger. I kept an eye to the shadows wherever I went, but he didn't show. He probably finished with me as soon as Ruiz stopped paying me. The whole business didn't make sense, unless—

Unless.

I checked the dive bars first. If the man needed to burn time, a stiff drink would help. Hallow Nicodemia's light gravity allowed faster, better transportation, so canvassing all the worst places only took me the better part of the afternoon. From the Sinless District to the Agricultural Quarter, I hit every working-class dive meant for non-Travelers. When I stepped inside each one, the light crowd would stop and stare. I was a Traveler to them. A cruel master looking to slum around in places they felt were sacred.

It was only when I spoke that they accepted me. "Looking for a guy," I said in a sharp Heavies accent. "Tough sort. Kinda older. Fedora."

"He in trouble?"

"Not from me." If I was right, I was the least of his concerns.

"Nobody like that around here." The answers were always vague and empty. True, but the kind of true that didn't give a person anything else to cling to.

Next, I checked the museums. If I was right about who he was, he'd have at least a passing interest in the arts. Hell, everyone around the Hallows had a passing interest. The stranger could have burned an afternoon at one of the many art museums.

Museums swarmed with natives of Hallow Nicodemia who were as tall as me but with their noses pointed permanently toward the ceiling. When I spoke to the museum hosts, they regarded me the way a servant regards a boss, and when I spoke to them, I dragged my vowels thick with the Hallow accent.

"Have you seen a man about this tall come through here today? Older gentleman? Likes to wear good-looking hats?"

"Like a bowler?"

"More the fedora type."

The host frowned as if trying to remember every guest they'd seen all day.

"About this tall," I repeated.

"Oh, no. None of the workers bother much with the arts."

"They're too busy?"

"Something like that."

By the time I finished with the museums, the sky was slate gray and the moons sat lazy in the projected haze.

As the last of the massive fiberoak museum doors swung shut behind me, an understanding blossomed in my brain. The stranger wasn't an art fanatic like Vitez. Vitez was passionate about art and dreamed of nothing more than to experience the various beauties of humanity's creation. He had been an art dealer simply so he could touch works of genius as they passed through his hands. Later, art had become an obsession for the man. He created his museum in space so that he could have, all to himself, the art that he had so often seen changing hands. He might have wanted to protect it for the ages, but something told me what he really wanted was to have it for himself.

The stranger didn't feel that way. That man was a hacker. He loved technology the way Vitez loved art, and he made it his life's goal to be the best of the best at mastering the machine. There was only one place in Hallow Nicodemia where such a man would go to spend his time.

The Apex.

Swift transport buzzed past me, but my feet carried me past the Cathedral of Saint Lucy of the Light. Even though I had been contemplating the chase all afternoon, this certainty of my success meant that I needed to really consider what I might say to the man. If he split before I could catch him, or if I caught him the wrong way, he might never give me the answers I wanted. I didn't know if he was a killer. My survival the previous night hinted that he would hesitate to kill, but what I had to say might put him over the edge.

A man protecting a secret was a deadly man indeed.

The priests of the cathedral still held Beck's crimson gun, but I didn't bother trying to get it back. They wouldn't be happy with how things had gone with Vitez. I was taking enough of a risk walking so close to the towering glass structure. I half-expected a gaggle of choir boys to chase me off.

Upspiral from the cathedral, the population began to thin. Hallow Nicodemia didn't have a dense population like the other nodes of the city, but even that turned into a downright suburb in the upper reaches. Plants swallowed every surface, starting with mossy grasses near the cathedral, then transitioning to dense vines over high arching trellises. The air was heavy with humidity and the scent of flowers. The path along the inner spiral thinned until it was nothing but a weaving trail through a dense forest. Above, the leaves of mighty oaks waved in the gentle wind, and my feet crunched a loosely packed duff layer of leaves.

Nestled in these many winding trails through the plants were mansions the likes of which residents of Heavy Nicodemia have never imagined. One of them, modest by comparison, was the one where my sister and I grew up. I remembered it for its high arching ceilings and the warm quality of its light. It might have been nice to visit the place, but I had a mission. I continued my climb upward.

There was almost no government district in Hallow Nicodemia. At the very tip of the upward spiral, seven brick buildings stood. Flying transports still carried a straggling trickle of government workers down to their residences below. Government was a farce in this node. Trinity truly ran everything for the Hallows. Trust in the machine was so deeply seated in every Traveler's heart that they were comfortable depending upon it for every aspect of their lives. It was a leftover cultural ideology from the Travelers' long voyage between the stars.

When I finally arrived at the top, the air warmed palpably as I pressed into the uppermost liminal space. Vegetation parted to reveal a domed room a hundred yards in diameter. Above, the great white sun shone through tinted glass. A polarized field below created night for the city, but above, it was always brighter than the brightest day. The light burned my senses, searing into my skull and scouring my soul down to the bone. It was fire on my skin.

In the center of the room, a circular railing stood around a hole in the floor. That hole overlooked all of Hallow Nicodemia, and a lone figure stood watching the city. Waiting.

The stranger looked up as I approached. His expression darkened as he saw me, but something in the hang of his shoulders looked defeated.

"I wasn't sure you'd come," he said.

"Couldn't pass up the opportunity to get some questions answered," I said.

"I figured."

His sad eyes caught mine, and for a moment I wasn't sure what he wanted. It should have been obvious. "The truth eats a hole in a person if it's bottled up too long," I said. "So tell me, Mr. Richard Ruiz, what really happened that day you stole *The Garden of Earthly Delights*? And why does your wife still think you're dead?"

Chapter 42

RICHARD RUIZ LEANED against the railing at the top of the world and stared up at the false sun above. Brilliant light played across his features, softening the creases of age and sharpening the color in his brown eyes.

"The job was bad from the start," he said. "I should have seen how ugly it was, but the price was too good. The challenge was too tempting."

"You had a buyer for *The Garden of Earthly Delights*."

"It was Vitez's job from the start, and Vitez had the contact. We were supposed to drop it off on the moon and be done with it. From there, we could collect our money and escape to the stars at our leisure. We'd live our lives out on a colony planet in luxury."

"A fine plan if you weren't married."

"Violet was supposed to meet me on the moon." He finally looked away from the bright sun to focus on me. "She knew every backup plan. I sent her the signal telling her where to meet if things went south. By then, I suppose it didn't matter."

"Why did this job go sour?"

"All we had to do was hit the transport flight. We had a ship to do the intercept, and with Violet's help, we had the math to make it click. Only, at the last minute I find there's a decoy transport. A second flight was loaded with forgeries. When I told Violet to redo the numbers, she was upset. Almost abandoned the whole job."

"Why would she be upset?"

"We were targeting the decoy, according to my source, but the same source hadn't mentioned before that there was even going to be a decoy. That kind of silence erodes trust, you know?" Ruiz strolled counterclockwise around the center railing, and I followed. When he touched a tablet, Trinity increased the tint of the overhead dome. The light became somewhat bearable. "Everybody knew the risk, but things kept getting worse."

"Did you know Vitez was a forger?"

He raised an eyebrow at me. "Would have been good information to have, don't you think?"

"That's the kind of thing that erodes trust."

"True enough."

"You fed Vitez the new trajectories, but still ended up at the decoy ship?"

"I was fooled right up until he panicked about our docking time. That was his ploy to hide the difference in the intercept window. The decoy ship had a later window, and we were all synced at that point. So, he docks us with the ship—which he had to have known was the wrong one—and the rest of the job went south."

"Why didn't you call it off?"

"He was our pilot. Once he had us in the air, we were at his mercy. I figured it was best if we picked up the forged goods and waited until we landed to confront him. He had other plans."

"They involved murdering you."

"Only he didn't count on Hector being so explosively violent. The big guy had a family, though. A daughter. He would have done anything to keep from getting caught." Ruiz smiled at that. "Anyway, we got the first panel out. It was a solid forgery. Soon as I saw it, I doubted myself. Maybe Vitez got us to the right transport after all."

I remember what Maurice Ribar had told me about the safe. "It was the wrong safe."

Ruiz raised an eyebrow. "Was it? Ribar never made a lot of sense to me, to tell the truth, but I wish he had said something to me. Finally, Vitez gave in and called for the cut-and-run. I think his plan all along was to convince one of us to back out. Get someone else to abort the mission so that it didn't look like he had anything to do with the failure."

If Ribar had called everything off, then nobody would have gotten murdered. Nobody would have been paid. He would crash the decoy transport, making it look like all that art was destroyed. "Vitez must have had another team hijacking the other transport."

"You met Vitez. Does he seem like the type to trust another team to cut him in if he's not there to supervise?"

"If there wasn't a second team, then how was Vitez expecting to get paid?"

"That's one mystery I've never been able to figure out. Maybe he just picked the wrong transport. Got outsmarted."

"You, Maurice Ribar, and Hector Chance got the first panel aboard your transport before Chance got shot. What happened after that?"

"Chance was in a bad way. Gutshot. Bleeding." Ruiz got a far-off look. "He was the only one of us who had a family. Grandkids, even." The old hacker drew a deep breath. "He asked us to look after them, and I promised I'd do my best. Do you ever feel like your best isn't all that great, Demarco? Maybe like your best is a bucket of shit."

"All the time."

"Chance was on his way out. Vitez had betrayed us. Ribar

must have known something was wrong, but he stayed in his own little world. Once we got that panel onto the ship, I was supposed to go back for the next one, but I didn't. Instead, I went up front to confront Vitez. By that time, I knew he had more to his plan than to hoodwink us with a forgery."

"Why the forgery, then?"

"Hell if I know."

I grabbed his shoulder and stopped him from walking so I could look him straight in the eyes. "What do you mean you don't know? All this time and you haven't figured out why he would put forgeries on a decoy ship if he was just planning on murdering you? It seems like a big mystery to leave unanswered when the man with those answers sat around in the lap of luxury just down the street."

He wouldn't meet my gaze. "It wasn't something I wanted the answer to. Some questions—"

"Did you kill him?"

He blinked rapidly and took a step back. Shock, if ever I'd seen it. "Why would I do that?"

"You cut him bad last night. Stabbed him in the back. What did you find out, Ruiz? I know you went back there. What did he tell you that got you so upset you killed him?"

Ruiz shoved me away. "Vitez was an asshole and he betrayed me, but I didn't kill him."

"He ruined your life. Tore you from Earth, stole your chance at a retirement job, and ripped you from your wife. You'd have to be a damn saint not to hurt him when you had the chance."

"I've had the chance!" Ruiz's voice echoed off the dome. "I've had the chance a hundred times and I never took it. There's a million ways I could kill him without anyone ever taking notice. I'm excommunicated, remember? Trinity doesn't care what I do to correct the problems of this station. If I decided that Trey Vitez's continued existence was a threat to community stability, then he'd be a dead man and I would face absolutely no consequences. Why would I go in during an auction and slash the guy's throat if I could do it any other time, cleanly and without any problems?"

"Rage," I said quietly. "Trey Vitez was killed by someone who hated him. With passion and fury. What did he say to you?"

"Nothing."

Now it was my turn to shout. "What did he tell you?"

Fury boiled in the old man's eyes, but he kept his lips closed tight until it passed. "We fought on the ship after the job. Shook things up bad, and Vitez had to tell Ribar that reentry had started. Vitez tossed me into an airlock and hit the cycle sequence, but when he went back to piloting, I was able to override his commands. I already had root access to the ship, so countering his actions was nothing. I thought about killing him then. That, I'll admit." His shoulders slumped. "I was afraid. I couldn't fly the ship. Whoever he was working with probably would have killed me."

"Is that when you went into hibernation?"

Ruiz looked up at me, sadness in his eyes. "I never did. It was the prison I deserved, alone in the vast expanse of space. Ribar and Vitez didn't find me on the ship. I heard them debate about landing on the moon or escaping to the stars. They even thought about landing directly on Earth, but their ship was never designed for that kind of abuse. They never would have survived. Ultimately, they decided to follow the backup plan, heading out to Nicodemia, where they could start a new life. Ribar wasn't happy about it."

"He's not doing too bad down in the Heavies," I said, calm now.

"I visit him sometimes. He doesn't know it, but I like to help him out when I can."

"It's nice to have a man walking around in the dark for you," I said.

"Sure is."

"How did you manage to get excommunicated when you arrived?"

Ruiz drew a tablet from his pocket. "I told you, it's a maintenance routine. It lets an engineer sit outside the normal permissions infrastructure. It's just a matter of spoofing the right trust level." On the screen, he scrolled through lines of code until he found what he wanted. "With some program routines I brought from Earth, this wasn't such a hard hack. It'd be difficult to manage with the resources available on ship, but I had no trouble at all."

"Do I need to worry about anyone else spoofing this access?"

"I doubt it. The key is, they would have to already be an outsider." He pushed a button. The dome above darkened further, and a rain of green text displayed on it as if it were a giant screen. The code cleared away to reveal one huge sentence.

Reconcile Jude Demarco?

"Are you ready to rejoin society, Mr. Demarco?" Ruiz asked.

"I've got more questions."

"It's crowded here in the dark," Ruiz said. "Starting to be a bit of a pain if there are too many people wandering around. Your help has been a real pain lately."

"Why have you been following me? Were you the one following Vitez?"

"Yeah, Vitez's people might have spotted me a few times. I'm getting sloppy in my old age."

"Is that why you started working for Lauder?"

"Frank Lauder doesn't know how much he's disrupting the established power structure of the Heavies. He thinks he's arranging for a hostile takeover of the district, but really what he's doing is making the district ripe for takeover." Ruiz's finger hovered over a button on his tablet. "Right now, what I need is for you to be out of the way for when that happens."

"Who burned *The Garden of Earthly Delights?*"

Ruiz hesitated. "What?"

And that's when I slugged him. My fist connected hard with his jaw, sending a spray of dark blood through the green-lit air. I brought a chop down at his hand, trying to knock the screen free, but he recovered faster than I expected and drew back.

I kept close, crowding him back, and swinging furiously. He ducked and dodged. His hand brought up the stunstick, but I slapped it away. The weapon skittered across the floor.

Then, he struck back. A fist flew past my nonexistent defenses to slam into my gut. He stepped past and elbowed hard at my kidney. Pain raged through the side of my body, dropping me to one knee. I pushed through it, throwing a block back behind me as I turned. It worked, deflecting another swing of his fist. He couldn't fight properly with the console in his hand.

So, I helped him with that. I took his wrist in one hand and squeezed, twisting until he couldn't maintain his grip. The little screen fell, its flashing *Reconcile* dropping to black as it struck the floor.

The move left me open, and he used the opportunity to land a series of hard strikes to the side of my head. Lights flashed behind my eyes. Pain burned. His wrist twisted out of my grip, and he reached for the screen.

Too slow. I kicked out, and it slid across the floor, stopping teetering on the edge of the hole in the center of the room.

"Not so special without your fancy toys, are you?" I asked, spitting blood.

"You're a goddamn fool, Demarco. You deserve what's coming."

He dove for the screen, but I tackled him, using my bulk to fling him across the room. He slammed into the wall, his head smacking hard. It had to hurt, but it didn't slow him at all. In a deft maneuver, he rolled and launched himself in the low gravity and grabbed my arm.

"Jujitsu," he said. "Pretty rare it comes in handy, but sure is nice when it does."

He had the position on me, and he had a decent joint lock, but

I was much bigger than him and significantly stronger. Instead of fighting his lock, I moved my whole body into it, lifting him.

"I don't want to hurt you, Demarco."

"And yet."

"*You* attacked *me.*"

I put a surge of strength under me, shifting him up and back. In response, he placed more pressure on my joint. My tendons screamed in protest. He had me.

He breathed hard. "You need to give up. You could say it right now and Trinity would let you reconcile."

"It would," I said. "But what's keeping me from getting excommunicated again?"

"You can't go back. Not without help."

"Fair enough."

I drew a deep breath, centering myself and steeling my resolve. Reconciling with Trinity meant forgiving myself for what I'd done that day my parents died. It meant taking the first step on the path toward redemption for what I'd done to my sister and all those people who might have survived if the ship's coupling had held.

But what if it hadn't? If I hadn't disengaged and the supports had failed, how many people could have died in Nicodemia? How much of Nicodemia's resources would be lost into the void if the ship had torn the airlocks? What kind of cascading failure might have happened? Legends told of the generation ships that didn't make it. Final broadcasts told of hull failures and collapsing resources. Even with their seven layers, the hulls were vulnerable. Space was a cruel master.

"Trinity," I said, my voice low and serious.

"Jude Demarco," said a voice from all around. It was Trinity's Hallows voice, which rang like the bells of angels. "Do you wish to reconcile?"

When I didn't answer immediately, Ruiz tightened his grip. Pain lanced down my arm.

I closed my eyes and pictured those final moments as the ship tore away from the station, inertial force carrying it far past the coupling. Maybe I had done the right thing. Maybe I could be forgiven for it. Someday.

Not today.

With every bit of strength I had left, I heaved upward. Something tore in my elbow, but I reached up and around to grab Ruiz with my right hand, lifting him high into the air. His face was a mask of fear and rage.

"Trinity," I said. "Catch." I threw Ruiz as hard as I could.

His feet struck the railing on his way over, and he spun head over heels as he dropped over the edge into the vast, empty hollow below.

The vibration from his hit rattled the railing, and the tablet wobbled. Tipped.

I dove for it, biting back the pain in my injured elbow.

My hand closed on air. Ruiz's screen fell into the city below.

As the tablet fluttered like a falling leaf, a hundred questions ran through my head. *If Ruiz hadn't burned the painting, then who? Who murdered Trey Vitez?*

I stuck my head over the ledge and watched the device dance through the flying traffic. Ruiz was gone. Either fallen out of sight below or captured by the rescue drones. The problem of what to do about him was something that I'd have to deal with later. If he hadn't killed Vitez…

Only one answer made everything fit. I didn't like it for two reasons.

The second reason was that it meant I needed to hurry if I wanted to save Maurice Ribar's life. He was the last of the thieves to survive, at least of those known to be alive. Even if Ruiz survived the fall, he didn't count so long as I didn't spill his little secret.

But Ribar? He was a good man. The thief had moved on from his life of crime. He didn't deserve the death headed his way. If I wanted to save him, I needed to run faster than I'd ever run before. There was only one reason Maurice Ribar hadn't been murdered already, which brought me back to the first reason that I didn't like this answer.

Charlotte Beck didn't want me to know she was the killer.

I picked up Ruiz's stunstick and fedora from the floor, fixed the hat on my head, and ran.

PART V

the case of the widow's truth

Chapter 43

THE RUSH from the tip of Hallows to the bottom of the Heavies left an ache in my bones and a pain in my knees. A couple of painkillers kept the agony of my back in check, but it did nothing for the throbbing fire in my injured elbow. Ruiz had cranked on the thing, and every time I moved it, there was a worrying click to the joint. Despite the pain, I moved faster than I had ever traveled from the top of the Hallows down to the bottom of Heavy Nicodemia.

By the look of their gutted home, Maurice and his family had scattered as soon as Beck and I had walked away. The other members of the small settlement fixed me with their blank stares until I stopped asking. They didn't know where Maurice went. When I left, the desperate addicts lingering at the edges of the small community saw me and let me through. Something about the look in my eyes must have told them they'd get nothing from me.

I moved back up the spiral.

Retch lounged in a wide hammock, pulling a needle through cloth with so much intensity I wasn't sure he heard me squeeze through his secret entrance. When I was halfway across the wide expanse of the warehouse, he looked up with a raised eyebrow. He had a new black eye and a couple of sloppily applied stitches in his eyebrow.

"Rough couple days?" I asked.

He held up the cloth he was working on. It was a cross stitch in the form of an elaborate skull, with the words *FUCK YO* in decorative lettering across its forehead.

"Fuck yo?" I asked. "Not sure what that means."

"Listen, asshole. I've had enough trouble from you."

I stepped forward but stopped when he took a meaningful glance at the pistol on the table next to him. Instead, I said. "Who gave you that shiner?"

"Just some friends."

"You have an interesting idea of friendship."

"You have an interesting idea of being an asshole." His heart clearly wasn't in the conversation. For several slow heartbeats, the kid didn't say anything. Then: "They took your papers."

Damn.

"No refunds."

"Nobody knew you had those. That was the deal."

He shrugged and pulled a long thread through the cloth.

"I was hoping to finally give those papers another look," I said. With the right leverage, Saint Jerome's people might help me find Maurice—or at least stop trying to kill me while I made the attempt. "The guy I want to help is missing, the painting I'm supposed to track was a fake all along, and that woman I was with might be a killer."

"No kidding," he deadpanned. "The woman who beat the shit out of me?"

"She's usually much nicer than that."

"It's the gang war," Retch said. "The Saints are split down the middle, and a whole lot of them are throwing support at the Gentlemen."

"Is that Frank Lauder's new gang?"

"It's been busy since you left." He pulled another stitch. "You look good."

"Thanks."

"The trench coat never really did anything for you. This is much nicer." Without looking up, he said, "I read the papers before they got took."

I moved forward into his home again, and this time he didn't warn me off. I settled my aching bones into one of his chairs and leaned back. "Learn anything interesting?"

"I learned that a person desperate enough for reading material can make it through some pretty boring shit."

"I'll bet."

"And I learned that there's proof that Saint Jerome is embezzling Karma from a system designed to help poor shits like me find a place in this fucking world. It all centers around the movement of goods." He glanced up to make sure he had my attention.

"How the hell does someone embezzle Karma?" I had a pretty good idea already, but his take might confirm some ideas.

"Body, soul, community. It's an obvious loophole. Jerome gets a hold of religious art of a certain value to the soul, and he's able to use it to raid a fund designed to support the community. Only, it's a lot more complicated than that. Everything runs through restaurants like the Pelican, and it involves exchanging art and food."

"Food that's supposed to feed people who need it."

He shot me with a finger pistol.

"How the hell do you know this much about Karma algorithms?"

"How do you know about art?"

"Let me get this straight. He's making himself rich by raiding a fund that's designed to help everyone around him." If what Retch claimed was true, then he had broken the case. Unfortunately, since the papers were gone, there was no proof. "I'm not sure if those were the original papers or forgeries, so even if you held onto them, there wouldn't have been proof."

"Proof is just going to get you killed," Retch said. "Saint Jerome might not have the pull he did a few days ago, but he's still got a whole pile of goons. That Wash shit still licks his heels. That guy was always an asshole."

"Wash still works for the Saint?" He hadn't sounded like it last I'd seen him. What had changed?

"That's the word." Retch sounded angrier than I had expected.

"He's the one who took the papers."

"Like I said, Sam was an asshole. Loved being the biggest guy in the group, but after a while, he traded up. Who wouldn't do that?" He jabbed a needle in and yanked it through. "The Saint robbing us kids is one thing. Wash doing it…"

"He was one of you."

"Yeah."

I wondered why Wash would go out of his way to claim to have left Jerome. "Lauder must have figured out the Saint's ploy, and he's using it to recruit people."

Retch concentrated on the needlework, tongue sticking out the side of his mouth.

"I don't have time for this," I said. "There's something more urgent, and I need your help."

"What are you paying?"

"Don't you want to know what the job is first?"

He pulled another long stitch through. "Wanna know how picky I can afford to be right now?"

"You've always got your art," I said, gesturing at the cross stitch.

Retch held up the cloth, which now clearly read, "FUCK YOU."

"Very nice," I said.

"It's abstract expressionism."

"That's not very abstract. It just says *fuck you*."

He grinned for the first time ever, dimples and all. "Written language is a form of abstraction."

I dropped my voice an octave so he'd know I was serious. "It's actually really good, Retch." I gestured at his piles of artwork. "Really. You should show it somewhere."

"I had to do a little stitchwork, and there was extra thread." He poked at his torn eyebrow, wincing. "Didn't want it to go to waste."

"Mind if I look at that," I offered. "I'm a med tech."

At first, he looked like he might refuse, but then he relented. He knelt in front of me so I could lean down and shine a light on his cut. He'd done a better job than I initially thought, stitching a fairly straight line across the cut.

"Is it going to make me look badass?" His voice wavered.

I met the kid's eyes and saw real worry there. "You *are* badass, kid. How you look doesn't mean a thing." I peered closer, touching the skin around the wound. No response. "It doesn't look like it's picked up any infection, and it's healing nicely. There'll be a scar, but it's not going to be an ugly one."

He flopped back into his hammock. "They got the jump on me. I don't know how, but they did." Real emotion seeped into his cracking voice. For a second, he wasn't the tough boy I'd come to know. He was just a vulnerable kid trying to survive in a harsh world. "I had your papers with me on the roof because I was reading them. I should have left them hidden."

"A stunstick," I said.

"What?"

I detached the stick from my belt loop where I'd stowed it after the fight with Ruiz. "A stunstick. That's your payment for helping me find a couple of people. Keep it charged and you can give a bad day to anyone, whether or not they deserve it. Even if they sneak up on you."

He gave me a wary look. "He didn't sneak up on me."

"You trusted him?"

His brow furrowed, and I knew I'd hit it on the head.

I handed Retch the stunstick, handle side first. "I need to find two people. The first is a guy named Maurice Ribar."

"So, check Trinity."

"Can't. Anyway, I think he'll avoid the system as best he can. Do you have anyone you can trust?"

"Not one damn person."

"I mean allies. Your gang. I'd like you to get an image of the guy and show it around. He's gone to ground, but someone in the city might have seen him."

"Who else are you looking for?"

"Charlotte Beck."

He grinned. "She got you good, huh?"

"That she did."

"I could have told you not to trust her."

"I wouldn't have listened."

"Do you always have such poor taste in women?" Retch pushed the button on the stunstick, causing it to extend to its full length and crackle with power. "Holy shit."

"You shouldn't stay here," I said. "There's a place I know. A diner my sister owns."

"Will I get free food?"

"Not with your Karma." I picked up a drawing from his collection. It portrayed a bedraggled man sitting alone on a pew in Saint Francis while a short distance away a priest celebrated mass with a collection of rapt parishioners. "Bring a few of these."

He waved the stunstick around, grinning at the sound it made as it hummed through the air.

"Are you going to be able to get others to help you or not?"

Retch hefted the stunstick. "I am now."

"I mean by paying them or cashing in favors. Not bludgeoning them into submission."

"I'll be paying with the opportunity to not be hit with a stunstick."

"That's not what I meant."

He looked affronted. "When you pay with dimes, you're giving people the opportunity to not starve on the streets. How is that any different?"

"I'm not really up for a fraught ethical debate right now, Retch."

"Who says it has to be fraught?"

"Meet me at Angel's Diner, down by the docks." I stood, my bones aching.

When I left, Retch returned to his cross stitch, finishing the final flourish on the last letter. That's all the world needed. One more artist.

Chapter 44

A BRISK WIND circled Heavy Nicodemia's downward spiral carrying a thick fog and frigid droplets that bit whatever flesh they touched. The air reeked of the salty fresh scent of the docks below, even up as high as the cathedral. The building's spires disappeared into the mists above, their upper reaches as concealed as the false stars. Somewhere, a blues trombone burdened the night.

When I entered the massive church, my footsteps rang against the fiberstone floors. Night had fallen, and when life got hard, the residents of the Heavies fled religion like rats fleeing a sinking ship. Inside the church, Cecilia Cano stood facing the altar, her priestly robes lit by the dim flame-like flickers of the artificial lighting.

I opened my mouth to speak but closed it again when I heard the click of a cocked weapon to my right.

"It's good of you to come," said Saint Jerome from his seat on the back pew. He wore a pristine white velvet suit trimmed with gold. "Saves my boys the trouble."

Cano turned, and the haunted look in her eyes turned fast into a scowl. "We have sanctuary here."

I raised my hands, palms out. "It'd be a shame to get blood on that nice new suit."

"You have a lot of nerve, Demarco," said the Saint. "Betray me and then walk back onto my turf? Takes a lot of balls."

What lies had Wash dropped on him to make me out to be disloyal? Better yet, why did Saint Jerome think I was ever on his side? "I did your job just like you said, Jerome. Swapped the papers and got out."

Jerome pulled himself to his feet. "I saw the papers you had your kid working on. A hell of a workup, if you ask me. You were going to take it all, weren't you?"

I furrowed my brow. The papers Retch was looking at were the originals.

Or were they?

"We were trying to figure out your game," I said. "I was curious."

"Curious," Jerome spat. He shuffled forward, his grim eyes fixing mine with a death glare. "Is that why your documents clearly rerouted the Karmic balance to your people?"

"Rerouted?" Then it clicked. I hadn't taken the original documents from the archives. I had taken Ruiz's copy, which held changes that would reroute credit to Lauder. "Wait?" I asked. "People? Who did it route to?"

The Saint jabbed the gun at me. "You know damn well who. How long have you been in Lauder's pocket, Demarco? And who the hell is Maurice Ribar?"

"Ribar?" If the balance was split between the two, then Ruiz was sending credit to his old partner. Maybe paying a debt.

Or relieving a lingering guilt.

"We'll find him," said Jerome. "And your papers were never placed."

"The originals are still there," I said. "It has to be."

"And that's why I'm ruined," said Jerome. "That record was full of discrepancies. Now, even the slightest hint of trouble and Trinity's going to turn on me."

"All that record shows is the truth."

His face turned red, and spittle flew as he spoke. "Paper lasts forever, Demarco. That record will outlive us both."

"Maybe that's not so much of a feat."

Saint Jerome raised the crimson-barreled gun, smooth and steady. Despite the rage apparent on his face, his aim stayed rock solid. "Things got complicated when you bugged out, Demarco. I don't like complicated."

Somewhere deep in the church, a door slammed. By the smug look in Saint Jerome's eyes, I figured his goons were on their way back.

I needed a new tack, and fast. "You're not going to disrespect the cathedral's sanctuary, are you, Jerome?"

"He's not," snapped the priest. She stepped between us and glared at Jerome.

"No need to if you stay put," the Saint said to me.

I glanced at the exit. If I ran I had about as much hope as a fresh-caught salmon in the cold hard vacuum of space. "What if I don't feel like standing still?"

Cano said, "Both of you stop. Jerome, if you shoot him, you're done here. Your sanctuary from Trinity in this church will be void. Jude, if you make him shoot you—"

"You're as bad as the priests upstairs," I said. "I should have seen it coming. Are you going full machinist like the others?"

"What are you talking about?" Cano's brow furrowed in anger and offense.

"Machinist. You must have heard. It's all the trend in the Hallows these days. They're even starting to convert down in Haven." I stepped to one side and leaned against the high back of a pew. I almost got away with lowering my arms, but a gesture from the Saint told me not to push my luck. "Seems there's nothing wrong with conflating the Holy Trinity and the Trinity of the station's AI. Makes for an interesting philosophical debate, doesn't it?"

"Shut it," said Jerome.

I said, "Priest, will you listen to my last confession before this guy plugs me?"

"Of course."

"Forget it, Demarco," said Jerome. "I've heard enough."

I said, "I wasn't talking to you, Jerome, though I've had some very sinful thoughts you might be interested in."

"I said enough!" Saint Jerome's face reddened. In the church's flickering lights, he looked like the devil himself. "You're going to walk out the back door right now, and I'm going to follow."

"Since when do you do your own dirty work?" I asked. My feet moved as slow as I could manage, but we moved toward the back door. "Where are your goons? Where's Wash?"

"Jerome," Cano said, her voice brooking no dissent. "Stop."

To my absolute surprise, Jerome stopped.

She continued, "We can fix this with Demarco's help. He can get what you need to make things right."

"I never shoulda trusted him."

"Think about it, Jerome. He can stop Lauder. He can change your paperwork back." Priest Cano put a hand on my shoulder. "I've known him for a long time. He's always trying to put things right, even if he doesn't always succeed."

"Bullshit." Jerome jabbed me in the back with his gun. "He messed up the papers."

"There was someone else in the government center," I said. "Someone like me." I turned and faced Cano. "How many others are like me? How many are excommunicated."

"The Church isn't involved in that, and you know it."

"Like hell it isn't. The Church and the AI are one and the same. Religion is just another branch of Trinity's community and soul mandates mixed together. If Trinity excommunicates some-one, the Church knows it. It must."

For several long seconds, she showed no expression, then she gave a slight nod. "Ten," she said. "There are always no more than ten."

"Plus Richard Ruiz," I said. "The hacker. I saw him in the government center. Those were his papers you saw."

Cecilia swallowed. "For years we've used our influence for the betterment of our community by bringing in art from outside."

"From Earth," I said. "Stolen fair and square."

"Provenance isn't the important thing," she said. "Authenticity is."

Something finally clicked. "And discovering that something you've traded is fake would make your immunity diminish. Suddenly you can be held accountable for your crimes, and it just happens that you're in the middle of a turf war."

Jerome said, "The source dried up a long time ago. That's *why* we're in a turf war."

"That's why you started trading in electric mud," I said.

Cano shot Jerome a look so fierce, hell might have swallowed him whole and it wouldn't have surprised me.

"Mistakes were made," was Saint Jerome's only explanation.

"How did you get involved in all this?" I asked Cano.

Before she could answer, Jerome jabbed me in the ribs with his gun. "Walk."

I walked. The back entrance to the main sanctuary stood only a dozen feet away. Once I stepped from the sanctuary into the church's inner hallways, there might not be a reason for Jerome not to plug me.

"I do it because it's the right thing," Cano said. "Bringing our past forward allows the Church to better establish its dominion. The art we bring preaches the word of God and shows everyone that the Catholic Church has inspired people for thousands of years."

"You mean it shows that the Catholic Church has always hoarded its treasures," I said.

Before I reached the door, it burst open and Wash thundered in. He took in the situation and said, "Sir, Lauder's guys are trying to get in."

"Wash," I said. "Working for the Saint again?"

Wash shot a nervous glance at Jerome.

"No, I get it," I said. "You thought you'd take a shot at independence. Now you see the advantage of a continued alliance." The air in the room was as tense as a badly tuned guitar. "Does the Saint know what you said about him when you found me in Haven?"

This time, Wash's glance at the Saint had a hint of fear in it—the kind that dripped with guilt.

But the Saint laughed. "One of the first steps to keeping your Karma clean is making sure your employees don't mess up your good name."

Realization dawned on me slower than a fall from the top of the Hallows. "He was faking it."

Wash opened his mouth to answer, but the Saint gestured for silence.

It was all the distraction I needed. I lowered my shoulder and bowled forward through Wash. He shouted. Saint Jerome fired two shots, missing wide. Running, I let the dark of the church corridors swallow me.

"Get him!" roared Jerome.

They followed, lights flaring as they approached, but I was too fast. I knew these hallways. They were the same as the churches in Haven and the Hallows. Only these were decorated with the paintings of local artists. Abstract, blocky images of crosses and gods. Stations of the Cross were revealed as Saint Jerome moved closer. Simon picking up the cross. Jesus wearing the crown of thorns. I ducked down another hall, sure that I could remember where the paths led.

All I needed was a way out.

Somewhere far away, the sound of gunshots echoed through an

open space. It could have been in the sanctuary or outside of the church. It could have been anywhere.

Darkness embraced me. Saint Jerome and Wash fell far enough behind that the lights surrounding them didn't reach me.

More gunshots, closer this time.

I stood in the dark, waiting for the world to move on, taking slow breaths of stale air. Deep under the church where nothing ever moved, I could finally consider what Saint Jerome's plans meant for the greater community. He made himself valuable to Trinity by bringing in the art that eventually got traded up to the Hallows, only to be sequestered in a museum and never appreciated by anyone. Right there was a reason to doubt the long-term stability of his plan, but what if a painting traded in this way was discovered to be a forgery? What would Trinity do?

This explained why Saint Jerome had holed up in the church. The sanctuary of the citadel made it someplace he could exist even if his status with the AI had dropped significantly. But how much could it possibly have dropped? He had been part of a system that brought in dozens, if not hundreds, of works of art. When I stared out into the dark, my eyes focused on the memory of *The Garden of Earthly Delights*. That third panel was a squalor of pain and darkness writ large in oil and color. Its gruesome images danced before me, a promise of a hell to pay for our earthly excess.

But it was the back of the painting that interested me most. That faded image on the wooden panel depicted something I'd seen before, and there in the dark, my brain felt like it might finally make the connection. The picture on the back was half of a world in a bubble. The bottled landscape. I'd seen the whole thing somewhere.

Then, I knew. The whole plot fell into place. In order to untangle it, I was going to need help. My first thought was of Beck. With her at my side, we could accomplish anything. But she wasn't at my side. She was part of the problem. Saint Jerome clearly didn't consider himself an ally, and his enemy Frank Lauder likely wouldn't be much help. Retch—well, I figured I could count on Retch, but he was only able to do so much.

It was time to depend on the last best hope of the private investigator. The police. Maybe it was finally time to step up and have a chat with police officer Anders.

Once the gunshots stopped, I worked my way through the cathedral's tunnels to a back exit. An eerie silence lingered over the darkened streets. Lights along the fiberstone cobblestones flickered yellow like the flames of a dying torch. Far away, police sirens sounded, echoing off mist-shrouded buildings. I stood, unsure where to go in the darkening night. I chose to go back into the warehouse district to make a wide circle around the area immediately surrounding the church.

After only half a block, I found the first body. A man in a suit sat slumped against the warehouse wall, plastic gun still gripped in his dead fingers. He had a gray fedora that matched his loosely tied tie. One of Lauder's men.

Not far from him lay one of the Saint's people. A young man wearing a cross. His weapon was missing, and his pale face pressed against the cobblestones. These boys were dead because of Jerome's war. They were dead because for years he had siphoned the funds that might have raised them from poverty. Instead, he had used their poverty to recruit them into his gang. He had created a community for them that would eventually lead to their deaths.

I continued. The blue would come to deal with these bodies, but this wasn't the circumstance I wanted to be in when I had my chat with them. They'd see me as a suspect. I picked up the plastic gun Lauder's man had used in the fight. It closely resembled the gun Beck had used, but the barrel was a deep orange. The man carried his extra bullets in the pocket of his suit, so I took them. Sin hadn't finished with me yet.

More bodies lay in the streets. Either nobody had survived the battle, or the injured had been taken away already. These gangs took care of their own. They likely had ways to help those in need. I could only hope. The police closed in, their lights flashing over the rooftops above. Picking up my pace, I jogged farther from the cathedral.

Right into a cluster of Frank Lauder's men.

A dozen guns pointed my way as soon as I rounded the corner. Frank held up a hand to signal his people not to shoot.

"Jude Demarco," said Frank. "Good to see you again."

"Wish I could reciprocate."

His smile widened. "You'll be our guest."

"I'll take a rain check," I said.

"We need to have a chat." Lauder drew a small pistol and pointed it at me. "Now seems like a good time, don't you think?"

And that is how I discovered the location of Frank Lauder's hideout.

Chapter 45

"SAINT JEROME HAS GOT TO GO." Lauder's pencil-thin mustache twitched with irritation. "He's a blight on this city. He and his fish-smelling thugs need to take a step aside so that we can run this city like the city of the future it was always meant to be."

Lauder's hideout was in an old pita shop that smelled of gyro meat and black pepper. His men had carted me upspiral to the place, nestled in among residential districts adjacent to the government center. This was the neighborhood where I had met with Matthew Williams. Frank's people looked a whole lot like Jerome's, and I recognized a few faces in the crowd. There really had been a fair number of defections.

"Let me take a look at your injured," I said.

Lauder narrowed his eyes. His thin form towered over most of his gang, but as tall as he was, he couldn't look down on me.

"Why does everyone think I'm up to something?" I wondered aloud.

Lauder's thin lips broke into a smile. "Word on the street is that you usually are."

Fair enough. "I trained as a medic. These people are hurt."

"Your buddy is still out there causing trouble for us."

"Saint Jerome's no buddy of mine."

The door crashed open, and two men hauled a woman in, laying her on a table. She bled from a deep wound in her leg, and her face was twisted in a silent scream.

"Let me help her," I pleaded.

Lauder nodded. "Fine. Help my people. I'll pay you."

"I don't want your money."

"I don't trust a man I can't pay."

"You mean you don't trust anyone you can't buy. I'm not loyal to you, Lauder, and I'm never going to be. I'm not loyal to Saint Jerome either. Sometimes I help him. Sometimes he helps me. That's the end of it."

"Sometimes he tries to have you killed," Lauder drawled.

"If you want your people to suffer from their wounds, then I'll leave them be. If you want them to get better, let me work."

The woman's silent scream transformed into a very loud one. The men at her sides held her down as she thrashed from the pain.

Lauder pointed to a man lingering in the corner. "You. Keep a gun on Demarco. If he does anything funny, give him some better injuries to start working on." With that, he left the room to shout down his troops. He'd always seemed so calm and collected. It was interesting to see him close to cracking under pressure.

The woman's skin had gone pale and cold. Blood poured from the wound, which someone had inexpertly bound with a bandage. I pushed on the artery to slow the bleeding. "Where's the nearest medical station?"

One of the thugs who had brought the woman in said, "Couple blocks away there's a clinic."

"Go there. Pick up bandages and painkillers."

"We're not supposed to use it."

I grabbed a handful of his lapels and pulled him close to my face. "Listen to me. You're going to go get me some decent supplies. Pick up a full surgery kit." I glanced around at the other injured people. "Five surgery kits. You're going to order them up with a provisional code. Tell Trinity that medic Jude Demarco requests the supplies. I'll check in later and make sure it's squared away."

"What if it won't give me the supplies."

"Then next time you're in charge of making supper you don't have to make quite so many gyros."

He blinked.

"Go!"

The thug disappeared into the dark streets. I gave it only about a 10 percent chance that the med station would supply him with surgery kits, but it was worth a shot anyway. The woman screamed again, and I did my best to adjust her bandages. I recognized her. It was the woman Saint Jerome had trusted as his bodyguard when he'd ambushed me in the tailor's shop. A bullet had shattered against her hip bone, and ceramic shards were shredding any attempt I made to staunch the bleeding. After several minutes, I got her bound up and stable.

A familiar voice carried from the kitchen. "I don't care if you're in the middle of a war. I told you to find him, and I expect results."

Charlotte Beck. My heart pounded, but I didn't know if it was rage or fear or something else. I moved around the table to get a better look into the well-lit kitchen. She stood there in a sapphire suit with matching gloves and pumps. It was a stylish outfit that showed off her sleek form.

It wasn't rage or fear making my heart pound. This was definitely something else. I had asked Retch to find her, but now that she was there, I couldn't move.

Part of me wanted to go to her, help her, maybe talk about what to do. Part of me knew how stupid that was. Beck was up to no good. She was after Maurice Ribar, and I didn't think it was for another round of chit-chat and sausages.

"I told you," Lauder growled. "I have half my people searching for this guy. We haven't seen him."

"Things have changed. My boss is leaving in the morning," Beck said. "She gave me three hours to find him, kill him, and get back to the ship for your payment."

"Maybe I should demand more payment up front."

Beck's knife moved so fast Lauder hardly had time to blink. She pressed it to his neck and leaned down so her face was close to his. She whispered something I couldn't hear, but the expression on Lauder's face was enough to tell me it was a threat. It got to him too.

As fast as it came out, Beck's knife disappeared. She took a step to the side, and I couldn't see her behind the gyro station. "You'll get it all, Lauder. Everything I promised. The node, the whole city if you want it. I can give it to you. All you need to do is find one man."

"It's a big city."

"Excuses!" she snapped. "Don't give me excuses! This is harder for me than you can possibly understand, and in three hours I'll be on a ship destined for the stars. You know what you need, Lauder. You know what I can get you." Her voice cracked a little, but I couldn't tell if it was due to regret or just the massive weight of her stressful situation.

"I understand," said Lauder.

"Just find him and bring him to me at the ship. Once it's done, you'll get your payment." She stepped back into view, and I caught a glimpse of pain in her expression. A tear threatened to spill onto her heavily made-up cheek. "Just find Demarco for me, Lauder. That's all I'm asking."

"You're going to kill him," Lauder said.

"I'll decide what to do with him."

"What about the other guy?"

"Ribar? I know where he'll be. Don't worry about him." With that, she exited through the kitchen door, leaving Lauder standing alone.

Now, my heart pounded for an entirely new reason. Beck was

after me? It didn't make sense.

Then again, maybe it did.

The thug returned with a single surgery kit. I worked on the worst of the injured with what I had, rationing painkillers to those in the worst shape.

After a while, Lauder came back into the dining hall. "Seems you're a popular man, my friend."

"I heard." I didn't look up from my work.

"Now will you make a deal with me?" His voice sounded exhausted, on the verge of giving up.

"How did you get involved with her? She hasn't been in town very long."

Lauder held a man's hand as I removed a bullet from his leg. The man swallowed a scream and clutched his boss's hand. When the worst was over, Lauder said, "Tell me what you know about Saint Jerome's scam."

"It has to do with art," I said. "He traded art for Karma, bolstering his own importance to the ship's community, allowing him the luxury of threatening body and soul on a regular basis."

Lauder said, "He's been doing it for years. It wasn't hard for Beck, who had all the connections of the original thieves, to discover who was affected by it on our side. We've been in communication for the past year as their ship approached."

"So, she used you to form connections in Heavy Nicodemia."

"She knew my parents had been murdered by Jerome's gang. She helped me trade up so that my people have some of the same capital Jerome enjoys."

"The guns came from her ship," I said. "Only, Jerome's men intercepted one of the shipments, didn't he?"

"The Saint grasps at power like a greedy hog. If we're going to win, we need more Karma. More capital. That means we need access to new art."

"Saint Jerome's supply ran out a long time ago. His hold on the node has been weakening for years." My tongs snagged the bullet fragment in the man's leg, and I extracted it. "He depended on the thieves for a constant supply. He didn't have much spare Karma when Trinity learned that some of the art he brought in was fake. Forged art meant that what he had left went away fast. Perfect time for you to strike."

"Except the discovery of all that forged art meant an erosion of the confidence behind what I traded."

"Which is?"

"Music. Analog music recordings dating all the way back to the twentieth century."

That struck me as particularly funny. "You're trading the blues to the devil for the right to murder people."

"We're not killing anyone who doesn't deserve it, Demarco."

My instinct told me it wasn't his decision to make, but I didn't think he wanted to hear it. "Why does Beck want me?"

"Same reason she wants all of them."

"All of who?" Then it clicked. "Violet Ruiz thinks the art thieves were responsible for murdering her husband. She sent me to look for the painting knowing that it would lead Beck to everyone involved in the trade. This has never been about recovering art."

I remembered that moment speaking with Violet in her ship. Violet Ruiz had seemed distant and cold, except when she turned her attention to the art. Was she really capable of such a plot? Then I remembered the art on her ship. Paintings and statues. Strange things to haul around on a spaceship, given how heavy and breakable they were.

"My father was involved in the trade," I said. "He found buyers for the art up in the Hallows. She probably wants me dead because of him."

Lauder shrugged. "Not my problem."

"Then why didn't you turn me over?"

"Jerome only survived these last few years because he had

someone outside the system to help him out. If I don't have that, I won't be able to keep a hold on this place."

"Is that why you hired the other guy?"

"Richard?" Lauder pressed his lips together.

"He double-crossed you, didn't he? You sent him looking for dirt on the Saint, but he's been using you."

"Everybody has their own agenda," Lauder said.

"No," I said. Things were starting to click into place. "He came to you first, didn't he?" Ruiz knew that his wife was approaching, and this was his chance to set things right.

"I need a man in the dark," said Lauder. "It's our only chance to take down Jerome."

"Ruiz was getting his affairs in order," I thought aloud. "He was tying up all his loose ends because he was planning on leaving with his wife." I wondered if she knew about this plan. Probably not, I thought. She wouldn't have needed to hire me.

"I think you'll be easier to work with than Richard," said Lauder.

"You want all the power of being excommunicated without the inconvenience."

"I want you on my side. When I figured out what you were capable of, I finally understood how the Saint's whole organization functioned. Trinity's everywhere. It's impossible to get around without the AI knowing. But you. You can do it. You can get the supplies needed. You can solve things that need solving. Trinity doesn't come after you for anything."

"Even murder."

A smile crossed his lips. "A well-run organization doesn't need to rely on murder."

"Everyone thinks their organization is going to be well-run, don't they?"

"Work for me."

"No."

He drew his pistol and pointed it at my chest. "One way or another, you're working for me."

"So much for a well-run organization."

I closed the injured man's wound, stitching it as neatly as I could. The man didn't even flinch as I pulled the needle through, so I knew the painkillers were working. Half the people in the room were on one painkiller or another now, and those I hadn't treated would heal on their own.

"The final panel of *The Garden of Earthly Delights* that Trey Vitez brought to the Hallows was a forgery," I said, "but I know where the real one is."

Lauder raised one of his perfect eyebrows. "It's on the widow's ship."

"True," I said. "But I can get you and your people onto that ship."

He leaned forward over the table. "I'm listening."

Chapter 46

AS I ENTERED THE DINER, Angel watched me with an icy expression that I knew only as a prelude to the storm of her rage. She sat in her wheelchair in the corner of her diner and made no attempt to berate me for my many sins.

That worried me.

The rest of the diner was empty but for Retch, who sat among the remains of several pot pies. He grinned at me, and said, "I like your sister, Demarco. She's a lot nicer than you."

I shot Angel a glance in time to see her brow furrow. I said, "Don't let it fool you."

Lauder swished through the open diner door and wordlessly gave the diner a scathing assessment. He wore a pristine pinstripe suit and carried a pistol fully visible on his hip.

I sat across from Retch, and Lauder joined me. When Helen cleared away the remnants of Retch's meal, we ordered some coffee.

"Just curious," Helen said, "because I don't want to get in trouble. Are you able to pay for this?"

"He's paying," I said, gesturing at Lauder. "We'll have pie too."

"Don't push your luck, Demarco," Lauder said.

"Saint Jerome never bought me pie," I said. "Seems like a loose alliance might be a little stronger if it involved pie."

Retch said, "The apple pie is decent."

"I'll have two slices," I said when Helen came out with the coffee. "One apple, one cherry."

Helen pursed her lips. "We're out of cherry."

"Two apple, then, and bring a lemon custard for Lauder here. Retch?"

"Apple."

"Three apple, one lemon custard," Helen said. She cast a questioning glance at my dear sister, who nodded. "Coming right up."

When she left, I turned to Lauder. "Lauder, this is Retch. Retch, Lauder."

Retch grinned. "I'm familiar."

"Pleased to meet you." Lauder's expression betrayed the lie, but Retch either didn't notice or didn't care.

"Aren't you supposed to be in the middle of a gang war?" Retch asked. "Last I heard it was going pretty rough."

Lauder went cold. "What's with the kid, Demarco?"

"I'm his boss," said Retch.

Before I could respond, Lauder sneered. "What are you, ten?"

"I'm fifteen," said Retch. A lie, I figured, but almost plausible. "And age has nothing to do with it."

I cleared my throat to get their attention. "Lauder's going to get a hold of the painting, which will let him trade up for Karma. That will give him leverage to negotiate for his power."

"Without violence," Lauder explained, as if to a toddler.

"Oh, everybody wins," Retch said dryly. "Except for the people who think your Gentlemen are a bunch of assholes."

"Right," I said. "This will keep organized crime in place. Things won't change, except that it'll be Lauder on the top." I leaned close to Retch and said, "Non-organized crime won't be affected."

"I'm organized!" Retch protested.

Lauder cleared his throat.

Retch said, "So if this guy's gaining leverage to run half of the Heavies, what do I get?"

"Excuse me?" I said.

"What am I getting paid?"

"You get free pie," I said.

As if on cue, Helen arrived with the pie and more coffee. I took a sip of the bitter, nasty stuff, and decided that it tasted like home. It made me feel like I was finally back where I belonged. My first bite of pie tasted that much sweeter with bitter coffee lingering on my lips. My head cleared, and the world settled into place.

I excused myself from the table and made my way over to my sister. "Angel, I need your help."

"There it is," she drawled.

I almost shot back a retort, but the memory of my parents' deaths ran through my head. How much worse must it have been for my sister, who lost not only her parents but also the use of her legs? She had always taken care of me. My older sister had been a powerhouse in political circles, lined up to take over my father's business—a business that I now knew to be corrupt and dangerous. She probably hadn't known that. She probably had never needed to know that.

"I found out something," I said. "About Dad."

"He dealt in stolen art," she said.

Shit. "You already knew?"

"Suspected." Something in her eased, and her shoulders slumped. "He always kept parts of his business secret, even when he was training me to manage the whole operation. It was suspicious, but I never really figured out what he was doing."

"I could have saved them," I said.

She went quiet. Extremely quiet. Dangerously quiet. I had never told her this. The topic was taboo between us.

"There was an override. After that first impact—the one that broke your back—I could have kept the ship from disengaging. There was a chance of saving everyone aboard."

"But you chose not to." The weight of her judgment was ten times the gravity crush of the Heavies. Her gaze bore a hole right through the side of my skull because I couldn't bring myself to meet her shining eyes. They reminded me too much of our mother.

"The pressure might also have ripped a hole in the station." The excuse tasted like sand on my lips.

"Jude," she said.

I finally met her gaze, and what I found there surprised me. Tears. Soft, merciful tears.

"Come here." She opened her arms wide. I leaned forward and she hugged me. It felt better than anything I could remember, and I hugged her back. My eyes blurred with tears, but I blinked them back. Angel said, "Sometimes the right choices are hard, bro."

I didn't have any words.

After a long time, she pulled back. "I'm still not forgiving you for gambling away our inheritance, though."

"Fair enough."

"What do you need help with?"

I told her what I needed, complete with how the timing had to work. "I also need you to help me look after Retch when this is through. He's just a kid and could use the occasional pie and wisdom."

A weak smile crossed Angel's lips. "I can probably help with the pie."

"You're such a dear," I said, imitating our housekeeper's voice.

She punched me in the shoulder. "She was a thief, you know."

"Oh yeah?"

"Stole from our parents constantly. I might have blackmailed her for a few years about it."

"That explains why she always gave you extra desserts."

Back at the table, Retch was telling Lauder about a time he

stole a purse full of counterfeit dimes and had to try to find clever ways to spend them that didn't reveal where they'd come from.

"They were fibersteel," he said. "Someone printed them as if they'd pass through any kind of inspection."

"Didn't they?"

"They did if you dunked them in fish guts first."

Lauder crinkled his nose at the thought. "Demarco, I take back everything. Your urchin friend is rather interesting."

Retch clenched his fists. "Who are you calling an urchin, you piece of shit?"

Lauder's smile widened.

It was my turn to clear my throat. "Retch, seeing as how you've already eaten my second piece of pie, maybe you'd like to start the business portion of this meeting."

"Sorry," Retch said. "We found your guy."

"You did?"

"Yeah. Guy fitting his description passed through Wailing Sinner turf. Holed up right outside the docks."

"The docks?" Lauder asked.

"Not the fisheries," Retch said. "The actual station side port."

"He's going to pay Violet Ruiz a visit," I said, thinking out loud. Maurice was a damn fool if he thought that was a good idea. "Was he able to get through any of the locks?"

"Nope. He's still hunkered down just outside. He thinks he's well hidden, but we know all the good hiding spots."

"Perfect. I'll need you to take me to him, and that's on the way for what Lauder needs." If Ribar was so interested in getting to see Violet Ruiz, maybe he would help us. "Lauder, you need the painting, but it's big. Are you going to have your people come with?"

"I have a team in mind. They can meet us there."

"All you need to do is get your people in, grab the painting, and leave. It's all yours."

Lauder didn't seem convinced. "This seems too easy."

"It'll be anything but." I swallowed the last dregs of coffee. "Pay the bill, Lauder, and leave a good tip. We're taking a walk."

Lauder paid without further complaint, and the three of us made our way upspiral, where the cathedral stood sentinel over a restless city. The mist had cleared, and the false stars gazed down upon us like a million uncaring angels. Stale air blew a constant wind, not cold, but cool and unforgiving. This was my city. We walked through the streets like ghosts carried on the empty wind, rising in our restlessness to haunt the hallways of the discontent.

Maurice Ribar's hiding place wasn't very good. For one, he was within view of the false storefront that led to the dock where Violet Ruiz's ship sat. I don't know how he learned the correct location, but across the street, there were only two buildings that would give him the view he needed. One of them was the home of an ongoing block party, complete with live music and an open bar.

The other building stood completely empty, and Maurice's nest sat at the very top. I left Retch and Lauder down below so I could confront the man. He huddled under the cover of a black shroud, peering out at the empty storefront.

"Ribar," I said as I approached.

He startled, pitched backward, and jumped to his feet, hands balled into fists. His eyes rolled around in his head with a crazy, haunted look. After a few seconds, he calmed and squinted at me in the shadows. "Demarco?"

I stepped forward to where he could see me. "You need to melt into the woodwork, old man. There's trouble coming."

"Not until I can talk to Violet."

"She know you're here?"

"I sent a message. She'll send someone out for me when she gets it."

"She'll send someone out to kill you when she gets it."

He shook his head. "No, I don't think so. Violet—she was always nice to us. She kept an interest in her husband's work, and she always helped us out. She'll help me now."

"Trey Vitez is dead."

Ribar's hands shook. "It's a damn shame."

"He betrayed you. Left you to live in the dark."

"Vitez wasn't such a bad guy. He did what he had to do."

A stiff breeze blew across the rooftop.

"I'll talk to Violet about your situation," I said, "but you need to disappear for now."

"I'm coming with."

"You can't, Maurice. She'll kill you. She already had Vitez killed, and she sent someone down into the tunnels to kill you."

"Who?"

"Charlotte Beck."

Ribar stood silent for a long time. Finally, he said, "I liked her."

"Yeah," I said. "Me too."

"She's really a killer?"

"Working for Violet. There's no way this ends well, Maurice. You need to disappear. The ship is scheduled to leave in an hour, and after that, you might be safe, but Beck is close and now she knows where you are. She's probably planning on taking care of you on her way out the door."

He chewed on that for a few seconds. "Then I gotta come with you." Before I could refuse, he continued, "There's nowhere I can go that'll be safe. She can track me wherever she needs. If I don't talk to Violet and make peace, she's never going to leave me alone. She'll just hire someone else to do the job once she's left. That's how she always did business. Hire experts to do the hard stuff. That was her thing."

I crossed to the edge of the building and looked out at the ongoing party across the street. A shirtless, well-muscled man drank beer from a glass the size of his head while others cheered him on.

Ribar thought he could convince Violet Ruiz to back off, and it occurred to me what information he must have had to bargain with. "How long have you known about Richard?"

He swallowed. "He's been down in the tunnels. I told you, the excommunicated sometimes go down there to talk to the big guy."

"So, you saw him walking through your tunnels. You ever talk with him? Did he know how you lived?"

"No, sir. I steered clear. I told you, I don't want that kind of life anymore. I don't want anything to do with them."

"You can come with," I said, "but it's going to be dangerous. Things just got more complicated."

"Why's that?"

I pointed down below to the false storefront that led to the locks. Saint Jerome, Wash, and half a dozen thugs passed into the first airlock. "We're going to have company when we get there," I said, "and it's not the friendly kind."

Chapter 47

"THERE ARE NINE SPHERES," I said to Retch as we passed through the false storefront. He and Maurice accompanied me along with Lauder, who conferred with three of his best goons. Saint Jerome and his goons were ahead of us in the airlock system, at least another room away. "We live in the ninth sphere, and the void beyond is the first. That means there are seven airlocks between us and the ship."

Retch scrunched his nose. "This isn't a sphere."

Maurice said, "Dante's Paradiso has a sphere called the Fixed Stars, so that's not exactly accurate either."

I checked the pistol I had picked up from one of Saint Jerome's men. Lauder had hesitated before giving it back to me, but in the end, he decided I was as trustworthy as a person could get. "Our understanding of space wasn't perfect in the fourteenth century."

"Is that when Nicodemia was built?" asked Retch.

"No." Maurice and I both snapped.

The first gateway opened, revealing a room filled with the false stars of a Nicodemia night. "This is the fixed stars now, actually," I said. "It's the eighth sphere, and this is where faith, hope, and love are supposed to live."

As one, we stepped in.

"Which one of you is faith and which is love?" Retch asked.

"Demarco!" Charlotte Beck approached the storefront as the airlock door descended. I stared at her as she rushed toward us. The blue of her suit shone against the dark of the gray city. Despite everything, something tugged in my chest. All I needed to do was reach out a hand and the airlock would wait for her.

The door slammed shut seconds before she arrived.

I hit the intercom, surprised when the touchscreen worked for me. We were in a liminal space already. "Beck," I said.

"You can't be in here," she said. A hint of desperation found its way into her voice. "It's not safe."

"Is it safer out there?" I tried to keep the hurt from my voice, but judging by the look Retch gave me, I'd failed miserably.

"Things are going to get ugly, and you don't want to be around for it."

Lauder made a point of rechecking his pistol.

"Is that why you left?" I asked. Somehow it was easier to talk through the intercom than face to face. "Trying to keep me safe?"

"No."

"I didn't think so."

Beck's silence was a noose around my neck.

"This has been great," said Saint Jerome through the intercom. "But can we please keep this channel clear?"

The next gate of the airlock opened, and Retch, Maurice, and I moved forward along with Lauder's thugs.

"Saturn?" Retch asked.

Maurice grinned. "How could you tell?"

Retch said, "It has the same picture of the ringed planet that's on one of the strip clubs downspiral."

"You go to strip clubs?" I asked.

"I'm a pickpocket," said Retch. "I go wherever people are distracted."

"Fair enough."

I pushed the intercom. "We could have worked something out, Beck."

She said, "Is it too late?"

Now it was my turn to pause. I wanted to say it was never too late, but something deep in my gut thought otherwise. "I don't know."

The airlock cycled, and we stepped into the next room.

"Jupiter," Maurice said as the room filled with an orange gas. The moving images of Jupiter's red storm swirled along the wall as red gas whirled around us.

"It's a decontaminant gas. Nothing to worry about it," I reassured Lauder and his men. "As long as you aren't too dependent on your lungs having living cells or anything like that."

When one of them opened his mouth to respond, Lauder waved him back. "Cut the crap and get us inside, Demarco."

I shushed him. "No talking. If you breathe too much of this stuff in, you're a goner for sure."

The gas cleared, and the next lock opened to a view of red Mars. Its dusty waste appeared to stretch forever once the airlock doors were closed. Domed buildings dotted its surface.

"This is the heaven for warriors of the faith," Maurice mumbled. "According to Dante."

Retch scowled. "Why would warriors of the faith end up in heaven? Aren't they murderers just like anyone else?"

"They get a special pass," I said. "The Church sells discounts to anyone who kills in their name."

"That's messed up."

The intercom came alive. Saint Jerome said in his gruff voice, "Lauder."

Lauder had a supremely annoyed look on his face. "Jerome."

"How about you take out that assassin behind you and I'll cut you into a big chunk of the business."

"I've heard this story. Nobody who's worked for you trusts a word you say."

"No, but they trust my dimes and my Karma. It's a good system, Lauder. It's also your best chance to get out of this alive."

"Alive? You think trying to kill that woman is my best chance to leave alive? I'd have a better chance stepping into the void for a bit of a drift with nothing but my skivvies and a pair of goggles."

"You paint quite a picture, Lauder," said the Saint. "Quite a picture indeed."

The airlock cycled. The next room we stepped into was the bright one, with walls that glowed searing yellow. As soon as the doors sealed behind us, the glow intensified, brightening to sear off whatever microbes might have been left after the orange gas of Jupiter.

"The sun," Retch said. "I know this one. Earth people rotate around a big old ball of fire, just like us."

Maurice said, "This is where the wise go after death."

"How do you know so much about Dante's Paradiso?" I asked.

"I wrote a paper about it in college."

"Must have been a hell of a paper."

"I have a good memory. It's part of what makes me a good safecracker."

The airlock cycled, and we stepped into a green room. The floor hummed with power and a scan passed over each of us in turn.

"Venus," Maurice whispered to Retch, "is for lovers."

The kid smiled.

"Demarco," Beck said, with an air of long suffering. "You don't have to turn back, but just wait for me. Don't step through when the next airlock cycles. We can talk."

"We could talk now."

"Not with everyone listening. Look, I'm sorry. I did what I thought was right, but I was wrong."

I swallowed the lump in my throat. "Sorry about what?"

"About leaving. About cutting you out when I needed your help. I couldn't let you get close because——"

"Because you're leaving."

"Violet hired me to collect her paintings. Part of my payment is that I never have to go anywhere near Earth again, and I can travel the colonies with her. She needs me, and I belong in the stars."

"Forget that anyone else might want you to stick around. Nobody would ever want to settle down in a slum like Nicodemia."

"That's not what I said."

"It's what you mean." My mouth had the consistency of damp cotton. "You're leaving because you can't imagine being happy here. That's all I needed to know."

Lauder stepped up to the intercom. "Jerome, how about this? Have your men lay down their guns and I'll let you have a healthy chunk of my new empire."

I stepped back.

"You gotta be kidding," Saint Jerome said over the intercom. "By the time you step out of that airlock, it'll all be over."

Lauder looked at me. Then at Maurice and Retch. I didn't like the cold, calculating malice in his eyes. "Wash," he said into the intercom. "It's time to earn that payment."

Gunshots. The heavy airlock door muffled the noise, but it was unmistakable. I lunged at Lauder but drew up short as his thugs—ready for me—leveled their weapons. One of them pointed a pistol at Maurice and Retch.

The airlock cycled. As one, we moved forward into Mercury. The searing heat of the room cooked us right down to the bone. A body lay on the floor, crumpled against the wall in a mess of black clothes.

I walked to it, careful to move slowly, so as to avoid spooking

Lauder's men. With my toe, I nudged the corpse, rolling it onto its back.

It wasn't Jerome. Nor was it Wash. One of Wash's gang lay with a still-smoking wound in his chest. The only guy I knew who owned a weapon big enough to make that wound was the Saint himself.

"Seems your plan didn't go off so well," I said to Lauder. "Was that all you had?"

"Care to join him?" Lauder said.

"Wash doesn't work for you, Lauder," I said.

"Sure, he does. He's been on my payroll since he was a kid. I've helped him work up through Saint Jerome's ranks all his life, feeding him ideas of triumph over the guy who kept him and his friends in squalor. I taught him that the only way to get ahead was to fight Saint Jerome's organization from the inside. Now, it's finally time to turn things around in this damn city." He turned to Retch. "Kids like Wash are going to have a better chance of moving ahead in this world."

"Under your organization?"

"That's right. Because I'm not a greedy bastard like the Saint."

Retch said, "You're a different kind of greedy bastard?"

Lauder let his cold gaze linger on the boy. "I know you've had it rough, but things are going to get better. Wash is on our side. Even if he didn't outright kill the Saint, he's got him on the run. We'll chase him down together, grab the painting, and leave."

"What about Violet Ruiz and her security detail?" I asked.

"She'll stay out of the way. She doesn't need the painting like we do, and she doesn't rightfully own it. Why shouldn't we take it?"

I pressed against the wall until I was as hidden from the door as I could manage, gesturing to Maurice and Retch to do the same. "Because Wash's only goal is the big score. He's a damn fool trying to buy his way out, but you can't buy your way out of this kind of debt. This hole only digs deeper. You're building your castle on sand, Lauder. That's one thing Saint Jerome had right. He built his criminal enterprise atop one of the greatest criminal enterprises ever in the history of man: the Catholic Church."

"Fuck the Catholic Church," said Lauder. "It can burn, as far as I care."

"Fair enough, but there's some good that comes from it too. It's a cultural touchpoint. Sure, there are other religions in the area, but everyone here knows the Church. Everyone has experiences with it, good or bad, and there's one thing I know: nothing draws people together like a central organization about which to complain. That's the real service the Catholic Church provides to Nicodemia. Body, soul, community. The Church provides for all three. No matter what you do, you're never going to beat that."

"People complain about Saint Jerome and his organized crime."

"Jerome's gang is nothing compared to a good, fully functioning Catholic Church."

Lauder studied me as if discovering an alien specimen for the first time. "I could use you, Demarco. Are you sure you won't join?"

"It's an interesting proposal," I said. "Do I want to be a part of a corrupt organization? I've considered my options, and I don't know that it seems all that bad. Luxury and ease with the occasional terrifying takeover attempt? That might let me live longer and happier than my current gig. I mean, there would be food every single day."

"That sounds nice," said Retch.

"But there's something I need to know before I join."

"What's that?" asked Lauder.

I swallowed the sandpaper in my throat. "What I need to know is, are you the kind of guy who knows when a person is just stalling for time?"

"What?"

The final airlock opened onto the *Thirty Silver*'s foyer, and bullets started to fly.

Chapter 48

THE OPEN FOYER to the Ruiz space mansion was exactly as it was when I visited before. The sleek shining walls swept outward from the dazzling radiance of the three steps to the wide doors. Glass displays of ancient art stood to greet visitors with a mix of the beautiful and the mundane.

The biggest difference was the active gunfight.

The velvet settee lay in shreds across the floor, and several display cases sat sideways as barricades. Ceramic shards of a porcelain God littered the floor. Above, a red light flashed with alarm, and the exits into the ship proper were all closed.

A bullet struck Lauder in the chest, and he staggered back. One of his goons stepped forward to protect him but took a shot to the skull and dropped like a broken drone from the gray Heavies sky.

"Stand down, Wash!" shouted Lauder, apparently unfazed by being shot. A blossom of blood spread across his expensive shirt.

Wash shouted, "I should have known you were just as bad as the Saint, Lauder."

Lauder cast me a furious glance, and I shrugged. Honestly, I had expected Wash to last a little longer before going completely unhinged. "He wants an equal share," I suggested.

"Split it three ways," shouted Wash. It was, honestly, the most reasonable any of the potential crime bosses had been, which is why I knew it would never work.

Our position was poor. Maurice and Retch stayed mostly hidden behind the outer airlock door, but I didn't fit. It was only a matter of time before Wash decided to start taking shots at me. I still couldn't see Saint Jerome, but I didn't like my chances with him either.

Glancing back at Lauder, I spotted the gateway terminal. That terminal—or its equivalent in Haven—had been the death of my parents. This was the same room, and the event flashed before my eyes like it had happened yesterday. One second, I was a wealthy aristocrat's son, the next I was an unwanted orphan. That fateful day I'd made the decision to murder my own parents—along with hundreds of others on that ship—all in the name of saving Nicodemia. Saving Trinity.

Maybe Trinity really was my god. It was the higher power for which I had sacrificed everything. Maybe one day there would be a reckoning for the sins of that day and all the sins since.

But not today.

I drew my pistol. "Maurice, Retch, I need you two to get to that door on the left. It's got some cover, and you should be able to open it. I'll cover you."

By the last word, Retch had already reached the door. Maurice shrugged at me and did his best crouch-run. When Wash—who hunkered down behind a shattered display case—spotted him, I fired a couple shots to get his attention.

Unfortunately, that got his attention.

"Demarco," he growled.

"How come all the other would-be crime bosses want to hire me and you just want me dead?"

In response, he fired. I dove out of the way, making the best of the cover that a shattered display case could provide. The distraction left an opportunity for Lauder and his remaining guy to duck out of the airlock into the relative cover of the room.

Wash unleashed a barrage of bullets. I ran. Behind me, the airlock started to cycle. I dove into cover with Maurice and Retch.

"The ship is locked down," Retch said, wrenching the door's control panel open. "But Mo's going to show me how to get through."

"Just get the door open." I popped my head out of cover and took in a glimpse of the surroundings. From there, I saw Saint Jerome, bleeding by the red door on the right. He shifted. Still alive, then. "We need to get out of here fast. Wash's backed into a corner. He finally figured out he can't trust anyone."

The airlock door slammed shut. Beck would join the party as soon as it cycled, and I wasn't sure we wanted to be around for that. The display above the airlock showed that two other chambers behind her were occupied. It would take them time to work their way through the system, whoever they were. Maybe too long.

Maurice said, "The *Thirty Silver* is built on the chassis of a Mark IV Cruiseliner. Standard stuff. These systems all have an open mode that they use during construction and big maintenance activities."

The words didn't sink in right away. His voice was chatter in the background of a gunfight. I fired two more shots at Wash, hoping to distract the raging idiot before he got anyone else killed.

"Thing is," Maurice told Retch, "open mode isn't supposed to be available post construction. It's dangerous. It was always a long, slow transition from wide open to full lockdown. Right now we're in lockdown, and if the airlock blew we'd suck void in one, maybe two rooms. Everyone else on the ship would be safe."

"But if all the bulkheads are all open," Retch said, "everyone's doomed."

"That's never a state an occupied ship should be in," said Maurice. "Ever."

Lauder's last bodyguard took a bullet to the neck, pasting the wall with blood. His body fell to become a grisly work of art on a broken display case.

Retch said, "You know how to override the lockdown?"

"All we have to do is bypass the system and revert the ship to maintenance mode." With that, he flipped the pins on the console, pressed the hard reset, and said, "Please let this work."

All the lights went dark.

As Maurice's words sunk into my head, I said, "Did you say this was a Mark IV?"

I knew there was something familiar about the layout of the ship. This was the same design that I'd been in so many years ago. It was the ship where my parents died. This was the ship that had failed to properly section off to compartmentalize during the disaster. This ship ruined my life.

Maurice had just shown Retch how to override every safety measure aboard the ship. He'd overridden the bulkheads.

The overhead lights flared to a shocking white. The door slid open, as did the others in the room. As we hurried through, the airlock cycled again.

Beck's voice rang down the hall, "Enough!"

I drew to a halt.

Silence hung in the air. All gunfire stopped. For the span of one held breath, nothing moved in the entire ship. It was the peace of the endless void—the deep echoing silence before the roaring cataclysm.

Tap, tap, tap of Beck's heels in the entryway. She didn't have a line of sight to me, but she would soon. "None of you are welcome on this ship. Lauder, you're here for a painting that isn't yours. Did you think it wouldn't be defended? Jerome? You think you can cut a deal with my boss? You're wrong. She's already made her decision. We're leaving, and you're not coming with. Take what's left of your goons and go. We'll let you live, and that's generous. Demarco." Her voice cracked, and the powerful demeanor shattered. "Demarco. We need to talk."

I met Maurice's eyes and saw the fear there. "We need to go," I whispered.

"Not until I see Violet," said the old man.

"Retch, you…" But Retch wasn't there. He'd disappeared while Beck was speaking. "Fine." I waved Maurice forward, deeper into the belly of the ship. As quietly as we could, we hurried down the weaving passages.

Now that I knew the truth, it was impossible not to recognize the ship for what it was—the same model I'd flown in before. There was the passage where I chased my sister on the last day she had functioning legs. Behind that was the cabin where the adults would gather for drinks and gambling. My father had been an avid gambler. That memory rattled in my brain after a decade of suppression. He'd been losing that day. He'd lost on a lot of days.

Maybe I was more like him than I thought.

Because I knew my way around the ship, I knew exactly where to go. Violet's central art display sat where the ship's biggest lounge met the helm. With Maurice at my heel, I stalked directly to it, rounding the corner to find two of Violet's guards blocking the path.

"I'm here to speak with the boss," I said.

After a brief pause, a voice from the other room said, "Make him leave his weapon."

I flipped my pistol around and handed it to the guard handle first. He took it and waved me through.

"Welcome back, Mr. Demarco," Violet said. She was lounging on one of the red sofas, a bowl of grapes at her side. "Forgive the confiscation, but we can't have anyone firing weapons in here."

"No, I suppose not," I said, walking into the center of the room. From there, I had a good view of each entrance, as well as the bulk of Violet's collected art. "This is where you keep the real stuff, isn't it?"

Maurice followed me into the center of the room, and when Violet saw him, she smiled. "Maurice Ribar. How lovely to see you again. My husband thought very highly of you and your skills."

"He's a good man," Maurice said.

"He was, wasn't he?" Violet's back stiffened. "If only he'd been just a little smarter."

"Or a little stupider. It would have been a good plan if he just hadn't tried to be so damn smart about it."

A sliver of a smile crossed Violet's lips before it faded. She approached Maurice. "What is it you came for, Mr. Ribar?"

"I came to apologize. I should never have agreed to the job. I knew it was dangerous. Then, when things started to seem off, I should have called the whole thing down. I didn't stand up to your husband, and that caused a whole pile of trouble. When we fled to this station, well, I think we were fleeing the humiliation of all our stupid decisions more than any real retaliation from law enforcement."

The flicker of a frown crossed Violet's brow, and everything I suspected about their job fell into place.

"You don't need to apologize to her, Maurice," I said, strolling across the room. "Violet here knew everything all along."

Violet picked up a half-empty glass of champagne and took a sip, raising an eyebrow with a question.

"She was working with Trey Vitez," I said. "The forger. You see, not only did the job go south once you breached the ship, but it was the wrong ship to start with, full of Trey's masterful forgeries. The real transport ship was somewhere else entirely, being taken wholesale by Violet." I gestured at the art all around us. "You see here the entire contents of that transport, minus a few valuables that must have paid for the ship itself and a few other luxury items."

Maurice's eyes narrowed.

I continued, "Violet fed the wrong telemetry data to her husband. Were you having an affair with Trey?" She didn't bother answering, but she didn't need to. It was the one thing that I could think of that her husband needed to know from Vitez. He'd trekked all the way up to the Hallows and followed his former colleague for weeks just to learn whether Vitez was still in contact with his wife. "It doesn't really matter if you were. For this to work, all you needed was Richard's trust. Your husband trusted you completely. When you fed him the data, it shortened the intercept window. What you weren't counting on was the team continuing the mission, even after things went south. They'd always been so professional."

"They got greedy," Violet said.

Maurice gestured at the art all around them. "Says you."

I walked to the tall wooden box with the faded painting of the bubble landscape. Pulling it open, I revealed the full triptych of *The Garden of Earthly Delights*. It was even more breathtaking together in one piece. "The false ship crashed, but the idea was to keep enough forged art intact that inspectors would assume that it was the real deal. Meanwhile, you and yours make off with the real thing, keeping everything aboard. You make your way across the stars, visiting all the colony planets and luxury stations you've always wanted to see. The art becomes a commodity for you, both in its beauty and its value to those poor art-starved elites of the outer planets."

Violet took another sip of her champagne.

"What I don't figure, then, is why you'd have Trey Vitez killed."

This time, she stopped with her wine halfway to her mouth. "Excuse me?"

"Trey Vitez, murdered. Why?"

After a long pause, she said, "I would never have murdered him. You were right. We had an affair. It was years ago, and it was a mistake, but he meant everything to me at the time. The theft of the art was exactly as you said, but it all went wrong. Trey chose to flee rather than circle back as we had agreed. He felt a life of wealth on a station somewhere out in the void was preferable to risking himself for me." She swallowed another gulp of wine as if it were a bitter medicine. "But I didn't murder him."

"I did that on my own," Beck said, stepping into the room from a side door. "I murdered him, and if I had the chance to do it again, I would."

"You *what?*" said Violet.

Beck's lips smiled, but her eyes stayed entirely flat. "You never knew. All this time, and after all that vetting. You never knew who I really was, did you?"

Violet's lips tightened to a thin line.

"Hector Chance had a daughter," I said.

"My mother waited for him to return. She waited and waited. Nobody ever told her he'd died. Nobody told her he had lapsed back into his criminal habits. We still had financial problems. Worse with him gone." Beck ran a finger along an ancient Ming vase. "She left a letter when she killed herself, you know. A letter to *him*. She didn't even mention me."

"How did you discover what your father had done?" I asked.

"I bounced around foster care for a few years until I aged out, but one of my foster parents was a journalist. He showed me how to dig through articles using facial recognition. That's when I found the old information about my father. From there, I was able to track down the rest of the crew and learn what happened. I learned about how he was betrayed."

"I'm sorry," Maurice said. "I'm so sorry."

Beck raised her gun, but before she could pull the trigger, I stepped between them.

I said, "Maurice is a decent man."

"A decent man wouldn't have gotten my father killed," she said. "A decent man would have at least told his wife of his death."

Maurice said, "She has a point."

"You're not helping," I growled.

To me, Beck said, "You know what it's like." Her voice held a hint of desperation. "When you're a kid in that stage where you hate your parents more than anyone else in the world. Where all your teenage angst and anger gets directed at them and then one day they're gone. Dead. Murdered. Where does all that anger go? Do you turn in on yourself? Do you impotently hate the parents who left you?"

"Or do you hate the people responsible for killing them?" I said. "I get it."

"But you've chosen to hate yourself, haven't you?"

Had I? Beck's rage was apparent, but my own? Mine boiled deep inside my gut. "It's different."

"Not even a little." Beck crossed the room and placed a finger on my chest. "You've hated yourself all these years, Demarco. Why not turn that rage outward?"

"Because I'm the one who killed my parents. There's no such thing as *outward*."

She took a step back and tilted her head. Her eyes bored a hole right down into my soul, and it hurt. "It must be hard being you."

"A lot easier than you think." I met her gaze. "Let Maurice go, Beck. He has a family. He has kids."

For a long time, she didn't move. The noise of a commotion outside the room almost drowned out the pounding of my heart. Beck held the tension of all those years on her shoulders. Clenched it in her jaws. Letting Maurice go took everything from her. Her revenge. Her identity. Her mother and father. Everything.

I'd given up all those things without a fight. In all my stubbornness, I'd abandoned the things that should have mattered to me. Why were the bulkheads all open in the ship that killed my parents? Why did the landing come in so hot? I may have pressed the button that killed my family, but I didn't create the conditions that made that button-press possible. Maybe there was something in Beck's attitude that I could learn from.

Maybe I needed to start thinking about revenge.

Or justice.

Beck lowered her gun. "You're right," she said. "I need to let this go."

I drew a deep breath. "The police are on their way."

She smiled. "Not if someone blocked the final airlock."

Clever. "What's happened to Lauder and the Saint?"

"Gone by the time I got through."

"All right." I looked around at the art. "Where's Violet?"

"This ship is full of secret passages, and she knows them all."

The main entrances to the room stood wide open. A tense silence hung around the whole gallery. Where Violet had been standing, another door hung open. Her way out. It might be ours as well.

"We need to leave," I said. "Whoever wins out there is going to come here for the art."

Gunshots rang through the hall. Violet's two guards dropped in a spray of blood.

Saint Jerome and Frank Lauder stepped into the room side by side. They leveled their weapons at Beck.

"Drop the weapon, sweetie," said Lauder. "It would be a shame to make a mess among all this art and culture."

Chapter 49

"IT'S a regular peaceable kingdom in here," I said.

Saint Jerome grinned like a shark. "A real businessman knows when to cut a deal."

"Fifty percent's not a bad cut," Lauder said. "He gets everything below the church. I get everything above."

"Seems fair," I said. "As long as you don't think Jerome here's going to stab you in the back, first chance he gets."

Lauder said, "Deals forged in fire are often the strongest."

"He's not really a saint, you know," I said.

"That's enough," snapped the Saint. "Let's get moving." He disarmed Beck and patted Maurice and me down. All around us, the art of old Earth sat ready for the taking. He looked up at *The Garden of Earthly Delights*. "Ugly thing, isn't it? Can you believe there's all this fuss?"

"It's considered revolutionary for its time," I said. "A real insight into the nature of heaven and hell."

Lauder stepped up next to us. "Is that a pig wearing a nun's habit?"

"It's symbolic," I said.

"What about the knife with ears?"

"Close it up," Saint Jerome said. He gestured with his pistol at Maurice and me. "You two move this thing. The lady can carry some of these smaller relics."

To my surprise, Beck obeyed. She picked up the ornate box—the one that contained a relic of Saint Catherine of Bologna.

The painting was heavier than it looked, and once removed from its sealed case and detached from its mounting brackets, it swayed dangerously in my grip. The pain in my injured elbow flared, even through the pain meds. Luckily, Maurice was in better shape than he looked, and we were able to get it under control while I shifted my weight to my other arm. Both crime bosses led us out at gunpoint.

As we left, out of the corner of my eye, I spotted movement. Something in the lower ventilation shaft.

"I used to fly in ships like this back in the day, you know," I said to Saint Jerome, who walked next to me. "My family didn't like waiting in customs like the commoners."

"Keep walking," Jerome said.

"It's interesting, all the places you can go in these ships when you're small enough. You can crawl all the way down to the control center and mess with the lights. You can throw the whole ship into lockdown too. It's really something they should have considered when they designed it. Gotta think of rats when you design a ship, right?"

The Saint jabbed his pistol into my ribs, causing me to stumble and my end of the painting to dip dangerously.

"You can't shut him up," Beck said. "Believe me, I've tried."

I smiled. "I'm just saying, it'd be a shame if anyone triggered the lockdown."

Lauder narrowed his eyes at me. He knew Retch was around but couldn't do anything about it.

When we got to the foyer, we found both the Mercury and Venus airlocks standing open. A knife jammed into the bulkhead track prevented the door between Venus and the ship's foyer from closing. That must have been Beck's handiwork.

But somehow the door after that stood open.

"That shouldn't be possible," Lauder said as we passed the foyer into the sprawling Venus compartment. "The airlock can't cycle if the next door won't close."

"That's what I thought too," said Beck. "Guess I was wrong."

"More of your people?" Saint Jerome asked Lauder.

"Not mine," said the gentleman. "Might be the blue."

The police didn't have the authority to override the airlock mechanism. Only one man I knew could do that. Only one man had the ability to be ignored by Trinity's safety mechanisms. He had the skills needed to hack the airlock consoles and the moral fiber to put the station in danger to do it. There was only one man I knew who could and would break through the airlock.

Last I'd seen I'd tossed him over the longest fall in the entire city.

"Richard," I called, my voice booming in the open lobby. "Come out so we can talk."

After a stutter of a heartbeat, Richard Ruiz stepped out from behind the display case of an enormous marble statue. "I was hoping to slip past," he said. The man's gray hair was frazzled and his face was covered in bruises. He looked almost as bad as I felt.

"How did you override the airlock?" I asked.

A mischievous smile crossed his lips. "I'll be out of your way, Demarco. No hard feelings."

"You tried to kill me," I said.

"So, we're even."

When I didn't respond, he took it as an affirmative and stepped past me. When he reached the bulkhead, I said, "She might not be happy to see you."

He ran a hand along the painting's heavy frame and let out a long sigh. "No," he said finally. "I don't imagine she will." With that, he disappeared into the ship.

"What the hell was that about?" asked Saint Jerome.

Before I could answer, the lights died and plunged us into darkness.

Beck moved the fastest, slamming her relic box into the Saint. A gunshot went off, and Maurice grunted. His half of the painting dropped, so I lowered mine as well as I could, leaning it against the wall.

Another shot—aimed at me this time. The muzzle flash blinded me, but the bullet didn't hit. Another shot.

I was already on the move. Lauder's shoe scuffed the steel floor. He stood feet away. I swung, blind in the dark but with a burned memory of his location in the back of my eyelids. I struck something. Hard. His gun flew away.

A red light flashed down one hall. Retch had triggered the lockdown sequence. The ship was going to prepare for launch.

Too soon.

I grabbed Lauder and threw him against the wall. Behind me, Beck fought Jerome, but the man was a sturdy fibersteel wall. He shrugged off blow after blow, advancing slowly to corner the woman.

The bulkheads descended. "Retch!" I shouted. "Get back here now!"

The room strobed between emergency red and complete black. I moved. Lauder disappeared. He had to be close. Behind the display cases.

Or behind me.

He struck hard and fast, fists pounding into my kidneys. A kick crunched against the back of my knee. He was damn fast.

Luckily, I could be fast too. When the lights went black, I swung a fist, pounding his solar plexus. My fist struck the light layer of armor under his chest and came back wet with blood. He flailed wildly at me, but nothing connected. I grabbed his wrist and twisted, feeling bones pop. Lauder screamed. Keeping hold of the wrist, I shoved, walking him back into Mercury.

The bulkheads between the entryway and the ship were halfway down. The outer airlock shield hadn't closed yet, but it would start soon.

"Retch!" I shouted. He had to get back before the lockdown completed or he might not get out at all.

Saint Jerome heaved Beck over his head and threw her into the entryway. She'd opened a dozen cuts on the man's arms and torso, but, pale as he was from blood loss, he still had the advantage of strength. A solidly built Heavy wasn't anything to scoff at, even if he was the kind of guy who usually ordered others to do his dirty work.

There wasn't time. I shoved Lauder farther back into the wide-open Venus airlock and slapped a hand on the airlock console.

Trinity's cheery font appeared. *Reconcile?*

"Not today, Trinity," I growled. "Close the airlock door between Mercury and Venus." If I could trap Lauder I could go back to help Beck. The giant airlock door complied.

But it was too slow. Lauder scrambled to his feet, favoring his broken wrist. His eyes locked on the pistol Saint Jerome had dropped in the center of the Mercury airlock. It lay next to the massive painting and Saint Catherine's ornate relic box. The three items were arranged almost as if on display. A work of art, a relic of the dead patron saint of artists, and an implement of death. My father, the curator, couldn't have assembled a better arrangement.

The *Thirty Silver*'s main bulkhead was closing. Fast, but not fast enough. Lauder lunged, his foot slipping at first, but he got his momentum. He scrambled forward. I dove too.

We hit it at the same time, just as the Venus airlock door sealed. My elbow hit the box as I scrambled for the gun, sending it sliding toward Beck and Saint Jerome. Lauder grasped the pistol's grip. I had a hand on the barrel. I twisted.

Not fast enough.

Lauder fired. Fired again. The barrel grew hot in my hand. Burned. He fired again and again until I smelled the burning flesh of my palm. Still, I didn't let go, and I didn't break eye contact with Lauder. The pain became a purgatory in my journey to redemption. It grew into the only thing I ever knew or felt.

Then, the gun clicked empty.

A grin grew up from deep in my chest to spread across my face. It must have been a frightening thing because Lauder crumpled under it, dropping to his knees. I threw the gun away, hefted him to his feet, and tossed him through the airlock back into the ship's entryway.

Saint Jerome shoved Beck to the ground. She slammed into the ornate box, which cracked open, spilling its contents across the floor. Jagged bones and desiccated leather wraps scattered across the thick carpet. Beck lay in a crumpled heap, and Saint Jerome, the monster of Heavy Nicodemia, stepped forward, ready to stomp her head.

I wanted to call out to her. Warn her that he was coming. My voice failed me. Beside her, the broken bone of Saint Catherine lay in a haze of dust. A real relic, passed down through thousands of years of the Catholic Church, only to be deposited gracelessly next to a dying assassin.

But Beck was more than an assassin, wasn't she? She was a woman wounded by the loss of her family. She was a lover, and she was the only woman able to ever break me out of my shell, if only a little. I cared about Beck. Loved her, maybe. She was more than a killer. More than the assassin traveling across the stars to seek revenge for her parents' death.

Or was she?

Beck's fingers wrapped around the shard of bone. As Saint Jerome raised his boot to stomp her, she spun and stabbed the bone deep into the Saint's calf.

He collapsed backward, landing in a heap, yowling in pain. The bone shard jutted from his bleeding leg. The Saint grasped it with one hand and yanked it from his wound.

But he was too slow. Beck pounced, shoving the big man backward onto the shattered remains of a display case. He slammed, splintering wood and shattering glass. With a single smooth movement, Beck snatched a falling shard and slashed the big man's throat. Saint Jerome burbled in horror, gasped in a last fit of rage, then collapsed to the floor in a bloody heap. His lifeblood mixed with the dust of the true saint and the sparkling remains of a shattered porcelain god.

Lauder moaned at Beck's feet and struggled to rise. She kicked him so that he stayed down. "Not now, asshole."

Beck stood very still, her eyes searching mine. She shot a glance at Maurice, who was still cowering in the corner of the Mercury airlock.

I nodded to Jerome. "He had it coming."

Tension fell from her shoulders. She had been expecting harsh judgment. "He did."

The lockdown bulkhead continued to grind down. Inside the ship, the boom of several bulkheads closing resonated outward. The entire ship was prepping to disengage, locking down bulkheads slowly in preparation for the shift back into the void. In a matter of seconds, the final entryway bulkheads—those three doors that separated the ship from Nicodemia—would finally close and Violet Ruiz's ship would leave forever.

Chapter 50

BECK STEPPED through the double bulkhead that would soon separate the foyer from the rest of the ship. To the sides, the two other doors still stood open, ready to shut when the big one finally closed. Behind me, the massive outer shell of Nicodemia prepared to seal the final airlock by moving smoothly into position. Maurice leaned against the Mercury airlock door. His bleeding had slowed, but sweat was beading on his pale brow.

I took Beck's hands, trying my best not to wince at the pain of my burnt skin as my adrenaline rush subsided.

"You've had your revenge," I said. Warmth flowed from her fingers, and I longed to pull her close. "Violet's ship can take you to whatever the next colony is, and when you get there, you can make a new life for yourself. You can move on and become the person you think your parents might have wanted you to become." I swallowed my own emotions. "You can even be better than that if you want."

Her eyes searched mine. "Come with, Demarco." She bit her lip. "Jude."

I had been hoping she wouldn't say it. Putting it in words made it a tangible, tempting thing. We could travel the galaxy. Visit strange and wonderful places. Something deep in my chest twisted at the idea of spending my nights in her arms and my days by her side. I could leave behind the endless slog of Nicodemia. No more would Trinity's judgment weigh me down. Crush my soul. I could leave behind this broken city.

"Nicodemia is *my* broken city," I said. "It always will be. I live and breathe this place from its darkest corners to its brightest heights. I *am* this city." When I saw the question lingering on her lips, I continued. "And you can never stay here."

She let go of my hands and took a step back. Her eyes searched mine.

"McCay," I said. "He was innocent. A go-between who didn't have a clue about this whole art ring. Now he's dead. If it hadn't been for Retch's theft, I might not even have known about him." I shot a glance at the side exits leading from the foyer, but there was no sign of the kid. "But you knew that, didn't you? You were the one who planted the information so Retch would steal from McCay as a way of flushing Ruiz out of the woodwork. I can only imagine your surprise when I showed up instead.

"I kept thinking, who would off a guy whose only goal was to trick his way into the upper reaches of society? What ambition could this guy have had that might put him on the wrong side of the gangsters and thugs of our district? He had his drugs, but I checked. Those drugs were harmless and not particularly valuable. Lauder's gang had access to a decent supply of painkillers, so why worry about McCay's supply? And he had been doing his best for years to stay under the radar. The man wasn't dangerous to anyone."

Beck's expression hardened.

"Then it occurred to me, that McCay *was* in the way. When I told you I couldn't work for you because I already had a job, you went and eliminated that job."

"You never stopped when McCay died."

"No, I didn't. That's how I am, isn't it? But you didn't know that at the time. You thought killing McCay would get me to help you faster, given that you had a limited amount of time to get your job done before Violet Ruiz gave up and left with your ride. You made it look like a random robbery when you stole McCay's gun, and hey, that gun came in handy."

"So you say." She took another step back. On the floor, Lauder let out another moan and shifted. The ship boomed as it shifted to another phase of its slow lockdown process.

"And the guns. Nicodemia's been flooded with a fresh wave of cheap guns. That was your mass exchange, wasn't it? You put the citizens of my city at risk just so you could have a little spending cash." I took the remaining dimes from my pocket and threw them at her feet. Nicodemian dimes, every last one of them. "And you made sure both Lauder and the Saint had access so that there would be enough chaos to cover your tracks."

"Ruiz wouldn't sell one of her artworks to fund my work." Beck's deflection made me even angrier, and she saw it. "Jude, I'm sorry. I shouldn't have—"

"You killed that guy in Haven. Shot him up close, like it was personal."

"He was a *monster*," she spat. "Their whole plan wouldn't have worked without the leverage that guy had over his victims."

"Then I got thinking," I snapped, "Why me? Why work so hard to get my help in this whole business? Was there some reason you couldn't hire someone else to be your guide through the city or was there a reason you wanted me in particular?" I paused as the alarm blared a warning of the imminent disengage sequence. "You knew I was Wilson Demarco's son. You knew I was meant to be his successor, and if he was dead, you wanted me close so you could kill me as well. Revenge demanded its price."

"Your father was a terrible man." Her voice lacked conviction, but her words still stung. "He drove the entire operation, funding everything and creating all of the right conditions for an art thievery ring that spanned several solar systems. He was the cause of my father's murder as sure as any of those other bastards." She paused, stepping back from the bulkhead. "But I couldn't kill you, Jude. You lay helpless in that bed, and I couldn't do it. You mean too much to me. You always will."

"A part of you still wanted to plunge that knife in my heart."

"I can change."

"Goodbye, Charlotte," I said. "Go be a different person if you can, but don't come back here."

She looked at me with those big blue eyes. With a blink, she saw right through me, down to the bruised and broken core of my torn-up soul. Her lips parted slightly, and her words of redemption hung from the tip of her tongue, ready to be loosed into the world. One dark apology was all it took. All she had to do was step forward and I'd forgive her. I felt it in my heart.

Then, the *Thirty Silver*'s big central gate closed, and Charlotte Beck was gone.

Chapter 51

THE DISENGAGEMENT SEQUENCE PROGRESSED, and red
flashing lights flared over the two side doors. Retch was out there
still. He should have been able to find his way back already. I
couldn't stop the ship from disconnecting, but I could slow its
progress with a word. Trinity would hold the doors for me. I didn't
know how long the ship would stay.

The open airlock would just vent into space, including all the
art, debris, and people in it. Same as what would likely happen to
the contents of the foyer.

A shouted curse rang down the hallway from the door to the
left. Retch's voice at first, and then someone bigger. Deeper.

Sam Wash stepped into the foyer, his boots crunching broken
glass. In his grasp, Retch struggled and kicked. Wash pressed a
plastic gun with a crimson barrel hard against the boy's head.

That gun. Had he picked it up from Saint Lucy of the Light?
Was it another carbon copy like a hundred others? He was too far
for me to read the inscription etched on the barrel.

The side doors slammed shut with a resounding boom. Above,

the clear shielding that would separate the ship's foyer from Nicodemia started to move.

A hollow expression haunted Wash's eyes. He was slipping down the slope of desperation, and I didn't much like where he was going to land. "Back away, Demarco," he hissed. "Or the kid gets it."

I raised my hands and stepped back. Retch struggled and kicked, but Wash was a solid guy with a good grip. When the two reached the center of the room, Wash paused, and without taking his eyes from me, lowered the gun and shot Lauder in the back of the skull. The plasti-ceramic bullet scrambled Lauder across the stark white floor.

Retch screamed in righteous fury, but Wash returned the pistol to its previous position.

"Looks like there's going to be a new boss in town after all," Wash said, glancing at Saint Jerome's body. Blood matted the big man's bright white suit. It was a damn shame. "With Lauder and Jerome gone, you're going to want to start working for me."

"Not a chance, asshole," Retch said.

"I wasn't talking to you, kid."

"This isn't what you want, Wash," I said.

"How would you know," he sneered. "Money. Power. This is what it takes to be safe."

"You won't be safe."

His brown eyes glistened, even in the dry ship air. "There's no other way."

"Stop fighting," I said, locking gazes with Retch. The clear station shell was already halfway down. I didn't have time for this. "Trinity?"

"Reconcile?" said a booming voice.

"Not today. Stop closing the outer shielding." My heart pounded in my chest.

The shielding stopped above my head.

"Stop struggling," I repeated.

Retch put out one final burst of a flail, then stilled. He stared me down but stopped moving. He trusted me, and the weight of that trust pressed down on my shoulders.

In my calmest tone, I said, "Sometimes we need to stop struggling to get our bearings. We need to take a step back from the chaos around us and make a good assessment of our surroundings. Figure out what side we want to be on and consider the best way to accomplish our goals. It's not an assessment devoid of emotion, but emotion is only one part of the bigger equation. A person has to think: What *can* we do? What *should* we do? And what's worth trying even if our chance of success is very low?"

"You're going to work for me." Wash nodded toward the airlock, where the display still showed one occupied compartment. "First thing we're going to do is get back into the city."

I drew a deep long breath. "Retch, relax."

The boy calmed down. His fingers released Wash's muscular arm and his arms fell to his sides.

His hand touched the stunstick hanging there. His eyes went wide. Wash, in his idiocy, hadn't disarmed his captive.

I tipped my hat at Wash. "Wash," I said, "it's been a pleasure, but one word from me, and Trinity will close the airlock and detach the ship that you are currently standing in. I'll rid the city of your violence and get rid of this pesky thief all at once. I'm asking you one last time to stop fighting."

Wash's expression went from confused to understanding to rage. He pulled the pistol from Retch, pointed it at me—

Retch jammed his stunstick into Wash's hip and pulled the trigger. A pulse of power surged with a pop. Every muscle in Wash's body convulsed. His gun fired.

A pain bloomed in my shoulder. Retch ran to me and slowed my fall. I landed in a heap in his arms, but he barely slowed my fall to the hard floor.

Pain blackened the corners of my vision.

Wash writhed on the floor, his limbs flailing. He got an arm under himself. The gun lay a few steps away.

"Demarco," Retch cried. "Close the shielding."

I opened my mouth to talk, but a wave of pain shut it.

Wash's arm flopped forward. His fingertips touched the pistol. His legs propelled him forward.

"Trinity," I whispered.

Trinity's serene voice reverberated in my skull. "Reconcile?"

"Not today, asshole."

Wash clutched the gun. He got his knees under him. He was one good lunge from the gate.

"Trinity," I said, "close the shield and detach the ship. All emergency overrides."

The clear outer airlock slammed shut as Wash fired. The shots sparked against the station's clear outer shell.

Then, the ship detached. A hard vacuum hit Wash, freezing him in death in an expression of rage and horror and confusion. All the art and saints and bodies in the foyer were blasted away into the great void. The *Thirty Silver* fell hard, tearing loose of Nicodemia and falling outward into the stars. In less than the span of a gasped breath, we were looking out upon the vast nothing.

"It's beautiful," said Maurice from the corner.

"It is," I said, struggling to sit up. "It is."

"I've never seen stars," breathed Retch. "There are so many of them. We're so small."

"That we are, kid. That we are."

The airlock door behind Maurice opened and Anders entered, leading a dozen blues.

"Well, I'll be damned," said the cop when he saw the bloody mess surrounding us. "The lady in the wheelchair was right, then."

"Perfect timing," I gasped as Anders knelt at my side. "And you brought backup."

"They wanted to help," said Anders, slipping an arm under my uninjured shoulder to help me up. "A lot of people wanted to help."

"Good." My foot slipped under me as I tried to rise, and he struggled to support most of my weight. He lowered me back to the floor, where I let out a long breath. "Good."

With that, I lay back and let the blackness take me.

Chapter 52

OFFICER ANDERS TAPPED his worn pencil against the side of his cooling coffee mug. A blues tune wailed on the diner's tinny speakers. Outside the window, the Angel's Diner sign flickered, pushing a halo of light out into the gloom of another misty Heavy Nicodemia night. He hadn't had any coffee since the first sip, but, really, that was for the best. Of all the bad coffee in Heavy Nicodemia, my sister Angel's was the bitterest, the grittiest, and the most dangerously acidic. I wouldn't want her getting arrested for assault.

"All right," Anders said. "Why don't we just start at the beginning again."

After the events in the airlock, I'd given the police the general details of what had happened. A beautiful assassin came to town to clean up an errant art thievery ring. In the process, she had flooded the town with guns, disrupted the entrenched crime bosses of the Heavies, and caused a whole host of other problems that our closed system wasn't accustomed to dealing with.

I winced as a dull ache ran through my bandaged wounds. The bullet wound definitely hurt worse than the burn. I filed both under the category of things I would rather not experience again. That list was getting pretty long.

"When I'm dead and gone to the great beyond," I started, "somebody at my funeral, as my body slides into the great recycler, will say, 'Jude Demarco was a nobody, but he was the best damn private detective Nicodemia ever had, from Heavies to Hallow. He was the bulldog who tracked down every lead and never let go until the bloody truth died dripping in his jaws. That man would never stop till he saw the way things really were, even if it meant someone got hurt. Even if it got someone killed. There was something we could all admire in Demarco, just as well as there was always something to hate. He saw the good in people, even if deep down he always believed that that same good would eventually lose out against greed and vice.'

"More likely they'll stop at *nobody*."

"More like they'll stop at *asshole*," said Retch, refilling my coffee cup.

I looked up at him. "*Asshole* wasn't even in the original quote, kid."

"I'm pretty sure that quote was all asshole."

"Shouldn't you try to be polite so you can get a tip?" I asked.

"You don't tip." He paused. "You don't even pay."

"My charm is payment enough."

"Officer," Angel said from behind the counter. "I'd like to report a brutal murder."

"Who?"

"The truth."

Anders's cheeks turned a deep red. "I'll make a note of it, Angel."

"She's joking," I whispered, leaning forward.

He deadpanned, "We'll see what a judge says about that."

Maybe Anders could handle himself after all.

I glanced over at the back side of Angel's flickering "OPEN" sign. Right below it hung my sign that read: *Demarco: Detective.*

Medic. Handyman. All things found. All things fixed. A lie, really. I couldn't fix everything. I couldn't fix the rift between myself and Beck after I'd seen in her eyes that she'd needlessly murdered McCay. I couldn't fix the hole left in my family after my parents died.

I could try, though. When I approached Angel with the idea, she had accepted me without a second's hesitation. Retch and I could help out at the diner, and she would let me live upstairs. In exchange, I would get to run my business from a stable location, no longer needing to move from one vacant storefront to the next.

Oh, and free coffee. Free terrible, *terrible* coffee.

Helen stuck her head in from the kitchen. "Jude, you got a call."

I excused myself from Officer Anders and made my way back into the kitchen. There, in the far corner, stood Helen's grease-smeared video screen. On it was the image of Violet Ruiz, looking as beautiful and impatient as ever. To her side sat Richard Ruiz, a smug expression on his face.

"Seems you have some explaining to do, Mr. Demarco," Violet said.

"You hired me to find the painting. It took a longer walk than maybe it should have, but I found it."

She frowned. "The idea was that I'd keep the original. It was the forgery we needed you to find."

"I don't think that was in my contract, ma'am. Anyway, I found a nice museum in Haven that was happy to take it off my hands. Everybody wins."

Richard said, "I'm sure we have enough priceless treasures to last us a few years."

"Richard," I said. "Nice to see you made it back to your wife."

He tipped his hat. I pretended not to notice the line of Violet's lips tighten.

"Does he know everything?" I asked. Violet Ruiz had double-crossed her husband. She had sabotaged the heist that had ended in his exile and even had an affair with Trey Vitez.

Violet's eyes narrowed. "Our marital relationship is none of your concern."

Richard said, "We're focusing on the future."

"And where would that be?"

"There's a nice little planet called Blue Haven," Violet said. "They have a forest and cliffside waterfalls that fall for miles."

"Lovely."

"One more thing," said Violet. "Why didn't you tell her?"

I knew exactly what she meant. Why hadn't I told Charlotte Beck that Violet had been at the heart of the betrayal that had killed her father? Why hadn't I given her the closure she needed to resolve all that pain and anger she'd worked up over the years? I could have told her of Violet's part. I could have told her that Richard was hiding on the ship. I hadn't.

"Is she in hibernation for the next leg of your trip?" I asked.

"Yes," Violet said, "and she'll be leaving the ship at our next stop. She was a good employee, and I love her dearly, but this business with her father makes her too dangerous."

"Make sure she's set up someplace nice before you let her go," I said. As much as I wanted, I couldn't bring myself to cut her loose. "Use my payment if you need."

Violet's lips tightened into a hard line again, but Richard grinned at the audacity of my statement.

"He *did* find the painting, dear," he said.

"Goodbye, Demarco," said Violet.

And with that, the screen went dark.

Back in the other room, Retch had made himself at home as my replacement across from Officer Anders. "Then, when he was rummaging around in my stuff, I pointed my gun at him."

Anders made a note with his pencil. "You have a gun?"

"No! I have a piece of metal that I twisted to be shaped like a gun, and Demarco bought it. So, anyway, I'm pointing this fake gun at him and he's all blubbering and pleading for his life. I almost think he's going to throw up right there he's scared so bad. Then this lady shows up out of nowhere. She smacks me so hard the gun goes flying."

I slid into the booth next to Retch. "That's basically how it happened," I said.

"And now you two work together?" Anders asked, a smirk on his smug face.

"We do," I said. "I'm able to accomplish a lot. Being excommunicated is a tremendous honor and grants me an amazing amount of influence in Nicodemia, but there are things I need help with. Retch here has agreed to be my assistant."

"Partner," Retch said.

"Same thing."

The door opened, ringing the bell. A boy stepped in from the cold drizzle, wringing his narrow-brimmed hat in his hands. I recognized his shabby button-down sweater. It was the teen from the clothing shop where I'd picked up clothes for Retch.

"Mr. Demarco?" he asked.

"We done here, Anders?" I asked.

"I think I have enough for now," Anders said, dropping a dime for his coffee, and then another dime for the excellent service. Retch snatched them up as the officer passed the government man.

As Anders opened the door, I called out one more question, "Hey, Anders, in the McCay crime scene, did you ever find the gun?"

He removed his hat and scratched his curly hair. "We did, actually. Buried under a bunch of junk in the office."

"Crimson barrel?"

Anders nodded. "And it said *Forsaken* on it. It's a McCay family heirloom, but we've found a dozen copies around town. Someone with the same print data has been churning out guns and selling them."

"Thanks."

Beck hadn't taken McCay's gun. Had she killed him? The gun had been my best evidence, but if not her, then who? I remembered her words before she left on Ruiz's ship. *So you say.* Not a confession, but not a denial either. Maybe she left because she killed the man. Or maybe she left because I had no faith in her.

Either way, she was a killer. I had to remind myself of that. She'd killed Trey Vitez. Even if she hadn't committed the worst of the crimes accused of her, she'd sinned enough. Somehow that knowledge didn't make me feel any better.

Anders left, and I searched my soul for a way to smother my doubts. "What can I do for you, kid?"

He said, "It's my sister. She's missing."

"Any idea where?"

The kid chewed his lip and twisted his hat. "I can show you."

I fixed my hat on my head and my coat on my back. With Retch at my side and a client following close, I stepped out into the swirling drizzle of the Heavy Nicodemia night.

All things found. All things fixed.

Bonus Content

Demarco's not done yet.

Interested in more? You'll get an extra author's note, huge discounts on more books, and access to piles of exclusive material.

You'll also get All Things Found, a short story about Demarco when he picks up a job investigating a murder that happened right there in the Saint Francis of Assisi cathedral. A priest is dead. A relic is missing.

There are some things that aren't so easy to fix.

https://anthonyeichenlaub.com/all-things-found-newsletter-signup/

Also by Anthony W. Eichenlaub

Short Stories

Not Done Yet: Sci-fi Stories of Wisdom and Fury

All Things Found

The Man Who Walked in the Dark

Devil in the Gravity Lounge

Old Code Series

Grandfather Anonymous

Grandfather Ghost

Grandfather Guardian

Grandfather Zero

Grandfather Crypto

Cascade Crash

Colony of Edge

Of a Strange World Made
Upon Another Edge Broken
On a Forsaken Land Found
From a Barren Seed Grown
Above a Distant Sky Seen

Metal and Men

Justice in an Age of Metal and Men
Peace in an Age of Metal and Men
Honor in an Age of Metal and Men

Acknowledgments

We like to think of writing as a solitary activity, but nothing in this world gets made without help from others. My writing world exists because of the hard work of my wife, Carol, and the grudging tolerance of my fantastic kids. Without their amazing support, none of my books would get anywhere.

I also want to thank my editor Scott Alexander Jones. No matter how good I think my writing gets, he always finds the little tweak that will make it ten times better.

My communities of writers also get a huge shout-out. SFWA has kept me connected to a worldwide network of writers. The Rochester Writers Group has been fantastic for helping me stay in touch with the local crowd. I don't think I would get anywhere without both.

Finances are tricky for writers, and because of that, I must thank my Patreon supporters. There's not much I could do without the steady paycheck that you all give me.

Readers, I need to thank you most of all. Would I still write if I didn't have all of you reading my work? Maybe. But it wouldn't be as fulfilling, and it wouldn't be anywhere near as much fun.

All the best,
Anthony W. Eichenlaub

Milton Keynes UK
Ingram Content Group UK Ltd.
UKHW020004090324
439162UK00004B/349